Ready for your close-up?

In one swift motion, Vader swept Cherie into his embrace, one arm under her legs, the other supporting her back. The breath whooshed out of her in a gasp of surprise. Her hands clutched his shoulders. Cherie was tall and she was all woman, an overflowing armful of warm flesh. He'd bet anything not many men would try to carry her like this. He, on the other hand, barely noticed the weight. Those workouts sure paid off when he wanted to sweep a woman off her feet.

He stepped in front of the backdrop, where he braced his legs apart in a heroic stance and bent over her. She stared up at him, her pupils widening until her eyes were storm cloud gray. He knew this look. That look made hope pound feverishly through his veins. She still wanted him, no matter what she said.

He leaned his head close to hers, so mere fractions of an inch separated them. She might try to hide it or deny it or laugh it off or any of the other wacky things she'd done since they'd met. But he knew their crazy chemistry worked both ways.

FOUR WEDDINGS
and a
FIREMAN

A BACHELOR FIREMEN NOVEL

Jennifer Bernard

AVON

An Imprint of HarperCollinsPublishers

AVON BOOKS
An Imprint of HarperCollins*Publishers*
10 East 53rd Street
New York, New York 10022-5299

Copyright © 2014 by Jennifer Bernard
ISBN 978-0-06-227367-3
www.avonromance.com

First Avon Books mass market printing: March 2014

Thank you to everyone who helped in the creation of this book, most especially Tessa Woodward, LAFD Captain Rick Godinez (any errors are mine, not his), my agent Alexandra Machinist, the fabulous Avon team, and my ever-supportive family. Thank you to Lizbeth, Tam and Maxine, the Homer Public Library for the writing haven, and everyone involved in the production of chocolate. Thank you to Kristan Higgins and Eloisa James for being my idols. Most of all, thanks to the readers I've had the joy of meeting, either virtually or in person. This one's for you.

FOUR
WEDDINGS
and a
FIREMAN

At the wedding of Sabina Jones and Chief Rick Roman . . .

Derek "Vader" Brown could bench-press nearly twice his own weight and heave an unconscious fire victim of any shape or size over one shoulder, but weddings turned him into a ball of mush. When a bride walked down the aisle, he might as well be some mutant combination of puppy dog and marshmallow, especially when that bride was his best friend, Sabina Jones, joining in true love and matrimony with Chief Roman.

If only Sabina hadn't begged Vader to be her "man of honor." If only he hadn't invited Cherie Harper, the girl he'd been seeing off and on for a year, the girl he couldn't stop thinking about even during those "off" times. If only he hadn't happened to glance her way while the preacher discussed good times and bad.

But he did, and the dreamy smile on Cherie's face was the nail in the coffin of his dignity.

Blame it on the orange blossom high. Blame it on the look of rapture on Sabina's face as Roman claimed his first married kiss. Whatever the reason, soon after

the "I do's" had been said, Vader found himself circling the dance floor with Cherie in his arms, blurting
words he hadn't consciously decided to utter.

"Marry me."

Cherie stumbled. Not a good sign, since she taught
dance. Her gray eyes flew to meet his, and all he read
in them was wariness. "What did you say?"

Slightly shocked, Vader replayed the words in his
mind and decided that he stood by them. Despite
their ups and downs, he loved Cherie passionately.
He knew she loved him too, even though she fought
against it.

"Marry me. Be my bride." His heart swelled. This
was right. It *felt* right. Saying those words aloud made
all his confused emotions about Cherie settle into
place, like puzzle pieces fitting together. Cherie was
the right woman for him, the only woman for him. "I
promise I'll take care of you and make you happy, all
that good stuff."

But Cherie seemed to be going through an entirely
different set of emotions, judging by the anguish on
her face. "Honey, you know how I feel about you. But I
can't marry you," she whispered gently.

Vader's world went still, as if a bubble had dropped
around the two of them. Outside the bubble, everyone else grooved to the tune of "Love Will Keep Us
Together." Inside, things were a lot more confusing.
"Why not? I'd be a great husband."

"You'd be the best husband in the world." Tears
welled in her eyes, turning them silver. "But I'm not
interested in getting married to anyone. Please just believe me, Vader, please?"

She seemed so upset, he swallowed back his protest.
He looked away, only to encounter one blissful couple

after another. Captain Brody and Melissa glowed with the joy of brand-new parents. Ryan Blake and his wife, Katie, were cracking up as they tried out some complicated new dance step. Thor and Maribel, who had flown down from Alaska for the wedding, beamed with their own good news: pregnant with twins. Captain Jeb Stone was whispering something to his brand new fiancée, Nita Moreno. Everywhere Vader looked, happy faces stared back.

Except for the one in front of him. Cherie had gone pale with distress. "Can we just erase the last two minutes?" she asked in a pleading tone. "Go back to how things were?"

Erase his proposal? He wrestled with that one for a long minute. Granted, he hadn't exactly meant to propose. It was a spur-of-the-moment thing, and obviously a huge mistake. Why did the thought of marriage get her so upset? Didn't most people want to get married?

He squinted at her, slightly dizzy from spinning across the dance floor under the influence of many champagne toasts. He hated upsetting Cherie. He'd jumped the gun and fucked this up. He had only himself to blame.

Even though it hurt his heart, he forced himself to nod. "Forget it. Weddings always mess me up. Now what were we talking about? *Grey's Anatomy*, right?"

Her face lit up and she threw her arms around him. The feel of her curvy body, so warm and womanly, took some of the sting out of the moment.

He gathered her close and rested his cheek on her soft hair, which was currently blond with pink stripes. He inhaled a deep breath of lilac-scented essence of Cherie. They'd survive this. He didn't give up that easy. At the right moment, he'd try again. In the meantime, he'd stay away from weddings.

Four months and twelve days later, from the wedding of Patrick Callahan IV and Lara Nelson . . .

The ring of her phone startled Cherie awake. Disoriented, she scrambled for it, squinting at the name that flashed on the screen. *Vader*. What in blue blazes? Vader was in Loveless, Nevada, at the wedding of his friend Patrick. And it was three in the morning.

Oh, sweet Lord. *A wedding*. She'd nearly forgotten what happened at the last one. The smart thing would be to ignore the call in case Vader did anything reckless like throw their relationship into chaos again.

Still, it was Vader, her own personal version of catnip, the only substance in the world she couldn't resist for long. "Hello?"

Vader's deep voice rumbled from her phone, sending the usual shivers down her spine. "We should get married, Cherie."

Crap.

"I mean it," he continued. "Why don't you fly down here right away and I'll pick you up in Psycho's tractor and we'll get ourselves hicced. I mean, hitched."

"Vader, are you drunk?" Was Vader drunk-dial-proposing to her? Despite her sinking heart, a little snort of laughter escaped her.

"Oh come on, Cherie. You know we're meant to be together. You *know* it. Hang on. Some dude's banging on the door."

"Where are you?"

"Bathroom."

"You're proposing to me in a bathroom?"

"*Dude!* Find yourself a bush. Toilet's taken." He returned to her. "Some guys have no manners. Frickin' embarrassment."

Cherie clapped a hand over her mouth to keep from giggling out loud. "Let's talk later, okay?"

"I can't stay in here all night. People won't like that."

"No, I mean, let's talk tomorrow. When the wedding's totally over and you've had a good night's sleep."

Vader went quiet. Then, "Aw, hell."

"What?"

"I proposed again, didn't I? And you rejected me."

"*Vader.* I didn't reject you because you didn't propose. You're a little buzzed, and I'm half asleep, and none of this counts." *Please, just let him forget the whole thing ever happened.*

"You wanna erath . . . erase it, don't you? Just like last time?"

Cherie groaned silently. "Could we?"

"Guys don't like having their proposals erased. Feels bad."

No, no, no. Cherie hated hurting anyone, but hurting Vader was the worst of all. She couldn't bear it. "Please don't feel bad, sweetheart. You know how I feel about you. This is just bad timing, that's all. We'll talk about it later." She cast around for a distraction. "How was the wedding?"

"Beautiful. That's the problem, right there. *Weddings.* I can't take it. They're too freaking beautiful. The way Lara looked at Psycho, like he's made out of stardust or something . . . and the llama . . . the cute little llama had the ring tied to her collar and she trotted up right when she was supposed to, and—" He broke off.

"Vader? Are you okay?"

"I better go."

"Are we cool? Still friends?"

Vader let out a long groan. "We are what we are, tha's all. Whatever that is. And don' ask me to figure it out. I'm done trying, Cherie. Done." And the connection ended.

Cherie dropped back on her pillow, then grabbed another one and clamped it over her mouth so she could let out a frustrated scream. If only she could explain everything to Vader . . . but she couldn't . . .

This was a disaster. Vader had now proposed twice. In the morning, he'd probably hate her. What if he hated her so much he decided to call it quits, for real? The thought gave her a horrible chill. Life without Vader . . . she didn't want to think about it. Vader was too important to her.

They'd survive this. She didn't give up that easily. At the right moment, she'd try to get their relationship back on track.

With her natural optimism flowing back, she searched for a bright side and finally found one.

Vader was one of the famous Bachelor Firemen of San Gabriel. *Bachelor* Firemen. As in, *single*. Surely that meant no more weddings for a while. If the Bachelor Firemen would just stop getting married, Vader would forget about proposing and they could go back to normal. She floated a tiny prayer into the heavens. *Let the Bachelor Firemen curse last just a little bit longer.*

Chapter One

Vader, wearing firefighter's pants, suspenders, and nothing else, bent the giggling blond girl backward over his left arm, flexed his right biceps, and grinned for the camera. "How does that look?"

Stupid, mouthed Fred, also known as Stud, who was manning the Firefighter Photo Booth.

"Perfect," squealed the girl. "It looks like you're saving me from a fire, right?"

"Well, I normally wouldn't fight a fire without my shirt on." He lowered his voice to Elvis Presley range and wiggled his eyebrows. "Except on certain special occasions."

She laughed and playfully swatted his chest, letting her hand linger. Vader plastered the grin back on his face, added a little Elvis lip curl, and jerked his head for Fred to take the photo. As soon as the telltale *click* had sounded, he dropped the pose and planted the girl back on her feet.

"Whew," she said, a little breathless at the speed with which she'd been righted. "You sure are strong. Do you work out?"

Vader caught a spluttering sound from Fred's direction.

"In our job, it pays to be fit," Vader told the girl. Her gaze drifted back and forth over the musculature of his torso. He fought the urge to say, *Eyes up here.* "The better to rescue pretty girls from all those fiery infernos."

She sighed at the prospect of a fiery inferno. But Vader wasn't paying attention to her anymore; Cherie was somewhere in the crowd. He knew it, even though he couldn't exactly say how. Maybe he'd caught a glimpse of her red hair, the color of Hot Tamales, through the throng of visitors. Maybe he'd heard a thread of her voice, that silvery, tender, maddening voice of hers, between the shouts of the Muster Games participants scrambling to don turnouts. Or maybe it was his sixth sense that always responded whenever Cherie was near.

Stud brought the photo to the blond girl, who by now had realized that Vader's gaze had wandered. She shifted her attention to Fred.

"Hey, you're kinda cute too," she told Stud. "Are you a Bachelor Fireman?"

"We don't really call ourselves that." Fred reddened. According to local legend, a volunteer fireman from the 1850s, thwarted in love when his mail-order bride ran off with a robber, laid a curse on the station. Since, in the time-honored tradition of firemen everywhere, his fellow firefighters had relentlessly teased him about his broken heart, he'd vowed that every San Gabriel fireman forevermore should suffer in love the way he had.

The curse certainly seemed to apply to Vader and Fred, both of whom were still single.

"You want a picture with Stud too? I'll take it," offered Vader. Normally he liked feminine attention. In fact, he loved it. But this thing with Cherie had been knocking him off his game for a while. Two failed proposals took it out of a guy. He'd been avoiding her since Psycho's wedding two weeks ago. He wasn't sure what she was doing here. Hope for Firefighters was *his* turf.

He realized the girl was waving a hand in front of his face. "You all right there, big guy?"

"Sure. Little thirsty. Hot day, huh? Hey, you have fun today. Thanks for supporting the San Gabriel Fire Department, we sure do appreciate it." He moved her away from the backdrop under the guise of reaching for a water bottle. With a sulky pout, she snatched up her photo and wandered to the next booth, where Ace, the blond surfer-boy rookie, was serving up his mother's Southern fried chicken.

"I need a bathroom break," said Fred, slapping a "Closed" sign on the photo booth. "Be right back." He hurried away as Vader slouched against one of the sawhorses that partitioned off their area. Three city blocks had been cleared of cars for the Hope for Firefighters event. White canopied stands lined both sides of the street, and happy crowds of sweaty San Gabriel residents strolled from one to the next. Vader loved this event, because he actually got to talk to people when they were in a good mood, rather than terrified, traumatized, or unconscious.

He tilted his head back and let the water flow into his mouth. It was a scorching hot August day. The force of the sun overhead was nearly physical, reminding him of the way air heated by a fire beat against his body. A few stray drops of water rolled down his throat and chest, offering some welcome relief. He should have signed up for the dunk tank. But since he, more than anyone else at the station, fit the image of a macho, ridiculously muscled superhero-type, once again he'd been given photo booth duty.

Last year. He swore it. He was becoming a cliché.

"Isn't that your friend, Cherie?" A smirky male voice caught his attention. "I think he's trying out for a Crystal Geyser ad. Hand me the camera, Nick."

Vader groaned. He knew that voice. While he didn't hate anyone—it wasn't in his nature—*if* he'd hated someone, it would be the owner of that voice, Soren. He was one of Cherie's housemates, the other being Nick. Soren and Nick had an emo-goth-trance band called Optimal Doom, which for some reason they thought was super-hip.

Vader refused to say what he thought. Cherie's housemates were friends of her brother Jacob, and she was fiercely, unshakably loyal to her brother.

Reluctantly, he turned his head. And there she was, standing just behind the two weedy guys in their black T-shirts, her cinnamon-red hair in a haphazard pile, a little sundress the color of pink lemonade skimming her generous curves, looking so delicious every muscle in his body clenched.

She smiled uncertainly at him and gave a little wave. He frowned at her. How dare she smile at him, after shooting him down a second time?

She lifted her chin and intensified her smile. That was Cherie. Always determined to make the best of things and stay friends, no matter what. "Yes, that's my buddy Vader."

Buddy? *Buddy?* Vader saw red. She didn't call him

her "buddy" when she screamed his name in mid-orgasm, she didn't call him "buddy" when he tied her to the bedposts—granted, she'd been pissed that he'd used his socks, but that hadn't stopped her from coming three times and . . .

He shook himself to attention just as Soren took a picture of him, most likely looking like an idiot as he gaped at them over an empty water bottle. "That'll be five dollars for the photo," he told Soren.

"But I didn't pose with you."

"Doesn't matter. If you want a picture of me, it's five dollars."

"Dude, get real. This is a public place. I can take whatever pictures I want."

Vader's jaw tightened. "This is a charity event. It's five dollars."

"Then I take my picture back. Here." He deleted the photo from his camera. "Gone." He smirked. "No more Poland Springs ad for you."

"Hey," Cherie protested. "Was that necessary?"

Vader would have liked to pick the loser up and launch him toward the dunk tank, but he reminded himself that Cherie appreciated Soren's prompt rent payments. "Let me guess. You guys have been walking around here, taking pictures and making fun of stuff, and you haven't bought one thing yet."

The two guys looked at each other, smirking. "Yeah, pretty much."

He shook his head, disgusted, and turned away. They weren't worth his time. He didn't know why Cherie put up with them. Maybe it was just one more indication of how wrong for each other he and Cherie were.

Too bad the rest of him didn't seem to believe that.

Even now, a little current of electricity was racing through his body.

"Don't you worry, I'm spending enough money for all of us," said Cherie, with a trace of a Southern accent and another determined smile. "I got a Sloppy Joe from Ryan that was pretty much out of this world. I bought a whole strip of those raffle tickets. They said the prize was a Firefighter for a Day." She gave a nervous little laugh. "No wonder they're going so fast."

Cherie was always innocently making comments that others could interpret as lascivious. Then she'd realize it, and two spots of pink would appear on her cheeks and . . .

Vader didn't want to look back at her, fought not to do so. He fixed his gaze on the orange and black swirls of the photo backdrop, but damn it, when it came to Cherie, his willpower evaporated faster than mist in the August heat. He gave in and let his eyes travel back to her. She was digging in her little silver purse, the one that was shaped like a dog bone. She triumphantly held up a twenty-dollar bill.

"And now I'd like a photo with San Gabriel's sexiest fireman."

"You're going to pay twenty bucks for a picture of you and your ex?" Soren laughed.

Nick chimed in. "Maybe he'll make his pecs do a little jig for the camera."

Vader clenched his hands into fists so tight, they could have broken through steel. Sure, he played the clown sometimes. He liked to bring a smile to people's faces. That didn't give them the right to—

A soft hand on his forearm interrupted his train of thought. "Ignore them," Cherie whispered. The scent of lilac, her favorite, surrounded him, making him feel as if he'd just lain down in a spring meadow, with

Cherie beside him. "They're just being jerks. Because they can. Now come on, let me make it up to you. Twenty dollars for a photo."

He pulled his arm away from her touch. "I don't think so, Cherie."

"Why not, for mercy's sake? It's for charity. Think of all those widows and orphans."

He pulled her aside, well out of earshot of her house-mates. "Why did you come here?"

Her lips parted, as if he'd taken her off guard. They were distractingly curvy, just like the rest of her. She studied him with serious gray eyes. They weren't really gray, he knew. One afternoon, during a picnic, he'd spent a long time studying them, noticing concentric rings and identifying their colors. The shimmery green of dew-covered grass, the deep gold of an antique picture frame, the gray of evening fog over a lake. "Vader, please. I support the fire department just like everyone else here. I support you. And I wanted to see you. I . . . I missed you. Vader, you're . . . well, you're very dear to me. You know you are."

He groaned out loud. *No freaking willpower.* "You turned me down, Cherie. Twice."

"I thought we were going to erase all that. Besides, I wouldn't put it like that. What I said was that I wasn't interested in getting married. Lots of people aren't."

"Yes, but your eyelid twitched."

"Excuse me?"

"Don't you know that your right eyelid twitches when you're not telling the whole truth? I've really got to get you to a poker table one of these days."

Her hand flew to her right eye. "It does not."

"Fine. Five-card stud, dollar a point."

Just then Fred came back and flipped the sign back to "Open."

"Hey, Cherie." He glanced at Vader, clearly looking for a cue as to how friendly he should be to her. Vader shrugged, and Fred's smile broadened. "Great to see you. Ready for your close-up?"

"You know it. Now, Stud, I'm paying extra for this baby, so make it good."

He handed her a helmet. "Why don't you put that on? It'd be cute."

Vader knew plenty of girls who wouldn't have wanted to mess up their hair with a clunky, heavy old fireman's helmet. But Cherie was game for anything. She grinned at Fred, then gave Vader the helmet. "Hold it for a sec, please."

She reached into her pile of hair and pulled out the pins that were holding everything in place up there. A torrent of spicy, sun-spangled hair came tumbling down over her bare shoulders.

Vader ground his teeth against the inevitable hardening of his body. Did she have to be so damn sexy? She planted the helmet on her head, and he lifted his eyes to the heavens, wondering just what he'd done to make the Almighty torture him like this. She looked . . . adorable. And he adored her. That's all there was to it.

And that's all there'd ever be. Him, adoring her. Her, back and forth about him.

He took a deep breath and stepped toward her. He could suffer a little more, for charity. *Widows and orphans. Widows and orphans.* "Come on. Let's get in front of the backdrop."

Cherie glanced at the sheet of plywood behind them. It featured dramatic flames and billowing smoke taken from a close-up of an apartment fire. "The photo's going to show a fire raging behind us?"

Hopefully it wouldn't also show the fire raging

inside him. He wondered if she felt a fraction of the lust scorching through his veins.

Soren hooted with laughter. "That's called the fire down below, babe."

She shot her housemate a scathing look. "Shut up, Soren. You're acting like an idiot."

Instantly, the guy piped down. Vader rolled his eyes. Cherie loved to mother people, and in the case of her housemates, that included trying to correct their rude manners. Maybe he should let her boss him around too. But no. He had too much leader-of-the-pack, take-charge, tough-guy in him. He'd tried to tone it down, but what was the point? He'd never be the emo type. He'd never be Nick.

Which gave him an idea. In one swift motion, he swept Cherie into his embrace, one arm under her legs, the other supporting her back. The breath whooshed out of her in a gasp of surprise. Her hands clutched his shoulders. Cherie was tall and she was all woman, an overflowing armful of warm flesh. He'd bet anything not many men would try to carry her like this. He, on the other hand, barely noticed the weight. Those work-outs sure paid off when he wanted to sweep a woman off her feet.

He stepped in front of the backdrop, where he braced his legs apart in a heroic stance and bent over her. She stared up at him, her pupils widening until her eyes were storm cloud gray. He knew this look. He'd seen it many times, in the throes of arousal. It meant she wanted him. It meant if they weren't in the middle of a crowded charity event, they'd be on each other in a millisecond.

That look made hope pound feverishly through his veins. She still wanted him, no matter what she said.

He leaned his head close to hers, so mere fractions

of an inch separated them. At this distance, he saw the tiny pulse that beat at her temple, the glimmers of moss green in her irises, the dimple by her chin, the hint of sunburn at the peak of her cheekbones. He felt her heart skitter, her body tremble. Deep satisfaction settled in his gut. No doubt about it. She felt the pull just as much as he did. She might try to hide it or deny it or laugh it off or any of the other wacky things she'd done since they'd met. But he knew their crazy chemistry worked both ways.

Mutual knowledge hummed between them. Both were attracted; both were aware the *other* was attracted.

Cherie splayed her hand on his chest, as if to push him off. But the hell if he'd let her. He was tired of that inevitable arm's length she kept putting between them. She'd come here, into his territory, and she could damn well deal with the consequences. He tightened his grip.

"What are you doing?" she whispered fiercely.

"Giving you your money's worth," he growled. "Now smile for the camera."

She started to look toward the camera, but he shifted her so she was angled his direction. "*For* the camera, not at it. Look at me. I'm the one rescuing you from certain death."

She regained a bit of her usual bravado. "Certain death? My, my. That does sound dire."

"Oh, it is. You see, we were making love in the third floor bedroom. We were a little distracted." He adjusted his grip so one of his hands cradled her head. He knew how much she loved his hands.

"Let me guess. Things got so hot there was a spontaneous combustion."

"As soon as I saw the flames, I leaped into action."

"And put a helmet on me?"

"Sure. And some clothes. That part was a mistake." He let his eyes rake down her body and caught her shiver.

She swatted him on the chest, exactly how the other girl had, but with completely different results. Under his padded firefighter's pants, he went rock-hard and aching. If only they were alone, if only he could turn this little scene into something real, something that involved nothing but their two naked bodies and lots of moaning.

He bent his forehead to hers, fighting to get a grip on his hot need for her. "What is it? Why do you keep running away from me? It's like you're afraid of something."

"I'm not—"

"Are you afraid of some*one*?"

"Of course not," she said quickly.

Her right eyelid twitched.

The camera clicked.

"Awesome shot," said Fred. "We should put this one in the calendar."

"No," said Cherie quickly. "It's strictly personal." Her eyelid twitched again.

Vader knew he was on to something. Cherie was afraid . . . of something or someone.

As Vader let her slip back to her feet, he decided that one way or another, he was going to get the truth out of Cherie Harper. Once a man had been turned down twice, he deserved some answers. It was time to haul himself out of his funk and take some action.

He was damn tired of being underestimated.

Chapter Two

By the time they reached the Muster Games, which were being held at the small park at the end of the street, Cherie finally managed to get her breath back. Every time she stole a look at the photo Fred had taken, her breathing did more funny things, like make her voice sound strange and her cheeks go hot.

Vader had that effect on her. Every single time. It was the most impossible situation.

In the photo, he looked like a cartoon image of male hotness, like an old weight-lifting advertisement a scrawny kid might gaze at longingly, wishing he could someday look even a little like that. Cradled in his strong arms, she looked positively tiny. No mean feat.

She tucked the photo into her purse. It had cost her twenty dollars, a fight with Optimal Doom, and two weeks of trying to forget Vader. If she was smart, she'd use it as a reminder to avoid him. But she'd probably just drool over it like a lovesick idiot.

One whole section of the park had been set aside for the Muster Games. Firefighters in San Gabriel Fire Department T-shirts were yelling and clapping for the daring civilians who were trying to pull an old-fashioned wooden cart with a hose coiled inside. Everyone was laughing and hooting and hollering.

"This is weird, man," said Nick, aiming his iPhone at the scene. "I didn't know they did this shit anymore."

"They don't, that's the whole point," said Cherie, more sharply than she'd intended. "That's old-school equipment. That's how they did it back in the old days."

"Check you out. Been boning up on firefighters? Or just boning 'em?" Soren snickered.

Cherie set her jaw. Soren and Nick were at their most irritating when it came to Vader. "Leave it alone, why don't you? Can't you just enjoy the sunshine and the pretty park and all the families having fun?"

They both looked at her as if she was nuts. "We're creatures of the night, Cherie," said Soren. "If we could be vampires, we would be."

Nick added, "Too bad that kit we ordered on the Internet didn't work. Or did it?" He bared his teeth, Dracula-style.

She shuddered. "You guys are weird enough without going supernatural."

"That's why you love us, right?" Soren winked.

Right now, she wasn't so sure. Soren and Nick were friends with her brother Jacob. When Jacob had enrolled in Santa Cruz College, he'd insisted she find suitable housemates to take his place. For six years, ever since they'd left Arkansas, they'd stuck together and protected each other. He refused to let her live alone. But then he found a problem with every candidate she interviewed. Female housemates might bring unvetted guys around; male housemates might come on to her. Finally Jacob had solved the whole dilemma by picking Soren and Nick, who inhabited a sexually ambiguous, body-pierced, spoken-word gender nether land.

For sure, it wasn't safe for her to live alone, though she wasn't sure how much help Soren and Nick would be if the man she still had nightmares about—Frank Mackintosh—showed up.

"I think I've had enough for one day. You guys ready to roll?"

"No, wait. I can't leave until I see how many people that dude manages to spray with the hose."

The hose had now been dumped off the cart, and an older man was aiming it at an orange cone. Water sprayed everywhere, but the cone remained stubbornly standing. To the side, a couple of firemen—she recognized Vader's friend Ryan Blake—laughed so hard they had to bend over and rest their hands on their knees. The sight gave her a pang; Vader laughed like that too, with wholehearted joy and fun, the life shining from his eyes.

Forget about Vader.

She checked her watch.

"I have to get going, guys. Tango class. And Nick, you promised to help me."

Every Saturday, she taught a Singles Tango class at the Move Me Dance Studio. So far, the class had produced three engaged couples and countless successful dates. Word had spread, and her classes had gotten bigger by the week.

"Oh fine," Nick grumbled. "Pick on the one-sixteenth Colombian guy. We don't even do the tango."

"I'm from backwoods redneck-ville. If I can tango,

anyone can." She often said that exact same thing in her classes. It always made the students relax.

Nick spent the entire drive to the studio harping on her relationship with Vader. He didn't stop even once they pulled up outside Move Me.

"Jacob left us in charge. He said to watch out for you. Especially when it comes to men. He said you're naïve and not cynical enough. Lucky for you, I have extra cynicism to spare." Nick was the quieter, more angst-ridden of the duo. He wrote the lyrics of their painfully morose songs. Generally, she preferred Nick's company to Soren's more abrasive personality, but not if he was going to talk about Vader.

"Don't be such a Nosy Nellie. I don't need you guys getting in the middle of anything."

She stalked out of the ancient Mercedes she'd converted to run on veggie diesel. Nick slouched after her.

"Oh, believe me, I don't want to get in the middle. I hear the noise you freaks make at night. I'm not touching that."

Cherie felt her face go pink. Despite her six years in California, her strict upbringing still made her blush over certain things. Nick followed after her. "Seriously, what is it with you two? You ought to either cut him loose or marry him."

"Excuse me? You're telling me to marry Vader? I thought you hated him."

Cherie hurried toward the entrance of Move Me. Of her many jobs—she had a patchwork quilt of them around town—teaching tango was her guilty pleasure. She loved the provocative music and the way the dance suggested all sorts of naughtiness without ever getting too blatant about it. Move Me had become a haven to her, a place where she could lose herself in music. She also practiced her self-defense moves here, the one thing that gave her a small sense of security.

"You don't get a vote. Vader and I are none of your business," she told Nick over her shoulder. "So how about you guys back off?"

"Can't. Jacob told us to—"

"Well, I'm firing you from whatever Jacob thought he was telling you to do. Vader and I . . . we're cool. We understand each other." She opened the glass studio door, knowing that if Vader were there, he would have opened it for her. Cool, lemon-scented air rushed past her face. The cleaning people must have come in last night.

Nick followed her down the hall to Studio A, where her class would take place. "What I don't get is why you're so different with him."

Cherie frowned as she struggled with the persnickety studio door. Lord forbid that Nick help her for one second. "Different how?"

"Normally you're like everyone's mom. You know, a sexy mom. MILF type. The young, hot mother of the kid next door, who makes cookies for you and gives you haircuts and always smells nice. And spreads a blanket over you when you're cold, and lets you pick the movie, and doesn't mind if you play your music a little loud and—"

"Is there a point in here somewhere?" Cherie finally got the door open and plopped her dance bag in the corner of the studio. Light glowed from the freshly polished hardwood floor and bounced off the wall of mirrors. Her students would be arriving any second. She needed to focus on preparing for the class, not listen to Nick babble.

She searched through her bag, looking for the twirly,

parrot-print skirt she'd brought to teach in. Maybe if she ignored him, Nick would stop talking.

No such luck. "The point is, you're not so motherly with him. You don't seem like super earth mother with her hand on the pulse of the universe anymore. You're more like a regular girl. You get kind of flirty and fluttery around him. And you forget about everyone else."

Cherie straightened up, her hands filled with her dance outfit. "Let me get this straight. You don't like Vader because when I'm with him, I forget to cut your hair and rub your feet?"

Nick smirked, hands in the pockets of his tight black jeans. "You've never rubbed my feet, and Vader'd probably rip my throat out if I asked you to, and *that's* my point. He acts like he owns you. So that's why Optimal Doom is taking a stand. If you're not getting married, and he doesn't own you, then why doesn't he hit the road, toad? Don't look back, Jack."

Cherie felt the tips of her ears burn. Uh oh, not a good sign. She took a deep breath, but it was too late. A wave of heat traveled from her ears all the way down to her toes. She threw her dance clothes onto the floor. A student opened the door, but Cherie put up a commanding finger that made the girl snatch her head back and close the door.

"First of all," she told Nick furiously, "you have no 'stand' to take. It's *my* life. I do what *I* want. I've come too far to let any man, even a pretend one in a lame black T-shirt that says 'Suck My Blood,' tell me what to do."

"Why are you dissing the shirt?"

"Second, I don't want Vader to leave. I like him. He's *good*. Do you know how hard it is to find someone *good* in this world? No, you wouldn't know. Everything comes easy for you. Well, it isn't like that for everyone. Some people are born in a big pile of crap and have to fight their way out and—" She caught her breath in a gulp of air. Nick, his shoulders caved forward, was looking at her with a mixture of bewilderment and hurt feelings. How could he possibly understand? Nick, despite his posing, was a rich kid who wouldn't understand the first thing about where she came from.

"You know what? I'll find someone else to do the class. You don't have to stay." She bundled him toward the door. "I'll be home late, so you and Soren can make your own dinner."

She closed the door behind him, then plopped down onto the polished hardwood floor. Catching a glimpse of herself in the mirror that stretched across the opposite wall, she gave herself a scolding shake of the head.

Nick was an innocent, if annoying, bystander. And the fact was, he had a legitimate point. She ought to end things with Vader once and for all. She'd *tried* to end things. But it never seemed to work. Somehow they always ended up together again. And each time it got harder to keep things casual.

Deep in her dance bag, her cell phone rang. She scrabbled through it, found her purse, and reached her phone just before it went to voice mail.

"It's Jacob." Right away, she knew something was wrong. Since he'd gone off to college, her brother called only about important things like his breakups and new boyfriends.

"What happened?"

"I got a call from Arkansas. Humility ran away."

"*What?*" Humility was the next youngest sister in their family—eighteen, a year older than Cherie had been when she and Jacob had fled Pine Creek, Arkansas. "Did she run away with Robbie Mackintosh?"

"No. But he's gone too. Apparently their engagement was a sham. They were both biding their time until they could make a run for it."

"Wow." Cherie ran her thumb up and down the edge of her phone. Clever trick, she had to admit. In her crazy family—she thought of it more as a cult than a family—early marriages were mandatory. "Has she called you?"

"No ma'am. I was checking to see if she'd called you."

Cherie shook her head, realized he couldn't see her, then kept on shaking it as she spoke. "No. Holy smokes. What should we do? *What should we do?* Oh no, Jacob, Mackintosh is going to be furious. Robbie's his oldest son and the only one with any brains. What if he comes looking for him?"

"Shhh. Calm down, Cherie. You're scaring your fairy godmother. Or at least your fairy brother." She closed her eyes and tried to conjure her beloved brother's wry smile and twinkling blue eyes.

Instead, Frank Mackintosh's grimy, whiskered face filled her mind's eye, the way she'd last seen him, looming over her with a whiskey-slobber leer, smelling of chicken poop and evil victory. Reaching for her, sure he had her cornered, trapped. Then the terrible sound that old pipe had made when she'd flung it at him.

She drew in a shaky breath. It was okay. She'd gotten away, and now she was here. Safe. Sort of.

"Here's what we do," said Jacob. "We don't do anything. Humility knows how to find us."

"Yeah, but what if she does find us, and Mackintosh follows her here?" She was having a hard time catching her breath. Her throat seemed to have a vise around it.

"If she comes to San Gabriel, and he follows her, *then* you can get hysterical, 'kay? But not until then."

As always, Jacob's lighthearted approach made things look better. She blurted out the first thought that came to mind. "If only I could tell Vader everything, I'd feel—"

"*No.* We agreed. He's a fireman, that's too close to cop for comfort."

"We can trust him. I swear to heaven we can."

"Cherie, Mackintosh filed charges against us. *You can't tell anyone.* Besides, we promised in blood. Harper family vow, can't be broken."

The memory made her shudder. "I can't believe you made me do that. That was so disgusting."

He snorted. "Everything will be fine. Call me if you hear anything."

"Sure."

But it already wasn't fine. It hadn't been fine since she'd fallen for Vader.

*I don't get you and Cherie," said Fred from the passenger seat of Vader's baby-blue Ford 350, as they headed back to the station to return their gear. "You're either flirting or breaking up. Or getting back together. What's the story?"

"No story. I'm done." Vader steered his truck past Engine 1 and waved at Double D in the driver's seat. "Don't worry your pretty little head about it."

Fred fussed with a bag of ruffled potato chips he'd found in the backseat. All the firefighters knew Vader kept a stash of staples in his truck: chips, energy drinks, a case of beer buried beneath that. "You aren't going to distract me with mockery, Vader. I've known you for like, eight years."

"How quickly they grow up." Vader gave a mock-sob. "Seems like just yesterday I was waving you off to firefighter kindergarten."

"Funny. Now back to the topic of our conversation, are you and Cherie really through? For real? Like I could ask her out?"

Vader felt his entire body go rigid. He loved Stud like a brother, but at that moment he would have cheerfully tossed him out the window. "If you go near Cherie, they'll have to urban-search-and-rescue *you*."

Fred was training to join San Gabriel's new Urban Search and Rescue Squad. Vader was all for it, but that didn't mean he'd pass up the chance to ride him about it.

Fred let out a hoot. "You don't scare me, big guy. You don't fool me either. After all this time, you're still hung up on Cherie."

Vader honked, long and hard, at a driver who had veered too close to his lane. In his opinion, horns had been invented to help drivers release their frustration. "I am not 'hung up' on Cherie. I only want one thing from her now."

Stud gave a snort.

"You have such a dirty mind," Vader said piously. "Does that mean you've gotten to first base with someone by now?"

Fred muttered something under his breath. Vader caught the words "Not rising to his bait, not rising to his bait." He hid a smile. Fred was a constant source of entertainment.

"Fine," he finally said, through gritted teeth. "What one thing do you want from Cherie?"

"The truth." It came out more grimly than he'd intended. But when he thought about everything Cherie had put him through—the hot and cold, in and out, back and forth—he knew he deserved the fucking truth.

He felt Fred's surprised gaze and scrambled to paper over the too-serious moment. "And one more bone for the road." He winked.

"You don't fool me, Vader," Fred said. Vader stared straight ahead, refusing to give away any more. "You haven't fooled me for a while. You know what you should do?"

"If it has to do with Cherie, don't bother."

"It's nothing to do with her. It's about you. You should go for captain."

"*What?*" Talk about left field. In his shock, Vader turned too quickly and shaved the curb on the way into the station parking lot.

"Captain Kelly's retiring. Captain Brody said he's giving it one more month and then he's going to be fulltime at the Academy. A couple of guys on the B shift already took the exam, but neither of them passed. You're the man, Vader. Besides, you'd be a good captain."

"I would?" Vader twitched his head, feeling like a dog shaking off water. He thought the guys all saw him as a muscle-bound, gym-obsessed party boy. How did Fred get from there to captain? He pulled into his parking spot in the lot alongside San Gabriel Fire Station 1. It was a tidy brick building with a flagpole and red geranium-filled planters out front. Its lawn was immaculately mowed and unnaturally green. Every other lawn in San Gabriel was brown this time of year, but the firefighters of Station 1 had devised a sprinkler system that kept the grass a sparkling, almost obnoxious teal.

"Yeah, you would. If you don't believe me, ask around. You'd be surprised, Vader. Don't sell yourself short."

With that, Fred jumped out of the truck, grabbed his gear from the backseat, and loped into the firehouse. Vader stared after him. Captain? Was he for real? Then again, why not? He was a good firefighter. Damn good. He knew the job inside and out. He could practically fight fires in his sleep. He'd never thought about going for a promotion because . . . well, other things had taken up his time. Things that were a lot more important than advancing up the firefighter career ladder.

As if on cue, his cell phone beeped; text message coming in. As he read it, the blood drained from his face. It was from his mother.

Fell off my throne. I'm ok, but hurry pls.

Chapter Three

Vader tossed his cell phone onto the passenger seat, put his truck into reverse, and floored the accelerator. Ginny Brown was the master of putting a brave face on things, but falling out of her wheelchair couldn't possibly be good.

He lived about ten minutes away from the firehouse. He'd bought the house because of its proximity to the station, not wanting to be too far away in case something happened while he was on shift. But his mother had a bad habit of refusing to bother him when he was working. As much as he'd lectured her about it, she'd put up with a lot before she notified him.

Which made him even more worried right now.

He screeched to a stop in the driveway of the pleasant ranch-style house draped in his mother's favorite magenta bougainvillea, a color so intense it appeared to vibrate. He parked behind the blue Suburban van specially modified for his mother's wheelchair.

"Mom?" he called, bursting through the door.

"I'm in the living room," she called in her usual cheerful voice. "Don't blow your top, I'm okay, hon."

She didn't look okay, Vader thought when he reached the living room. She lay on the hardwood floor next to her wheelchair, both legs bent under her. His first instinct was to panic, but that wouldn't help anything, and she hated it when anyone made a fuss.

"Geez, Mom." He crouched next to her. "What'd you do, take a corner too fast?"

"You know me and my speed demon ways." She raised her arms so he could lift her back into the wheelchair. He put his forearms under her armpits and maneuvered her gently into the seat, taking care to keep her legs from bumping against the wheels. She wouldn't feel it, since she'd been paralyzed below the waist for seventeen years, but he couldn't bear to see her hurt.

She'd lost weight again, he noticed with a pang. Sometimes he thought she deliberately tried to shed pounds to make things easier on him. He'd have to start sneaking flaxseed oil or coconut milk into her smoothies.

"There, that's better," she said with a bright smile. "Now tell me everything, hon. How'd the photo booth go?"

He gave her a swift once-over, ignoring her effort to change the subject. "You have a bruise on your cheek."

"I do?" Her hand flew to the side of her face. "Hmm."

He gently pulled her hand away so he could get a better look. She had a stubborn set to her mouth that told him all he needed to know. "What happened?"

"Izzy and I were racing and—"

"Don't blame this on the cat." As if he knew he was being discussed, Izzy, a fat, orange pasha of a cat, rubbed against Vader's shin. Absentmindedly, he reached down to scratch between his ears. "Besides, Izzy's nearly a hundred in cat years. He couldn't run if a mouse was doing a tap dance in front of him."

His mother fussed with her hair, which had gotten rumpled from her fall. Her hair was the same brown as his, a rich espresso shot with bronze. She refused to cut it, even though a shampoo girl had to come wash it once a week. Vader didn't have the heart to argue. She'd lost the use of her legs, and soon thereafter, her husband. Who was he to deny her one remaining vanity?

"Come on, Mom. I won't tell you anything about the fair until you give me the complete incident report. I'm an EMT just arriving at the scene. What do we have?"

His mother gave in. She loved anything to do with firefighting. "We have a fifty-five-year-old woman who lost consciousness for unknown reasons. She believes she was out for about ten minutes, but has no recollection of what caused her collapse. Pulse is racing, but blood pressure is probably normal."

"You *fainted*?"

She hadn't had fainting spells since the first year after the car accident, when he'd been fourteen and completely freaked out. At the time, the doctors had said that the results of her level of brain trauma were unpredictable. They'd said she shouldn't be left alone.

That had apparently been his father's cue to take a hike. Vader had been left alone with the duty of never leaving his mother alone.

"We need to call Dr. Swenson."

"Please don't."

But Vader already had his phone out. While keeping an eagle eye on his mother, who still seemed shaky, he explained to the nurse what had happened. She instantly put him through to Dr. Swenson. Vader did a thorough assessment of his mother's condition while she listened closely; she'd had seventeen years of hearing her body discussed in impersonal medical terms.

As a trained paramedic himself, Vader knew what to look for. After all these years, he and Dr. Swenson had a kind of shorthand together. He quickly communicated the fact that his mother seemed rattled but not disoriented, her pupils were not dilated, and the only apparent damage was the bruise on her cheek. He listened to what the man had to say, thanked him, then clicked off the phone.

"He wants you to come in for an MRI sometime in the next couple of days."

She made a face. "Him and his tests. They never actually tell you anything."

He couldn't disagree. And the tests cost a fortune. "Still, we should do what he says. He's kept you alive so far."

"No." A sheen of moisture glimmered in her eyes. "*You've* kept me alive."

His mother rarely got weepy. She must be really shaken up. He shifted into "Vader" mode. "Aw Mom! Don't start with the tears. Are you forgetting I'm a guy? You're trying to kill me, right? Just cut to the chase and drop me into a vat of battery acid. Or throw me in a . . . a bouncy castle with a . . . man-eating lion. Lash me to a TV playing nonstop shopping channel."

Finally she laughed. Reassured, he straightened up and put his hands on the handles of the wheelchair. "Now do you want to see the video I shot at the fair or what? You can check it out while I get you some ice for that bruise."

For the past couple of years, he'd been taking his

video camera to work and documenting the crazy antics that went on at Station 1. He never managed to shoot any actual fire footage, since he was always in the thick of that. But practical jokes, goofing around, handball games, firehouse dinners were all fair game. To his mother, those videos were better than a million soap operas or episodes of *Bones*, her second favorite form of entertainment.

The guys at the station had no idea they'd become a sort of long-running TV show in the Brown household. They didn't even know about his mother. As far as he was concerned, she was his responsibility, and he didn't want anyone feeling sorry either for him or for her.

"Fred said something funny today," he said as he wheeled her into the living room, which was dominated by a large flat-screen TV. Ginny spent a lot of time in this room, either watching TV or working out with her Wii. A desk in the corner of the room held a computer at just the right height for her. That was where she wrote her daily blog, "Cripple Creek," in which she offered advice to other wheelchair-bound people, and surfed the Internet for everything that caught her attention. Since the accident and his father's departure, she'd preferred to stay at home unless he dragged her out for a walk or a spin in the Suburban. These days, her friends were online instead of down the street. Vader shuddered to think what her life would be like without the Internet.

"Isn't Fred always saying something funny? He's such a cutie-patootie."

Vader gleefully pictured Fred's face if he heard that one. "Not that kind of funny. He actually said I should take the promotional exam." He crossed to the TV to hook up the cable of his video camera. "It's the exam you take when you want to be promoted to the next level. Captain I, in my case."

She gripped the arms of her wheelchair, nearly lifting herself off in her excitement. "You'd be the captain of Station 1, like Captain Brody?"

"Steady now. No more accidents. *If* I passed, *and* they gave me the job, I'd be captain of the engine company. On the A shift. But I'd have to be a Captain I for two years until I could be Captain II, like Brody is." Even saying the words made him uncomfortable. Captain Brody was a legend in San Gabriel. How could a goofball like Vader Brown ever take his place? "Ah, forget it. I thought it was funny, that's all." He cued up the clip from the event.

"It's a good idea," his mother said firmly. "Don't you laugh this off or you'll be needing ice for that thick head of yours instead. Of course you should be captain."

Aw hell. He should have known she'd latch on to this idea like a toddler with a teddy bear. "Here's the best part of the entire event. This is Double D in the dunk tank." He played the clip. On the screen, the big-bellied veteran was taunting the kid who was trying to unseat him. He put his thumbs in his ears and waggled his hands. "Wait for it, wait for it . . ." Finally the kid hit the target and Double D went down with a massive splash. "Shazam!"

He used the momentary distraction to disappear into the kitchen. "I'll be right back with that ice."

"Vader!" his mother called after him. "We're not through with this!"

Cursing under his breath, he slowly banged his head against the freezer door. He should never have mentioned this to his mother. Big mistake. No one was more persistent than a proud mama stuck in a wheelchair with not enough to distract her. How could he tell her that *she* was the reason he couldn't consider the captain gig? Captains had a lot more responsibilities than the guys at his level. The studying to *become* captain would take up huge amounts of time. How was he supposed to take care of her *and* commit to such a big change?

He reached into the freezer for the quick-freeze packs he kept for his many injuries. He was always bruising something. Digging through a drawer of dish towels, he found a soft one that wouldn't chafe his mother's head.

On the other hand . . . Captains got paid more money. He didn't know exactly how much more. Maybe it would be enough to bring back Betsy, the home health care aide. Their insurance benefits had run out last month, and he'd had to cut her hours. He shuddered, remembering the sight of his mother curled up on the floor. Since the age of fourteen, he'd been protecting her. That was his job. He'd even taken out a huge life insurance policy for himself, so that if he died while on a fire, she'd be financially secure.

But he rested a lot easier when he knew that someone else was keeping an eye on her while he was at work.

He wrapped the ice pack in the towel, grabbed a jar of salted peanuts, since he hadn't eaten since lunch, and headed back to the living room.

Ginny was replaying the epic splashdown of Double D in slow motion. "Do you know that I think he tripped the lever himself?"

"No. Really?" He squinted at the screen.

"See here? His hand goes behind his back? What's he doing?"

"Scratching an itch. Looking for a donut. Who

knows? It's Double D." He handed her the ice pack and settled her hand against her cheekbone.

"Is he still gluten-free?"

"Sure. If you don't count hamburger buns and 'everything' bagels. And a cruller or two. He's doing good though. I told you about the chicken wings he made last week, right?"

That was their cue to settle into the beloved routine they shared, in which he spun firehouse stories, some real, some exaggerated, some completely invented, until she dozed off for her nap, at which point he'd tenderly extract her from her chair and carry her to her bed. This time he stuck with reality, because half of his brain was still mulling over the captain idea. Maybe Freddie was right. Maybe he should ask around. Maybe he could pick up some moonlighting work while he was at it.

One thing was for sure. To properly take care of his mother, he had to step it up and make more money.

He must have dozed off in mid-story, because he was in the throes of a vague dream in which Cherie was steering a large wheelbarrow overflowing with hundred-dollar bills toward him, when a loud exclamation startled him awake.

"Well, look who the cat dragged into the fair." Ginny was stationed a mere foot in front of the flat-screen, which showed a clip of Cherie and himself as they talked by the Firefighter Photo Booth.

"Hey, where'd that come from?" Fred must have used his video camera without asking.

"What was *she* doing there?" His mother was not a fan of Cherie, though they'd never actually met. All her knowledge was secondhand, mostly obtained during the bleaker moments of Vader and Cherie's on-and-off relationship.

"Same as everyone else. Supporting the San Gabriel Fire Department."

"Hmph. So she's got red hair now? What happened to the pink streaks?"

"I forgot to ask her. I was too busy flexing my muscles for the camera." He watched the two of them on the TV screen, himself huge and shirtless but for suspenders, Cherie even more curvaceous than in person, filling the screen with summery pinks and hot cinnamon reds. He wouldn't be surprised to see bees hovering near her. The two of them were standing to the side of the photo booth. In the background, attendees wandered past, munching on hot dogs, carrying balloons. But he and Cherie seemed to be locked together in their own private world. Neither of them looked at anything but each other.

Watching the two people on screen, he felt excruciatingly awkward, as if he was invading his own privacy. The raw intensity vibrating between him and Cherie was embarrassing.

His mother fell silent, but she shot him a disapproving glance. After their second breakup, she'd stopped supporting his relationship with Cherie in any way, shape, or form. And she didn't even know about his two rejected proposals.

"We were just talking," he said defensively.

That was her cue. "There's never 'just' anything with that girl. Why don't you let me find you someone nice and uncomplicated? I know you, Vader. You might act like all you want is a party, but you'd give up all those crazy nights out for a nice girl to love. I've been surfing around on dating sites and I found one specifically for firefighters and—"

"No."

"Vader, you're my only child. Do you know what

it's like to see you eating your heart out for a girl who doesn't appreciate you?"

He opened his mouth to tell Ginny that he and Cherie were through, that she could stop nagging him on the subject. But something in him refused to say it. Because it wasn't true, damn it. He and Cherie were a long way from being through; he knew it in his bones. "Cherie and I are fine the way we are."

"Doesn't look that way to me."

She gestured to the TV screen. Vader looked, desperate for escape, and saw the camera zoom wildly in and out. Fred must have been fooling with the lens somehow. A close-up of the tendons on his neck turned into a panoramic view of the blue sky, then shifted back to a wildly tilted angle on Cherie. And there it froze. Or maybe Fred stopped recording at that moment.

At any rate, Cherie had just glanced toward the camera, though she didn't seem to realize it was there. Her head was tilted thoughtfully to the side, and underneath her bright, eager smile, a different expression lurked, like one of those "ghosts" captured during long exposures. She looked . . . hopeless? Desperate? Haunted?

Hell, he was no wordsmith. He didn't have the right vocabulary for that look. But all along he'd known it was there. He'd always sensed the vulnerability beneath her busy-ness, a sad, sweet wistfulness shadowing her fun-loving nature. Maybe that's what kept drawing him back for more.

His mother snapped off the TV. "If only I had a remote control for your hormones."

"Okay, that's the line, right there. The one you don't cross."

Wisely, she subsided as he stalked from the room. It was one thing to live with your mother, take care of her, entertain her. He'd accepted his lot in life long ago.

Discussing his "hormones" with her was another matter.

As soon as Ginny had eaten her dinner, he'd head for Firefly and see what trouble he could get into. His mother was all wrong about that part. He loved to party; he *needed* to party.

Hell, if not for his firehouse buddies, he'd have blown a fuse long ago.

Chapter Four

If Cherie were to be completely honest with herself, she'd started falling for Vader the first moment she'd ever seen him, more than a year and a half ago.

She and Jacob had decided to spend Thanksgiving playing pool at the local dive. Vader and a couple of his firehouse buddies had stopped in and immediately lit up the place. Try as she might, she couldn't keep her eyes off him. He was so . . . big. His muscles were enormous, his chest broad and solid and bursting with strength. He looked as if he could bench-press the pool table—for that matter, all the pool tables in a big pile. His appearance pleased some primal part of her; she kept stealing glances his way, confirming that some-one actually looked like that.

But it wasn't just his muscles. She was also fasci-nated by his exuberant personality, the big smile he beamed around the grungy pool hall, the warmth in his deep-set eyes. They were brown, she'd noticed when he leaned into the light for his first shot. A burnt-sugar brown, somewhere between caramel and milk chocolate, a brown that allowed no room for coldness or doubt. The phrase "hunk of burning love" popped into her mind and wouldn't leave—even before she knew he was a firefighter.

He must have caught her staring, because next thing she knew he was standing over her, blazing his smile down on her like sunshine and asking if he could buy her a Thanksgiving drink. "Cuz I'm giving thanks I laid eyes on you," he said with a wink.

Jacob had groaned and rolled his eyes, but she tuned him out. It wasn't hard. The force of Vader's personality made everyone else fade away. It was unnerving, really. It gave her the sensation of stepping into a whirlpool that could sweep her off somewhere she'd never been. Like Alice in . . . Vaderland.

He'd taken her home, but of course they hadn't slept together. She made him molasses cookies in the middle of the night and let him try every trick in the book to talk her into bed. And some new ones—fireman-style.

"This house of yours is Victorian era," he said, kissing the inside of her wrist, the heat of his breath making her squirm. "They weren't as strict about fire exits back then. If a fire broke out, what would you do?"

"I'd call 911."

"And guess who'd come? Me. So we're ahead of the game. I'm already here. And I don't have a bunch of other firefighters right behind me. So we can skip that whole step. And we can skip the step where you realize you could have died and you figure out what's really important."

"Let me guess. You?"

"You and me, baby. You and me is what's important. Life. Fun. Live it up. Drink it in."

She burst out laughing. He grinned widely. "That's a start. I like how you laugh. That little Southern accent of yours is adorable."

"No one has an accent when they laugh."

"You do. It's sexy. It's the kind of accent that makes me want to flip you over on this couch and find out what's under that blouse you're wearing."

"Take it easy, big guy."

As soon as she said that, he stopped teasing. "Am I scaring you? I don't mean to. I know I'm large. I can intimidate people even when I'm not trying to. If I make you nervous, just say so. I'll lighten up."

She eyed him as he shifted back on her sapphire velvet couch, moving his powerful body away to give her some space. "I'm not exactly tiny myself," she pointed out with a raised eyebrow.

"You're perfect," he said with such ardent, complete conviction that her heart did a little flip.

She held out for two torturous months, but inevitably their raging attraction won the day. While she didn't regret a single moment of the time she'd spent in bed with Vader, that slipping, whirlpool feeling had never left her. In fact, it had gotten stronger the more serious Vader got. Sometimes, when the edge got too close, when that rabbit-hole feeling threatened, she scrambled back in complete panic. She knew it hurt Vader, but it was better that way. Better for him.

How could she tell him that she wouldn't—*couldn't*—make any sort of real commitment? Even if she ached to do so. Even if she wished with all her heart that things had happened differently the night she ran from that psychotic madman. If only that blow on the head hadn't sent Mackintosh to the hospital. If only he hadn't reported her to the police. If only he wasn't famous for his grudges.

Better to hurt Vader's feelings than to put him in Frank Mackintosh's line of sight.

So when, a few days after the Hope for Firefighters event, she got a call from the San Gabriel Fire Department informing her that she'd won the raffle drawing for Firefighter for a Day, she didn't take another breath until they told her who she'd "won." Fred Breen would be her Firefighter for a Day. She nearly fainted with relief . . . or was it regret? When it came to Vader, she didn't know anything anymore.

The idea of going for captain wouldn't leave Vader's mind. He decided it was at least worth running by some of his firehouse peeps. He started with Joe the Toe, an engineer at the Rancho Camino Station, with whom he had a long-running pool competition going. So far, he'd won ninety-six games, Joe had won a hundred and ten.

"If it's simply a question of remuneration, why don't you give my company a go?" Joe, one of the few firefighters in Southern California even bigger than Vader, bent over the pool table. Not only was he huge, but he was black. Not only was he black, but he had a British accent and an extensive vocabulary. People found him confusing, which delighted him. He and Vader, being opposites in just about every way besides size, had gone from being bitter rivals in the gym to solid buddies.

"You still doing the moving thing?"

"You'd be surprised how much people will pay to simply transport their possessions from one place to another. But actually, I'm speaking of my new moonlighting project. I've been playing with stocks and doing quite well." He sank the six ball in the corner pocket.

"Count me out on that." Vader absentmindedly chalked his cue, his eyes scanning the table for angles. "I may be big, but I ain't dumb. No offense."

"None taken. At any rate, the best revenge is a—how do you Americans phrase it?—a can of whoopass." His next bank shot careened off the side and sent the last two balls into two different pockets. Satisfied, he began collecting the balls to rack them up again. "As for your original question, why would you want to be captain? A thankless task, if you ask me. The captain's the bloke everyone likes to whinge about, no matter who he is. You're sensitive, Vader. You wouldn't be able to let it roll off your back."

Vader leaned on his pool cue. "I'm proud of my sensitive nature. Helps me appreciate fluffy kittens and walks in the rain. Chicks are all over that shit."

Joe the Toe threw his head back with a rollicking laugh that shook his huge body and drew glances from whichever girls in the bar hadn't already checked them out.

"Did anyone ever tell you you're priceless?"

"No one who owns a pair of balls."

"Ask Roman. He went all the way to battalion chief. See if he thinks it's worth the agita."

Roman wasn't much more help. "It's the kind of decision a guy has to make for himself," he said as he bustled around the kitchen of Lucio's Ristorante Autentico Italiano. "Yeah, it's more responsibility. You can't be friends with the guys in the same way as you were before. And when I say 'you,' I mean you, not me. I was a captain before I was a captain, if you know what I mean."

"Yeah, I can see that." Roman had the most commanding presence Vader had ever witnessed. He'd probably told his mother how to diaper him correctly. "I like hanging out with the guys, but I'm getting older."

"And wiser?"

"Wouldn't go that far."

Roman chuckled and poured olive oil into a stainless steel pan. "If you decide to go for it, come back and I'll give you some tips. Most guys don't make it the first round, you know. Most have to take the exam a couple times before they pass."

"How long did it take you?"

"Once. But like I said, I was—"

"Right. Born a captain. Look, don't mention this to Sabina yet, would you? I'm trying to keep it quiet at the station."

"I'll try, but if she pries it out of me with sweet—"

Vader held up a hand. "You can stop right there."

If only he could talk to Sabina about this, he thought as he left the restaurant. This, and so many other things. Cherie, his mother, his money worries. But even though Sabina had been his best friend at the station before she got married to Roman, he'd never told her about his mother's situation. She'd probably be stunned that he'd kept it to himself. Everyone thought he was such an open book—and he liked for them to think that. Everything that happened to him away from home, including risking his life at a four-alarm fire, was a relief compared to his worries about his mother.

And if that wasn't fucked up, he didn't know what was.

For a relaxing vacation join the fire service! Learn how to carry a hundred pounds of gear on your back while breathing through a mask! Hold the lives of your fellow firefighters in your hands and trust them not to get you killed!

As he reached his truck, his cell phone buzzed.

"Yo, Stud."

Fred answered with exaggerated hacking. "I'm sick, dude. You have to fill in for me."

"Fill in for you where? We're off today."

Fred coughed with so much force that Vader pulled the phone away from his ear, as if the germs could fly through the atmosphere. "Firefighter for a Day. Can't do it. Don't want to infect anyone."

Vader rolled his eyes. He knew fake coughing when he heard it; he wasn't a trained paramedic for nothing. "Fine. Who's the winner? Give me the address and I'll head over."

"Fifty-eight Gardam Street," said Fred, then hung up in a hurry, before Vader a chance to say he knew exactly where that was, and exactly what Fred was up to, and that he really didn't appreciate it.

Or did he? When it came to Cherie, he wasn't sure of anything.

Ten minutes later he strode up the front steps of Cherie's three-story house on Gardam Street. Cherie and her brother Jacob had signed a lease on the old Victorian for practically nothing, when it was a falling-down wreck. They'd poured time and money into it, so at least it was no longer a death trap, although the graceful front veranda still sagged in the middle and a couple of the shutters hung crookedly. They'd painted it a vibrant lilac color with cream trim. In fact, when he'd met Cherie she'd had purple specks in her hair, like bits of confetti. You had to love a girl who didn't mind a little manual labor.

The inside of the house had received even more loving attention. Cherie's house was the most feminine space he'd ever entered; she had a weakness for bordello-red velvet and antique lace. He couldn't even name most of the fabrics she used, but she told him she'd picked up everything at various flea markets. The sweet scent of lilacs clung to everything, except when she was baking something. Then the whole house filled with mouthwatering buttery, cinnamon smells.

Spending time at Cherie's house was like mainlining pure womanhood. If they lived together, he'd have to have a man cave somewhere, a garage packed with tools and a refrigerator, maybe a pool table . . .

He gave that line of thought a ruthless karate chop. If Cherie wanted something permanent, she would have accepted at least one of his proposals. He was here in the capacity of Firefighter for a Day, that was all. Whether she wanted him or not.

Some kind of pulsing, exotic dance music was playing inside. Mixed up with it, he heard the irritated voice of Cherie and the sullen tones of her housemate Nick.

He knocked. When no one answered, he rummaged under a pansy-filled watering pot for the key, and let himself in. The entryway was home to a coatrack, a telephone stand, and a fish tank. He greeted his favorite, the angelfish who liked to nibble the newcomers, and strolled into the living room.

The rug had been rolled up and pushed to the side, and the dark wood coffee table lay upside-down on the couch like an upended beetle. Nick and Cherie faced each other in the middle of the cleared space.

To Vader's eyes, Nick was a blur. His eyes flew immediately to Cherie. She was barefoot, and wore a leotard the color of emeralds and a flowy sort of wrap skirt with parrots printed on it. Her hair was tucked into a little bun at her neck. With his habit of assessing her entire appearance instantly, he knew that she was wearing hardly any makeup, maybe just a touch of gloss on her soft, violin-curved lips. She was glaring at Nick, who was in the midst of answering a text.

"You can't text while doing the tango."

"The tango can suck it." Nick made a rude gesture with his phone.

"It's not that hard! If you'd just pay attention."

Just then, Nick spotted Vader, and pointed the phone his direction. "Get him to be your dance slave. I'm out."

Cherie whirled in Vader's direction. He folded his arms over his chest, ready for battle. "What are you doing here, Vader?"

"I'm your Firefighter for a Day."

"No, you aren't. Fred is."

"Unless you want the bubonic plague, it's me. Take it or leave it. Me, I mean." Maybe that wasn't the best phrasing, considering all she did was take him and then leave him.

Nick grabbed the opportunity to slide past Vader and head for the front door. They both heard it slam shut. They were alone.

The last time they'd been alone, they'd had mind-blowing sex and then he'd mentioned marriage. The hell if he'd make that mistake again.

"I mean, come on, Cherie. Do you think we can't handle a day together? I'm a big boy. You're a . . . well, we're both adults."

A smile of pure mischief curved her lips and made her eyes crinkle at the corners. "I could use some help with my tango lesson. But do you really want to do this? Ballroom dancing isn't exactly your cup of tea. Not that you like tea either. So maybe it *is* your cup of tea."

He gave her a hard look. "You aren't going to scare

me off with ballroom dancing. Sure, I'd rather fix a leaky faucet or double-check your fire extinguishers. But if want me to tango, I'll tango."

She tilted her head, considering. He could imagine the thoughts running through her mind. Tango wasn't the best way to maintain distance, but here he was. And here Nick *wasn't*. "I need someone for Saturday's class. I'm trying to demonstrate leading versus following. Today was just supposed to be a practice session because Nick . . . well, it didn't work out last Saturday. So I'd need your help for two days. I only won a fire-fighter for one day."

"I'll check with the department, but I'm pretty sure we can split it into two half-days."

Slowly she nodded. "You might even be good at tango. I know how well you move." A million images flashed through his mind, all of them including her naked and moaning beneath him. As usual, she was innocently oblivious to the effect of her words. "Maybe you'll have fun with it."

He knew exactly how to make it more fun, but he heroically suppressed that thought.

She read his mind anyway. "And we're not going there, Vader. Tango is the dance of passion, it's supposed to suggest the sex act, not actually demonstrate it."

"You just had to go there, didn't you?"

"I said we're *not* going there."

"I heard what you said. You said 'sex act.' How am I supposed to hear the words 'sex act' and not think of the sex act?"

Her eyes flared. "What difference does it make? You're always thinking of the sex act anyway."

"I might *think* about it, but you *said* it. That means *you* were thinking about it."

Two spots of pink appeared on her cheeks. She took a deep breath, visibly trying to control herself. "I was making the point that this is a professional session. So just tell me right now, so I can be prepared. Are you planning to do this the entire time?"

A slow grin spread across his face. "You got me for half a day, babycakes. That's four hours of nonstop Vader Brown. Can you handle it? Can you dig it?"

She set her jaw. Raised her chin. And one eyebrow. "The better question is whether you can handle it."

He flexed his chest. "There's only one way to find out."

"Okay, then." Her eyes glittered. "We start like this, facing each other, except"—she took a step forward, so the tips of her breasts came within millimeters of his chest—"a little closer."

He swallowed hard. *Lord in heaven*. What had he gotten himself into?

Chapter Five

Cherie put her left hand on Vader's muscled right shoulder. It tensed, going from steel to living titanium.

"I'm not going to hurt you, Vader," she murmured. "It's just a dance."

He said nothing, just looked down at her, waiting. Letting her make the moves. Secret knowledge shivered through her. Having a man of Vader's size and strength at her temporary command was an incredibly empowering feeling. There'd been a few times, in bed, when . . .

She shook off the memory. *Maintain your distance. Keep it professional.* She lifted his right hand, its weight heavy in her grasp, and placed it on her lower back. It settled around her in a warm curl. "You're going to be the leader and I'm going to follow. Right now I'm dictating, but as you get used to it, you'll take the lead. I want to show my class how the man leads, and how the woman should follow."

Vader coughed. "No comment."

She gave him a warning glance. "There better not be."

"I'm keeping it zipped."

She looked at him suspiciously—exactly what did that "zipped" refer to?—but he maintained an innocent expression. "Now take my right hand in yours, but keep your arm bent to the side. Keep it nice and rigid."

Oh sweet mama. She closed her eyes as she heard him smother a snort. What was wrong with her? She managed to get through entire tango classes without a single double-entendre. But as soon as Vader showed up, out they came. She gritted her teeth. "Maybe I'll just show you instead of talking about it."

"Sure thing, Teach."

He was enjoying this way too much. She shifted into a brisk, businesslike tone as she pulled him across the floor, demonstrating as she spoke. "I'll just explain the count first. The basic sequence is slow, slow, quick, quick, slow. A slow step is two beats, quick is one. Don't drag your feet, keep the steps what they call staccato. Firm and quick."

She hurried past that unfortunate phrasing. Luckily, Vader didn't react. He was now focusing on the steps, moving his body after hers. She hummed a tango tune under her breath, emphasizing the beats.

"Why don't you go ahead and sing it?" Vader asked.

"I don't sing."

"Never? Of course you do."

She didn't answer. For a fact, she knew Vader had never heard her sing, because she didn't allow herself to sing. When they glided past the entertainment center—Optimal Doom's principal contribution to the household—she leaned over and activated her iPod. She'd danced to the song a hundred times in class, but in the company of Vader, it acquired a new sensuality, a sort of suggestiveness amplified by his personality.

As the music played, the spell of the dance began to weave itself around her. As she'd known he would, Vader caught on to the steps very easily. He was such a natural when it came to anything physical, not just strong, but quick on his feet. And he really seemed to feel the unfamiliar rhythm of the music.

Or maybe it was that their bodies were so attuned to each other that he was easily able to follow her lead. As he assumed command of the dance, steering her across the floor, something within her relaxed. While teaching her regular tango classes, she never actually enjoyed herself. She was too preoccupied with her instructions, and monitoring the progress of the students. But here, now, with no one present but her and Vader, and the sense of physical harmony that always seemed to sing between them, she could devote all her senses to the dance.

Her eyes half closed, she allowed herself to feel the heat of his body, so close to hers. She could almost sense the steady, reassuring thump of his heart. He wore his usual off-shift casual wear, a white beefy-T and red board shorts. Soren and Nick liked to point out that it made no sense for someone as clothing-conscious as she to be with a guy like Vader, who had no qualms about wearing the same pair of board shorts for a month. But the secret truth was, she liked looking at him in these clothes. She enjoyed the sight of his sculpted legs powering out of his shorts like a freight train from a tunnel. The way his shirts hugged the muscles of his huge shoulders was a constant treat for her eyes. Better than chocolate.

Was it so strange that a woman would enjoy the physical beauty of a man, the way men did with women? In her family, neither sex was supposed to even notice such things. They called it vanity, and it would earn you a beating with a switch of witch hazel. But she'd always had that forbidden side to her, the side that loved the look of things, the feel of them, the sound and scent ...

With a long breath, she filled her lungs with the air hovering between her and Vader. Vader's smell was entirely male. Sweat, of course, and a hint of gym shoes behind the clean, soapy scent he always carried. Despite his obsession with working out, or maybe because of it, Vader loved showers, and took at least two a day. He always smelled freshly washed. Unable to stop herself, she leaned in closer. Even though she couldn't name the scents he carried, they brought to mind power tools and gearshifts, leather seats and other manly accoutrements. To her, it was a heady smell—in fact, it made her lose her head much too easily.

She took another deep breath, letting the scent filter to her mouth, which watered. Her tongue pressed against the back of her teeth. With a sudden fierce desire, she wanted to taste Vader's skin, investigate all the little permutations of his evocative aroma. Why power tools? If she ran her tongue across the rippling muscle of his biceps, she could figure it out. Why leather? Maybe it had to do with the stubble just appearing on his jaw. If she could bite his chin, lightly, hold it still with her teeth, and dart out her tongue in little exploratory trips, she could find out all sorts of things. If only ...

Her long, desirous exhale sent a puff of air across the short space between the two of them. Opening her eyes a slit, she saw Vader notice, saw him understand exactly what her sigh meant. When it came to matters of the flesh, Vader was quick as a fox. At least when it came to matters of *her* flesh.

He looked down at her, holding her gaze in a long, searing, questioning glance. Whatever he saw in her eyes made him tighten his grip on her. He pulled her closer, her body offering no resistance whatsoever, even though the tango wasn't meant to be danced *that* close. It felt so good to be pressed up against him, the hard ridges and valleys of his torso fitting so snugly against hers. One of her thighs slipped between the shifting columns that were his legs. Heat spangled through her lower belly, stoked by the movement of his thighs, the friction of his growing erection against her stomach.

She sighed and let her body flow against his. Her leotard gave her nipples no protection against the enticing heat of his massive chest. The opposite, in fact. Each shift of the clinging fabric pressed between their two bodies sent an electric charge from the peaks of her breasts to her sex. Every step the two of them took drove her higher, toward that mindless realm where all that mattered was touch and taste and feel.

"Vader," she murmured, with the last remnants of her willpower. "What are we doing?" The question had a desperate tone to it. *What are we doing? Why do we keep doing it? Why can't we stop?*

"Whatever you want to do," he answered, the devil. He made it sound so simple, but it wasn't, was it? More than anything, she wanted *him*, to be close to him, to take him into her body and her life. But she couldn't, not completely, and that's why she kept hurting him, and she couldn't stand that . . .

But all those mostly logical, semi-coherent thoughts disappeared like vapor in his arms. He moved his hands from the rigid hold of the tango to a more blatantly sexual embrace, in which one hand pulled her hips flush against his lower body and the other cradled her skull. With a sigh of pure pleasure, she rested the back of her head against the solid warmth of his hand. In her humble opinion, Vader's hands were a miracle of nature. So large that they spanned her head from ear to ear; so sensitive as they molded to each delicate little bony plate. At Vader's touch, every forgotten part of her felt like Sleeping Beauty, awakening only under his attention. With every movement, his hands spoke to her, telling her how beautiful he found her, how much he wanted and revered her.

And, as always, she responded like a spoiled cat, greedily accepting every caress as if it were her rightful due. She was born to be petted by this man. While in his arms, she could never doubt that. Out of his arms . . .

She didn't want to think about the cold world outside the magic circle of his embrace. Reality would intrude soon enough.

"I have a few ideas," she murmured, her lips curving in anticipation, her heartbeat doing its own tango of excitement.

"Fire away, Teach." He tilted her head back and mumbled the words against the skittering pulse in her throat. Farther down, with no apparent effort, his other hand gripped her buttocks and moved her in a smooth circle against the hard rise of his erection. She let out a deep groan, the kind of noise she made only in Vader's presence.

"Soren?" She heard his question vaguely, past the savage pounding of the blood in her ears.

"Gone," came her answering squeak.

"Good." And he swung her backward, so her feet flew off the ground and the breath whooshed out of her. She clung to his wide shoulders, which had become her only anchor. Her hair came loose from its bun and tumbled down her back.

"Your hair says it wants me," said Vader in a growl that seemed to rise from deep in his chest. He bent over her, the way he had at the photo booth, hovering his mouth over hers.

"My hair talks too much." She giggled, but her eyes had gone wide from the desire pounding through her. Held securely in his arms, she felt herself being transported across the room, toward the couch. But the couch was full, she'd stashed her coffee table on top of it . . .

With an awesome demonstration of sheer muscle power, Vader shifted her so he held her in one arm, while with the other he plucked the table off the couch and set it on the floor with a clatter. Then she was swooping through the air onto the crushed sapphire velvet surface of the couch, which was soft as kitten's fur against her skin.

"Here's what I want," said Vader, hands on hips, standing over her like some kind of conquering Viking. "I want to see your red hair spread across that blue couch, with all your white skin in between. Naked white skin," he added, with a meaningful lift of his eyebrow. He bent over to put his hands to the waist of her skirt.

"Very patriotic."

"God bless America." A few deft movements of his hands and her skirt was gone, tossed through the air like so much dandelion fluff. He paused, and she glanced up at him. The perplexed look on his face as he surveyed her leotard made her burst out laughing.

"Hit a roadblock, Mr. Universe? Has the mighty Vader been brought down by a ballet outfit?"

"Down, but not out." He crouched down before her and slid his big thumb along the leg hole, where fabric met skin. Being on the curvy side, her flesh swelled outward from the leotard. With some people, she might be shy about that fact. But she knew Vader appreciated every excess inch of her. His thumb traveled in a slow traipse across the sensitive skin of her groin, across the taut tendon, and into the valley where arousal already ached.

His hot gaze met hers as he investigated her wetness. She didn't have time to be embarrassed, because he found her pulsing clit and circled it with his knowing thumb. Her lips opened on a moan. Slowly, with ruthless teasing intent, he moved aside the damp fabric and the panties she wore underneath, pulling her open, exposing her completely to his voracious scrutiny. Lightning flashes of taunting pleasure streaked through her being. With her hands flung to either side, she clutched at the couch, the soft velvet slipping through her fingers. Her body was so eager for him, she felt the climax already building, that bright sun rising behind her eyelids.

He slowed his strokes; she whimpered in disappointment. "Baby, I could keep this up all day. I'd sacrifice my left nut to make love to you like this. But I had that picture in my mind, and remember how I said 'naked'? That means no clothes, not even something as sexy as this." And he stroked her sensitized cleft until she cried out. "Cute as this little outfit is, you're even cuter naked." He withdrew his hand and gave her a little pinch on the thigh.

She tried to glare at him, but she was too turned on to manage it. Instead she made a striptease out of it, sliding the leotard off one shoulder, then another until both breasts crested the neckline. After all the teasing of the dance, her nipples greeted the open air with embarrassing exuberance.

His eyes lit up, but she held up a hand to stop him. "No interfering with my process."

His Adam's apple moved as he gave a hard swallow. "Hell no."

She inched the leotard down her body, lifting her hips to ease it off her butt. Nothing could be more satisfying than watching his eyes go more hot and feral the more naked she got. Finally he couldn't take it anymore. He planted his hands on her upper thighs, where the leotard was bunched, and whisked it down her legs.

"That's interfering!" she protested.

"No, it's not. It's stripping." He stripped too, with dizzying speed. With a few quick movements, his shorts were off, his T-shirt flung across the coffee table, and his spectacularly honed form stood naked before her. It was a good thing she was already sprawled on the couch, because the sight of Vader with no clothes on was enough to make any woman feel faint.

All those acres of muscle contained within tight, browned skin, the ridges parading up his rib cage toward those mountainous shoulders, the massive thighs spread apart, and at the center of it all, an erotic punctuation mark, his emphatically thickened penis, so aroused it curved up, up, up toward his taut belly.

She rested one foot on his thigh, her artistic eye appreciating the contrast of her paler skin against the bronze of his. He bent down, his erection bobbing against his stomach, and spread her hair out behind her. When he straightened up, he wore a different look, utterly absorbed in his cataloguing of her exposed parts. Under his inspection, she felt abandoned and dissolute, like a courtesan posing for her patron.

Amused by the thought, playing the role to the hilt, she ran her foot up his thigh, into the bed of brown curls. When her big toe touched his penis, waggling against his hot flesh, his nostrils flared. He hooked his hands under her knees, spreading her legs apart and shifting her forward on the deep couch. She locked her legs around his hips, freeing up his hands.

"You're teasing me, aren't you?" He growled.

Only because he'd teased her. But she was suddenly too breathless to say so.

"You know what the rules say. Don't play with the animals in the zoo." He took his shaft into one hand. She didn't know where he'd gotten it, but he was maneuvering a condom onto his erection. When he was done, he ran his hands along her inner thighs, his thumbs tracing the tendons all the way to the throbbing heart of her craving.

"Stupid rule," she gasped.

"And what happens when you break the rules?"

She struggled to form thoughts through the desire clouding her brain. "Go to jail?"

"Yup. Sex jail." He gave a devilish laugh and spread her open with his fingers, easing the way for his cock. It felt so unbelievably good to have him back inside her, thick and probing, his heat parting her, penetrating her. A long, low sound came from her throat, like some kind of wild animal mating call.

In answer, he thrust further, deeper, while his fingers played with her clit, rubbing and teasing, finding a rhythm that matched the flexing of his thighs. A rumble of primitive satisfaction rippled through his chest.

"Play with your nipples," he urged in a thick voice.

"No."

"Yes. Do it."

"But . . ."

"I know. It's okay. Just do it." They were speaking in shorthand now, brief words laden with meaning. They both knew what happened when her nipples were touched when she was this close to the edge. She'd fly over like a bottle rocket. But right now, in this moment, he was the boss. Holding his hot gaze, she put her fingers to her nipples.

"Squeeze them," he ordered, nearly choking.

"Vader," she whispered helplessly. She'd lost all control of her reactions; her body quivered and jumped from need.

"Just do it."

She squeezed. The searing arc of heat acted like the spark to a bomb. She absolutely detonated, her body arching with the force of her climax, sweet, drugging pleasure flooding her brain. He came too, deep spasms racking his magnificent body, his hands digging into her upper thighs.

Finally he went still. "Sweet baby Jesus," he gritted, eyes closed, his head thrown back, his strong throat muscles moving hypnotically. "What you do to me, Cherie."

She flung the back of her hand over her damp forehead, and uttered a helpless moan of a laugh.

That made two of them.

Chapter Six

Vader was pretty sure the woman he'd just made fierce, passionate love to was muttering, "Crap, crap, crap," under her breath.

He eased her into a more comfortable position on her couch, then collapsed next to her. In the time that they'd been immersed in lovemaking, dusk had fallen. Ghostly blue shadows gathered in the corners of the room. He knew what was coming next. Instead of enjoying a blissful afterglow, and maybe sharing a pan of peanut butter brownies, as he'd prefer, Cherie was about to head straight for a massive dose of self-recrimination.

Right now, with everything going on in his life, he didn't want to go through that cycle one more time.

He cleared his throat and spoke before she could shift from "Crap, crap, crap" to something more specific. "Look, Cherie. We just had sex, and it was awesome, as always. Why don't we just let it be? Let's skip the part where you beat yourself up and make us both swear we're never going to touch each other again."

She lifted her head, her mouth dropping open in a rosy oval of surprise. "Am I really that predictable?"

Vader looked at her soberly. "If you were predictable, this would be easier. I know you, that's all. Or at least certain parts of you."

Even though he hadn't intended any kind of sexual innuendo, a flush gathered on the pillowy flesh of her chest and made its way up her throat. He wanted to follow it with his lips, but he restrained himself. "I'll make a deal with you, Cherie. You know how you keep telling me you want to be friends?"

"Yes, and I realize my behavior hasn't exactly backed me up, but . . ."

"That's okay. I get it. I'm such a virile, handsome devil you can't resist me." He put up a hand before she could laugh too hard at his mocking self-assessment. "No need to argue, we both know it's true. Moving on. I'm willing to be your friend, on one condition."

She sat up, pulled a silky scarf off the arm of the couch, and gathered it around her shoulders. He'd never understood why she draped the scarves everywhere, but now, seeing the way the iridescent fabric shone against her skin, he was glad she did. "What condition?"

"You tell me the truth."

An odd sort of flinch rippled across her face, so quickly he wouldn't have noticed if he didn't know her so well. "What do you mean?"

He had to steel himself for this next part. This was what he'd wrestled with late at night. "I want to know why you don't want me."

And yes, it hurt just as much as he'd predicted to say those words out loud.

"I want to know why you keep pushing me away. Even when things are going great. No, *especially* when things are going great. That's when you always drop the hammer. It's fucked up, Cherie. And before you say it"—he put up another hand as she opened her mouth—"I know you don't mean to hurt me. I'm a big boy. I can take the hurt. Fuck, I *have* taken it. Now you owe me something. You owe me the truth."

Her gaze fell away from his, color coming and going in her cheeks. She fiddled with the long fringe of the shiny silk scarf, then bent forward to gather up her clothes.

Bull's-eye. He was on to something. No doubt.

She clambered off the couch and bunched her clothes in front of her like a shield. "I've told you. It's not that I don't 'want' you, you know that. I don't think we should get married."

"Why?"

"Because I don't want to get married. We're very different. We have different goals in life." She took a shuffling step backward. "I should go change before the boys get back."

He'd come this far, he wasn't going to let her off the hook now. Especially when her right eyelid was twitching. "What goal do you have that means we can't be together?"

"I have responsibilities. Students. All my jobs take up a lot of my time."

True, she held down about six part-time jobs at any given time. She was always running from one class to another, one shift to another. But it wasn't as if he didn't have responsibilities too. "I have no problem with all your jobs. I think it's great that you do all that stuff."

Her gaze darted here and there, everywhere except

his direction. "Look, Vader, you know I care about you. You know I enjoy . . . getting intimate with you."

His mouth quirked. At least her eyelid didn't twitch when she admitted that part. "Yeah, I got that. I enjoy it too. But it doesn't make me turn into a crazy person who has to call it quits every week or so. I want to know what's really going on. Because I know something is. I may be a big, dumb guy who doesn't know how to tango and has trouble watching *Brokeback Mountain*, but I'm not blind."

"You're not dumb, Vader." She blinked, as if chasing away tears. "You're not anything bad. There's nothing wrong with you. And you're pretty darn good at tango, considering you just learned it today. And you did watch *Brokeback Mountain*, because I wanted you to. And I was wrong about you and my brother. You didn't mind that he's gay. And you know what? You are handsome and virile and irresistible and all those things you said before. And if there was anyone I could—" She broke off, biting her lip. "But I can't— and I can't explain—if I could tell you everything, I would—" She took a long, shuddering breath, then cried, "Why are you doing this? Why are you putting me on the spot? I don't want to hurt you. I hate hurting you! It's the worst thing in the entire world and I don't want to do it ever again . . ."

"Okay, okay, shhh." He stood up and pulled her into his arms. "Don't worry. You're not going to hurt me. We're friends, right? No one's hurting anyone. We're friends, we care about each other, and we're not going to hurt each other." He said the words soothingly, the way he would speak to a child in a medical crisis. She trembled, then slowly relaxed against him. He blocked out the delicious sensation of her half-naked body against his entirely naked self. Not the right moment for another hard-on, though really, he had only so much control around Cherie.

Firmly, he set her away from him, at a safe distance of at least two feet. "Friends probably shouldn't do naked hugs."

"Right." She wiped a trembling hand across her eyes. In the blue twilight illumination filtering from the window, he caught a silver flash of moisture on her fingers. Damn it, he'd made her cry. As always, he'd taken the direct, head-on, balls-out approach. He should have known Cherie wouldn't be that simple. Extracting her secrets would be like picking a lock, not kicking down a door.

As he released her, bittersweet determination made his jaw clench. He might have lost this particular battle, but he'd be back. And he'd win the war. Losing was not an option, not when the prize was Cherie.

That same never-say-die attitude stayed with him over the next few days. He took his mother in for an MRI and learned . . . nothing. The doctor couldn't say whether she might lose consciousness again, and recommended keeping a close eye on her. No doubt about it, he was either going to have to draw a bigger salary or begin moonlighting as a male stripper to afford the extra help.

He began his next shift determined to talk to Captain Brody and get his advice. But before lineup had even ended, they'd gotten their first call.

"Structure fire for 32 Westhaven. Task Force 1, Battalion 9. Respond to Thirty-two Westhaven. Reported people trapped. Time of incident 7:03 a.m."

"Someone's coffeemaker explode?" Ace the rookie grumbled as the firefighters ran into the apparatus bay to change.

"My money's on burnt bacon," said Sabina.

"I call after-sex cigarette in bed," Vader chimed in.

"Vader! Focus." Captain Brody gave them a scorching look as he slid his feet into his boots.

"Sorry, Cap," Vader muttered. Doubt cratered through his gut. If he became captain, that would be *his* role. He'd have to make sure no one was joking around at inappropriate moments. He'd have to stop goofing around and playing the clown. Did Brody ever dance around in a bar wearing nothing but his fireman's helmet over his dick? No. Did Brody let Lula Blue, the porn star, put her hand on his ass at the Firefighter Photo Booth? No. Did Brody win the nickname Vader by making spooky breathing sounds through his apparatus? No. Did Brody pose wearing nothing but an oven mitt for the firehouse cookbook? No no no.

The thought of his checkered past taunted him as the crew loaded into Truck 1. Either he was completely unsuited for the role of captain and would never get the job—or he was going to have to overhaul his personality. Maybe the fun-loving part of his firefighting career was over, and he should just accept it. Maybe he should resign himself to a life of heavy responsibility at home, heavier responsibility at work . . . and no Cherie.

He continued the debate in the tiller bucket, where he steered the back end of Truck 1 through the early morning sunshine gilding the streets of San Gabriel. Vader was proud of his role as the tillerman on the truck company. "Truckies" were known as hard-charging, invincible, excellent firefighters, and his nature suited the position. He'd have to switch over to the engine company if he got promoted, which meant no more working the aerial. He loved his job, loved his crew, but maybe a change would be good. Or maybe not.

He abandoned the issue when they reached the scene. Thirty-two Westhaven was an apartment building that housed twelve families. Even though the building was only partially involved, the entire structure had to be evacuated. Some of the residents already stood in tight clusters on the lawn, others were leaving to grab coffee or head to work early.

The incident commander briefed them on the initial size-up. The idea was to keep the flames contained to Apartment 3D, which was in the back of the twelve-unit building. The truck and the pump took the Delta side of the building, where smoke swirled in witchy spirals out the back window. A nearby propane tank posed the biggest worry. They had to make sure not a single spark got close to it.

Still in the tiller bucket, Vader waited until Fred, the Apparatus Operator, had maneuvered the ladder to the right, then busied himself hooking up the ladder pipe assembly to the aerial. The pump engineer attached a supply line from the hydrant to a Y-shaped cluster of valves, where Sabina, the "inside man," stationed herself, ready to open the flow of water. Meanwhile, Mulligan, the new top man who'd taken Psycho's place—and who was almost as crazy—set up a ladder to access the roof.

"Load it," Vader called when he'd clamped the ladder pipe assembly to the top rungs of the ladder. "I'll see you in a second," he said under his breath to the nozzle. So he liked to talk to his equipment, so what? Down at the cluster, Sabina opened the valve and loaded the line. Fred rotated the ladder and extended it to its full length of a hundred feet, working the controls to maneuver the aerial, nicknamed "the Stick," into the perfect position.

Now it was Vader's turn to do his thing. As soon as

the Stick was locked into place, he began climbing its rungs, breathing apparatus on his back, with the agility on which he prided himself. This was his specialty, and everyone knew it. There was nothing he loved more than standing on the top rungs of the Stick, feet braced like that guy on the *Titanic*, shooting water at a vicious, nasty dragon of a fire.

His muscles flexed as he mounted the Stick. Step by step, into the world that he knew and thrived on. Into smoke and flames and adrenaline and muscle power. If you thought about it, the aerial was his happy place. The place where he did his best work. Where he could roar back at the flames, sing to them, yell at them, and no one blinked an eye.

The higher he climbed up the Stick, the more optimistic he felt. Of course he'd win over Cherie. Of course he could take care of his mother. Of course he could make captain. And there it was: his decision. Crystal-clear, a sparkling oasis on the horizon. He was going to go for that promotion. He'd work hard, he'd do whatever it took. When he put his mind to something, he always accomplished it.

Hell, maybe he could kill two birds with one stone, so to speak. If—*when*—he became a captain, maybe Cherie would take him more seriously. Maybe he could order her to spill her secrets.

At the top of the "Stick," gripping the nozzle, completely caught up in his thoughts, he didn't catch the warning from Captain Brody until it was a split second too late.

"Safety harness!"

Just as he realized he'd forgotten to strap himself to the Stick, a surge in nozzle pressure made him lose his footing. He fought to keep his balance, but it was no use. He went sliding ignominiously down the rungs of the ladder, then, perhaps out of sheer embarrassment, blacked out.

When he came to, only a few moments later, he was flat on his ass on the ground. His helmet and face mask were off and Sabina and Fred knelt next to him. Fred was feeling his pulse and Sabina was waving her hand over his eyes.

"I'm fine," he growled. "Go fight the fucking fire." He sat up, brushing them off. What a freaking idiot he was. That would teach him to get crazy ideas.

"He's good to go, Cap," said Sabina into her helmet mic.

"Tell him to sit in the engine until the paramedics get here."

"I don't need paramedics." Vader grabbed his helmet.

"It's procedure," said Sabina roughly. He noticed that she looked a little shaken up. "You scared the crap out of me."

"I'm fine. A little bruised, that's all. Nothing some ice can't take care of. I wasn't that far up. Now get the hell back to work." He shook off Fred. "I can make it to the rig by myself."

He did, though he could already feel the bruises forming. His left hip in particular was going to be a purple mess. But he knew his body, knew nothing had been broken or torn. Ice, ibuprofen, and a soak in a hot tub would do the job.

In the engine, he found the first two items in the first aid kit. By the time the paramedics arrived, he'd already cracked an ice pack, applied it to his hip, and downed three ibuprofen. With the fire winding down, Captain Brody came over to listen to their assessment.

"He's in the clear," said the lead paramedic. "You

got a strong guy here. Sometimes those muscles pay off."

"Told you, Cap," said Vader, grimacing, as he re-applied the ice pack. "Told you I wasn't wasting my time."

"Never thought you were. Nor did the female population of San Gabriel."

He let out a snort, then leaned his head against the back of the seat. He fully expected Captain Brody to head back to the fire, but instead he propped himself against the gleaming red engine. "You seemed a little distracted up there."

Vader grunted.

"What was going on? I'm not prying, but it's the kind of thing I need to know." The captain fixed him with level charcoal-gray eyes. Vader knew Cap wanted to move on, that he wanted to go back to the academy and have more time at home with his wife and brand-new baby. He was probably sick of moments like this, sick of supervising clowns like him.

Maybe his fall had knocked something loose, or maybe it was the ibuprofen, but Vader felt ironic laughter bubble to the surface. "You wouldn't believe what I was thinking about."

"Try me."

"Taking the promotional exam for captain."

A spark of surprise lit up Brody's eyes. He tilted his head and seemed to consider the idea seriously. "Good for you."

"Good for me? Are you serious? I just fell off the freaking Stick. Captain material, I ain't."

"Because you had a fall?" Brody's dry tone made Vader do a double take.

"Because I'm a goof-off."

"Yes, well, you'd definitely be your own kind of

captain. But everyone is. I'm not like Captain Kelly, am I?"

"No, but . . ." Vader fell silent.

"You want to be a captain? You can do it, Vader. But it's not easy. The exam is just part of it. You'll have to study for it, of course. A lot. There's also the civil service exam and the 'three whole score' interview, when the Deputy Chief rakes you over the coals with fire ground questions. You want to know the books inside out. But it takes more than that to get the job. You also want to impress your superiors with how serious you are about it. You might want to consider volunteering for committee assignments. Take on a few special projects. Supervisors want firefighters who do more than just show up for the job. They want the firefighters who go the extra mile, the ones committed to the department, the ones who always show up and give one hundred and fifty percent. You have a degree, right?"

"Yes."

"A master's wouldn't hurt either. You could take night classes, or complete them online on your days off."

"I can't," he said in a flat, final tone of voice, so the captain wouldn't ask why not.

"Well, it's not necessary. It's just one more piece of the puzzle. What it boils down to is that you want people to take you seriously. And you know where that starts, right?"

Vader shook his head.

"It starts with taking yourself seriously."

Every bone in his body shied away from that prospect. Home was serious. Firefighting was serious. But Vader? Vader was never serious. Except about bodybuilding. And beer. And closing down bars.

"Oh, I take myself seriously. Serious as an STD," he quipped, because that's what Vader did.

Brody gave one of his enigmatic smiles and straightened up. "Don't sell yourself short, Firefighter Brown. I think you'd be a helluva captain. If you want it."

Chapter Seven

*C*herie spent an anxious few days worrying about two things—if Humility was going to show up, and if Vader wasn't. She knew that she'd upset him during their postcoital confrontation. But as soon as she saw him stride up the walkway to the studio, wearing jeans and a SGFD T-shirt, exuding muscular, wild-animal energy, she knew that once again she'd underestimated him. She should have known better.

When Vader said he'd do something, he did it. She couldn't think of one instance in which he hadn't. But what mood would he be in? Would he be resigned to performing his civic duty as her Firefighter for a Day? Would he be going through the motions, stifling his exuberance, breaking her heart in the process?

She channeled her confused emotions into the biggest smile she possessed. He stopped in his tracks and fixed her with a stern look. "You're not going to turn this into *that* kind of tango lesson, are you?"

About to protest, she caught his little wink. The tightness in her chest, the fear that she'd finally driven Vader away for good, eased. Maybe they could resume their usual playfulness as if nothing had happened—as if they hadn't backslided into sex just days ago. "Don't tempt me," she teased.

"That's my line, babe. And I'm serious." He reached her side. All her nerve endings flared to attention. "Don't play with the animals, remember? The sexpot voice is off-limits. And you'd better put your hair up in that school principal bun of yours." His warm brown gaze raked her up and down. "And I think I have an old canvas tent you can wear."

She laughed, in that despite-herself, goofy way only Vader inspired.

"I'll teach class in your turnouts if you want."

He took her by the elbow, opened the door, and steered her through. "See, you just don't get it, do you? You—in my turnouts—that's hot. That's damn hot. Now you got me going, babe. We need an empty studio, and we need it now."

As she giggled, warmth spread through her with the speed of a shot of brandy. No one else had ever made her feel like this, as if she were floating in some kind of golden bubble, buoyed by his warmth, his desire, his appreciation. If only she didn't love being with Vader so much, if only his particular brand of lust and goofiness didn't touch some sweet spot deep inside her.

And then there was his unbelievable physique. As they stepped into the studio where a few students had already gathered, she witnessed the impact he had on strangers. Saw eyes widen, heads turn, lips lick. Felt the very air turn charged. She was used to Vader's intensely male presence—not that it didn't still affect her—but for the rest of the class, it was like a shot of adrenaline straight to the vein.

It wasn't every day that a six-foot-plus, bronzed, expertly sculpted work of art walked into the room.

Her male students didn't look happy at the sight of Vader. They were here to meet women, after all, and right now all female attention was on the broad-shouldered, narrow-hipped, mouthwatering hunk of man aiming a wide smile in their general direction.

She'd better move quickly, before she lost the male half of her class. Putting a possessive hand on Vader's ridged forearm, she said, "This is my partner, Vader Brown." It was true enough. He was her *dance* partner. They could draw whatever other conclusions they wanted. "He's a firefighter here in town and he's taking valuable time away from his duties to show us how a man leads the tango."

Vader stood with legs apart, hands linked behind his back, and offered a friendly nod to the class. "Howdy."

Tara, a buxom brunette, raised her hand. Cherie's hackles rose. Tara was a player; she was pretty sure Tara had already slept with at least two other students.

"Have you been dancing the tango for a while, Vader?"

"Nope." He winked. "But I promise I know what I'm doing. I had a good teacher."

Before Tara could get too much of a flirtation going, Cherie jumped in. "Before we start, I wanted to share the results of the research I did after our discussion of the health benefits of tango last week. One study showed it helps Parkinson's patients with their balance. Other studies say it can make you feel more relaxed, less depressed, and sexier."

"I'd say it's working pretty well," Vader joked, scanning the class. Cherie noticed the disgruntled look on the faces of the single men in the class.

"And here's something just for you guys," said Cherie. "Can you believe tango may also increase testosterone levels?"

"I think we're looking at Exhibit A," purred Tara.

Cherie was starting to dislike her student. "Okay, everyone find a partner." She started the music playing on her iPod, which she'd hooked into the studio's sound system. As the provocative notes flirted through the room, she stepped into the opening pose with Vader—just to emphasize the point that everyone else would have to find their own partners.

"Now don't worry too much about the steps yet. The most important thing is to listen to the music. That's what it's really all about. Listen to the music and the beat, let that other part of yourself take over, the part that doesn't live here"—she tapped her head—"but here." She jabbed her fist into her stomach. "Or even a little lower down."

The class laughed. Vader's left eyebrow quirked upward.

A new student, an awkward, thin girl with a terribly unflattering haircut, whose name tag identified her as Cathy, waved her hand. Cherie walked over to her iPod and stopped the music. "Yes, Cathy?"

"What if you come from a family where dancing means snapping your fingers to 'Jumpin' Jack Flash.' You know, the white man overbite?" She demonstrated, shifting gracelessly back and forth while biting her lower lip.

Cherie smiled at her, experiencing a rush of compassion. It could be difficult to do something out of your comfort zone, something you hoped desperately would find you true love. She had complete empathy for her students. "I know exactly where you're coming from. You know, I never danced one step until I was seventeen years old. Where I came from it was considered a sin. You know that movie *Footloose*? I lived that movie, except there was no sneaking out of the house in my family. If I could learn to dance, I guarantee all of y'all can."

Cathy looked at her with wide eyes. "What happened when you were seventeen?"

Cherie bit her lip. Something about dance class— the shared sweat, the intimacy created by making a fool of yourself—made it tempting to say too much. She had no business spilling personal details when she was working. Especially with Vader listening. She'd promised Jacob.

"I left home," she said, simply. "Now come on. From the top." She started the music again. Turning back to Vader, she caught the arrested look on his face. *Stupid, stupid.* She should have kept her mouth shut.

"How come you never told me any of that?" he murmured as she moved back into position.

"Never came up."

"You tell your tango students more than you tell me? What kind of sense does that make? Why'd you leave home? How'd you end up here?"

With a pointed glare, she turned up the volume on her iPod. "Okay, class. Pay attention, now." She faced Vader, raising her hands into the starting position. Vader instantly did the same, as if he'd been dancing the tango for years. With a narrow-eyed look that declared their conversation far from finished, he stepped forward. At her nod, he took the opening step. "Gentleman, watch how Vader holds his right arm. In that position, it's easier to guide your partner across the floor. Watch how he assumes command, but also how he pays attention to his partner. Both leading and following come down to one thing. Anyone know what it is?"

Nothing more than a sigh fluttered across the room as the two of them glided and turned across the polished floor. Why wasn't anyone answering? Weren't they paying attention? She caught her and Vader's reflection in the mirror, and nearly missed a step. Even though Vader was keeping the exactly perfect distance from her, every line of his body—the tilt of his head, the slight hunch of his huge shoulders, the way he angled toward her—screamed of possession and . . . well, passion.

Which was exactly what the tango was all about, but still . . .

She swallowed hard. "Anyone? What's the key to leading and following?"

Still no answer. Above her, Vader cleared his throat. "Can I take a guess?"

She gave him a gracious nod of her head. "Please."

"It's listening. Hearing what your partner is telling you. Not with words, but with their body." They reached the turn, and he dropped her backward, maneuvering her smoothly with arms like bands of iron.

She gave a little squeak, unable to manage more. Once again, he stepped into the breach. "You can't just haul her around like a dead ox, dudes. It's about the C word. You know, communication." He winked at the class, breaking the spell. A ripple of laughter swept through the room.

Tara raised her hand, slanting an avaricious look at Vader. "Cherie, don't you think all of us ladies should get a chance to be partnered by Vader, so we can see what it's like?" Cherie gritted her teeth. Vader was like catnip to women like Tara. They saw him as a fun, no-strings, surefire roll in the hay.

But Vader was more than that, much more. She resolved to keep Tara far away from Vader.

"No," Cherie said quickly. "All the men in this room are more than capable of leading. Let's see what y'all can do now." Her Arkansas accent was intensifying—a sure sign she was rattled. What was so wrong with Vader partnering the other women in the room? She shouldn't mind. She didn't mind. Well, she wouldn't mind if it were any other girl but Tara, and of course Tara would be first in line.

She restarted the track, then stood back and watched as couples formed. As always, there weren't quite enough men to go around. Vader squinted down at her, hands hooked in the back pockets of his jeans. "Something's not making sense here. You sure you want me holding up this wall while those poor girls look so lonely?"

"I don't want to take advantage of your time. You came to help me out, not dance with a bunch of strangers."

"I'll probably survive. Now come on, who should I dance with first?"

Admitting defeat, she heaved a sigh. No way could she admit the real truth, that she shied away from the thought of him touching another woman. She was here to teach, not to hover over her assistant like a jealous high-schooler. "Take your pick."

"Really? Fireman's choice?"

He'd probably go for Tara. Tara was the hottest girl in the room, and she'd been flirting with him ever since he walked in.

But Vader surprised her, as he had a way of doing.

He walked over to Cathy, the awkward new student, and gave her that friendly grin that no shy person could resist. Tara looked fit to be tied, and managed to miss a step, which meant that her partner stumbled into her, causing the two of them to crash into another couple. Cherie rushed to sort out the aftermath before any blood was shed.

When she looked up again, the room was humming with excitement. Vader and Cathy were at the center of an admiring ring of students. They were prancing cheek-to-cheek across the room with no sign of awkwardness. Vader's rough-hewn features were set in a concentrated expression, while Cathy's cheeks held two bright spots of excitement. When they reached the center of the room, he whispered something to her, she nodded, and at the next turn he lifted her off the floor, whirling her around in a perfect spin.

Everyone applauded. Cherie experienced a moment of sheer, crazed envy. That ought to be her flying through the air, weightless in the arms of the strongest man she knew.

As Vader set the breathless Cathy back on her feet, his step faltered, as if his leg had nearly buckled. He covered it up quickly, but too late.

"Break time!" Cherie called, turning off the music. "Vader and Cathy, great job. I haven't even covered spins yet. I'd prefer if you'd wait until I instruct you in the more advanced moves. Vader, can I talk to you outside for a minute?"

Vader scrunched his eyebrows, but his usual playfulness seemed a little forced. "I guess I'm in trouble now."

"Take five, everyone! We'll be right back."

Vader followed her to the hallway. With her expert eyes, she knew he was trying not to limp. As soon as they were alone, she turned on him. "What were you thinking? Are you okay?"

"I'm fine. I was just trying to show her a good time. She seemed so nervous." His coffee-brown eyes flicked away from her. She reached up and took his chin into her hand, turning her face back toward his, refusing to let him avoid her scrutiny. This time, she saw the pain lurking in the tightness of the skin around his eyes.

"What's wrong? You tell me right now, Vader Brown. I'm serious."

"It's a little bruise, that's all. Happened a couple shifts ago. No big drama, Cherie. Just another day in the life."

"Let me see."

"That's not a good idea."

"Where is it, on your dick?" She knew that would wake him up, since she usually stuck to her religious upbringing and avoided such language.

"Close enough."

"Fine." She took him by the hand and dragged him to the men's room, locking it behind her. "The other guys can go pee outside. Now drop 'em."

"You know how long I've been waiting to hear that from you?" He waggled his eyebrows again, this time with a little more verve.

She put her hands to his belt buckle, which featured a bronze ram's head. Vader was the most loyal of men; when he liked something, he liked it forever. He'd told her he'd owned this particular belt buckle since his grandfather had given it to him for his eighteenth birthday. She'd always found that story very endearing. "You want me to do it for you? Because I have to warn you, I'm not in the mood to be gentle."

Again, he winced. "Normally, I'd say it was worth it. But this time, I'll do it. It might be a little tender."

He unfastened his belt buckle, unzipped his pants, and peeled off the left side of his briefs. She tried to ignore the sleek muscles and curving bone structure he uncovered. And then—she forgot about all that and sucked in a breath at the sight of the biggest bruise she'd ever seen. Raging purple and deepest magenta, with an edge of mustard yellow, it spread the length and breadth of his hip and upper thigh.

It looked horrible and painful, and the thought of how much it must have hurt—still hurt—just about broke her heart.

Tears sprang to her eyes. Impulsively she took up his hand and cradled it against her chest. It was either that or whack him, and she didn't want to inflict any more pain on him. "Why didn't you tell me? Why didn't you cancel? You shouldn't be dancing around with an injury like that."

"This is not an injury." He looked offended. "It's a slight discoloration. If I can handle two shifts, I can handle tango class."

"Shifts . . . you've been *working*?" Outraged, she dropped his hand. She wanted to shake him like a naughty little boy. "What's *wrong* with you? You need to take care of yourself. You can't just throw yourself around like a piece of . . . piece of . . ."

"Hot man flesh?"

"Don't joke."

"Cherie. Honey." He cupped her face in his hands and captured her gaze in the brown warmth of his. "It would take a lot more than a bruise to keep me away from you. They'd probably have to cut my legs off. And even then, my upper body strength is outstanding, and . . ."

"Stop it." Tears spilled over, running in hot, embarrassing rivulets down her face. She hated how easily she cried. "Don't talk like that. You're a firefighter. Anything could happen out there."

He froze, still cupping her face. "Is that why?"

"Why what?" She sniffed, trying to call back those tears.

"Why you push me away. Because I'm a firefighter. Because I have a dangerous job."

A hiccup shook her. That wasn't it, but it was close, in a way. "I hate the thought of you being in danger." She especially hated the thought of *putting* him in danger. If Mackintosh ever did find her, who knew what he'd do to Vader? "But they train you guys really well, right?"

"Yeah, we got drills coming out our ass. Training bulletins up the shebizzle."

"And you have a great captain."

"The best."

She made herself look at his bruise again, even touch it gently, using no pressure. If only she had healing powers. She imagined white light streaming from her hand to his thigh, erasing the discoloration, easing his pain. But when she drew her hand away, the bruise was still there. So she wasn't magic. The love she kept hidden away couldn't make his wounds vanish.

He ran a thumb across her cheekbone, the warmth of it like a soothing hot stone. "You like helping people, don't you?"

"Well, sure. Of course I do."

He gave her an odd look, then muttered something under his breath. She thought he said, "I'm so dense," but she couldn't be sure.

"Actually," he said, then hesitated. Her eyes flew to meet his; it was unusual to see him so tentative. "I could maybe use your help."

"You want me to ice your thigh? I could make my

great-grandmother's tonic for that bruise, if I can find the ingredients. Works like a charm. I have to find some arnica and some comfrey, I think I saw some right outside of town on the way to the Roadhouse, and boil it up together . . ."

"Don't worry about my thigh." He waggled his eyebrows. "But if you want to worry about my dick, go for it."

She rolled her eyes. Only Vader could find a way to turn an injury into a come-on.

"This is something different," he continued. "I've been . . . well, I'm going for a promotion to captain."

Amazed, she scanned his face. She'd never heard him mention anything so ambitious before. He'd always behaved like a live-in-the-moment sort of guy, completely happy with where he was. What she saw in his expression—vulnerability and a touch of anxiety, as if her opinion really mattered to him—made her heart somersault. "That's cool, Vader. Really cool."

"You think I could do it? I mean, I'll have to give up on my promising male stripper career. The one I keep threatening to try."

"San Gabriel will go into mourning."

"I'll still be available for private shows, of course." He winked.

"I don't get it, though. You said you wanted my help. How can I help you make captain? You want me to help you study?"

"It's not that." His strong jaw tightened. "To make captain, people have to see you a certain way. They have to think you're up to it. They can't think of you as a party-boy muscleman."

"People know there's more to you than that."

"Do they? Do you?" He fixed her with a direct stare.

"Of course I do."

"Not enough to hitch your wagon to, though."

She drew away a few steps. Her shoes clicked against the tile floor. In her anxiety over Vader's condition, she'd forgotten they were in the men's room. The unfamiliar, sweaty smell made her suddenly claustrophobic. Digging in her purse, she found a travel bottle of perfume and sprayed a few whiffs into the air. "Please don't start that. If you want me to help, just tell me what I can do."

He pulled up his briefs and gingerly refastened his pants. "It's like what you did just now."

"What do you mean?" She stuffed the little atomizer back in her purse.

"You made it smell nice. You fixed it. Improved it. I'm going for a full-scale overhaul. Top to bottom. I have a three-point plan."

"A three-point plan," she repeated numbly.

"Oh yeah. I'm not messing around. I've got it all planned out. And when I put my mind to something, it gets done. The guys at the station can tell you that. Everything on the inside is my responsibility. Experience, skills, studying. I need your help with the exterior part of the operation."

"The exterior?" She frowned at him in the mirror, then turned so she was staring at the real thing, not the reflection. "Are you saying you want me to give you a makeover?"

Chapter Eight

*H*ell no, it wasn't a makeover, but Vader considered it a stroke of genius. Watching her get so worried over an ordinary bruise had switched on a light bulb in his mind. Cherie had a soft heart. All her mismatched jobs had a common theme—helping people in some way. Her dance classes helped people with their confidence. Her hot stone massages helped people relax. Movement therapy helped heal emotional problems, or so she said. Babysitting for the Hendersons . . . well, she did that because she loved their kids.

She liked to mother people, even irritating people like her housemates. So—why not let her help him? Not that he needed it, of course. But if she wanted to mess around with his appearance, he could live with that.

The next night, she led him into her third floor bathroom. Vader's nostrils flared, his sense of smell alerting him to his entrance into alien territory. Wafts of fragrance floated around them. He spotted lemon-grass hand lotion, rose-petal oatmeal exfoliating mask, ylang-ylang persimmon body wash, whatever ylang-ylang was. Along with the jumbles of cosmetics, hair products, hair ornaments, cotton balls, and random assorted essentials, the room was a nest of femininity.

Cherie sure did love her girlie stuff.

Gingerly, he lowered himself to the chair she'd set up for him, his long legs barely fitting between the chair and the sink cabinet. He seemed to take up half the space in her tiny bathroom.

Cherie set her cell phone on the bathroom shelf. He wondered if she was waiting for an important call.

"You seem a little nervous." Cherie stood behind him and sifted her hands through his hair. It felt so good he nearly moaned.

"Well, the last girl who tried to spruce me up was Danielle, Captain Brody's daughter. I let her put nail polish on my left hand when she was in the hospital. It was hot pink. I couldn't get it off and the guys ragged on me for a month."

"That's adorable." A cooing sort of smile, the kind girls gave to babies, came over her face.

"Take that back."

"Oh stop. Your manhood is safe. It's adorable because you're so masculine. It's the contrast."

That was a little better. He allowed himself to relax.

"You've gotten haircuts before, right?"

"Of course. Man's haircuts. Vinnie over on Main. Charges me two bucks." Vinnie didn't fondle his hair the way Cherie was doing.

"Hair tells a lot about a person. Unconsciously, people pick up on the signals your hair gives and make judgments about you."

"Oh yeah? What does mine say about me?"

"That you don't really care about your hair."

"I don't."

Now she was testing different lengths, squinting at him from one angle, then another. He watched her in the mirror. She was dressed about as casually as he'd ever seen her, in a V-neck T-shirt and what looked like loose, silky pink pajama bottoms. When she bent over to pick up a comb, he saw the shadow in the deep crevice between her soft breasts.

He yanked his attention away from her much-too-tempting cleavage, back to the words she was speaking.

"But people might also think you don't really care about anything else either. We can't have that. From now on, you do care. You care about getting that promotion. You care about the department."

"Of course I do. I always have."

"And now you're going to look like it."

He screwed up his face. "My hair is going to say all that? More than showing up for work and risking my life?"

She abandoned his hair, turned aside, and grabbed her best towel, made from thick, creamy cotton. "Of course not. It's more like . . . an exclamation point."

Warily, he ran his hands through his hair. "You're going to make my hair into an exclamation point? Like some kind of Mohawk?"

She buried her face in the towel to stop her giggles. Smiling to himself, he watched her in the mirror. God, he loved making her laugh. Almost as much as he loved making her . . . *Don't go there, Vader.* Not the right time or place—hell, he'd end up breaking every perfume bottle in the joint if he tried to make love to Cherie in here.

She wiped her eyes, then draped the towel around

his neck. "No Mohawk, I promise. Now, you'd better not make me laugh while I've got scissors in my hand."

She prowled around him, examining the shape of his head.

It occurred to him that he'd never get a better opportunity to ask a few questions. She was relaxed, maybe even distracted. "How'd you get into cutting hair?"

"Oh, I've been doing it my whole life. I cut all my brothers' and sisters' hair," she answered absently.

Yes! *Good call, Vader.* Now to see how much more he could pry out of her. "How many brothers and sisters do you have?"

Cherie paused in mid-snip. Vader's eyes were half closed, and he'd asked the question in an almost lazy manner. Normally she never talked about her past, because she was afraid she might let the wrong bit of information slip. But it was an innocent question. Jacob wouldn't mind if she answered it, would he? She glanced at her phone. No more calls from Jacob, and nothing from Humility. It was a little bit like waiting for the other shoe to drop.

"Thirteen."

"Thirteen?" He swung his head around; she pulled the scissors away just in time to keep them from jabbing him. "*Thirteen* brothers and sisters? Where do they live?"

What harm would it do to tell him that? "A homestead in Arkansas."

"With your parents?"

"With my father and stepmother. My mother's dead. Now can we change the subject? Keep your head still. What about you? How many siblings do you have?"

"None." It sounded so empty and sad, the way he said it. "I wanted some. Someone to play with, make forts with. Fight with. Whatever. I used to bug my parents about it. But they . . . I don't know what happened. Then my mother—" He broke off with a helpless gesture. "None," he repeated.

She wondered what he'd nearly said about his mother, but decided not to press the issue, considering she didn't want any more questions herself. "What about your firehouse buddies?" she asked instead. "They're almost like brothers."

"They are. They're the brothers of my heart." A husky edge roughened his voice. "And sisters. I'd die for them. And them for me." In the midst of trimming the hair behind his right ear, she caught the movement of his Adam's apple. Vader was the sort of man who didn't mind being swept away by emotion. She'd seen it a few times, and it always made her want to throw herself at his feet.

She glanced at his reflection in the mirror. He was looking down, his square-jawed, open face as serious as the statement he'd just made. It was so matter-of-fact, the way he'd said those words, as if it was unquestioned truth, some kind of bedrock belief. And just like that, something about Vader shifted into focus for her. All joking and partying aside, this was a man with an enormous capacity for love, but even more than that, for sacrifice. She had no doubt that he would do exactly as he'd said, and lay down his life for someone else.

The thought made her heart practically split in two.

Oh, Vader. Why couldn't he be the goofball she'd originally thought he was? Why did he have to turn out to have so many more . . . *layers*?

It was getting harder and harder to keep her distance.

She cleared her throat. "Be still now. No more talking. This is the tricky part. Don't move a single muscle, especially anything involving your jaw."

Vader had to admit that Cherie's haircut did something to his appearance. It made him look—not older, exactly. Stronger. Like someone you didn't want to mess with. She'd cropped it shorter, so his face stood out more. Or something. He didn't have the vocabulary to describe it, but he liked it.

And he really liked the feeling of closeness they shared now that he'd put himself at her mercy. And she'd actually revealed a morsel of personal information. Was her family the key to her problem with him? He filed the moment away. He hadn't gotten as far as he wanted, but it was something.

He rose and dusted bits of hair off his clothes. "You did a good job. Nice exclamation point."

Delight made her eyes glow like moonbeams. Two dimples appeared on either side of her curvy mouth, one accenting her cheek, the other gracing the side of her chin.

"You could be a hotshot hairstylist if you wanted to. You know, for magazines and models."

"No, thank you."

"Seriously, if you could quit all of your jobs except one, which would it be? Which one is your dream? Do you want to be a dancer? A baker? A hair genius? What?"

Cherie stuck the scissors in a leather pouch and meticulously rolled it into a tight little bundle. "Nothing like that."

He persisted, frowning down at her. It was a harmless question, for Pete's sake. "What then? What's your dream?"

"I'd like to work with kids," she blurted. "You know

I teach movement therapy at the studio. I'd like to do the same class for traumatized children." She snapped her mouth shut, as if forbidding herself to say anything more.

Bewildered, he shook his head. "Then why don't you? Sounds like a great idea."

"Because . . ." She stared at him with a hopeless expression that he found completely incomprehensible.

Just then, the front door opened and footsteps clattered into the hallway. She started, and for a quick second he spotted that look he'd seen before—that hunted, afraid look. Her pupils dilated, her face paled. *What was going on?*

Soren called out, "Cherie? You here?"

And the look disappeared. Color flooded back to her face. "Upstairs," she called out.

"We're going out for a drink. You in?"

Great. Count on Soren and Nick to ruin everything. But then she surprised him and picked up one of his hands, which looked enormous in hers.

"Come out with us."

He made a face. "With the death-ghoul duo?"

"They're annoying, but harmless. Come on. I want to see how everyone reacts to your new haircut. I want to show you off." Her smile sent a sneaky tendril of sunshine into his heart. How could he say no to that? He could handle Soren and Nick. He had so far.

The four of them settled into a booth at the corner bar, which had the unfortunate name of Beer Goggles. Vader, who loved most nightspots, despised this particular bar. It had a meanness to it; the bartenders were rude, the patrons sarcastic. No one seemed interested in having a good time. Why bother, when they could look down on each other instead? Neon beer signs provided the only decor, along with two dartboards and an ancient foosball table.

Neither Soren nor Nick had any noticeable reaction to his haircut. If anything, it might have made them more obnoxious, since Cherie looked so pleased with herself. Honestly, they were like spoiled kids when it came to her.

Deciding the only way to endure the evening would be with a drink in hand, Vader ordered a Guinness. Cherie opted for red wine, Soren and Nick for bourbon, neat.

Soren slanted a half sneer at Vader. "Where's your balls, dude? Why don't you go for a real man's drink?"

Vader had no idea what that was supposed to mean and didn't care. "I don't drink much hard alcohol."

Nick settled his elbows on the table. "Now see, I don't mean to call a big strong firefighter like you a pussy, but—"

"Cut it out, Nick," said Cherie sharply.

"He knows I'm kidding around. Right, big guy?"

Vader took a swig of his beer, hoping it would drown the strong sense of dislike spreading through his system. Since he didn't usually feel that way about people, it disturbed him. "Let's just drop it. How about those Dodgers? Think they have a chance?"

"Is that football?" Soren asked, with a shrug that meant he really couldn't be bothered to care.

Vader shook his head and fell silent. He'd tried. Now it was their turn.

His cell phone, which he'd set on the table, beeped with an incoming text message from his mother. He dropped his head, scanning to make sure it wasn't urgent.

"Firehouse?" Cherie asked.

He shook his head. Soren leaned over and peered at his phone. *"We ran out of paper towels,"* he read aloud. "Holy hell, it's from his mother. You live with your *mother*?" Soren's eyes, which he'd rimmed with black eyeliner, lit up with glee.

Vader's jaw tightened. "Yes." Technically, his mother lived with him, since he owned the house. But he saw no need to explain anything to these assholes.

"How old are you? Over twelve, right?"

Oh, how he wanted to rip the guy's sneer right off his face. Then he felt Cherie's hand squeeze his thigh, which had gone as tense as rebar. "We're leaving," she said, glaring at her housemates. "If you can't manage to be polite for one lousy drink, we're out of here."

"But Cherie, *he lives with his mother.* I moved out when I was eighteen."

"Nineteen for me," said Nick, flopping his hand in the air.

"Bet she still does his laundry. Fess up, Vader. Does she do your laundry?"

Vader tried to crack his jaw open, to say something, anything, but it had gone as hard as concrete. He could brush off a lot of abuse, but if they said anything rude about his mother, he couldn't guarantee civilized behavior.

"You're being an ass, Soren," hissed Cherie. "I want you to stop this."

"Do you call her when you're going to be late? Does she give you a curfew? Does she give you cookies and milk after school . . . I mean, work?"

Vader leaned forward, gripping the edge of the table to keep from striking out. He let his narrowed eyes and deadly serious voice get his point across. "I'd advise you to stop. Right now."

"Or what? You'll sic your mother on me?"

Vader's hand whipped out and grabbed him by the throat. Soren's eyes went wide as beer goggles. The fierce satisfaction of it nearly made Vader dizzy. He wasn't a violent man, really he wasn't. Most of the time. "You got anything more to say, let's go outside and take care of this. Much as I hate this bar, I don't want to make a mess of it."

"You see, Cherie?" Soren tugged at Vader's wrist, but had about as much effect as a mosquito. He squeezed out more words in a thin wheeze. "This is what he's really like. A big, dumb, violent moron. You can't be with someone like him. Look, he's trying to strangle me."

"If I wanted to strangle you, you'd already be unconscious, instead of just an idiot," Vader said tightly. "I'm not even breaking a sweat. Now you want to do this or what?"

"No," said Cherie, distress trembling in her voice. "No fights. Vader, let him go. He's not worth it."

"Ain't that the truth," Vader muttered. But it felt too good to have the little asshole right where he needed to be—at his mercy.

"I'll let you go if you apologize to Cherie for ruining her evening out. Then apologize to the Dodgers for not knowing who they are. And you can damn well apologize to me too, for making me put up with your crap."

Soren narrowed his eyes, and again tried to pry Vader's fingers away from his neck. He only succeeded in making Vader tighten his grip.

"I'm not hearing any apologies. You ready to go out back and settle this?"

"What are you talking about? No one does that anymore. Does this place even have an 'out back'? What's back there, Dumpsters and shit? That's so old school, dude."

Vader had to give him credit for hanging in there. "I guess I'm just an old-fashioned guy. Now what's it going to be? I don't care either way."

Soren's mouth opened and closed as if he were a desperate fish. Vader didn't look forward to thrashing him; it would be no challenge, and Cherie wouldn't like it. He'd probably end up putting a scare into him instead of actually fighting him. The guy needed to learn a lesson, and if he had to be the one to administer it, he'd do so. And enjoy every moment. He was mentally readying himself for battle, when Cherie tugged frantically on his sleeve.

"Vader, something's wrong with Nick," she cried.

Chapter Nine

Keeping his grip on Soren, Vader swung his head toward Nick, who was slouched sideways against the wall, his body stiff as a plank of wood, his neck arched, and his eyes rolled back so far that only the whites showed. His limbs spasmed and his eyes blinked uncontrollably.

Instantly he dropped Soren. "Get out," he ordered. "Out of my way."

Soren scrambled to obey. Vader swept everything—napkins, ketchup bottles, salt packets—off the table, then clambered over it.

"Has he ever had an epileptic seizure before?"

He loosened Nick's jacket. The T-shirt underneath didn't constrict his airways, so he left it alone. When he waved his hand in front of Nick's face and got no response, he knew the guy was having a full-blown seizure. Mentally he began a count, figuring he'd already been seizing about a minute, depending on how far into this episode he'd been when Cherie first noticed

He looked back over his shoulder. Soren appeared to be completely shell-shocked, staring at his friend as if he were watching a horror movie. "Soren! Here!" Vader snapped his fingers, dragging Soren's attention his way. "Has this happened before? Does Nick have epilepsy?"

"I . . . I don't know."

"Not as far as I know," said Cherie. "He never mentioned it. Should I call 911?"

"Yeah. You'd better."

If this was his first occurrence, he needed to see a doctor. If Vader was wrong, and it wasn't epilepsy but some kind of drug reaction, Nick needed an ambulance right away.

"Soren. Has he taken anything? Any sort of drug?" When Soren gaped in confusion, he elaborated. "Ecstasy, meth, crack . . ."

"What? No. He had a quad latte with sprinkles, that's it."

Vader nodded. "Back away, you two. I need some space." In one strong movement, he lifted Nick's still rigid, spasmodic body off the cramped booth and lowered him to the floor. He turned Nick's head to the side in case he vomited. When he pulled his hand away, something wet clung to his hand. Blood was dripping down his fingers from the back of Nick's head.

He glanced up at Cherie, who was speaking into her cell phone. "Tell them suspected epileptic seizure and a head injury. He's been at it for about three minutes, but I think he's coming out of it now."

Nick's eyes fluttered open. "You got light all around you . . . I'm dead, aren't I?"

"You're not dead. You're having a seizure, but you're going to be fine."

"Dead and gone. All y'all are ghosts. Ghosts made of light. Did you know ghosts are made of light? I'm so tired."

And then he was seizing again, his body racked with more convulsions. "Tell them to hurry," he ordered Cherie.

"They're on their way. Is there anything else we can do?"

Vader tilted Nick's head back to the side, crouching close enough to monitor him, but far enough not to get in the way of a stray limb. "Just keep him from hurting himself. Seizures usually only last a few minutes. Would he have told you if he'd had them before?"

"I think so. I hope so. I don't know why he wouldn't."

He had to give Cherie credit. Although she was clearly frightened, she wasn't making things more difficult. He couldn't say the same for Soren, who flopped to the floor with a wad of napkins in his fist. When he tried to stuff them in Nick's mouth, Vader shot an arm out and pushed him away.

"I read about this," Soren protested. "We're supposed to keep him from biting his tongue off."

"He could choke on those. It's the worst thing you could do. I know it looks scary, but he'll be okay."

"What about his tongue?"

"His tongue'll be fine too. Just let him be."

Luckily, the familiar sirens of the San Gabriel Rescue Squad grabbed Soren's attention just then. As soon as Vader saw the first paramedic, he identified the squad as Paramedic Unit 3.

"Laney," he greeted the paramedic. "Victim's been seizing off and on now for about six minutes. He became fully conscious once for about ten seconds.

He seemed delusional. Blood on the back of his head. His friends say he's never seized before, at least that they've witnessed, and that he hasn't taken anything."

"These are his friends?"

"Yes. Soren and Cherie."

Soren jumped to his feet. "I tried to help him but Vader wouldn't let me." He waved the wad of napkins in the air.

"You're fucking lucky he didn't." Laney bent next to Nick and felt his pulse. Three more paramedics arrived with a gurney. "Now move back, everyone. Vader, good job. You got blood on you, need help with that?"

"Nah. Where are you taking him?"

"Good Sam. You guys can follow. No napkins though." She winked at Vader. "Never off the job, huh?"

"You know it. See you in a few."

In their quick-moving, bustling way, the paramedics whisked Nick onto a gurney and out the door. Vader straightened up, feeling a kink in his back from being hunched over so long. All activity in the bar had stopped; everyone was staring in their direction.

"That'll teach him to order a chick drink," Vader said mournfully, adding a comically sad shake of his head for good measure. Someone chuckled, and the tension left the room as if he'd popped a balloon with a pin.

"Is that really appropriate?" Cherie hissed.

"Why not? People need someone to tell them it's going to be all right. Dumb jokes do the job quicker than anything else."

She gave him an odd look, as if she was trying to figure him out. He didn't think there was much to figure out, but whatever floated her boat. He gave her a crooked smile and threw enough bills on the table to cover their drinks.

Cherie was relieved when Vader offered to drive to the hospital. It had been such a shock to see Nick's head jerk against the wall like that. At first she'd thought he was joking around, then she thought he'd been shot. She'd seen deer twitch that way, after her father or brothers had shot them in the woods. The sight had always upset her, especially because she or one of her sisters would have to field-dress it. It had almost—but not quite—been enough to turn her into a vegetarian.

When she'd heard Vader call Nick's fit "epilepsy," she'd been hugely relieved, though Nick might not feel the same way.

"Do you know much about epilepsy?" she asked Vader. He lifted one huge shoulder in a shrug. She noticed that he still had a streak of blood on his T-shirt.

"The seizures usually only last a few minutes. Once he gets a real diagnosis, the doctor will tell him how to handle them. You guys will have to know too. It's important that the people close to an epileptic are prepared."

His serious tone matched his demeanor during the entire incident. Truly, it had been a real eye-opener to see Vader in action.

"How'd you know what to do?"

He shot her a slightly amazed look. "I'm a trained paramedic. Just got my recert last month."

"Oh." Should she have known that? Probably so. For a moment, she felt ashamed of herself for not educating herself more about what Vader did at work. But the topic always made her anxious. She hated thinking of him in danger. Besides, the more questions she asked, the more he might ask. So she'd kept her curiosity to herself.

"It's a good thing you came out with us," said Soren from the backseat. "Without you, I don't know, man."

Vader lifted his gaze to the rearview mirror, as if trying to make sure Soren wasn't being sarcastic. "Glad I could help. But he would have been fine. Someone would have called 911. He wasn't in any real danger."

"We don't really know that yet, right?" Soren's voice sounded thin with anxiety.

Cherie jumped in. "They said he'd be fine, so we shouldn't even—"

"Actually, Soren has a point," said Vader. "Until they do a real workup on him, we don't even know if it's actually epilepsy. That's just my off-the-cuff assessment, and I ain't even close to being a real doctor."

Cherie put her hand on his forearm, where ropes of muscle and tendons intertwined. "You got it right," she said with a sense of complete and utter confidence. "Even the other paramedic thought so. I have no doubt. None whatsoever." And she really didn't. Watching Vader move so quickly, so precisely, with so much confidence and knowledge, had probably cured her of ever doubting him again.

"No one gets everything right." Vader waggled his eyebrows at her as he pulled into the parking lot of the Good Samaritan emergency room. "Even the King."

For some reason, the sight of Vader's Elvis-like lip curl, the one he pulled out when he wanted to be especially goofy, reassured her all the way to the soles of her feet. If Vader could joke around, then everything was going to be fine.

The benefits of being with a firefighter kept piling up. Inside the hospital, the charge nurse, who had to be at least fifty, greeted Vader with a wide smile. "Just can't keep away, can you?"

"If I'd known you were on shift, I'd have been here hours ago."

"You sweet-talker. But hell, after the night I've had, I'll take your flattery."

"Rough one?"

"Big accident down past Burtonville. Your guys were on it. Ten injured. No firefighters though," she added quickly, as Vader tensed. "Now who are you here to see? Besides me, of course."

"Epileptic seizure at a bar. His name is Nick—"

"His full name is Nicholas Willingham, the Third," said Cherie. For a moment, the nurse actually seemed surprised to find someone else with Vader. "Has he regained consciousness yet?"

"I don't know," said the nurse, after giving her a very hard once-over. "Why don't you wait here while I find out what I can. Vader, you can come with me if you want. Lord knows you've been back there enough times. Hey, did you get a haircut, honey? Looks good. Wait'll Tracie gets a look at you."

And she whisked him off through the big double doors that swung open into the forbidden land, leaving Cherie to wonder who Tracie was, and just what she'd unleashed with her barbering skills.

"Well, that takes the cake." Irritated, Cherie plopped down in an uncomfortable gray molded plastic seat. "*We're* his friends, not Vader."

"If it weren't for Vader, we'd probably still be waiting for her to notice us," Soren pointed out, slouching into the seat next to her.

"Hmph."

"You know what? You're not going to hear anything bad about Superman out of this mouth for the next . . . oh, I don't know. At least a week."

"Superman?"

"It fits. He's crazy strong, and he has a secret identity." Soren hunched over his iPhone. A glance at the screen told her he was updating his Facebook page.

"Are you telling everyone Nick had a seizure?"

"Yeah, so?"

She snatched the phone from his hand. "Don't you dare. *He* doesn't even know he had a seizure yet. What is wrong with you?"

"Chill out. He won't mind."

"Don't you take anything seriously? What if he'd died?"

"You are seriously demented." He shifted one seat away from her, crossed his arms sulkily, and stared at the muted TV, which was tuned to a *Jeopardy!* episode.

"What did you mean about Vader having a secret identity?"

"You know, he acts like a player. Then he turns into Superman. Now give me my phone back."

"Fine. But no Facebook until Nick says it's okay."

Soren snatched the phone out of her hand, but she didn't get a chance to make sure he obeyed because just then Vader, surrounded by nurses, came bursting out the double doors. The sight was like something from a music video; time seemed to slow as she watched. He could have been a rock star in the midst of an adoring harem of nurses and a patient in a wheelchair. He towered over them like some sort of sexy giant. They were all gazing in his direction, all smiling with varying degrees of delight combined with exhaustion.

Then time sped back up and he was in front of her, then bending down to look her in the eyes. "You okay?"

"Me?" She snapped out of her trance. "Yes, of course. How's Nick?"

"He's fine. The doctor's with him now. They want him to spend the night here, so I thought we could go grab some of his stuff for him. Soren, do you mind staying here? He'll probably want to see you as soon as the doctor's finished."

"Yeah. Sure. Is he, like, normal and all?"

"No. Neither of you is what I'd call normal."

The worry immediately cleared from Soren's face. Vader really had a gift for this, Cherie realized. She took the hand he offered and let him haul her to her feet.

Back in the truck, she spoke that thought aloud. "How do you do that? How'd you know what to say to Soren so he'd stop worrying?"

"He'll still worry. But even a short smile can make a big difference. Hospitals are stressful."

"I know. And he was being a total jerk. He wanted to put Nick on Facebook!" The thought still made her furious. She fully expected Vader to share her disgust.

But he just shrugged. "People react to trauma in different ways. I've seen all kinds of crazy-ass shit. Fire's eating up her house and some lady's looking for the coupons she clipped that day. A lot of people put up a shield. It looks like they don't give a shit, but they're just protecting themselves. That's his best friend in there and he's freaking out. Give him some slack."

She screwed up her face and pretended to check her watch. "About a half hour ago, didn't you have your hands around his throat, about ready to haul him out back and beat the tar out of him?"

"Yes. That was different. He was being an ass for no reason, except that he needed a good ass kicking. If I had to be the one to do it, I wasn't about to back down."

As if drawn by a magnet, she glanced over at him. The lights from the big dashboard silvered his face, molding the strong lines of his features. The haircut really did wonders for his face, bringing out the beauty of his eyes and balancing his muscular jaw with his jutting cheekbones.

"How did Tracie like your haircut?"

"What?"

"That nurse said Tracie was going to love it. Did she?"

Vader slanted her an enigmatic stare. "Yes. She said she wants to paint me after she's done with her next round of chemo. She's an artist."

Oh mercy. Tracie must have been the woman in the wheelchair. How could she be so shallow as to immediately jump into jealous-woman mode?

"Did you rescue her or something? How do you know her?"

Vader hesitated a long time, all the way from San Gabriel Boulevard to the turnoff to her street. "I've been to the hospital a few times. You start to recognize people. Sometimes you get to be friends. Tracie's in that category. She's a friend of my mother."

"Oh." She puzzled over that for a moment. Vader never talked about his mother, but now she'd come up twice in the same evening. "Is your mother an artist too?"

"No."

Monosyllabic answers were not Vader's usual style. Determined to get a real answer out of him, she waited. Finally, reluctantly, he added, "She's in the hospital a lot. For tests and things."

Cherie remembered Soren's stupid teasing about Vader's living with his mother and wished she'd throttled him. "I'm sorry," she stammered. "What . . . how long . . ."

Vader pulled up in front of her house with a jerk. "Here we are." He swung his big body out of the driver's seat before she could protest. How very odd. Vader was usually such an open book. Why didn't he want to say any more about his mother's hospital visits? Much as she wanted to pry, she forced herself not to push it. She certainly understood wanting to keep certain things secret.

But why on earth had Vader asked her to marry him, if he didn't even want to talk about his mother?

She hurried after Vader as he ate up the dark walkway with his long legs. None of them had thought to leave the light on. The bougainvillea that arched over the front door dangled creepy tendrils in their path. Vader brushed them aside like cobwebs.

"You need the key, silly," said Cherie, catching up. She elbowed him, which had about the same effect as nudging a boulder. It wasn't until he stepped to the side of his own accord that she reached the door. "And if you don't want to talk about it, just say so. You don't have to run away."

"I'm not running away. I'm trying to perform our errand in an efficient manner. I'm sure Nick is waiting for his toothbrush and pillow. He'll want some different clothes. Underwear. Any medications? What about a favorite teddy bear?"

"Are you joking?" In the darkness, she fumbled through her purse for the key. An odd sound, like that of someone clearing their throat, caught her attention. Must be Vader. More of his strange behavior. "How would I know? What grown man has a teddy bear?"

"Um, Cherie . . ."

But the tension of the evening was finally bursting

out of her. "Why do you always have to think the worst of Soren and Nick? I know they act like juvenile idiots, but they're not that bad, in fact they have their good points, if you'd only let yourself see them."

"Cherie."

"What?" At the glint in his eye, she realized she'd been successfully distracted. He didn't want to talk about his mother, so he'd shifted the conversation to Nick's hypothetical teddy bear. How infuriating. She clenched her teeth. "Oh, very clever. But if you didn't want to talk about it, all you had to do is say so, not accuse Nick of having a teddy bear."

"What's wrong with having a teddy bear?"

The noise came again, and this time she was looking right at him, and didn't see any sign of his Adam's apple moving. "Did you make that sound? That *hmm, hmm*."

"No. That's the girl behind you, the one who's been trying to get your attention for the last two minutes."

"What?"

She swung around wildly, nearly colliding with a girl in the shadows. She was slender and light, and had somehow managed to hide on the front porch without Cherie suspecting a thing. Cherie screamed and grabbed at her, peering into her face.

"Holy catfish on a spit. Is that you, Humility?"

Chapter Ten

"As of eleven days ago, I'm not Humility, Chasti—"

Cherie clapped her hand over her little sister's mouth. "It's Cherie." She couldn't think straight. Trust Humility to show up in the middle of a crisis. But at least she was safe. But what if Mackintosh had followed her? In the end, relief won out, and she pulled her sister into a tight hug.

When her sister gave a strangled screech, Cherie released her, but kept her hands on her shoulders. "What in blue blazes has been going on? We've been worried sick."

Humility sucked in a breath, and said in a tone of hushed excitement, "You aren't supposed to use profanity. Is that profanity?"

"No, it is not. Blue blazes is just . . . just a phrase. And anyway, I can use profanity now. I do it all the time."

"No, you don't," came Vader's warm, rumbling

voice from behind her. "She never uses bad words, cute little stranger. Take it from me."

Cherie swung around. For a moment she'd forgotten Vader was there. Crap, there was no way she could keep him out of this. He was about to get a big ol' dose of Harper family craziness. "This is my little sister," she told him. "So you shouldn't talk to her like that."

"He can talk to me like that," said Humility, quickly. "I don't mind. I think I might actually like it."

"Let's go inside," said Cherie. She gave a quick glance around the front yard. Was that a man's shadow behind the camellia bush? Or was it just the potato vine?

While she was squinting into the suddenly ominous landscaping, Vader took Cherie's purse from her unresisting fingers, found the key, and disappeared inside. When he turned on the front light by the door, a yellow shaft of illumination flooded the porch. Cherie caught her breath. Her sister was an absolute mess. Her dress—the pinafore required in the family—was streaked with dust, and the long-sleeved blouse underneath was ripped at the elbow. Her fine, light brown hair hung in clotted shanks around her shoulders and her small, kittenlike face looked pale and pinched, as if she hadn't eaten in a while.

"Sweetie, are you okay?" Cherie cupped Humility's cheek, needing to feel for herself that her sister was in one piece.

"Yes, but why'd you have to live such a long ways away?" The hometown twang in her sister's voice brought Pine Creek rushing back in all its wooded loveliness—the crowded homestead where they all lived crammed together, the old junkers behind the house, the chickens pecking in the yard.

Dizzied by the rush of remembrance, Cherie tried to let go of her sister but couldn't.

"Are *you* okay, Ch— Cherie?"

"Yeah. Yes. Fine. Come on in, Humi— Okay, so you're no longer Humility. What do you want me to call you?" She steered her sister through the door, then cast another quick glance behind her. Gardam Street, with its mix of older Victorians and newer tract homes, looked as placid and quiet as ever. Maybe they'd gotten lucky and no one had followed Humility. She shut the door behind her, then locked it for good measure.

"I was thinking about Trixiebelle. Wow, this is some house." The thin girl cast a wide-eyed glance around the large, brilliantly colored, velvet-draped living room. Cherie imagined it through the eyes of someone who'd never worn anything other than washed-out hand-me-downs. She must be awed by its beauty, stunned by its luxurious textures and lush tones. "Looks like a whorehouse."

"Humility!"

"Trixiebelle. And look at your hair! Prophesize would send for the razor if he saw that color." She tilted her head. "I like it, though. Reminds me of the red fox that used to eat our chickens."

"Where'd you get Trixiebelle from?" Cherie winced at the extra dose of Arkansas that had suddenly appeared in her own voice.

"I just always liked it. Remember my pet mouse, from way back? I called her Trixiebelle."

"Seems kind of complicated. Why not something plain and simple?"

"Like Cherie? What is that, Italian or something?"

"It's close enough to my real name, but completely different, that's why I chose it."

"Real name?" Vader, in all his testosterone-packed glory, stood in the doorway with a can of Coke. "You mean I've been calling you a fake name all this time?"

"It's not fake. It's the name I chose. The name I prefer."

Frowning, he handed the Coke to Humility-Trixiebelle. "Here. You look like you could use a pick-me-up." Humility stared at him as if he were a king-size Justin Bieber.

"I'm not calling you Trixiebelle," said Cherie. "How about just Belle?"

"No. But Trixie'd be okay."

"Fine. Trixie."

"Okay." Humility, now Trixie, guzzled her Coke, her gaze riveted to Vader. When she finished, she handed the can to Cherie, then stuck out her hand. "Hi there, handsome. My name's Trixie. What's yours?" As an aside, she added, "That don't sound half bad, does it?"

Vader, after an amused glance at Cherie, played along. "My name's Derek, but most people call me Vader. Even my mother."

"I'm not most people. Or your mother." She lowered her eyelashes and gazed demurely up at him, like a Southern belle who'd just been dragged through a dusty cornfield.

Every warning bell in Cherie's brain started clanging in double time. "Humility . . . Trixie . . . come with me. Vader, give us a few minutes. Come to think of it, don't you need to get back to the hospital?"

"You want *me* to get Nick's stuff? He might not like me pawing through his underwear drawer."

"Grrr. Fine." She grabbed her sister's wrist and pulled her down the hall to Nick's room. No way was she leaving her alone with Vader until she had a grip on the situation. In a flurry she grabbed a change of clothing and a pillow and snatched his toothbrush from the boys' bathroom, never once letting go of her sister's wrist.

"You live with *boys*?" Trixie asked, with breathless awe. "Boys who aren't brothers?"

"They're very brotherly. They might as well be brothers." She didn't want Humility—Trixie—getting any wrong ideas.

"What about the big, handsome one in the living room? Does he live here?"

"No. He doesn't. And put Vader right out of your mind. He's too old for you and . . . what am I even talking about? What are you up to? Have you forgotten the whole Creed?"

The Creed, which their father had developed when he'd moved them all to the backwoods and decided to create his own personal cult, didn't permit flirting or ogling or any attention to the opposite sex before marriage. Of course, marriage happened young.

"No, I haven't forgotten. I came here so I *could* forget. You're not the only one who had enough. If I'da stayed one more week I'd be married by now. And probably pregnant."

A shudder passed through Cherie's body, head to toe. That's exactly—well, almost exactly—why she'd left.

"You'd better tell me the whole thing. Come on."

She dragged Trixie back to the living room and thrust the armful of Nick's things at Vader's chest.

"I'm coming back," he said firmly.

"There's no need."

"The hell there isn't. There are a few little details someone better fill in for me."

Cherie looked in despair at his rock-solid body. His legs, bulging against the fabric of his jeans, were planted on the floor like young oak trees. Nick's toothbrush looked like a twig in his huge hand. "Like what?"

"It's a long list, but we'll start with your real name."

"It doesn't matter," she hissed. "I don't use that name anymore."

"It matters to me."

They glared at each other, until Trixie threw up her hands in exasperation. "Oh for mercy's sake. Her real name is Chastisement."

"Chastisement? That's not a name."

"I agree." Cherie marched to his side and tried to tug him toward the door. Nothing doing, of course. When Vader didn't want to be tugged, nothing could budge him. "Why don't you take that toothbrush to Nick before his teeth rot out of his head?"

"I'm not done yet. What kind of family names their daughter Chastisement?"

"That's nothing," said Trixie. "Our youngest brother's named Celibacy, 'cause after he was born that's what my father said he was committing to. We call him Cel for short. We got another sister named Forgive-Our-Sins."

"Thirteen," said Vader. "You said you had thirteen brothers and sisters."

"Yes, but you're not going to meet any others . . ." Another horrible thought struck her, and she swung around to Trixie. "Is it just you, or is anyone else about to show up?"

"Just me. I guess I'm the only other sinner in the bunch, except Jacob. Everyone else either toes the line or cozies up to Father while acting up behind his back."

"You just came here from Arkansas? Alone?" Vader asked.

"I been saving up. The Greyhound bus don't cost that much. But it took a lot of eggs. And I could only skim a few every day. It took me a coupla months. I thought about stealing it from the bed mattress, but I just couldn't."

The mattress, Cherie remembered, was where their father kept all the important things, from birth certificates to cash. She'd snuck in to grab her birth certificate before she'd left, and it had been the most nerve-racking experience of her life.

She had a lot to talk to Trixie about, but she couldn't say a word with Vader still here. Squaring off with him, she raised her chin. "I'll call you, Vader. I promise. But right now, my sister and I really have to talk."

His warm brown eyes seemed to penetrate all the way through her soul. For a moment, she wondered what it would feel like to actually tell him everything. Shivering away from that thought as if from a hot iron, she held his gaze. Finally he gave a reluctant nod.

"I'll bring Soren back, then leave you guys alone. One thing, though."

Cherie relaxed, letting out a pouf of breath. If Vader said he'd leave them alone, he would. He was always true to his word. "What?"

"I want Trixie to have my phone number."

"Excuse me? She doesn't even have a cell phone."

"Yes, I do!" Trixie dug in the pocket of her dull blue pinafore. "It's a disposable one, I picked it up for fifteen dollars at the bus station in Little Rock."

"Get rid of it," ordered Cherie.

When Trixie didn't react quickly enough, Cherie snatched it from her hand and dunked it in the fish tank. "It's disposable, so we're disposing of it."

"But *Cherie*!"

"I don't want anything here that can be traced. Your being here's bad enough. I mean, it's good, and I'm glad you came. And I'm going to take care of you. But I don't want anyone else following behind. You know what I mean."

Huge storm clouds gathered on Vader's forehead

as he shoved his hands in his pockets. "Well, I don't know what the hell is going on here, but is there some kind of danger to worry about?"

"No," said Cherie quickly. The last thing she needed was for Vader to get involved.

He narrowed his eyes at her, clearly unconvinced. "Listen, Trixie. Do you know anyone else in San Gabriel?"

"Just my sister. I would have known Jacob if he hadn't left for college. And you!" Her face lit up. "My first real live San Gabriel man."

"He's not a man," said Cherie quickly.

Vader looked offended by that news. But Trixie was hitting the ground running in terms of flirtation, and this particular one had to be nipped in the bud.

"I mean, he is a man, a fireman, a very nice, *older* man than you. Too old."

"A *fireman*?" Trixie's eyes, blue where Cherie's were gray, acquired a blatant sheen of hero worship. "He's so tall and strong, *and* he's a fireman?"

Vader raised an eyebrow at Cherie. With that one gesture, the heaviness in her chest eased. She knew Vader's ways; with anyone else, he would have curled his lip or plastered a leer on his face. But obviously, he realized Trixie was an innocent, and he had no intention of playing any games with her.

Although Cherie had to wonder just how innocent the former Humility Harper actually was. She seemed ready to flirt with a lamppost.

"Trixie, even though I'm not as old as your sister makes me sound"—Vader frowned in Cherie's direction—"I want you to think of me as your older brother."

"Which one? Justice-Denied? Righteous-Be-Thy-Name?"

"Huh?" Vader shook his head. "Doesn't matter. Think of me as a whole different kind of brother. One without a weird name."

"Vader ain't exactly your common run-of-the-mill name either." Trixie opened her eyes wide and fluttered her eyelashes.

Cherie ground her teeth. "The point he's trying to make is he wants you to look on him the same way you would if he was your brother. For instance, if you need help. Right, Vader?"

"Right." He approached Trixie. "You have anything to write on?"

She held out her arm. "Better write it there, so I don't lose it." She snatched up one of the Bic pens Cherie kept in a vintage jelly bean jar next to the telephone. "I always wanted to do this. If I had my druthers, it'd be on my bosoms instead . . ."

"Trixie," said Cherie sharply.

"What? Are you planning to be Pine Creek, the Sequel? 'Cause if that's the case, Mr. Fireman better take me home with him right here and now."

Vader finished imprinting his phone number on her hand and backed away. "Sorry, that's not going to happen. Now make sure you write that number down somewhere safe before you wash your hand. It's for emergencies, since you don't have any other family around."

"I get it, I get it."

Vader gave Cherie one last, lingering look, as if he didn't want to leave her alone with her own sister. She walked with him to the door, where he bent and whispered in her ear. "Something tells me that girl is trouble."

"Really? What clued you in? The eyelash-batting or the cute little Southern accent?"

"Her resemblance to you." With that, Vader stepped onto the porch. "I'll bring Soren back, then leave you alone. But I'm not forgetting your promise. You'd better call me."

"Look, Vader. She might be trouble, and I'm not going to deny it, but she's *my* trouble. You don't need to worry about us. Don't go all manly and protective on me. I got this. I'll call you soon." She shut the door on him, steeling herself against his wounded expression, then turned to face her long-lost sister.

While much of Vader's job as a firefighter involved putting out fires, it also included a certain amount of cleaning up messes. Fires always left stinking, smoldering chaos in their wake, and firefighters did what they could to leave a fire scene as tidy as possible. Fire engines had to be kept polished, hoses stowed, gear maintained. As first responders, firefighters were used to showing up when things were at their absolute worst, and leaving when some order had been restored.

But Cherie's mess, that was another matter. How had Vader wound up fetching her housemate's underwear, after enduring endless abuse from her other housemate? And what had inspired him to give his number to that little bundle of wild-girl hormones called Trixie? Especially since Cherie had basically just told him to keep out?

The things a man did for the woman he loved.

Fuck. He loved Cherie, and until ten minutes ago he hadn't even known her real name. How screwed up was that? Did Soren and Nick know her real name? Was he the only one she'd left in the dark?

These and similar thoughts churned through his brain as he hurried down the hospital corridors. Nick was awake, looking much better, and very happy to have his things. Vader had stuffed them in a plastic grocery bag that used to hold potato chips, so Nick didn't think he'd been handling his tighty-whities.

"I called Serafina. She's my mother," Nick told him. "She has a gap in her schedule so she's taking the Lear-jet from LA first thing tomorrow."

Vader nodded. He couldn't imagine any statement that would make the difference between him and Nick more clear.

"Are you ready to roll?" he asked Soren.

"Thanks, dude," Nick called as they left. "I don't re-member much, but I know you're made of light. We're writing a song about it. 'Beer Goggle Hero,' we might call it."

Vader shook his head, more than a little amused. He hadn't done much. Any first responder would have done the same thing. He and Soren headed back to his truck. Vader wondered if there was a way to ask him about Cherie's real name without giving anything away. But by then he was too exhausted to come up with anything. He let Soren ramble on about the song he and Nick were writing about the seizure.

"The whole thing was like, profound, man. Opened my eyes even more than ecstasy. I'm playing with 'sei-zure' and 'seize,' like 'seize the day,' since you never know what intense shit might go down."

By the time they reached Cherie's house, Vader's head was pounding like a drum set. Soren hopped out of the truck, but before he could disappear down the pathway, Vader called out. "Soren. Hang on. One of Cherie's sisters showed up. Thought you should know."

"A sister." Speculation gleamed in Soren's dark-rimmed eyes. "I knew Jacob and Cherie had a big family, but they never talk about them. It's all some kind of big secret."

The promise of knowledge about Cherie dangled before him like the forbidden apple. He shouldn't try to get information from Soren; Cherie wouldn't like that. Besides, she'd promised to answer his questions herself. If he asked Soren any questions, he'd be admitting that he wasn't in Cherie's confidence. And yet, the temptation was too great. "Do you know why they left Arkansas?"

Soren pursed his lips, which made his scraggly soul patch wiggle in the breeze. "All I can say for sure is a man was involved. I used to hear them arguing about a 'he.' But I was doing a lot of Turkish hashish back then, the fake stuff that has cherry flavor and shit. I kind of dug the hazelnut best."

Vader had had enough. Already he felt dirty for asking Soren anything. "Okay. Good night." Barely giving the guy enough time to close the door, he pulled away with a loud squeal of tires, feeling vaguely disgusted. He hadn't liked prying for information about Cherie's life. He shouldn't have to do that.

Most of all, he hated the fact that things between him and Cherie had just been thrown into even greater chaos. For the first time, he actually felt angry with her. He didn't like the way she'd wanted to shove him out the door. Didn't like the fact that she'd hid her real name, as well as just about everything about her family. Who was she, really? Did he even know her at all? Who had he been pining over all this time?

He set his jaw and reminded himself that he'd wanted to pry the truth from her. Now it was coming out in ways he hadn't expected in a million years. *Be careful what you wish for, because you might get it.*

Chapter Eleven

*E*ven though she hadn't seen her sister in six years, Cherie quickly figured out that Trixie had inherited the Harper family willfulness. They'd all gotten it from their father, who was so pigheaded he hadn't been able to function in normal society and had retreated to the backwoods. A big streak of nutty eccentricity also ran in the family. What else could explain how Justice-Denied had invented a way to turn old dryers into chicken-plucking machines? And why her sister Faithful sold paper flowers made from dyed toilet paper at the local farmers' market?

Their father, who'd adopted the name Prophesize when he'd settled in Arkansas, did his best to control his progeny, but he wasn't much good at it.

Which was no doubt why Trixie was now the third Harper to make her way to San Gabriel. Remarkably, she'd come alone; at least Cherie and Jacob had had each other.

"You sure no one knows you came here?"

"Mackintosh has no idea, Cherie. I know he still has a grudge against you because of how you hit him on the head and gave him brain damage."

Cherie winced. "Really? Brain damage?" She hadn't known it was that bad.

"Oh yes. He's not only mean now, he's even crazier. I talked another girl at the station into switching bus tickets, so I bought hers and she bought mine. If anyone asks, they'll think I've gone to Gatlinsburg, Tennessee. Plus I pulled a whole bunch of other tricks. No one followed me."

"That's good thinking, Trixie." She and her sister were holed up in Cherie's bedroom. Until she warned Soren and Nick, she had no intention of letting Trixie near those two. Since she had a big four-poster bed, they had plenty of room. In the old days, they'd slept five to a bed. Trixie wore a pair of Cherie's pajamas— her favorites, blue silk with capering white lambs— and sat cross-legged in a nest of pillows, brushing her long hair.

Cherie couldn't help greedily examining her little sister. She'd missed having her siblings around, especially the girls. They'd had plenty of unauthorized fun behind her stepmother's back. They'd built fairy houses in the woods, made up goofy songs, experimented with forbidden curlers.

"But how did you find me?"

"It was that phone message you left for us with Mr. Olson at the feed store. About the angels and the setting sun. Pretty clever that I worked it out, ain't it?"

She and Jacob had spent hours composing the perfect message that the Harper kids would be able to interpret, but no one else. They'd left the message for this exact purpose—so that other siblings would be able to escape if they wanted to.

"How are the others?"

"Growin' up fast. Cel's seven, and he's a complete scamp. He drives everyone crazy, especially me since I'm the one that's supposed to watch him." Trixie drew the brush through her long, honey-brown hair, the same color Cherie's would be if she let it grow out.

"You're eighteen now, right?"

"Eighteen and ready to rock," said Trixie cheerfully. "After you left, I set my mind to do the same thing, come hell or high water. Me and Robbie Mackintosh came up with our scheme to pretend to be engaged so everyone would leave us alone. Especially Mr. Mackintosh. Robbie told me he was heading to New York City, can you imagine that? Cherie." She put down the brush and began braiding her hair. "I'm ready to have some fun. I been feeling like a water balloon ready to burst. I want to jump around and scream and cut my hair and laugh and stay up all night and meet some boys. What about that good-looking fireman? Vader? He's . . ." She hesitated. Harpers weren't used to talking this way. "Hot. Very hot. I think he might be the handsomest guy I ever seen."

"That ain't saying much." Hearing the way she slipped back into their backwoods cadence, Cherie corrected herself. "*Isn't* saying much. You've probably only seen about ten men outside the family."

"I've seen enough to know the real deal. I'm serious, Cherie. Are you together with him? Because if you're not, I wouldn't mind that he's older, and . . ."

"*No.* Big N-O. Vader and me . . . it's complicated. But he's definitely off-limits."

Cherie got up and went to her dresser, where she kept an assortment of hair dyes stored in a basket.

"Complicated because of Mackintosh?"

Cherie fumbled with the bottles of dye. How much did Trixie know? How much did everyone in the family know? She and Jacob had fled without a single extra second to explain what had happened. "How do you mean?" she asked carefully, eyeing her sister's reflection in the old-fashioned oval mirror over her dresser.

Trixie blithely finished one braid and tossed it over her shoulder. "Just that he wanted to marry you and you didn't want to, so you bonked him on the head and ran. And Jacob helped. Is that right?"

"Yes, that's about right."

For certain, it was all her little sister needed to know. As she sorted through her hair dyes, more disgusting images from that night assaulted her. The stench of Mackintosh's sweaty armpits as he grabbed her arms, the suffocating darkness in the henhouse where he'd cornered her, the woozy way the room kept spinning around her.

"What are you doing over there?" Trixie's voice brought her back to her task.

"We're going to dye your hair."

"Really?" Looking thrilled, Trixie scrambled to her knees. "Sinful red, like yours?"

"I was thinking dark brown. Like a"—she scrambled for something appealing—"mink coat."

Trixie's face fell. "I don't want hair the color of roadkill. Give me platinum blond or nothing."

"How about a dirty blond?"

"No dishwater. I wanted to leave the boring stuff behind, remember?" She tilted her head, measuring Cherie's determination. "How about we compromise with strawberry blond?"

"Fine." It would probably be different enough to throw off any pursuers. "But we're going to cut it too.

You probably pissed off Mackintosh when you ran away. You need to change your basic appearance in case he's on your trail."

"Of course I made him mad. But he won't find us. Robbie said he hasn't left Arkansas in twenty years."

That was good to hear. But she wasn't taking any chances. "Where's Robbie?"

"He said he was off to find the love of his life. Someone he used to be with. He wouldn't tell me who. I have no idea where he is, but if Mackintosh goes after anyone, likely it'll be Robbie."

"Well, better safe than sorry."

She beckoned Trixie over and sat her on a chair angled to face the mirror. She lifted one braid, feeling the silky weight of it, so like her own. A tremor went through her. There was nothing like the blood and bone connection of family, of flesh that looked like your own, a voice that sounded like your own. Tears welled, straight from her heart, and she silently thanked the Universe—she didn't like to mention God, in case He reported back to her father—that her sister had made it here safely.

And now it was her job to make sure she stayed safe.

As she performed her second haircut of that endless day—had it really only been this afternoon that she'd cut Vader's?—she went over the ground rules with Trixie. No talking to strangers. No mentioning Arkansas to anyone. No phone calls home. Keep the door locked. Always tell Cherie where she was going. In fact, try not to leave the house.

Trixie's hysterical laughter was not exactly encouraging.

Fortunately, without a driver's license or much money, Trixie couldn't get into too much trouble. For the first week, she went out of her way to behave like a perfect angel. She cleaned the entire house while Cherie was at her movement therapy class. She whipped up some biscuits and chicken gravy that had Cherie's mouth watering with the taste of home. Cherie got a little suspicious when Trixie began churning out batch after batch of oatmeal raisin cookies, but decided it was a harmless hobby that at least kept her inside.

They got a stroke of luck when Nick's mother, a paper company heiress, made the executive decision that Nick should stay in her Malibu compound so her own doctors could tend to him. Nick refused to go without Soren, since they were making such good progress on their new, seizure-inspired songs. With both of her housemates gone, there was plenty of room for Trixie, and Cherie didn't have to worry about boys corrupting her vivacious little sister.

All in all, Trixie's blithe nature made her a pleasure to have around. And when an entire week passed without a peep from the backwoods of Arkansas, Cherie began to relax.

But she still didn't know what to tell Vader, so she didn't call him. It was getting harder and harder to hide things from him. In fact, she hated it—but not nearly as much as she hated the idea of Mackintosh going after him.

While Vader's goal of learning the truth about Cherie had hit a major roadblock, things were proceeding well at work. He took the first step toward making a good impression when Captain Brody announced the newest "learn not to burn" program. At lineup, the captain read out loud from the bulletin.

"This is a school outreach program. We need volunteers to talk to kids in kindergarten through third grade at each elementary school in San Gabriel."

Vader's arm shot up. "Count me in, Cap."

The entire company looked his way. In the past, he'd been pretty choosy about his off-shift commitments—though no one knew the real reason why. They figured he preferred to spend his time partying.

Captain Brody nodded and made a note. "The battalion chief has also asked for a volunteer to coordinate the volunteers. Each school needs two firefighters, and we have twelve elementary schools in town. You'll have to work with the captains from each station to determine availability and—"

"I'll do it." Again, Vader shot his hand in the air.

"What'd you have for breakfast, scrambled suckup?" Sabina whispered out of the side of her mouth.

"Ha ha. You were a lot funnier before you got married."

"Really, that didn't work? I guess I left out the side of brown nose."

"From not-funny to disgusting. Wrong direction."

Captain Brody raised his voice over their muttered squabbling. "Next up is a call for committee members for a new community relations manual. As you all know, the fire department is a vital part of this community. The committee will be tasked with writing clear guidelines on how best to interact with the citizens of San Gabriel, including the various ethnic groups that—"

"I'm in," Vader announced. "I'm all over that one."

Stunned silence settled over the crew. Then one of the new guys broke it. "By 'the citizens of San Gabriel,' the captain doesn't mean just girls."

Vader stalked toward him, until he was chest to chest with the guy. He wanted to pound him into the ground, of course, but that's exactly what the others would expect from him. He needed to show a different side. A smarter, less impulsive side. "What's your name? Mulligan?"

"Yeah, what about it?" Mulligan, whose broken nose and clenched fists screamed *fighter*, didn't back down.

"You're interrupting the captain. He's asking for volunteers, not wiseass comments." Vader kept his tone firm, giving Mulligan no leeway to get crazy on him. This was about keeping order in the firehouse, not kicking some guy's ass.

Mulligan dragged his eyes away, nodded in acknowledgment. "Sorry, Cap. I'll sign up too."

When Vader returned to Sabina's side, speculation glinted in her turquoise eyes. "You're up to something."

"Don't you worry your little newlywed head about it."

She made an irritated face at him, but didn't tease him anymore. And she kept giving him odd looks as lineup ended and various groups split off to work out or check equipment. He didn't care. He was used to odd looks; they came with the territory of being Vader.

At his locker, he gave his old video camera a longing look. The crew was used to him sticking the camera in their faces, shooting random moments of idiocy. He only did it for his mother. But if he wanted to be captain, he'd probably have to lighten up on the amateur filmmaking.

So be it. His mother would just have to live without the home movies. If the payoff was a higher salary, she'd understand.

For the rest of the shift, he applied himself with a new sense of devotion to the familiar routines of the firehouse. Truck 1 fielded three calls, none of which posed any challenge. The aerial wasn't needed, but if it had been, Vader was prepared to battle the whole crew for the chance to reclaim his turf. After the third call, a drunk driving accident that didn't wrap up until late, he eased himself into his bed at the firehouse. He gave a deep sigh and stretched every tight muscle in his aching body.

What he wouldn't give for one of Cherie's hot stone massages. He loved the flower essence she used, and the way she kept his body relaxed with warm towels as she worked. He loved the way she started out all business—using him to practice her techniques—but then her touch would shift from nurturing to lingering, and her breath would come more quickly, and before he knew it, she was sliding her hand underneath him.

As he'd warned her from the beginning, he wasn't capable of resisting her touch. A stiffie was inevitable. What she wanted to do about it was up to her.

They hadn't once completed a massage without ending up in bed. Or on the floor, or wherever was most convenient.

Did "friends" rate massages? He was drifting into a blissful dream in which a naked Cherie knelt before him, holding a bowl of steaming water, when the sound of his cell phone yanked him awake.

Panic racing through his veins, he fumbled for his phone. Something must have happened to his mother. Why else would anyone call so late?

"Hello? Mom? What's wrong?"

"Is this Vader?" a light, Southern-tinted voice answered. "Did I get the wrong number?"

"No. This is Vader." He forced his galloping heart to slow down. "Who is this?" It wasn't Cherie, he knew that much—he'd know her voice in his deepest sleep. But the rattled pieces of his brain couldn't place her.

"This is Trixie. Cherie's sister. You said to call if I needed help."

"Yeah." He sat up and swung his legs over the side of the bed. Then, goofily, he drew the sheet over his bare legs, as if she could see him over the phone. "What's up?" He checked his watch. Five in the morning. "Where are you?"

"In a phone booth. My phone's still in the fish tank. I hate to bother you so late at night, but can you come pick me up?"

Vader groaned. "I'm on shift, Trixie. I can't leave. Did you call Cherie?"

"No. She's working too. It's her night at the Hendersons."

He thought quickly, running through the options, other firefighters who could pick her up. But it was solidly the middle of the night, and he didn't feel right bothering anyone at home.

"I can get off in an hour if one of the early relief guys show up. Brett usually does. What phone booth are you at?"

There were only a few left in San Gabriel.

"It's inside an all-night coffee shop. I was sorta surprised it even worked."

He sagged with relief. "Stay there. Hang out, order what you want, I'll be there in an hour."

"But I don't have any money. I barely had change for the call."

"I'll take care of it. But you're going to tell me everything. That's my price for bailing you out of trouble."

"Yes, sir," she said meekly.

His plan had been to volunteer for overtime, not take off at the first sign of an early relief guy. But he didn't have a choice; he couldn't leave Trixie out there on her own. When he burst through the door of the Brite Spot coffee shop, Trixie nearly knocked him over by jumping into his arms.

"Thank you thank you thank you," she murmured. "I'm so glad to see you, I nearly peed my pants."

"Didn't need to know that." He firmly set her back down on the floor, then followed her to the booth where she'd been sitting. He slid in opposite her and signaled the waitress for coffee. With a scowl, he took in her appearance. "You look different."

Her hair was now somewhere between apricot and peachy yellow, and it hung halfway to her shoulders in a cloud of flyaway wisps.

"You don't like it? Cherie did it."

It wasn't that he didn't like it. But his job—keeping her out of trouble—had just gotten a lot more difficult. She no longer looked like an off-limits innocent. She looked like a girl who wanted to have some fun.

The waitress appeared with a carafe of steaming coffee. As soon as she was gone, he ordered Trixie to talk. Surprisingly, she did so. Too bad Cherie wasn't a little more like Trixie, at least in that respect.

If anything, Trixie shared too many details during her long, rambling account of a visit to a bookstore, at which she'd met someone who invited her to a dance party, where her new friend had disappeared, leaving her to pick her way through drunken bodies. As Vader listened, he downed his coffee and a couple of muffins.

"Did your sister know you were going out?"

"She probably figured it out."

Vader knew an evasion when he heard one.

"That's why you don't have to say anything." Trixie's utter confidence was almost amusing, as if she were a baby chick set to dive out of the nest, wings or no. "I got it handled."

"If you had it handled, you wouldn't have had to call me."

"That's how I handled it." She gave him a superior look. "That's what you told me to do, genius."

He gritted his teeth. "Yes, but now that you've involved me, I get to decide what I tell your sister. And I intend to tell her everything. Unless you want to do it first."

Storm clouds gathered on her pretty, exhausted face. He headed them off by tossing some bills on the table and rising to his feet. "You can think about it in the truck. But I'm serious. San Gabriel's a small town, but there's crime here like anywhere else. And you don't know how to take care of yourself. You don't even have a cell phone, for Pete's sake!"

"And whose fault is that? Not mine!"

He took her arm and hauled her out of the coffee shop. Normally he might be more patient, but he was running on about three hours of broken sleep, max. Trixie was Cherie's problem, Cherie had said so herself. She'd declared that she didn't need Vader. So he'd take Trixie home and let Cherie take it from there. End of story.

Chapter Twelve

Cherie's most lucrative job was watching the Hendersons' kids on the wealthy couple's weekly date night. They probably spent nearly a thousand dollars on that one night, between the expensive hotel room, their four-star dinner, and her hefty fee. They paid her so well she couldn't manage to quit, despite the challenge of dealing with four boisterous kids and their eighty-odd electronic devices. Besides, she loved those kids.

By the time she drove home around eight-thirty the next morning, she was completely drained and craved nothing more than a long bubble bath and a nap.

But it was not to be. As soon as she saw Vader's big blue truck parked outside her house, she knew something was wrong. Racing inside, she found her sister planted in a corner of the couch, her thin arms wrapped around her drawn-up knees. Despite her defensive posture, she held her chin at an angle that spelled big trouble.

Like a guard dog ready to pounce, Vader occupied the nearest armchair, legs spread apart, jaw clenched, tension rippling his strong body. The two of them barely stopped glaring at each other long enough to greet her.

Cherie dropped her tote bag and folded her arms. "What happened?"

Vader shot Trixie a pointed look.

She dropped her head to her knees, then yanked a fluffy blue pillow over her head. A frustrated, mewing sound rose from the couch.

"Don't you even think about lying, Humility," said Cherie. "'Cause I'll know. And I won't put up with it. I mean it."

All the Harper children were accomplished liars. They'd had to be, to avoid being whipped for insignificant things like forgetting to close the window at night. Over the years they'd developed their own version of the Creed. Rule number one: Lies told to save themselves from a beating didn't count. Rule number two: No Harper child ever told on another.

"My name is Trixie," muttered Trixie.

Cherie wanted to roll her eyes, but stopped herself. "That's right. You're Trixie now. And Trixie is a grown-up who takes responsibility for her own actions. Now spill it."

"Fine." She dropped the pillow and spoke in a rapid-fire burst of words. "I went to a party and started talking to a boy but he turned out to be a meanie-head so I hid from him in someone's closet until it was really late then tiptoed out of the house and walked to a coffee shop where they had a phone. Then I called Vader." She emphasized that last sentence with a venomous glare at her rescuer.

"And Vader, being the good guy that he is, dragged himself out of bed to pick you up?"

"He took his sweet time."

Cherie glanced at Vader, whose rugged face looked as if it had been assembled from quarry stone. "I came when I could," he said.

A horrible thought struck her. "You weren't on shift, were you?"

Though he didn't answer, she realized he must have been. "For shame, Trixie. And stop giving him those poison eyes or you won't be leaving this house for a month."

Her sister's cheeks went pink. "Sorry, Vader," she muttered. "And thanks for picking me up." She unfurled her legs and bounced to her feet. "I really need to catch up on my sleep, y'all."

"Don't even think about leaving," Cherie ordered. Trixie plopped back down on the couch. "How'd you get to the party?"

"I went with a girl I met at Starbucks."

"You've been hanging out at Starbucks? With what money?"

"I had a little bit left." Cherie folded her arms and summoned the eagle-eyed stare that Prophesize used to make them all shake in their shoes. Her version didn't work quite as well, but it was enough to make Trixie squirm. "Fine. Soren and Nick paid me to help them pack. And I sold some oatmeal raisin cookies to the neighbors. Lots of them."

Cherie flopped down on the love seat still shoved up against the wall from the day she'd taught Vader the tango. At the moment, the disorder in her living room felt like one more sign of her pathetic lack of control over her life. "For mercy sakes, I've been blind as a fruit bat. You've been selling cookies behind my back and sneaking out to parties? I ought to just send you back to Arkansas."

Trixie scrambled off the couch and stomped across the room until she loomed over Cherie. "You know you won't do that, so don't even bother to say it. And you can't expect me to just stay inside like a prisoner. That's not why I left home!"

Equally furious, Cherie surged to her feet. "Why'd you leave home, then? To make my life hell? Hear that? That's *profanity*!"

Trixie poked her in the chest, her face red with passion. "All I want is a little bit of what you have. *You* get to do what you want, and have pretty red hair and sexy clothes and . . . and makeup . . . and . . . and *sex*. You have sex with Vader, don't you? And don't you lie to me, sister!"

Hot humiliation coursed through her body until she wanted to melt into the living room floor like the Wicked Witch of the West. Back home, during Family Circle, Prophesize would list off their misdeeds and assign punishment. But no punishment could compare to the shame of being singled out in front of everyone else. Intense embarrassment rooted her to the floor. She couldn't even look at Vader.

But this was her house, her life. She shouldn't have to feel this way.

"My sex life, whether it exists or not, is none of your business, Trixie." Her voice shook, but she kept it even.

And then a warm hand settled on her shoulder and she heard Vader's deep voice.

"We're getting off the subject, Trixie. Your sister's just trying to keep you safe from horny guys like the one last night. Take it from me, there's a million more like him."

Trixie shot him a resentful look. "I just wanted a little fun. You don't know what it's like."

"*I* know," Cherie told her. "I know perfectly well what it's like. Look. How about we work out some kind of deal so I know you're safe and you get to have more fun?"

Trixie's exhausted face lit with joy. "Really?"

"Well, we'll see. Why don't you get some sleep now and we'll work it all out later." Trixie nodded, her gaze shifting from Cherie to Vader, then back again. Cherie wondered if this was what it would be like to have a teenage daughter. With Vader.

But that was out of the question.

With an ache in her heart, she watched Trixie drag her tired self down the hall toward Nick's old bedroom.

Vader watched her go, an ominous frown gathering on his wide forehead. "You sure about that? It seems like you're rewarding her for sneaking around."

"You're going to be one of those strict daddies, aren't you?" There she went again, imagining Vader as a father. Silly Cherie. Why was it so hard to let that thought go?

Completely exhausted by the long night, topped off by Trixie's drama, she let out an enormous yawn. The next thing she knew, she was being gathered into Vader's strong arms and lifted into the air. "What are you . . . ?"

"Shhh."

She subsided, her eyes drifting half closed. It felt so delicious to be transported this way, as if she were a bit of dandelion fluff floating on the wind. As a child, she'd loved filling her cheeks with air, then sending the white dandelion spores bursting off the stem. You were supposed to wish on something, and always, always, she'd wished for the same thing. *Freedom.* Was this freedom, this utterly secure, relaxed sensation? Was this freedom, this wonderful ride in Vader's arms up the stairs, into her bedroom, then onto the soft nest of her bed?

It felt like freedom, but also like something more, something infinitely sweeter and better. Vader straightened, looking down at her with a shuttered look. He was leaving, because she'd told him to earlier. But right now, she couldn't bear to watch him walk away. Dark shadows ringed his warm brown eyes. He was probably even more tired than she was. She opened her arms and beckoned him into bed.

He hesitated, but the pull between them was too strong for even a mighty fireman to resist. His long, hard body stretched next to hers, exuding heat like the molten core of a power plant. She snuggled against him and let blissful sleep steal over her senses.

When she rose through the deepest layers of unconsciousness, into the sunlight of half awareness, she was moving against Vader, or he was moving against her. It didn't matter. They were moving together, their bodies hot and longing. Her sex throbbed with a fierce, pleasurable urgency. She needed this man in her, around her, all over her. Vader braced himself on top of her, his arm muscles rigid as steel cords, his broad chest shielding her from anything outside their precious haven. His muscles strained, his breath rasped.

"If you want me to stop, you'd better knee me in the balls or something," he muttered.

"I don't." The word came as a soft gasp. "Don't stop. Oh. Right there." This, as he put his hand right where the need flared, in that soft place between her legs that wept for him.

"You want me," he growled.

"Oh yes."

"Tell me how much."

"The most. The most ever." She didn't have words to tell him how much she wanted him, how much he called to her, how much he tempted her, threatened her resolve. In this intimate circle filled with slick skin and hot want, she couldn't hide anything from him. And that meant danger. Real danger.

But before she could panic, he was sliding his thick length into her, driving all other thoughts to the wind. She arched to meet him, drawing him into her heat, into the pulsing core of her being.

She heard his sharp indrawn breath and slitted her eyes open. The strain on his face, the chocolate eyes gone hot, the tensed jaw, the tight lips, thrilled her to the bottom of her feminine soul. She'd done this, made this spectacular man want her this badly. And she craved more. She wanted him to drive himself into her, give her everything he had, all his strength and power and heart.

"Make love to me," she whispered to him. "Don't hold back."

As soon as Cherie said those words, Vader felt as if a dam burst inside him. He'd been trying so hard to restrain himself, to spare her the full force of his need. But now, he let his ferocious passion for her take the reins. She trembled under him as he drove his cock deep, then deeper still. This wasn't just sex. This was a tumble down a waterfall, a shrieking thrill ride that tossed them up and down until he didn't know what was what or where was where.

She came almost immediately, sobbing incoherently against his chest. But there was more, and he knew it, and he wasn't letting it slip away. He flipped her over, piled pillows under her hips, and stroked the creamy globes of her ass. Shivers swept across her flesh. With hungering hands, he roamed the full curves of her hips, tracing the crease between her upper thighs and her buttocks, then finding his way between her legs. She tightened her inner thighs.

"No holding back, sweetheart," he whispered. "Remember?"

"Yes. No. Yes." She gave a helpless sob as her thighs relaxed. He used his knees to nudge them further, opening her like the petals of a flower. With a sense of reverence, he searched the delicate folds of her sex, vulnerable and open before him, until he found the swollen nub of her clit. He rubbed it with his thumb, gently until she moaned, then faster, harder, sensing exactly how much pressure she wanted.

When she was right on the edge, quivering, desperate, he laid his body over hers and reached for her breasts with one hand, slipping a pebbled nipple between his fingers.

A long sigh left her lips as his cock joined his other hand. He stoked the fire from inside and out, with powerful, flexing movements of his hips, grinding her sensitized sex against his hand. He wanted more than an orgasm from her. He wanted complete surrender, complete acknowledgment of what existed between them, this insane, maddening, sweet, hot craving, this fever that wouldn't leave him, no matter how many times he spent himself inside her body . . .

And then he was flying apart, growling like a wolf over its prey, exploding inside her while she screamed and shook with the force of her climax.

Sweet Lord above.

When his head cleared, she was sitting bolt upright, a sheet clutched to her gloriously flushed chest. And she was groaning. "I can't even believe we did that. My sister is *right* downstairs."

He stroked a lazy hand down her back, shaping every curvaceous swell and dip of her flesh. "She's two floors down. And I'm sure she's dead to the world."

Cherie chewed at the fingernail on her thumb. "You don't know that."

"What are you so worried about? She knows we have sex. She said so. Even if she heard you making those cute little whimpers, it wouldn't be any big shocker."

She dropped her head into her hands. "Did I whimper? Tell me I didn't whimper."

"Of course you did." Maybe it wasn't cool to be so smug about it, but he couldn't help it. If nothing else, he and Cherie knew how to satisfy each other in bed. "You whimpered and you don't even remember it. Bonus."

"*Bonus?* This isn't a game, Vader."

"Would you relax, Cherie? I know it's not a game, but it's not life or death either. Sex is supposed to be fun, remember?" He ran a finger across the bold curve of her hipbone. "Just once, can we enjoy the afterglow without you going through some kind of nervous breakdown?"

She pushed his hand away from her body. "I'd better go check on Trixie." As she rolled toward the edge of the bed, he lifted himself on one elbow and pinned her in place with one long arm. "Sorry, Cherie. You don't get to fuck and run."

His choice of words made her draw in a shocked gasp. "Don't use that word."

"You're the one trying to turn this into something bad. I'm not ashamed of anything we do in bed. But you keep acting like we just broke all Ten Commandments at once. I'm here, Cherie. I'm here for whatever you want. You want to get married? I've already asked you twice. *You're* the one who treats this like dirty laundry. Like some kind of sweaty socks you want to bury at the bottom of the hamper."

Her eyes were fixed on him, wide and gray as the open ocean, a storm brewing in their depths. "I don't know what you're talking about."

"The hell you don't."

In a surprise move, she tried to dislodge his wrist with a sudden push, but he didn't bench-press three hundred for nothing. When she gave up trying to budge him and tried to squirm through the cage of his arms, he flung his thigh over hers and flipped her onto her back.

He stared into her eyes, refusing to let her look away. "Give me something here, Cherie. Give me one good reason why Trixie wouldn't be okay with us having sex while she's catching up on her sleep."

"You're not acting like a gentleman," she gasped.

"No. I'm just a straight-up guy who loves you. And you don't know what to do with that, do you?"

Flat on her back, caged beneath him, she bit her lower lip and glared up at him. "If you think this is going to make me talk, you don't know me."

"You're right. I don't know you. And every time I try, you throw up one roadblock after another." With a grunt of disgust, he sat back on his heels, setting her free. "I shouldn't have to freaking interrogate my girl to get some simple answers." He flung up a hand. "Don't say it. You're not my girlfriend. You never said you were my girlfriend. You have a heart attack when I talk about marriage. But when we're in bed it's a different tune. It's 'Don't hold back,' and 'Don't stop' and whimpers and screams and—"

"Shhh! My sister."

"That's it. I'm done." Vader scrambled over her and flung himself out of her bed. With this kind of fury raging through him, he couldn't be around her. Couldn't be around anyone. "You think you can control everything, don't you? You think your sister's going to sit at home and follow orders?"

"I can handle my sister."

"The hell you can. And what about us? You think I'm going to keep fucking you and never want anything more? Well, I'm not that guy."

He thrust one leg into his board shorts, then jumped on one foot while he straightened out the fabric of the other leg. His still-purple bruise produced a stab of pain.

"If you want that sort of guy, there's plenty of them out there."

What was he saying? Was he telling Cherie to go find some other man? Obviously, he'd completely lost it. He inserted his other leg into his shorts and fastened the Velcro at the waistband. Still bare-chested, he pointed at her. "But you're not going near them. Because they're not right for you. I'm the one you want and that's why we keep ending up *there*." He swung his arm to indicate the rumpled bedcovers. She sat, wide-eyed, in the middle of the bed, clutching the sheets around her like some sort of security blanket, her hair a vivid splash of wine red against the milky white.

"What I don't understand is why you don't see that? Why we keep ending up like this." He thumped his chest. "With me storming out the door and you telling yourself a big lie that it doesn't matter. That it's better this way. Well, baby." Two long steps and he was bending over her, nearly nose to nose. "It's not better. But if this is how you want it, this is how you get it."

He snatched up his T-shirt and wheeled toward the door.

"What do you mean?" she called after him. "What are you trying to say?"

"I'm saying what you've been wanting me to say. I'm leaving you alone."

"But Vader . . ."

His hand on the doorknob, he turned to face her one last time. "I'm a firefighter, Cherie. It's not in me to give up on a call. But when the commander says, 'Pull out, we're going defensive,' you have to get the hell out because there's no saving that sucker. That structure is going down. That's where we are, sweetheart. If you don't start getting real with me, this thing between us is going down in flames."

At her bewildered expression, he softened his tone, adding a touch of wry humor. "No matter what I do with that big hose of mine."

Even though it hurt like hell to leave her looking so shaken, he forced himself to turn the doorknob, push open the door, and heave his body through it. *Pull out, we're going defensive.*

Chapter Thirteen

It took all his considerable willpower, but Vader managed to put Cherie at the back of his mind while he tackled his other mission—convincing everyone that he could be captain. Not just any captain, he decided, but an outstanding captain.

The first session at the San Gabriel Elementary School went great. Vader and a couple of firefighters from other stations in town went from class to class, demonstrating how to use a fire extinguisher and teaching the kids about dialing 911.

"What do you do if you smell smoke?" Vader put his hands on his knees, bending down to their level, and making a comical smoke-sniffing face.

"Cough!" one kid yelled.

"Throw up!" said another.

One quiet little girl raised her hand. He pointed to her. "What would you do?"

"Tell my grandmother."

"What if your grandmother's in another room? How would you make sure she heard you?"

She thought for a moment. "I'd yell."

"Really loud, right? Like, how loud?"

Giggling, she tried a soft yell, what he would have classified as a loud whisper. He cupped a hand around his ear. "What was that?" He pretended he was deaf. "Come again, missy?"

This time, both her giggle and her yell were louder. He motioned to the whole class to join in, and soon the room was filled with shouts of "smoke" and "fire."

"Okay, so you've woken up the entire neighborhood. Great job! But now the fire has gotten into your room. What do you do?"

No one had an answer. Vader couldn't believe it. Didn't they teach kids fire safety anymore? At home, he kept a fire extinguisher in every room, and he'd trained his mother how to drop and roll, then drag herself across the room with her elbows. It was a damn good thing he'd signed up for this job.

"Have you guys heard the phrase 'Stop, drop, and roll'? No? Yes? Some of you? Well, this is how it goes. You can practice it at home."

He took a step forward, then came to an exaggerated stop, like Road Runner. "First you stop, so you don't make the fire worse. Then you drop to the floor." Making every movement like something out of a cartoon, he dove to the floor and covered his face. "And don't forget to roll back and forth, in case a spark landed on you. Like a Tootsie Roll. That's how you roll. Oh yeah, oh yeah."

The kids screamed with laughter as he bumped into a chair and knocked a pile of books onto himself. After an exaggerated double take, he rolled in the other direction, right into the feet of Joe the Toe. Joe, hands on his hips, glowered and shook his head at Vader's antics.

"Anyway, you get the idea, right?" Vader hopped onto his feet and straightened up. "Let's hear it. What do you do if there's a fire near you?"

"Stop, drop, and roll!" the kids shouted.

"You have to admit, they won't forget it," Vader said to Joe the Toe as they strolled away from the sunny campus, followed by a chorus of good-byes.

"You know what's worse? I won't forget it. It's branded into my eyeballs. Vader the bloody Tootsie Roll," said Joe.

"Don't go spreading that around, now." Vader's cell rang with the ring tone he'd assigned to Trixie—the theme of *Jaws*. "Uh oh, trouble."

"Of the female persuasion, I presume?"

"Not exactly. Cherie's off-limits little sister. Feel free to spread that around, by the way. Off-limits with a capital O-L," he answered. "What's up, Trix?"

Her Southern accent floated over the phone line. "Well, the thing is, Cherie wanted me to clean the bathroom, which is fine, but I needed some stuff from the supermarket, so I walked over there and only then did I discover that I left my little change purse back at the house, along with my house keys. Luckily, the sweetest bag boy is letting me use his phone."

"Why are you calling me? You know Cherie doesn't want me in the middle of anything."

"That's her problem. I don't know what bug crawled up her butt, but I think you're cute."

Joe cocked an eyebrow at him. "Trouble," mouthed Vader.

"Besides, she's in the middle of her bowel movement class."

Vader nearly choked. "Movement therapy, Trixie. Not bowel movement."

"I don't know, Vadie-poo. Have you seen the kind of moves they make in that class? I'm not sure it's decent."

"What'd you just call me?" Vader glanced over at Joe, who was doubled over with laughter.

"I'll tell you when you get here. I'm at the Red Apple on Main Street." And she hung up.

"Oh, hell no." Vader was pretty sure steam was coming out of his ears. He gave Joe a little kick in the side. "You laugh like a rhinoceros."

"I absolutely must meet this girl," gasped Joe, rolls of laughter rippling his huge body. "Red Apple, we're on the way. Brilliant."

Vader brandished his phone in the air. "This makes the third time she's called me for help. The last time I was in the middle of a committee meeting. Do you know what that made me look like? I had to pause my presentation just in case it was an emergency."

"Your *presentation*?"

"Yeah." Vader realized he hadn't told Joe the Toe about his plans to become captain. "I have to call Cherie. I'm not going to cover for Trixie, she knows better than that."

But Cherie's phone went to voice mail. Try as he might, he couldn't suppress his rescuer impulses enough to ignore Trixie's call. While he ferried her home from the Red Apple, he heroically managed to avoid asking her how Cherie was doing.

Even so, she dropped a cheeky "Cherie misses you like crazy," as she hopped out of the truck.

When Cherie returned his call later that day, he was

ready. "Thought you had your sister under control. Didn't you mention something about 'handling' her? That must have been someone else who called me for a ride, not Trixiebelle Humility Harper."

"I'll talk to her."

"Are you still making her stay home all day?"

"Don't worry about it," she said tersely. He could picture her hands going white-knuckled on her phone, her forehead creasing in that worried frown. The image twisted his gut.

Dropping his antagonistic tone, he asked, "Are you sure you're okay?"

For a moment she didn't answer, which made his imagination go wild. Something must be happening with Cherie, something she didn't want to share.

Of course she didn't want to. She didn't want to share anything. That was the heart of the problem right there. That was why he had to stick to the declaration he'd made while walking out of her bedroom. *I'm leaving you alone. Pull out, we're going defensive.*

"I'm fine," she finally said. "Don't worry about Trixie. She has a way of coming out okay. I'm not sure what she's up to, but we'll be fine. I do appreciate it, though, Vader. I'm sorry she bothered you."

The finality in her voice made panic race through him. He gripped the cell phone tight, hanging on to it like an anchor. What if his tactic didn't work? What if it backfired? What if leaving her alone did nothing but . . . leave him alone?

"Okay," he managed, and ended the call. For a long time he stared at the breaded chicken breasts he was frying for dinner at the station. A speck of grease leaped up and landed on his arm. He started.

"Yeah, yeah," he muttered to the chicken. "I'm on

it. Don't worry. I'll get over it. She's just a woman. Millions of 'em out there. Billions. I have other things to do than chase after a girl who doesn't want me."

The chicken sizzled—sympathetically, he thought. He picked up the spatula and eased it under one of the pieces.

"Thing is, she does want me. I know she wants me. *She* knows she wants me. But there's something stopping her." He flipped over the piece of meat, which settled comfortably on its other side. "I can't exactly tie her up and make her tell me."

Then again . . . tying her up worked for him. If he knew his Cherie, it worked for her too.

"You know something? That's genius." He poked at the chicken. "I think we're on to something. I just have to get her back into bed."

Someone cleared his throat. Someone very close behind him. He looked over his shoulder. Sabina, Fred, Ace, and Mulligan were all watching him, their faces red from the effort of holding in their laughter.

"Did you just call that chicken breast a genius?" Sabina asked in an unsteady voice.

He shrugged one shoulder and turned back to the pan. "Don't worry about them," he told the chicken, which was turning a lovely brown. "They wouldn't recognize genius if it laid an egg right in front of them."

All the firefighters lost it then, letting loose with howls of laughter. Vader ordered himself to keep his cool. Every firefighter was the butt of a joke at some point. The trick was to let it roll off your back.

A call came in just then, and half the crew took off. Vader finished frying the chicken, but no other brilliant ideas regarding Cherie occurred to him. He'd tried barging through her defenses, but it just didn't work. He had to hold firm and make her come to him.

If she didn't, maybe they weren't supposed to be together. Even though he knew in his bones that couldn't
be true.

In the two weeks since Vader had stalked out of her bedroom, nothing had gone right for Cherie. Trixie had
left "challenging" behind and zoomed toward "impossible." With no paying housemates and extra food
expenses, Cherie had to work extra shifts just to make
ends meet. In her absence, Trixie kept finding excuses
to leave the house. The second she got in a jam, she'd
call Vader with the new disposable cell phone she'd
somehow acquired. Vader, being the hero that he was,
kept rescuing her. How did he even find time for Trixie's drama when he was trying to win a promotion? In
two weeks, she'd called on Vader for at least five rides
and a few temporary loans. Which was mortifying,
since Cherie had essentially told Vader to mind his
own business.

Trixie, clearly, was not following that plan. And
Cherie had to admit she was grateful every time she
walked in and found Trixie on the couch, flipping
through TV channels. In her heart, she knew it was
thanks to Vader that Trixie was okay. But how could
she let Vader know that, without giving in to his
demand for more honesty? Without welcoming him
back on new, more intimate terms?

She wasn't ready for that. Not yet. Something told
her the other shoe from Arkansas hadn't dropped yet.
Until it had, she had no business involving Vader.

But all of that logic and reasoning had no effect on
what was going on in her heart. Her heart ached from
missing Vader. And not just her heart either. Vader had
invaded her mind. It was as if he'd strolled in, picked
out a comfy armchair, put his feet up, and refused

to leave. At night she dreamed of him, felt his hands soothing her body, his big chest under her cheek. She'd wake up with her leg stretched over the empty spot next to her, where Vader was supposed to be.

Scratch that.

Where Vader used to—occasionally—spend the night. It wasn't as if they'd ever had a permanent, official, defined relationship. She'd never even been to his house, for pity's sake. Until the incident with Nick, she hadn't even known he lived with his mother. Until he'd mentioned his mother's medical tests, she hadn't known his mother had health issues. And she didn't ask about that kind of thing because that would open the floodgates to *his* questions.

None of that added up to a solid relationship.

So why did she keep pining for Vader? Why did she keep going over every stupid thing she'd said to drive him away? Why couldn't their relationship have stayed exactly the way it was?

It hadn't been perfect, she had to admit, with those two rejected proposals hanging between them. But at least Vader had been part of her life, instead of hovering around the edges like Trixie's personal guardian angel.

But first things first. She had to deal with Trixie. She called in sick at the hair salon and sat Trixie down in the kitchen with a big bowl of popcorn with butter and Parmesan cheese. Cherie scanned her sister's outfit, which was entirely made up of items from her closet. But she put them together in a way Cherie never would have. That flowing white top that Cherie usually belted over a skirt—well, Trixie wore nothing under it but electric blue stockings and silver ballet slippers. With her tiny frame, the look worked on her.

But Cherie wouldn't want her leaving the house like that. She pushed the topic of outfits to a later date; right now they had more important things to discuss.

"Trixie, I know you're itching to get out there and meet boys and have fun, but I want you to take it slow. The way we were raised, you don't know anything about the dangers out there. And that's not even counting the Internet. You've been going online, haven't you?"

Trixie grabbed a handful of buttery kernels with her usual blithe obliviousness. "Well, of course I have, silly. Not much else to do when you're at work. Since you haven't let me go out *at all*, I'm taking advantage of my time at home. I'm learning *so much*."

Cherie dropped her head onto her arms. Mercy above, what had she unleashed when she'd given Trixie access to her computer?

"Besides, how else would I study for my driver's permit?" Trixie asked cheerfully.

"With the manual I brought you, that's how. You don't need to be online for that."

"But online they have all these cool reenactments of car crashes and stuff." She eagerly stuffed a handful of popcorn in her mouth. "Totally rad."

"That's not how we talk. We're not Valley girls." It was as if Trixie had learned a new language while surfing the Web.

"Listen to you, Cherie. You're not my mother. 'That's not how we talk.' We can talk however we want to talk! We're free! Or at least I thought we were. If we're not, then what's the point of all this? What's the point of this gorgeous house and all your pretty clothes if you're going to put yourself right back into prison, like you never left home?"

Cherie gawked at her little sister. Surprise, surprise, Trixie had a good point. She'd never thought of it like that. "I don't mean to put you in prison. I just don't want you to get mixed up with the wrong sort of men. You keep saying 'boys' but you need to think of them as men. Men with needs. Desires. Impulses."

Trixie stopped chewing popcorn and leaned forward with breathless anticipation. "Like what sort of impulses?"

"I'm not going into that right now."

"What about Vader? Does he have impulses?"

"I don't want to talk about Vader."

Trixie planted both elbows on the table and leaned forward. "If you don't want Vader, you should say something right now. Because if anyone's crush-worthy, it's that big hunk of fireman love."

Before she could stop herself, Cherie reached over and grabbed her wrist. "Put Vader right out of your mind. You hear me?"

"Aha!" Trixie bounced up and down in her chair. "You do like him. I knew you did."

Cherie tried to wrench the conversation back to its original topic. "Promise me you aren't talking to any 'boys' online. Because they're probably not boys, they're fifty-year-old perverts looking for young girls."

"Like Mackintosh?"

Cherie shuddered as a chill shot through her, the same chill she got every time that name was mentioned. "Pretty much."

"I wonder if he figures I'm with you."

"Let's pray not."

United for once, they both cast their eyes to the heavens above. "The thing is," said Trixie, settling back down to her popcorn, "it's fun to flirt on the computer. It's not like they're ever going to see me. You can say anything you want. Act like you're super-glamorous and sophisticated. You can even pretend you're, like, thirty." The way she said it, "thirty" was the next best thing to heaven.

Cherie realized she had some serious work to do. Trixie was even more naïve than Cherie had been at that age, and that was saying something.

"Trixie, listen to me. That stuff might be fun, but it's not going to make you happy."

"Why not?"

"Well, you know how Prophesize always wanted us to get married and start birthing babies. After I left home, I started seeing that there might be other things I could do too. When you're online, maybe you should think about that instead of boys."

"That's a rad idea." Trixie's face lit up. "Does that mean I can go online whenever I want?"

Oops. Cherie had the sneaking suspicion she'd fallen into a trap. She forged ahead anyway. "And you're going to have to get a job at some point. I'm going to need help with the rent and so forth. What interests do you have? What did you like doing back home?"

Trixie sorted through her handful of kernels, looking thoughtful. "I liked walking in the woods. I liked messing with Prophesize's traps so he couldn't catch rabbits."

"There you go!" Cherie gestured triumphantly. "Maybe you'd like to be a vet. You could start by volunteering at a pet shelter."

"Nah. I was thinking more like an engineer. I really liked figuring out those traps and how to wreck them so he wouldn't notice. Can girls be engineers?"

Progress! "Sure. But you'll need to go back to school for that."

"Like I said, maybe later." Trixie squinted, misty-eyed, as if looking into the future and witnessing exactly what she'd asked for. "In a couple of years. After I take care of a few things. But you don't have to worry about me being a burden. I won't be."

Cherie eyed her suspiciously. It sounded as if her willful little sister had some kind of master plan. What wasn't Trixie telling her?

Trixie swept the stray kernels of popcorn into a little pile on the table. "Thanks for the chitchat, sis. It's good to know I can turn to you for guidance and advice during my vulnerable teenage years."

"Uh-huh." Cherie watched as Trixie fetched the wastebasket and tidied up the pile. She shouldn't be so hard on her sister. Unlike many teenagers, Trixie was helpful around the house and never left a mess. And she was mostly cheerful, certainly better company than Soren and Nick. Trixie had already fixed more meals than the boys ever had. "You really can turn to me, you know. If there's something you want to tell me, I promise I'll listen. I won't freak out on you. Oh Lord have mercy."

She put her hand over her mouth as a terrifying thought struck her. Did she need to discuss birth control with her sister? What if she met someone as irresistible as Vader and got carried away? "Just so you know, I keep a stash of condoms in the medicine cabinet."

Trixie turned pink as a rhododendron and burst out laughing. "I wish I could see our stepmama's face if she heard you say that!" She dropped the wastebasket and skipped to Cherie's side. Like a kitten, she snuggled her cheek against Cherie's. "Not to worry, big sister. I'm a virgin and I intend to stay that way. For now." A funny look crossed her face, making warning bells chime in Cherie's brain. "But just so you know, you're my role model. Someday I hope to be just like you."

"But . . ."

Since Trixie was already halfway out the door and she was addressing her back, Cherie didn't bother to complete her thought, which was that Trixie could find a much better role model. Someone who could actually manage a healthy, honest relationship, for example. With a long sigh, she dropped her chin into her hand. That talk had definitely not gone the way she'd hoped. Instead of setting up clear guidelines and rules, somehow she'd offered Trixie Internet access and all the condoms she needed.

I'm handling it.

Vader would probably laugh his head off.

Chapter Fourteen

"She's going to ruin your chances of making captain, just you see." Ginny sat by the kitchen table slicing tomatoes while Vader grilled hamburgers at the stove. He was already regretting telling his mother about Trixie's arrival. He'd thought Trixie's escapades would entertain her, but they were having the opposite effect.

"How is one little teenage drama queen going to change anything?"

"How much have you studied since she got here?"

Vader made a show of creasing his forehead and counting on the fingers of one hand. "At least sixty."

"Hours or minutes?"

"Seconds."

"Hmph."

"Seriously, she's not anything to worry about. I've got my committees going on, I've been working on my new image." He ran one hand across his haircut, then made a "sizzling" sound. "Hottttt."

"The haircut's not bad, I admit. Vinnie changed things up this time."

"Vinnie nothing. This one was all Cherie."

His mother's hand slipped off the tomato, and her knife clattered onto the cutting board. Vader shot her a quick look to make sure she hadn't nicked herself. "Cherie cut your hair? I thought you dumped her."

"I never said that."

"You said you weren't going to play her game anymore."

Vader snorted. *Cherie's game.* If Cherie had a game, it would be Twister, where you got turned into a pretzel, then fell flat on your face. "I'm trying to switch us over to a new game, that's all. One we both enjoy."

Of course, there was a game they both enjoyed, and right about now, he was missing it more than he would have believed possible. How many nights had it been since they'd had sex? A couple of weeks. And for some unfathomable reason, he hadn't even been able to look at any other woman. All he wanted was to get back to Cherie's luxuriously soft bed, where everything smelled like flowers, and Cherie let all her worries and barricades fall away. Where they came together in sweet, hot, abandoned bliss. Where they—

"Vader," Ginny said sharply, waving the knife to grab his attention. "I want to paint you a picture."

"That's nice, Mom." He barely heard her.

"A verbal one. One in which you have a wife who thinks you're the center of her universe."

"Mom, get off my back."

But Ginny wielded her knife in the air, daring him to stop her. "One in which the woman you love loves you back just as much. One in which she knows all your favorite dishes and loves to make them for you."

"Cherie makes me peanut butter brownies all the time. You know how I am about peanut butter brownies."

"One in which she doesn't end things every other week."

Well, she certainly had him there.

"One in which you feel like a king instead of a beggar."

"A beggar?" Vader plopped a hamburger onto the bun he already had waiting. "I am a beggar. I'm begging you to stop." He placed the plate in front of her. "Eat up, Mom. While it's hot. I beg you."

She didn't even look at the hamburger, even though he'd added her favorite Worcestershire sauce to it.

"Wouldn't you like to know what it feels like to be with someone who thinks you're the moon and the stars put together, who treats you like a king and makes you chicken soup when you're sick, and leaves you little love notes on your pillow and—"

"No more Lifetime for you, Mom."

His mother rolled over that comment as if it were a speed bump. "Don't be cute. I want the best for you, Vader. That's all. You've been taking care of me since you were fourteen. You were a scrawny thing back then, remember?" She backed the wheelchair away from the table and cruised toward him.

"I was on the skinny side." None of his firehouse buddies would believe it, but it was a fact.

"And you started lifting weights so you could be strong enough to help me."

"Nah. I wanted the chicks to notice me." He hated when she started to reminisce. If he thought too much about that time, he got upset.

"You don't fool me. You started lifting after Ron left."

"So? What's gotten into you, Mom?"

"I haven't even gotten to the most important part, hon. *Don't you want someone who wants to have your babies?*"

Vader stared at her, blinking incredulously. "*What?*"

"You heard me, hon. You're thirty-one years old. Don't you think it's time you put your swimmers to work?"

Swimmers? "Is your grandmother clock ticking?"

"This isn't about me. It's about you." She was close enough now to jab him in the chest with her finger. "Can you look me in the eye and tell me you don't want children? You don't want a little boy you can show off at the firehouse? A little girl you can carry around on your shoulders?"

"Stop it, Mom. I don't want to talk about this." Feeling trapped, hounded, he wheeled her around and steered her chair back to the table. How the hell was he supposed to start a family, when he was either taking care of her, hauling hose at a fire, or letting off steam from those two activities?

Vader headed back to the stove, where he randomly clattered pots and pans around. This was why he didn't like reminiscing. Because it made him think of fathers who left and mothers who were suddenly helpless.

"I'm sorry, hon," Ginny said, though she didn't sound at all sorry. "My point is that you're a treasure, Vader. A bona fide, one hundred percent certified treasure. I know how lucky I am to have you. The woman you love ought to know it too."

Vader deliberately kept his back to her so she couldn't see the effect her words had. She meant well. Of course she did. She wanted the best for him. Completely understandable. But the picture she painted, of some perfect love in some ideal universe, a woman waiting on him hand and foot . . . damn, but he just couldn't see Cherie in that role. And if it wasn't going to be Cherie . . .

"See, that's the thing, Mom," he said, scraping hamburger grease off the frying pan. "You keep mentioning 'the woman I love.' But that's Cherie. Has been from the first moment. And it's not going away. I think I'm stuck."

Strained silence came from the table. On the off chance that she was filling her mouth with hamburger instead of pondering his statement, he risked a glance over his shoulder at her. She was chewing ferociously, frowning as if trying to work out the answer to a puzzle. Finally her face cleared. "Then we get you unstuck. We'll think of it like surgery. Speaking of surgery, that new nurse at the hospital—"

"No. No setups. If you try, I'll get myself snipped."

His mother straightened her spine. "What a thing to say!"

"Just showing how serious I am." He brought his burger to the table and sat down.

"Fine. I have another idea." At his menacing eyebrow lift, she threw up her hands. "You don't have to worry. It's a behind-the-scenes idea. More of a spiritual approach."

"Spiritual? Like prayer?"

"Yes. More or less."

No matter how much he pestered her, she wouldn't explain further. But since the whole scheme, whatever it was, had made her brighten, made the deep brackets around her mouth soften, he let it go. If she wanted to pray for him to get unstuck on Cherie, more power to her.

He called an early meeting of the Community Relations Handbook Committee before the next shift. The six firefighters on the committee, who came from stations all over town, gathered in a trailer behind Station 1. The trailer was set up to be an emergency headquarters for a disaster situation. Crammed with electronics, with a powerful generator out back, it also held a long table where the crisis managers would make their decisions.

Vader took a seat halfway down the table and passed around copies of a five-page list he'd made.

"I got ahold of all the old handbooks going back fifty years. I read them all and marked the areas that need updating. Some of the stuff is the same as it always was. But in some cases the demographic makeup of the community is different, so we have to adjust to that. We didn't always have so many Hmong in San Gabriel, for instance. The Hmong don't like to call in outsiders. So we have to figure out a way to win their trust."

Mulligan stared at the list, then stared at Vader. "You did this?"

Vader narrowed his eyes at him. He'd been worried when he saw Mulligan's name on the volunteer list. The guy had just moved to San Gabriel. What did he care about the community? "That's what I said."

"You studying for captain?"

Vader clenched his jaw. "Back to the list. Look through it and if you see an area you want to work on, shout it out. I broke it down into fire prevention, Emergency Ops, and general community relations like charity events, ride-alongs, station tours, and so on. Whatever doesn't get chosen I'll assign when we're done."

Mulligan kept shooting him curious looks while he flipped through the pages. "Not bad. Quite comprehensive. You sure no one helped you with this?"

"If you're looking for some kind of reaction, keep walking, dude. Doesn't matter what you say, I'm sticking to business."

Mulligan shrugged, and said nothing more until they'd finished doling out the various assignments. Then he raised his hand. "I got just one question."

"Yeah."

"You don't mention the Bachelor Firemen once in here. Kind of a big omission, don't you think? Considering the station's on the news all the time?"

Vader looked at his list in shock, as if it had just turned into a viper. No Bachelor Firemen. How could he have forgotten that little detail? "It's a legend. It doesn't belong in a manual like this. It's a mythical curse. Who cares?"

Vader had always claimed he didn't believe in the curse, but then again . . . he thought of Cherie, and how he could never get anywhere with her. Maybe he *was* cursed.

"*People* magazine cares about the curse," said Mulligan. "The *Today* show cares. Channel Six cares. Ella Joy cares." Mulligan rattled off the many news outlets that had covered the Bachelor Firemen story.

"Watch a lot of TV, do you?"

Mulligan shrugged. "I like to educate myself. I figure if there is a curse, this is the place for me."

"That's fucked up," said Vader. "But if you're so interested, you can work on that part. But keep your personal reasons to yourself. No one gives a shit."

"Ten-four, Cap'n." Mulligan gave a mocking salute. Vader was quickly growing to detest the guy.

"But I still think it's a waste of time," he grumbled. "We're a fire department, not a freaking reality show."

"If you say so, Cap'n."

Vader ended the meeting, setting the next one for a

week later. The other firefighters left to hurry to their own stations. Hands in his pockets, Mulligan ambled across the backyard toward the training room, where the crew was gathering for lineup. Vader followed a short distance behind. The guy got on his nerves almost as much as Soren and Nick did, and that was saying something. Of all the firefighters at the station, Mulligan was the one who looked at him with the least amount of respect. Maybe they hadn't fought enough fires together. They hadn't yet formed that bond that came with facing death head-on.

Vader put Mulligan out of his mind and focused on his firehouse duties. After lineup, he did a quick workout in the station's weight room. Then he reported to Brody's office to fill him in on his progress with both the school project and the handbook meeting.

"Do you think we should mention the Bachelor Firemen curse in the book?"

Brody went tense. Vader knew how much he despised the whole topic, even though he'd been the first to break the "curse" with his wife, Melissa. "I keep hoping it'll fade away and everyone will forget about it."

Vader made a show of scrawling a note on his pad. "So we'll leave it out. If we don't mention it, maybe it'll go away."

Brody let out a long-suffering sigh. "While that sounds appealing, that could be a case of wishful thinking."

"The mind is a powerful thing," said Vader, borrowing a quote from Ryan Blake, who used to be notorious for spouting affirmations at the drop of a hat.

Brody raised an eyebrow at him, but before he could say anything, Stan, the firehouse dog, who'd been napping in the corner of the office, shot to his feet and barreled past Vader. He shot toward the training room, where a Southern-tinged feminine voice could be heard.

"Those are molasses-ginger-chocolate-chunk, just like my mama used to make. Well, not my mama, my stepmama. Her name was Lily, as in Lily-of-the-Lord. Well, that wasn't her real name, but that's what we all called her. Anyway, help yourselves, Bachelor Firemen. And you too, older lady in a uniform. Do you know that I read online that older women are doing it with younger men nowadays? I never heard of such a thing back where I come from, but then again, I didn't hear much about anything. I didn't even know about the Bachelor Firemen until I went online and read all about y'all."

Vader stood rooted to the floor of Brody's office. It couldn't be Trixie. But it also couldn't *not* be. No one else would waltz into the station as if she belonged, bearing cookies and talking a mile a minute. He could only imagine what One, a veteran firefighter and woman of few words, must be thinking right now.

He and Brody shared a look of incredulous horror as One mumbled something sarcastic but inaudible.

Mulligan—of course it would be Mulligan—asked her something in a low rumble.

"I baked these myself, as my own personal little thank-you to the brave firefighters who keep our city safe. Well, it wasn't my city until up about a month ago. I'm here staying with my sister Cherie. Well, she wasn't Cherie before. She was Chastisement. But don't tell her I told you that. Y'all know Cherie, right? She and Vader have a thing going on, but don't ask me to explain it."

Brody gave a jerk of his head that broke Vader's paralysis. He vaulted out of the office. The last thing he needed was for Trixie to spill mortifying, intimate details of his relationship with Cherie to freaking Mulligan. He shouldered his way through the small crowd of firefighters that had gathered, as always happened when home-baked gifts arrived. Or pretty girls. A pretty girl bringing homemade cookies? Forget about it.

And Trixie had gone out of her way to qualify as pretty. She wore a sparkly silver top that left the tops of her shoulders bare, along with a pair of denim minishorts with striped purple leggings underneath. He fought the impulse to grab a blanket and wrap her up, stop-drop-and-roll style. Even though she wasn't his little sister, as Cherie kept pointing out, he still felt responsible for her.

"Trixie, what are you doing here?" He demanded when he reached her side.

"Vader!" Her face lit up. She put down the platter of cookies and threw her arms around him. He peeled them away; if he'd had handcuffs, he would have used them. "You aren't mad, are you? I was bringing cookies for your coworkers."

"Why?" His blunt tone seemed to confuse her.

"Why not? Where I come from, everyone loves cookies."

"Oh, we love cookies too," said Mulligan with a wolfish grin. He took a handful and stuffed one in his mouth. "Especially cookies with a Southern accent."

"Cookies don't have an accent." Trixie fluttered her eyelashes and giggled.

"What's your name, sugar pie?"

"You can call her OL," growled Vader. "Stands for off-limits." Vader grabbed her by the elbow and hauled her toward the corridor that divided the sleeping quarters. Then he changed his mind and headed for the backyard. Somehow it seemed safer.

Trixie didn't make the dragging part easy. She kept trying to twist her arm out of his grip, and grab on to various pieces of furniture to stop her inevitable journey out the door.

"What is wrong with you, Vader?" She burst out when they reached the pleasant square of green lawn, which retained only the faint marks of Psycho's failed attempt to dig a swimming pool with an excavator.

"What's wrong with *you*? I never said you could come to the station."

"It's not your private personal fire station! I read all about it online. The Bachelor Firemen. You're famous!"

Vader clutched his head with a groan. "Don't tell me you're looking for a bachelor fireman."

"Bachelor means single, right?"

"Does your sister know you're here?"

"Of course she doesn't." Trixie folded her arms across her chest. "She'd never let me bother you at work. I wouldn't have either, except it turns out that you work with a whole bunch of good-looking firemen who don't happen to be married. What's the blond one's name? I like him."

Blond. She must mean Ace, the rookie. Ace was also from the South, and was only a few years older than Trixie. In other circumstances, he might think it a good match. But with Trixie bouncing around town like a hormone-crazed pinball, not a chance.

"Tell you what. Why don't you write him a note and I'll deliver it to him during our next call."

"Okay, sure, but it seems like a lot of bother when you could just introduce me, since I'm here, and—"

"*Trixie.* A call is a fire incident. During a call we're too busy to pass notes. I was making a joke."

Completely unimpressed, she made a face at him. "Not much of a joke. Now come on. If not the blond one, then what about the scary-looking one who grabbed half my cookies?"

"I'm not introducing you to any of the Bachelor Firemen." Good grief, had he really called them that? "I mean, the firemen. I'll introduce you to One, if you want."

She brightened. "Which one's that?"

"The woman."

"That's not funny." She scowled at him and tapped her foot. "Why are you standing in my way? It's not like it's going to help you make points with Cherie. She's done with you."

That remark felt like a dagger to the heart, but he ignored it. "How did you get here?"

"Took a cab."

"Is it waiting for you?"

"I sure hope not. I don't have any more money. I had no idea cabs could be so expensive. I had to make up half the fare with extra cookies."

Vader shook his head. Somehow, he'd known it would come to this. "I can't leave work to run you home."

"No one's asking you to. I can hang out here and watch you guys. I don't mind."

"Sorry, we like to schedule tours in advance." Brody's cool voice came from the doorway, which he filled with his usual air of quiet command. "Vader, you can take her home in the plug-buggy. I've scheduled some drills out in the field today. Meet us at the training center when you're done."

"But Cap—"

"Go. It's fine. But don't let it happen again."

Vader stared after the disappearing back of his captain. His mother had been right. Between the two of them, Cherie and Trixie were going to take him down.

Drive him crazy and leave him for dead. "Are you trying to ruin my life, Trixie?"

She drew back, wounded. "No. Of course not. Why would you say something like that?"

He ground his teeth. "Never mind. See that red truck in the parking lot? That's the station pickup. We call it the plug-buggy. Go get in it. I'll be there in a minute. I have to grab some gear. Don't talk to anyone on the way."

"I swear, Vader, you are ten times worse than Prophesize and Justice-Denied, put together and puréed in the bossy blender." She spun around and flounced across the lawn toward the parking lot.

It took him a few minutes to gather his wits enough to say, "What?"

Chapter Fifteen

Trixie chewed on her thumbnail and stared out the window of the plug-buggy while Vader drove her home. He hadn't meant to rain on her parade, but she had no business tangling with a guy like Mulligan. His fellow firemen—much as he respected and trusted them—were guys. Guys who liked girls—maybe a little too much. Or too many at a time. That's how he'd been before getting involved with Cherie. Girls had flocked to him like hummingbirds to spilled sugar, and he hadn't made a habit of turning them down.

Now, of course, things were different.

"Why do you want to make trouble for your sister?"

She shot him an irritated look. "Why are you automatically taking her side?"

Vader had always wanted siblings; now he felt as if he was getting a crash course in how to be an older brother. It wasn't exactly what he'd imagined. "I'm not taking anyone's side. It's not about sides. I know how much Cherie has going on in her life, and I don't want her to worry."

"You don't know anything." Trixie flipped her ponytail from one shoulder to the other. "You didn't even know Chastisement's real name."

Ouch. Trixie really knew how to zero in on his weak spot. "No big loss. She doesn't care about that name, so I don't either."

"What do you really even know about my sister?"

"I know the important things."

"Do you?" She fixed disdainful blue eyes on his face. He could practically feel her scorn singe him like a blowtorch. "Have you ever heard her sing?"

"Sing? She doesn't sing."

"She doesn't sing *now*. Basically, everything you know about Cherie is stuff from the last six years. But there's a lot more, Vader. Have you even bothered to try to find out the rest?"

Now *that* was unfair. He'd done nothing *but* try to find out more. "She won't tell me anything."

"Yeah well, she probably has a good reason." With a dark look, she turned back to staring out the window, muttering something about "boys" and "impulses."

Vader turned his attention to the road ahead and ignored her mumbled insults. So Cherie had some secret singing ability that she wanted to keep hidden? Why? What would be the harm in sharing something like that?

No doubt about it, Cherie and Trixie were going to drive him insane.

When they pulled up outside Cherie's house, the sight of her ancient, mustard-yellow, veggie-diesel Mercedes parked out front made his skin prickle. Cherie was actually here. He hadn't seen her since he'd decided to make her come to him, instead of the other way around. Obviously, that plan had not worked out the way he'd hoped. And his plan hadn't taken Trixie into account.

Trixie hopped out of the truck and sped up the walkway. Vader put his hand on the gearshift, ready to take off. That's what he should do, instead of lingering outside her house like some sort of stalker. On the other hand, shouldn't he make sure Cherie got the whole story of Trixie's latest adventure? Before he could decide one way or another, the front door opened. Trixie brushed past Cherie, who was just stepping out, and disappeared into the house.

Vader's first dazzled thought was that Cherie was wearing sunshine. Her dress was the color of spring daffodils. It cinched at the waist, then flounced down to her calves, where it flirted with her bare legs as she descended the porch steps. A row of buttons skipped down her front, drawing his gaze to her full breasts.

As he watched her draw closer, he felt as if someone had reached inside his body and twisted his heart into a pretzel. She was so goddamn gorgeous—to him. He knew others might find her too curvaceous, not skinny enough. She wasn't one of those tight, athletic types. He'd never seen her wear jeans. She was always in dresses, or cute little skirts, clothes that embraced her curves and flowed with her movements.

The way she moved might be the most beautiful thing about her. Her dress hugged her body as if she were dancing a tango with it. As she reached the truck, his nostrils quivered, drinking in her fresh scent. Wildflowers and spring rain showers. Sugar and spice and everything nice. That was what Cherie was made of.

He, on the other hand, being a boy, was made of snakes and snails and puppy dog tails. If he'd had a real puppy dog tail, it would have been wagging up a storm as she leaned in the passenger side window. A hint of cleavage flashed in his eyes like an emergency beacon.

If he were in a joking mood, he would have said the emergency was in his pants. But mostly, he knew, the emergency was in his heart. He met her eyes and felt the impact of that misty, worried gray all the way to his toes.

"Hi Cherie."

"What is it this time? I almost hate to ask."

"She brought cookies to the firehouse. It's hard to get too mad at her for that. But then she started in about wanting to meet a Bachelor Fireman. I gave her a lecture and Captain Brody wasn't too happy either. She got the point."

Cherie frowned, two little lines puckering the wide expanse of her forehead. "I just can't figure out what she's up to." She ran her fingers across the side view mirror. With a sort of painful longing, Vader felt the movement across his own body.

"I hate to ask, Vader, but do you have a few minutes?"

Exultation nearly made him howl at the sun. *She* wanted to see *him*. Finally, his plan was working. But it was the worst possible moment. He was due at the training center. Brody had told him to drop Trixie off and join the crew right away. Someone who wanted the captain's job wouldn't linger with his on-and-off non-girlfriend.

But . . . but . . . He'd been waiting so long for this moment. "Sure. But just a few minutes. You want to get in? Or should I get out?"

She hesitated. He wondered if she was remembering the last time they'd been alone together in her house.

Lord knew he couldn't seem to forget about it.

"How about a cup of coffee? My treat."

Better and better. Now she wanted to buy him coffee. "Hop in."

She opened the door and slid onto the passenger seat, filling the cab of the pickup with her sweetness. The plug-buggy had never smelled so good. He could just imagine the ribbing the guys would dish out when they got a whiff. He didn't care.

He started the truck and cleared his throat. "Where to? I only have a few minutes."

"I'll be quick. The closest place is the Lazy Daisy on Main."

As he turned the truck toward Main, he felt her looking at him. He wondered if she was anywhere near as happy to see him as he was to see her. The sensation of her gaze made his body tense. Especially one particular part of his body. He hoped she didn't look in that direction.

She drew in a long breath, then released a torrent of words, her down-South accent transforming them into pure melody. "Vader, I really appreciate you being there for Trixie, and I'm sorry I told you to mind your own business. She's making it your business. I wouldn't blame you if you told her to get lost, but you never do that. You always make sure she's okay. I know it's because you're a good guy and a firefighter and you automatically want to protect people. I know it's not for me. But even so, I just want you to know how much it means to me."

Not for her? Was she crazy? When would she ever grasp the fact that he would do just about anything for her? "Don't worry about it," he said through clenched teeth. "Can't have her wandering around San Gabriel like a prom queen on the loose."

"See, that's the thing. She never went to prom. Or

school, for that matter. Neither did I. She's completely unprepared for life in the real world."

That little glimpse into her past was more than Cherie had ever revealed before. He kept his eyes on the road, afraid to overreact for fear she'd clam up again. "Were you like that when you first came here?"

"That was different. I didn't have a big sister to run to. And my brother and I left home together." She twisted her hands in her lap. "I know all this must seem crazy to you. You probably had a normal childhood with parents who weren't completely off their rockers."

Vader didn't answer. He had no idea what a "normal childhood" was, but he was pretty sure his didn't qualify. Many times, he'd wanted to tell her about his mother, but his pride had stopped him. He didn't want anyone feeling sorry for him, especially Cherie.

The silence stretched, until it was almost embarrassing. He kept hoping she'd say more.

"Fine. We don't have to talk about that." Cherie's voice cooled. Vader could have kicked himself. Another chance blown. Add it to the hundred others. "Anyway, since you've been spending so much time picking Trixie up and dragging her home, I wondered if you'd gotten any ideas about what she's got cooking in that busy little brain of hers."

"Are you sure she isn't just a horny teenager on her own for the first time?"

"I won't say that she isn't. But my ever-so-slightly psychic side tells me she's got some kind of a plan. She's on the computer a lot."

"She said that's how she found out about the Bachelor Firemen."

Cherie tilted her head back so it rested on the cloth-covered headrest. Her hair flowed in a coppery mass over her shoulders. He mulled the option of pulling over, yanking her against him, and burying his face in the aromatic warmth of those spicy waves. She'd go tense for a minute, while her mind rehearsed all the mysterious reasons that they shouldn't get close. Then, as always, she'd give in and they'd melt together the way they always did.

She was saying something else. He forced himself to pay attention. "Maybe she was curious about where you work?"

"Then why didn't she just ask me to show her the station? You saw her outfit. She was looking for action. And she had molasses-ginger-chocolate-chunk cookies with her."

Cherie drew in a shocked breath, as if he'd said she had dynamite with her. "Molasses-ginger-chocolate-chunk? Are you sure?"

"Yeah, so?"

"Well, that could mean only one thing."

"What? That she likes extra iron in her cookies?" Mystified, he pulled into a parking space in front of the Lazy Daisy. It was busy as always, although the crew rarely went there now that Thor had whisked the former waitress, Maribel, off to Alaska to get married.

"She's looking for a husband."

"Whoa." Vader turned off the truck and pulled the keys out of the ignition. "Is this more Harper family weirdness?"

She snorted. "There's plenty more where that came from. Everyone in the family knows that my stepmama made my father molasses-ginger-chocolate-chunk cookies that were so good he proposed right then and there. 'Course, little did she know what she was in for, since—" She cut herself off so abruptly someone might have slapped a gag over her mouth.

"Keep going," he prompted. "Don't hold back all those juicy crazy-family details."

"Maybe later. Right now I have bigger fish to fry." She stepped out of the truck, bright as a sunrise illuminating the drab parking lot. He followed, locking the plug-buggy behind him. As they walked side by side toward the coffee shop, he snagged her hand, engulfing it in his.

"I'm happy to see you, Cherie. No matter what."

Her eyes widened, and she swallowed, the muscles moving under the creamy skin of her throat.

"But don't worry. I haven't forgotten where we stand." He held the door open for her. As she walked past him, she gave a quick glance up; maybe it was his imagination, but he could have sworn there was a flash of regret in her lovely eyes.

"I'm happy too, Vader. You know how much I care about you."

He decided to ignore that, since it wasn't anywhere close to what he wanted from her. "Care" brought to mind Care Bears and nursing home care. Not the hot, sweet glory he experienced with her.

They chose a small table in the corner. As he pulled out a chair for her, he carefully kept his body from brushing against hers. He couldn't forget his determination to make her come to him—for more than help with her sister. But since she'd sought him out for advice about Trixie, he bent his mind to the problem.

"Why do you think Trixie's looking for a husband?" he asked as he sat down. "Most eighteen-year-olds aren't thinking about marriage. And she acts like a thirteen-year-old at her first boy-girl party."

"I know. That's what I don't understand. If she wanted to get married, she should have stayed home.

That's what they do there. They get married, the younger the better."

The hint of bitterness in her voice made him look at her searchingly. She was surveying the menu, running her tongue over her rosy-red lips. He allowed himself a moment to admire the sight, then forced his own gaze back to the menu.

"Why don't you just ask her? She's not exactly shy."

"And she's not exactly honest either. She's a Harper," she added, almost absentmindedly.

A Harper. As if that explained everything. Cherie's family was becoming more and more interesting. He was going to make her share the details if it killed him. "I don't get it. What nefarious purpose could she have, other than making some poor guy her chauffeur and wallet-carrier for life?"

"That's just it. I don't know why she's being so secretive. Maybe it's just habit. She's a—"

"Harper," agreed Vader. "Care to explain what that means, exactly?"

"It means trouble. That's all you need to know." She snapped the menu closed.

"Yeah. I already knew that part." He raised his eyebrows at her.

She made a little face, which looked so adorable he wanted to plop her on his lap. "Not me," she told him. "I'm the exception to the rule. I left home, remember?"

"Well, so did Trixie. But she's looking for a husband, and you're looking for anything but a husband. So put that one together for me."

He'd finally rattled her. Her eyelids fluttered down and a flush of pink warmed the upper curve of her cheeks. "It's not . . . I'm not . . . It's not that simple."

"It never is with you." He gestured for the waitress, a harassed-looking woman on the far side of the coffee shop. "I need to get going, Cherie, so if you think you've figured it all out, I'll take my coffee to go."

"*Vader.*"

Her soft cry of protest was interrupted by the tone of an incoming text message. Quickly he glanced at his phone, expecting a text from his mother, immediately relieved to see it wasn't. "It's Stud," he told Cherie. "Probably wondering why the hell I'm not at the drills with the others."

"You're on *shift*? Why didn't you tell me? I never would have dragged you out here . . . Vader? Are you okay?"

No, he wasn't okay. The words in the text message weren't making sense. And yet his body was responding on its own. He leaped up, knocking the menus off the table. "I have to go." Completely flummoxed, he turned toward the plate-glass window, as if he could dive straight through it into the plug-buggy.

A strong tug on his arm stopped him two feet from the window. Cherie was hanging on to him with both hands. He looked at her, barely aware of who she was, or who *he* was. "Let me go," he said in a strangled voice that sounded utterly alien.

"Sure, we can go. The door's that way, though. Come on, I'll take you there." He let her tow him away from the window. "What happened, Vader? Tell me what's going on."

"My house is on fire."

The fog in his brain cleared as soon he said it out loud.

"*What?*"

But now he was half running toward the door. He

tried to shake her off but she refused to let go. The two of them tandem-ed out of the restaurant.

"Is the fire department there? Your station?"

"Yeah. They're all there." Everything was hazy around the edges. He felt like he was drunk. He couldn't even walk in a straight line. The truck might as well be miles away and his legs had to be made of molasses. So slow. *Too slow.* Had to get there. *Too far.* "I should already be there." Why did his voice sound like that? So thin, so strange.

"We'll go. Right now. We'll be there in a few minutes. The guys are on top of it, Vader. They're the best, remember?"

"But they don't know." Somehow the truck was in front of him. He fumbled in his pocket for the keys. Dropped them on the pavement. Fuck, what was wrong with him? *Bend, damn it. Get the keys. Get in the truck.*

"Of course they know. They're already there. They know how to put out fires, Vader. Take a deep breath, come on, baby."

His mind whirled in crazy circles, occasionally spitting out a word or two. "You don't get it. My mother. Wheelchair. No text. Must be hurt." Ginny must be unconscious. No other reason why she wouldn't have called him or texted him that the house was on fire. She would have called 911, then him. Or maybe the other way around.

Cherie stared at him, then dropped to her knees, scrabbling on the ground for the keys. When she found them, she sprang to her feet and gripped Vader's forearms. The metal dug into his flesh. The slight edge of pain acted like a slap in his face.

"Look at me, Vader."

Blankly, he met her eyes, which were so focused they'd turned nearly black. "Your guys are there." She gave him a little shake. "You trust them with your life. You know how good they are. Brody's there, and he never loses anyone. Sabina, Fred, Double D. They'll take care of your mother. I'm taking the keys and I'm driving you over to your house. But you have to tell me where it is. Can you do that?"

The hell she was. *His* truck. *His* house. *His* mother. "Give me the keys."

"No." She snatched her hand away. "You can use the time to put your gear on, or text someone about your mother. Or to get a grip. You're in no state to drive. I won't let you."

Fuck that. He was a firefighter. He was always in a state to drive, and do everything else necessary to function. It was part of the job. But as Cherie slipped from his grip and climbed into the driver's seat, he knew she was right.

He'd never had a fire break out in his house before; never with his mother inside, trapped in a wheelchair.

With a quick prayer to God, the angels, and every divine power that might watch out for his mother, he grabbed his gear and jumped into the passenger seat.

Chapter Sixteen

Cherie had never seen Vader like this. Every speck of his usual fun-loving exuberance was gone, leaving a grim mask of terror in its wake. His jaw was set tight, his mouth white around the edges. As she drove, he pulled on his firefighter gear, twisting and turning to get the big padded jacket and pants onto his body. "Good thing I was on my way to training," he muttered. "But I should have fucking been there."

A horrible thought struck her. It was Trixie's fault that he hadn't been at the station when the call came in. And it was Cherie's fault that he hadn't gone straight back. Oh Lord, if anything happened to his mother, she'd never forgive herself. And why hadn't she known his mother was in a wheelchair? She'd never even been to Vader's house. He'd always picked her up at Gardam Street, and they'd either gone out or stayed in. How could he have proposed marriage to someone who'd never been to his house?

Maybe she wasn't the only one who was hiding a few things. What if she'd said yes to his proposal? When would he have told her about his mother, at the wedding?

As she watched him out of the corner of her eye, she realized that she knew the outer layers of this man. But so much more lay beneath. She'd been so busy with her own crap that she hadn't taken the time to know more.

"Why is your mother in a wheelchair?" Maybe this wasn't the best time for questions, but then again, she had him trapped in a fire department truck.

"Car accident. Take the next left." He gestured to the upcoming intersection as he pulled on some kind of neck garment made from a thin fiber material.

"What happened to her?"

"Spine injury. She's paralyzed below the waist. Some brain impairment too, but she's pretty sharp still. She always surprises people." The muscles in his jaw shifted as a grim look came over his face. "I should have told the guys, but I didn't want them looking at me different."

"Is that why you didn't tell me?"

He fastened his jacket, obviously uncomfortable with that question. "I'm the fun guy. Why would you want to hear about a wheelchair? I would have told you eventually."

A million responses rushed into her mind. Why wouldn't she want to know something so important? Did he really think all she wanted was "fun"? What kind of person did he think she was? And exactly when was he planning to tell her? But she shoved all those questions aside and stayed focused on his story.

"When was the accident?"

"Seventeen years ago. The doctors didn't think she'd live this long. Next right, then it's halfway down the block."

By now the sound of sirens filled the air, and they could see a plume of smoke rising over the rooftops. Vader fiddled with his helmet, his leg bouncing impatiently up and down, his entire body drawn tight as a bungee cord. She gave up on asking any more questions, especially because the last answer had shocked her. *Seventeen years.* Quickly, she did the math. Vader must have been fourteen when it had happened. And he'd never mentioned it. Not once. She never would have guessed that he was dealing with something so serious on a daily basis.

When she turned onto his street, a line of emergency vehicles came into view. Lights flashed in a hypnotic, alarming rhythm. Firefighters dressed just like Vader were hauling long hoses toward a house halfway down the street and shooing away curious neighbors. A tongue of flames leaped from the tidy one-story ranch-style house plastered in ochre stucco.

"That's your house?"

Vader nodded tensely, his eyes scanning the scene. Cherie, with a quick glance, saw no sign of a woman in a wheelchair in the crowd of curious onlookers.

"Where should I park?"

"Just pull over. I'll get out, then you can go home."

"I'm not going home, Vader. Anyway, this truck belongs to the fire department."

"Then drive it back there, catch a cab. You can't stay. It's dangerous."

She pulled to a jerking stop behind the last fire engine in the line. Vader burst out of the truck, letting in a blast of warm, smoky air. "I'll call you later," he told her. "Go home."

"I'm not leaving," she called after him, but he was already racing toward the burning house while jamming his helmet onto his head.

She parked the plug-buggy next to the curb, so the engine in front of her could back out if necessary. Then she sat for a moment, her throat going tight. It could have been from smoke or worry, or some combination.

"Please, Lord Almighty, let his mother be okay," she muttered under her breath. She'd lost the habit of spoken prayer after leaving Arkansas. There, she'd been forced to pray and sing hymns and confess her tiniest little sins. When she'd run away, she was afraid the Lord Almighty would be on her father's side and that someone would catch her. So she'd used a different part of her being, her most secret, silent, yearning heart, to beg for a chance. She'd gotten that chance, and ever since, she'd held that sacred space in her heart.

But this situation called for every kind of prayer she could come up with. "Vader's a good man, the best man I know. Please, Lord above, have mercy. Don't let anything happen to his mother."

She caught a glimpse of Vader's tall form, bulky in his turnout gear, saw him point toward the wheelchair ramp leading up to the side door of the house. He hoisted a tank onto his back as easily if it were a child's backpack, then strode toward the side entrance.

Oh God. He was going in. Of course he was going in. Why wouldn't he? He was a firefighter, and that was his house. His mother. He did this sort of thing all the time, except she'd never had to witness it before.

Her prayer changed. It became a desperate, urgent thing, repeated over and over in her mind. *Please take care of him. Don't let anything happen to him, please please please.*

Vader shouldered his oxygen tank, adjusted his breathing apparatus, and plunged into his burning house. At first Brody, as the commander on scene, hadn't wanted him there at all. He'd been pissed that Vader hadn't made it to the training center. But the instant Vader had explained about his mother, he'd waved him in. It would have taken ten armies to hold him back anyway.

As he entered the kitchen, thick with swirling smoke, he heard Brody's voice sputtering on the tactical channel. His comm must be damaged. "Be . . . lookout . . . possible vic . . . a fifty-five-year-old . . . wheelchair. She's likely . . . unconscious . . . paralyzed from the waist . . . Brown . . . Ginny."

The bare facts of his mother's existence, laid out for all to hear, shivered through Vader's panicked brain. *Likely to be unconscious. Paralyzed.* Why didn't they just say she was doomed? *No. Don't think that way. It's not too late.*

He didn't see his mother's wheelchair in the kitchen, but he looked under the table anyway. She could have fallen. But there was no sign of her. He flung open the door of the pantry, in case she'd gotten trapped in there. What if she'd hidden to escape the flames and something had fallen on her head and knocked her out and . . .

The pantry was empty.

Trying to escape the horrible images racing through his mind, he jogged through the kitchen into the adjoining dining room. The tall white candles his mother liked to keep on the sideboard were wilting from the heat. Blisters were rising on the surface of the table as the varnish ran from the heat churning through the house.

The furniture was doomed. His heart twisted. But there was nothing he could do. The only thing that mattered now was getting to his mother, wherever she was.

Where could she be? Why hadn't anyone found her

yet? Realizing he wasn't hearing anything over the tactical channel, he put his hand to the earpiece in his helmet. It crackled in response. Damn, his comm must have cut out altogether and he hadn't even realized. Now he was hearing all sorts of things.

" . . . unresponsive . . . unable to rouse her . . . burns on lower extremities . . ."

"Where the fuck is she?" he yelled into his helmet mic, tearing into the living room. The mess he saw there stopped him short. It looked as if the room had been gutted. The big-screen TV lay on one side, a blackened, blank shell. The couch smoldered in a cindery, sodden mess. The crew must have already come in through the front door and beaten back the flames. Which meant . . .

It must have started in his mother's bedroom. With a roar, he launched himself out of the living room into the hallway that led to his mother's room. A hose snaked along the floor. The flash of reflective tape on the dun fabric of padded jackets caught his eye. Firefighters in his mother's room.

It felt as if the hallway had expanded to twice its actual length. His body refused to move as fast as he wanted; it was a big clunky weight dragging him down. He roared in frustration, pushing himself forward, onward down the hall. And then he was there, and he was pushing aside the firefighter blocking his way.

"Vader!" Sabina yelled, righting herself. "Take it easy."

He ignored her, his gaze fastened on the sight now revealed. The French doors to his mother's outdoor, walled-in patio, where he'd planted jasmine and gardenia in planters, had been smashed open. His mother lay on the floor of the terrace, her favorite purple corduroy pants scorched and blackened. Her head was tilted sideways. Fred knelt over her. He was giving her heart compressions, sharp, regular jabs to the chest. Sabina was aiming a hose at the flames pouring from the corner of his mother's room, where she kept all her paperwork and files.

He couldn't speak, couldn't move.

"Get out of the way, Vader," said Sabina, not unsympathetically. "The fire's getting into the walls. If you want any house left, give us some space."

"Is she . . ." His voice was so strangled, he couldn't even complete the sentence.

"She's alive. Go. Go."

As if she'd set him free, he bounded across the room and burst onto the patio. Fred, his face mask off, was focused with complete attention on the supine figure of his mother. "Come on," he muttered fiercely. "You can do it."

Vader tore off his face mask and right-hand glove and picked up her hand, holding it to his cheek. "Come on, Mom. I know how tough you are. You gotta fight. You can't let some little fire take you out. Not after everything we've been through."

"This is your mom?" Fred asked, not taking his eyes away from her.

"Yeah."

"Mrs. Brown. I know you're a champ. You must be, with a son like Vader. You must be really proud of him. I bet you're even stronger and tougher than he is. I bet that's where he got it. Come on, don't let us down. Show us what you're made of."

Vader felt something wet on his face. He swiped at it, then realized it was his own tears.

"Mom, you can't leave now. Don't you want to see if I make captain? What about Cherie? It's like leaving before the story's over. I know how you love your stories. And this guy keeping you alive right now? You've seen him a hundred times in my videos. That's Fred. Remember him? We call him Stud, because no one else is going to."

"Very funny," muttered Fred.

His mother's lips moved. Was it from the impact of Fred's compressions, or an attempt to form words? With a hand that shook so much, he could barely find her neck, Vader felt for a pulse. There it was, faint but distinct. Giddy, delirious relief flooded him. "She's okay. You can stop compressions. Let's get her out of here."

Together, he and Fred lifted her off the concrete. She was so light, so fragile. His hands were still shaking so hard, he was afraid he'd drop her.

"You carry her, I'll clear the way," he told Fred, who nodded. He settled his mother into Fred's arms, realizing that right now, he trusted Stud more than he trusted himself. He pushed aside a huge wisteria planter and a white wrought-iron table where his mother liked to sit with her laptop. Behind it, set into the stuccoed wall, a locked door led to the neighbor's driveway. He kicked it open, putting all his fear and pent-up emotion into the action. The door splintered under his heavy boot. A few jagged pieces of wood remained. He broke them off with his hands, barely noticing that he'd never put his right glove back on. It didn't matter if splinters dug into his bare palm, so long as neither Fred nor his mother got jabbed.

He gestured to Fred to go ahead of him and spoke into his mic. "We're coming out the back door with an unconscious woman. Is an RA standing by?" If there were no rescue ambulance, he'd have to carjack a neighbor's vehicle.

No answer. He'd forgotten his freaking comm was broken. "RA," he bellowed out loud, making Fred start. "Unconscious woman coming through."

"I think they heard you in Spain," muttered Fred as he maneuvered Ginny through the door. Vader followed close behind, but as he stepped into the driveway, he remembered something, *Izzy.* Frantic, he scanned the patio. "Izzy! Here kitty, kitty. Come here, Izzy."

No flash of marmalade orange creeping from the crawlspace under the house, or jumping from behind a planter. He called to Sabina. "Keep an eye out for a big orange cat, would you? His name is Izzy."

"Will do," she answered. "The RA's here. Get a move on."

As Fred carried Ginny down the driveway, Vader ran ahead to signal to the paramedics where to go. They trotted down the driveway with a gurney. They strapped her onto it, fastened an oxygen mask over her face, and shuttled her into the ambulance. The EMT, whom Vader recognized but couldn't possibly name at the moment, held the back door for him. "You coming?"

"I gotta check with the Cap—"

"Get your ass in there, Vader," said Brody, through the static crackle of the tactical channel. "We'll see you when you surface."

"Thanks, Cap." Gratitude made his eyes sting. He jumped into the ambulance and crouched next to his mother and the EMT, who was securing the gurney for the ride. "Make sure it's nice and tight."

"Are you going to let me do my job or you going to watch over my shoulder?" The paramedic glared at him. John-boy, that was his nickname. He couldn't remember his actual name.

"As long as you do it right, we're cool."

"That's a given." Cocky bastard. But somehow, the familiar fire department bravado made Vader relax. The ambulance swung into the street and they wove through the melee of fire engines and milling neighbors.

At the hospital, it was as if a magic carpet had been laid out for their arrival. Doctors swarmed from the emergency room and helped transport the gurney into an exam room. John-boy rattled off her vitals on the way. Vader, still in his turnouts, followed a few steps behind, not wanting to get in their way.

And then a door closed in his face and a nurse he didn't recognize was telling him firmly, "The doctor will talk to you as soon as he can. You can wait over there." She gestured to the waiting room.

"I need to be in there. She's my mother. She's paralyzed from the waist down. When she wakes up she'll be in a panic. I can't leave her alone in there."

"She's not alone. She's with a very competent staff of doctors and nurses who have her medical records and know what to do. Go. Sit down. Relax. Are you hungry? There's coffee and vending machines."

Hungry? Was she insane? Of course he wasn't hungry. He was terrified, grubby, and a little dizzy, but hungry? No way. He was about to snarl something sarcastic, when he felt a hand grip his forearm. A husky feminine voice spoke next to him.

"That's a great idea. Thanks, we'll be waiting right here, won't we, Vader?"

He whirled around. Cherie, bright as a sunbeam in the dreary emergency room, stood before him, her hand fastened to his sleeve, her gray eyes fixed intently on his. "*Cherie?* What are you doing here?"

"I thought you might need some company. I hope

no one minds that I drove that red truck here, though it's probably against all the regulations. I didn't have any other way to get here. I saw you leave in the ambulance, so I followed y'all." She shifted her grip, so she was squeezing his hand. "How's your mother? I saw them put her into the ambulance, and I heard someone saying she was breathing again."

"Yeah." He held tight to her hand, even though he was getting her all sooty. She didn't seem to mind. "Fred saved her life. He saved her life," he repeated, the truth of it sinking through him. Tears sprang to his eyes. He blinked them away, but more came, then more, until one rolled down his cheek.

She lifted her other hand to his face and wiped the tear away. "That's what he's supposed to do," she said with a slight smile. "That's what you all do, right?"

He couldn't answer. His throat was too tight, too constricted with hot emotion. His mother had nearly died. *Nearly died.* Again.

Scanning his face, Cherie seemed to understand how close to the edge he was. She put an arm around him and guided him across the room, past the other waiting patients, some curious, some indifferent. At the far side, sheltered from view, stood a little alcove with a phone booth. They slipped into it, even though the two of them barely fit. She wrapped her arms around him, squeezing tight, so tight, as if to keep him from spinning off the planet.

Slowly, surely, it worked. The sensation of her pliant body conforming to his grounded him, tethered him to the present moment. Gradually the world reordered itself around him. This was where he belonged. Feet on the ground. Arms around Cherie. His mother in the hands of skilled professionals.

He relaxed into the embrace and rested his chin on

her soft hair. The scent of lilac floated into his brain, another sweet anchor to reality. He gave a long shudder, releasing some of the terror that had gripped him for the past half hour. They stayed that way for a long time. Cherie made no move to extract herself from the tight circle of his arms. She simply stood there, steady and comforting, giving him all the time he needed to get a grip on himself.

Finally, he let out a long sigh and leaned away, his back hitting the wall of the tiny alcove. She looked searchingly into his eyes, then nodded, seemingly satisfied. "You're okay." It was a statement, not a question.

He nodded, and amazingly, a bit of a smile hooked the corner of his mouth. "The sight of you always does wonders."

Miracle of miracles, she didn't back away from the expression of affection. She kept her eyes on his as a dimple appeared in her cheek, then another one on her chin.

"I still owe you a coffee. And that vending machine's considerably cheaper than the Lazy Daisy. I'll even throw in a bag of chips."

His smile broadened to include the other corner of his mouth. "Is that a proposal?"

"More like a proposition." And she took his hand and led him back into the busy hive of the emergency room.

Chapter Seventeen

Ginny Brown spent several nights in the hospital. Vader went back to the house to salvage what he could, which was mostly clothes and some mementoes he knew his mother would treasure. He whistled for Izzy, but didn't dare explore too much for fear the house would collapse. None of the neighbors had seen any sign of a big orange cat.

The insurance adjuster arrived to assess the damage. Despite all the fires Vader had experienced, he'd never been on this end of the process before. The source of the fire appeared to be candles, but Vader couldn't explain why his mother had lit so many. The only person who might know that was Ginny, and so far she hadn't uttered a single word.

Vader spent the first night in the hospital, draped uncomfortably over an armchair. When he woke up, his mother's eyes were open but she was staring vacantly into nowhere.

He swung himself off the chair. "Mom? How do you feel? Do you want me to call the nurse?"

Her gaze drifted over to him. She barely seemed to register his presence. He walked to her bedside and cradled one of her thin hands in his.

"Mom, the doctor says you're going to be fine. You had a very minor heart attack. You're probably a little shell-shocked right now. But we're going to get through this. I promise."

Her eyelids fluttered, then fell shut.

A horrible sense of déjà vu gripped him. Abruptly, he was fourteen again, facing an earth-shattering change in his only reliable parent. The same blank terror he'd experienced back then swept through him now. He knew what came next. People left. His father walked out. No one wanted the burden. At most, some pity would come his way. A few sympathetic looks. And lots of distance. Last time, his family had splintered. Now he'd face the same thing at the firehouse.

Except . . . it didn't happen that way. Fred was the first to visit his mother in the hospital.

"She's a lot better," Fred told Vader as the two of them checked their gear in the apparatus bay. It was the day after the fire, and Fred had just come from the hospital. "I think she smiled. She might have recognized me. I thought she was going to say something, but then she went back to sleep. She's probably just too exhausted to talk."

"Yeah, that's probably it."

"The captain said you and your mother need a place to stay until the insurance money for a new house comes through."

"Yes, it'll be a few weeks."

"I can clear out my studio. I could have it ready for you to move in by tomorrow."

Caught off guard, Vader studied his regulator more closely than necessary. He tried to speak, but couldn't.

"It's not a ton of space, but you're welcome to it," Fred added.

Vader cleared his throat. "It's not always easy, living with a disabled person, especially someone with as much energy as my mother."

"If I can put up with the A shift, I can handle your mother."

Vader heard himself laugh. *Laugh*. While talking about his mother. Something he hadn't done . . . well, ever. "You have a point there."

Fred continued. "How come you never mentioned your mom was paralyzed? We could have been helping out all this time. You never said a word."

Vader managed to summon his old party-boy laugh. "I'm a guy. Talking isn't my thing."

"That's a load of bull. You talk about everything else. Even Cherie."

Before the fire, he would have ignored Fred's question. But now things were different. Fred had saved his mother's life; Vader would owe him forever. From now on, he enjoyed special status in Vader's world. "I didn't want anyone feeling sorry for her. Or me. The firehouse is my fun place, you know?"

Fred scratched his chin. "Yeah, I guess." He gave Vader a dubious look. "You're a weird guy, you know that?"

It was a good thing Stud had attained special status, or he would have paid for that one. But since he had, Vader told him more.

"My father left us after my mother's accident. Made me a little gun-shy."

Fred gave a brief nod that conveyed complete understanding, finished checking the O ring on his regulator, and that was that.

The rest of the crew was the same. Several visited his mother. They offered help, but none of the pity he'd dreaded. He'd known the crew had his back at a fire call, but this was different. He'd never realized they'd be there for him in other ways too.

Never had he loved his fellow firefighters as much as he did now.

Fred was only the first to offer them accommodations. Sabina also stepped up.

"We're finally going on our honeymoon. You and your mom can have our house for the next two weeks, as long as you don't mind Roman's kid showing up now and then to grab stuff he forgot."

But two weeks might not give him enough time to find a new house, so he told her he'd think about it.

Ryan Blake and his wife, Katie, called to offer their spare bedroom. Psycho phoned from Nevada, offering them the guesthouse on the Callahan ranch if he wanted to take some time away from San Gabriel.

Captain Brody called him into his office and told him that his old silver Airstream could easily be made wheelchair accessible.

"Melissa would love the company. She's home all day with the baby and Danielle, and some adult conversation would be a godsend."

"Did you just put me and 'adult conversation' together in the same thought?"

"I was referring to your mother."

"Now that makes a little more sense."

On the third day after the fire, Mulligan announced over the intercom, "Visitor for Firefighter Brown. Firefighter Brown to the front desk. Soda pop."

Vader sprang to his feet. "Soda pop" was firehouse code for a female at the station. Hoping it was Cherie, whom he hadn't seen since that first day at the hospital, he dashed to the reception area.

As if he'd conjured her with wishful thinking, Cherie stood in the lobby, her hands clasped behind her back as she perused the vintage firefighter tools in the glass display case. She lit up the drab station entryway like a coppery-haired torch. She'd twisted her hair into a bright-penny, about-to-tumble pile on top of her head. As she turned to greet him, he noticed that her pansy-blue dress made her eyes look almost purple. She gave him a wide smile that might as well have been a right hook to the heart.

"Can I talk to you in private, Vader? There's something I want to discuss with you."

Unnerved by her serious tone, he guided her into the apparatus bay. He hadn't proposed to her lately, so she couldn't turn him down. Maybe something had happened with her sister.

But she surprised him. Shocked him, more like.

"I heard you need a place to stay," she said, twisting the fabric of her skirt with her hands, the way she did when she was nervous.

"We've gotten lots of offers. I'm just trying to decide what place would work out best for Mom."

She lifted her chin. "I know the best place. With me."

"*What?*"

"I'm serious. You can have the entire first floor. Trixie can switch to the second floor bedroom. It's a huge house, and we might as well put all that space to good use."

"But . . ." At a loss for words, he gawked at her. After all the times Cherie had put him at arm's length, now she wanted him to essentially move in with her? Him *and* his mother? What was going on?

Cherie refused to show Vader how nervous her proposal made her. This was the right thing. She knew it. She'd been thinking it over ever since the fire, and her conviction had gotten stronger each day. It would solve so many problems. Vader would have a place to stay. She'd feel a little safer with him around. Maybe Trixie wouldn't get into so much trouble. Most of all, she wanted to do *something* to help Vader.

But still, the thought of Vader being so close gave her an anxious thrill.

"I want to do this for you two," she told him. "It would mean a lot to me. I promise to give you plenty of space. We'll make whatever changes your mother needs. You could take the whole first floor, with your own bathroom and access to the kitchen. You could stay as long as you needed to, however long it takes to find a new house. I also thought that I could pay Trixie a little extra money to help your mother when you're working. She's not trained in home health care, but she's very reliable with that sort of thing. She took care of the younger kids after I left."

Vader's jaw set. "No. I'll pay her."

He must be considering the idea; her stomach filled with butterflies. "We can talk about that part later. It'd be good for Trixie. She needs something to do besides going online and inventing crazy outfits. But before you say yes, there's one thing I should tell you first."

She searched his face, but couldn't tell how he was reacting. When Vader chose, he could be very hard to read.

She forged ahead. "I can't explain everything, but there's a man with a grudge against us. We don't think he knows where we are. At first I was afraid he'd followed Trixie, but we haven't seen him. I think we're safe. And I doubt he'd bother your mother. But I thought you should know before you decide."

Gripping her hands tightly together, she waited, holding her breath. She'd struggled with how much to tell Vader without breaking her promise to Jacob. But she couldn't allow him to move his mother in without giving him some warning.

"This man is dangerous?" Vader asked, his face like stone.

"He's . . . unpredictable. Mean. But he hasn't left Arkansas in twenty years."

"If you were in danger, you should have told me."

Her temper flared. "And maybe you should have told me you're taking care of your disabled mother."

At an impasse, they stared at each other. He acknowledged her point with a dip of his head. "I'm starting to see that. I didn't know how people would take it. Guess I should have been a little more trusting."

The accusation hung in the air; *she* should be more trusting too. If only she could. If only he knew what a huge step this was for her.

Then again, maybe he did. His expression shifted, softening. "It's a nice offer, Cherie. I appreciate the thought. I'll have to think about it."

"Are you worried about us? You and me?"

His gaze flicked down her body, rendering her instantly aware of herself in a way only he could accomplish. "Why would I be worried?"

"You don't have to worry. You know how busy I am. And with your shifts, we'd probably hardly see each other."

Not that she wanted that. Or maybe she did. These

days, she was so confused she couldn't make heads or tails of her feelings. The only certainty was that she cared about Vader. No, it was more than that; she wanted to *take care* of him. He'd never needed her before, but now he did. Every particle of her being wanted to help him.

"Come to think of it, I am a little worried," he said, dropping his voice to an intimate husky murmur.

She was standing with her back to one of the fire engines, the polished steel brushing against her. He leaned in closer, putting a hand on either side of her head. She took in a big gulp of diesel and Vader-scented air. It was utterly, intoxicatingly male. "You might sneak into my bedroom at night and take advantage of me." He waggled his eyebrows. "Couldn't blame you. I'm a hard man to resist."

She cleared her throat, which had gone dry. He was making a joke out of it, Vader-style, but the nearness of his muscled frame had its usual effect. Light-headedness up above, restless pulsing down below. And a whole lot of shivering in between. "We'll just make a pact to stay away from anything like that. With my sister and your mother in the house, it shouldn't be hard."

"You might be underestimating the temptation." He deepened his voice to a low growl. The raspy sound scraped across her nerve endings and made her nipples rise. She put her hands on his chest, intending to push him away, but the second she touched those hard muscles, she was lost. Her fingers lingered, then spread across his broad rib cage. She felt the steady thump of his heart, the heat radiating from him.

"I'm sure we can handle it." Even to her ears, that statement held all the conviction of a kleptomaniac vowing not to shoplift. "We're adults."

"Oh yeah." His voice seemed to come from the pit of his stomach, from a place of molten heat. He leaned closer, dipping his forehead to rest against hers. "Consenting adults." Then he was touching her, shaping her body—the slope of her waist, the curve of her hips.

She let out an involuntary gasp of pleasure. "Stop that. This is your job. Your firehouse . . ."

Her words trailed away as he pressed his big thumbs against her hipbones, making her pelvis tilt forward. Pleasure streaked in knee-weakening flickers across her body. Merciful heavens, she had no self-control when it came to him. If he wanted to take her right now, against the side of a fire engine, she wouldn't say no.

The husky sound of his breathing penetrated her awareness. The desire it held echoed her own, and amplified it even further. Her eyes closed halfway, like a satisfied cat's, and a sense of luxurious anticipation took hold. Her body, held securely between Vader's strong frame and the cool steel of the engine, hummed with arousal.

Then his lips touched hers, just a whisper of a brush, firmness against softness. A sigh passed between them, slipping from one to the other, she wasn't sure which. Her eyes fluttered closed and her lips parted, giving him the welcome her soul demanded. He cupped her face, tilting it toward his mouth. He claimed his kiss like a king, like an emperor, as if he had absolute divine right to worship her, to possess her. His tongue swept through her mouth, chased by ripples of excitement dancing in its wake like drunken revelers.

The intoxicating taste of him went right to her head, straight to her sex. She kissed him back with naked hunger, baring all the sensual need that had been building since their last time together. They clung to each other, ravished by the heat that flared so quickly between them.

Then he stepped back, his chest heaving with harsh pants, his muscles jumping from the effort of ending the kiss. From inside the firehouse, she heard someone shouting about a ladder. For the space of one kiss, she'd completely forgotten where she was.

"Oh yeah," said Vader. "We'll have no problem living in the same house together."

She stared at him helplessly, knowing her arousal was written all over her face, in her darkened pupils and flushed cheeks. "Is that a no?" she managed.

"No. That's a yes. A yes, thank you. On one condition."

Her cheeks got even hotter. Her susceptibility to Vader was already off the charts. When he got into his dominant, demanding mode, she had absolutely no resistance. "What condition?"

"We'll talk about it later. I should get back to work. You'd never know I was trying to make captain." With a deep breath, he took another step back.

Risking a quick glance at his trousers, she caught the huge bulge. He was absolutely right. If they couldn't keep their hands off each other at his workplace, how would they stand a chance at home?

"I have a condition too. No sex while your mother's in the house."

"Unless you beg me." He winked.

She put her hands to her flushed cheeks. "I'll try to remember not to beg. So what's your condition? Tell me now, so we can settle this."

"My condition is easy. One night with you in your bedroom. That's it."

"But no sex?"

"Unless you beg."

She eyed him suspiciously. That innocent expression meant trouble. He had something up his sleeve, but she couldn't begin to guess what it was. As long as he agreed to the rule against sex, she couldn't imagine they'd have a problem.

"Agreed." She stuck out her hand to shake on it, but he hesitated, his playfulness gone for the moment.

"Also, I have to talk it over with my mother. I'm not sure she's going to agree."

"Why not?"

He gave an uneasy shrug. "She's been through a lot. I need to be sure she's comfortable with whatever I decide. I'll let you know tonight, okay?"

"Sure."

"And Cherie." He caught her hand and lifted it to his mouth. "Thank you. You're a true sweetheart."

"You're welcome." The sensation of his warm mouth on her palm made her giddy. Scolding herself for being a sex-crazed idiot, she pulled her hand away and waved good-bye. She was picking her way across the diesel-spotted concrete when she remembered the other part of her errand. "Vader," she called.

He was already halfway through the door that led into the firehouse. "Yeah?"

"I nearly forgot to ask you. Do you have a cat?"

He spun around and strode across the apparatus bay in about three longs steps. "Yeah. But I haven't seen him since the fire. Why?"

"Is he big and orange?"

Those brown eyes lit up with a joy that made her heart skip several beats. "Yes. That sounds like Izzy. Did you see him at the house?"

"No, but after I left the hospital I drove that red truck to my house to check on Trixie because she wasn't answering the phone. Then I took it back here to the firehouse and one of the firemen brought me home. The next morning I saw this orange cat hiding under the bougainvillea. I put out a dish of milk, but then I had to go to work. When I came back the milk was gone. Same thing with a can of tuna. I couldn't figure out where he came from, but then I remembered the truck, and thought maybe he was hiding in it during the fire, then hopped out at my house. Cats can be pretty smart." She grabbed his hand. "Are you okay?"

He was blinking rapidly, as if trying to bat away tears. "My mother loves that cat like nobody's business. If she knows he's alive . . . He's alive, right?"

"Oh yes. He was shy at first, but he got over that pretty quick. He runs right up to the food dish now, but he still won't let me get close enough to check his collar."

Vader squeezed her hand tightly. He seemed rooted to the floor, afraid to release her.

"Really, Vader, he's fine." She curved her other hand around his cheek and felt his jaw muscle jerk. "Cats are survivors. He probably has at least seven lives left. Do you want to come and see him? You want to make sure it's him? Oh, wait! Where is my brain today?"

She dug in her pocket for her cell phone and scanned through her photos. There it was, the big orange cat crouched over a dish of tuna. Vader grabbed the phone and enlarged the picture.

"That's definitely Izzy." He caught her up and swung her in a wide circle. Breathless with surprise, she gripped his forearms, clinging to their corded strength as she flew through the air. Like a pro, he landed her safely on her feet, then steadied her. "Thank you so much, Cherie. You have no idea what this is going to mean to my mom. I want to go tell her right this minute. But I have a whole shift to go."

"I'll take good care of him until then. Don't worry. He'll still be there. He's definitely adopted us."

"As my mother would say, 'Bless you, hon.' I'll call you tomorrow after I talk to her."

The news of Izzy's survival perked his mother up tremendously. She finally spoke, telling the nurse that her cat was so smart he'd recognized a fire department vehicle and hitched himself a ride to safety. She was so thrilled that she easily accepted the news that they were going to be staying at Cherie's house for a while.

"If Izzy trusts her, then I guess I can give her a chance," she said, her voice still raw from smoke. She poked at the plastic-wrapped dinner the nurse had left on the retractable tray. "Is her house wheelchair accessible?"

"We'll have the first floor. There's a nice backyard with only two steps down. I can rig up a ramp for you."

"This is what you want?"

"Yeah." He wanted it for several reasons. Being around Trixie might cheer his mother up and give her something to do. Also, if some crazy dude from Arkansas chased down Cherie and Trixie, he wanted to be manning the barricades. But most of all, he couldn't resist the chance to be so close to Cherie. Her barriers were starting to come down, he just knew it. If he was living in her house, he gave himself pretty good odds of kicking them down once and for all.

He decided to focus on the Trixie factor. "Cherie needs help with her little sister. I told you about her. She's a handful."

Ginny loved nothing more than being of use to someone. "She won't be a handful for me, hon. I have my secret weapon. My wheelchair. She won't know what hit her."

"You can't hit her with your wheelchair, Mom. Rules of the house."

She gave him a playful slap on the arm. "You're deliberately misunderstanding me, Vader. You know I'd never do a crazy thing like that, unless it was an accident, or Izzy got in the way."

"You can't blame it on Izzy either. I'm on to you."

When she giggled, the world settled back in its proper orbit. His mother was going to be fine.

A frown settled over her exhausted face as she fiddled with a container of chocolate pudding. "I wonder what went wrong?"

"You mean with the fire? I've been meaning to ask you what happened."

"Not the fire. Well, yes, the fire. But the feng shui ritual."

"The what?"

"I know you'll think I'm silly, but I was summoning true love, which requires plenty of red candles. I put them a little too close to my *Casablanca* poster. It caught on fire while I was chanting a love prayer, and by the time I realized it, I couldn't do a thing. It spread so fast." She began tearing at the napkin on her dinner tray.

"It's okay, Mom. Calm down. These things happen. I've seen it a zillion times."

"Yes, yes, I know." She dismissed the fire with a careless wave. "But what went wrong with the feng shui? I was trying to get you unstuck from Cherie. And now we're going to be living in her house! That doesn't make any sense. Unless . . ." Her face cleared.

"Unless what?"

"Living so close to her will finally open your eyes. You'll find out she's not the one for you. Just you wait and see."

Chapter Eighteen

When Ginny finally met Cherie, on the day Vader drove her to Gardam Street in the blue Suburban, the encounter went much better than Vader had feared. His mother took Cherie's hand in both of hers, called her "hon," and thanked her profusely. She showed off her bubbly chatterbox side, even though she still sounded as if she'd smoked a carton of cigarettes.

Cherie presented her with a welcome gift of lemon bars, which Vader had said were her favorites. Ginny took one taste, and proclaimed them the best she'd ever tried.

"Thanks for being so nice," whispered Vader as he wheeled her into her new bedroom. "You just earned yourself a box of mini-donuts."

She spun the chair in a circle, surveying her new domain. "I can afford to be nice. I still don't believe she'll last."

"I take it all back," Vader grumbled.

Cherie knocked on the doorjamb. "How does everything look? Do you like the table?"

She'd offered up an old drafting table she'd found at a flea market. By some miracle, Ginny's computer had survived and now sat on top of it, plugged in and ready for action.

"Everything looks wonderful," said Ginny. Vader could tell she was itching to get online and check her forums. When Izzy trotted into the room and jumped into her lap, things couldn't have been more perfect.

Although the house was workable as it was, Vader decided to make a few alterations for his mother. He bought the materials for a ramp to the backyard, a ramp onto the front porch, and safety bars installed in the shower and by the toilet. A couple of the guys from the firehouse—Fred and, surprisingly, Mulligan—showed up to help him with the construction.

While they cut the boards for the ramps, Trixie outdid herself bringing them snacks and homemade cookies. Every delivery seemed to come with a different outfit.

"Was she wearing that miniskirt last time she came in here?" Fred asked through a mouthful of shortbread.

"That's what they call a microskirt," said Mulligan. "They're getting shorter. Next they'll make a nanoskirt and no man will be safe."

At the table saw, Vader used the back of his hand to wipe sweat off his forehead. "Nanoskirt? Where'd you come up with that?"

"Science. Heard of it? I have a degree in it."

"Rings a bell. Like scientifically formulated energy drinks?" Vader winked at Fred. He loved tweaking his muscleman reputation.

Trixie reappeared with another platter, this one

loaded with roast beef sandwiches. "Red meat for you red-blooded American guys," she said, flirtation dripping from every pore.

Fred dropped his nail gun and bounded to her side. "You're a lifesaver."

Trixie batted her eyelashes, revealing bright turquoise eye shadow. "Thanks, hot stuff. You know, you should really take those gloves off when you eat. At least the left one. Unless there's a ring on it. Then you don't have to bother. Do you have a ring under there?"

"What?" Fred looked thoroughly confused, as any normal man would be.

Vader rolled his eyes. Trixie must still be husband hunting. He should have warned the other guys. Or made them all wear fake rings.

Ginny appeared at the doorway. "Oh Trixie, Izzy's stuck under that old curio cabinet. Would you mind helping me get him out, hon? You're such a darling, helping out an old crippled lady like me."

Vader nearly choked on his roast beef.

"Wow," said Fred, gazing at Trixie with reverence. "You are something special. Not only do you make killer roast beef, but you help out ladies in wheelchairs."

Trixie's kitten face lit up, and she practically danced into the house to help Ginny. Vader watched her go, realizing he'd just gotten a taste of life on Gardam Street, and it wasn't half bad. Ginny already had Trixie's number. He had a feeling they were going to be perfect for each other.

"Freddy, that girl is pure trouble," said Vader, feeling duty-bound to warn his fellow fireman. Then he caught Fred's wink. "Wait. You did that on purpose?"

"Redirection and positive reinforcement. Works great with kids."

Vader clapped him on the shoulder. He should have known Fred would get it. The more he hung out with the guy, the more he respected him.

"So how's the captain thing going?" asked Mulligan. "You schedule the exam yet?"

Vader adjusted the bandanna keeping the sweat off his face and bent over the table saw. "Next week. But I think I might have blown my chances. Fuck-up city every time I turn around. Brody asked if I wanted to back off some of my work commitments considering what I have on my plate right now. I told him no way. I need the promotion now more than ever."

Fred finished his sandwich and hoisted the nail gun again. "Everyone's saying you really opened people's eyes with all the committees you're serving on. They say the handbook's going to be the best ever."

"Yeah, I've been researching the Bachelor Firemen curse," added Mulligan. He turned a two-by-four resting on two sawhorses and brushed the sawdust off it. "Funny stuff. I'm starting to believe. Did you know the marriage rate for San Gabriel firemen is statistically speaking significantly lower?" He didn't sound at all disappointed by that.

"Well, just look at us," said Fred. "None of us are married. And some of us want to be."

Vader glanced at Fred in surprise. "You, Stud?"

"Why not? Are you saying you don't want a wife? A couple of kids to show off at the firehouse?"

The image was so similar to what his mother had said that he nearly laughed. And then everything else his mother had said came rushing back, and the answer burst into his mind with the clarity of a flashing neon sign. No, he didn't want "a wife and kids." He wanted Cherie. He wanted his and Cherie's kids. No one else would do. Not now, anyway. And not for a long time. If he couldn't bring Cherie around, it would take his heart years to adjust. Stubborn, pigheaded organ.

To hide his reaction, he turned on the table saw and ran the next piece of lumber through the blade. When he looked up, Fred was watching him with a knowing little smile. "You can do it, Vader."

"You mean make captain? You think so?"

"That too."

Vader's mother looked a lot like him, with deep brown eyes and a vivacious smile. While her face was worn into lines that indicated pain, Cherie hadn't seen her complain once. Mrs. Brown had a can-do, effervescent spirit that Cherie admired. She was a magician at finding things for Trixie to do. At the first sight of her little sister lounging on the couch, ten tasks would suddenly appear, from rolling balls of yarn to giving Izzy his worm medicine. In three days, more cleaning occurred on the first floor than during Soren and Nick's entire stay. Ginny had Trixie dusting and scrubbing and Lemon-Pledging until the entire house smelled like spring cleaning.

Cherie had no problem with that. She and Trixie had both grown up with lots of assigned chores. Keeping busy was much better for her little sister. Trixie seemed to know it too. Both Cherie and Vader offered to pay her to help Ginny, but to her credit, she refused to accept any money.

"You're putting me up and feeding me, Cherie. And Vader just lost his home. It's the least I can do. But if Vader wanted to hook me up with one of the Bachelor Firemen . . ."

"Not going to happen," Vader had told her, very firmly.

"Oh, fine. They're probably too old for me anyway." Trixie tossed her hair. "Cherie's right. I should focus on myself and developing my own interests. So if anyone needs me, I'll be online makeup shopping."

Best of all, she got to see Vader on a regular, almost daily basis. Watching him move his mother into her room, set up her knickknacks just so, hang family photos on the wall so his mother would feel at home . . . well, it would be enough to make anyone melt.

She missed him during his shifts, but when he rolled in the door after a night at the station, she experienced a rush of giddy pleasure. Whenever she caught the rumble of his voice in conversation with his mother, a smile would spread across her face.

Vader brought a companionable, fun-loving energy into the house, the spirit of a man who made everything into a party. He dug out the grill she never used and made steaks for everyone, wearing his "Stand Back, I'm a Fireman" apron. He brought home cat toys for Izzy because his mother found them endlessly entertaining.

And then there were the firehouse videos, Ginny's top form of amusement.

"I can't make them anymore," he told them gloomily as Ginny scanned through the files on her computer, looking for her favorites. Cherie had pulled up a chair next to Vader and was busy trying to ignore his nearness. "Not if I want to be captain."

"Once you're captain, you can make your own rules," said Ginny.

"I can't make my own rules. Captain doesn't mean dictator."

"Aha. Here's one. Remember your Ella Joy investigation?"

"Yep. Came up empty."

"Investigation?" Cherie inquired.

"Someone kept feeding Channel Six inside information on the firehouse. I interrogated everyone at the station on camera and asked them incriminating questions. I'd start them off with softball questions like, 'How do you like your peanut butter sandwiches?' Then wham. I'd slam them with something like, 'Speaking of food, are you feeding information to Ella Joy?'"

Cherie laughed. "How'd that work out?"

"See for yourself."

He gestured at the computer, where a short clip had just started. It showed Sabina flipping the bird at the camera, followed by a shot of Double D doing the exact same thing. Then came Fred, who gazed thoughtfully toward the ceiling, finger tapping his chin. "Do you need the question again?" asked Vader from off screen.

"No, no. I'm just thinking." Finally he seemed to come to a decision. "Strawberry jam, with a glass of cold milk. Has to be whole milk. And I like cracked wheat bread."

"That was the first question. What about the next one?"

"You mean the one that's too stupid to answer?" With a roll of his eyes, he wandered away from the camera. "I'm hungry. Did anyone pick up more peanut butter?"

At that point, the camera turned a hundred and eighty degrees so Vader could address it. "And there you have it. Who is the traitor? Inquiring minds want to know. But inquiring minds still don't have a clue. As you can see, this inquiring mind"—he knocked on his head—"got shut down like a leaky nuclear reactor. In the meantime, he—or she—is still on the loose, spilling firehouse secrets and royally pissing me off. Until next time, reporting live from Station 1, I'm Vader Brown."

Ginny closed the file and beamed. "He's good, isn't he? My boy could have been a newscaster. So photogenic and well-spoken."

"Definitely network material." Under her lashes, Cherie looked sidelong at Vader, who made a face at her.

"Don't encourage her. I did it purely for the love of the art."

"He did it for me," corrected Ginny. "It was like my own personal soap opera, those videos. I never liked the soaps much, but I could watch those firehouse videos for hours."

The affection between mother and son was, quite frankly, adorable. Damn the man.

She wondered why he didn't come to her bedroom the way he'd promised—or was it threatened? Whatever the reason, she spent each night of that first week alone, wishing his big, warm body was next to hers, dreaming of the touch of his skin, his heavy bones and hard flesh and hot mouth.

Then one night, it wasn't a dream. His mouth really was planting warm kisses along the inside of her arm. He really was naked in her bed. The night air really was charged with electric excitement.

"Vader?" That part wasn't in doubt; she'd know the feel and scent of him anywhere. But she wanted to make sure it wasn't a dream.

"Shhh." He pushed her nightgown up to her chin, exposing her body.

"What took you so long?"

He nestled his face into the softness of her stomach. "Did you nearly give up on me?"

"Yes." He licked the outer swell of her breast, close enough to her nipple to make it sing. "No."

"You'd better not. I told you I was going to come."

He reached between her legs and dragged his hand across the soft furrow, already wet. "Mmmm. Have you been thinking about me?"

"No." He pressed the heel of his palm against her pulsating clitoris. She groaned. "Yes."

"Thank you. The truth, Cherie. The truth will set us free." Her hips lifted against him, longing for a taste of the silky, hot skin of his pelvis.

"Is that right, Fireman? Then why didn't you ever tell me about your mother?"

He paused, and she could have kicked herself. The last thing she wanted was to make him stop the delicious things he was doing. "I should have. I didn't tell anyone. I didn't want anyone seeing me as some kind of charity case, I guess."

She squirmed under him. "Can you . . . ?"

"What?"

"Can you . . . um . . . keep doing that thing with your hand?"

"I'm pretty sure that qualifies as begging, so sure." He resumed the steady, circling pressure of his palm against her sex. Pleasure flooded her senses. Maybe it was begging, maybe it wasn't. Maybe he'd kept his distance for a week so that as soon as he touched her, she'd ignite. She didn't care. Right now, she wanted him.

She held on to his shoulders with a kind of death grip. With anyone else, she would have worried about hurting him, but Vader was so built, his muscles so rugged. He was like a Mack truck of male flesh.

"Oh, sweetheart," she murmured. "You have no idea what you do to me."

"I just hope it's enough."

"Enough for what?" She felt drugged by the sensations flickering from her sex.

"Enough to make you do what I want."

"I'll do anything you want." She sighed, because in that moment it was completely true. She couldn't deny him anything. "What do you want?"

"First I want to lick you until you scream. Quietly, of course. Then I'll tell you. Deal?"

The word "deal" rang a distant alarm, but she didn't listen. She was too riveted by the way he was shifting his body toward the foot of the bed, his hair brushing against her stomach as he settled between her legs. With strong hands that heated her inner thighs, he pressed her legs apart.

"Oh mercy me," she muttered, and dug her fingers into his hair.

"Oh no, you don't. We're doing this my way." With a sudden surge of movement, he rose to his knees, swept her hands over her head, and pinned them together.

"Don't you dare use your socks again, Vader."

"Hey, I learned my lesson. I'll use this." With his other hand, he dragged her nightgown all the way over her head and maneuvered it up to her wrists. Somehow, in that ingenious Vader way of his, he snagged her hands in it, completely immobilizing them. She responded with a soul-deep sigh of relaxation, every muscle giving up a bit of its tension, every bone luxuriating. He traveled back down her body, swirling a path of flame with his tongue. By the time he reached the apex of her thighs, her body was jumping with eager pulses of anticipation.

"You know, I love seeing you like this," he murmured, the stubble on his chin brushing her sensitized sex. "My own personal juicy little shish kebab. You're my Cherie kebab. Tastiest thing I ever nibbled."

With exquisite stabs of his tongue, he parted the folds of her sex. How could such a muscle-bound man be so very sensitive with his tongue? It made no sense, and yet when she looked down her body and saw his large frame bent over her, his dark head between her legs, her eyes wanted to roll back in her head. The way he licked and soothed, tormented and tantalized, made her lose all pretense of control. As the sharp pleasure built, she twisted against the bedcovers, urging him on with thrusts of her hips and incoherent babbling.

He doubled her legs back against her body, bending her knees, manipulating her as if she were a rag doll. In his hands, she was. He gripped her hips in those huge, powerful hands, thumbs digging into the quivering flesh of her inner thighs. And all the time he kept his mouth latched to her sex, lapping and suckling, the maddening friction driving her up and up until her head wanted to explode.

She needed to scream, to shout out the extremity of her pleasure, but some part of her was still tethered to reality. She pressed her lips closed, so nothing more than frantic whimpers came out. Until he put two fingers inside her, sandwiching her clit between his hot tongue and the teasing pressure from inside. Then, helpless as a kitten in a tsunami, she let out a cry, her body arching in utterly abandoned bliss.

"Next to you," growled Vader against her sex. "Pillow." She buried her face in her pillow and let the long, racking convulsions lift her up, spin her around, and cast her down in a roller coaster of release.

"Oh my heavenly angels," she murmured as she came down from the intoxicating rush. "Mercy on me," she managed when she recovered her breath. "That was incredible. Lord, I missed you, Vader." He rested his chin on her knee, which was splayed open, and grinned. Lazily, she rubbed her other calf along his strong, brown back. "Your turn now."

Chapter Nineteen

Cherie narrowed her eyes at him. She should have seen this coming. Vader was persistent, and at the moment he had her utterly sated, her defenses down. In the intimate darkness, the soft, cocooning privacy, it would be so easy to let go of her resistance.

He reached up and untwined her nightgown from her wrists. "One question, that's all."

"What kind of question?" Her Arkansas accent thickened, the way it always did when she was relaxed.

"Something that tells me a little more about Ms. Cherie Harper. I am living in her house, after all. Trusting my mother with her. Seems like I ought to be able to ask a few questions."

"You said one question."

He smiled, clearly sensing victory. "We'll start with one. But I'm off shift tomorrow, so I got all night. You never know, you might get inspired."

She hauled herself into a sitting position and

wrapped her arms around her bent knees. The moonlight filtering from the window kissed his muscular torso with silver. He was rock-solid, this man. She could trust him. "Fine. What's the question that's so important it beats an orgasm?"

"Who's the man with a grudge against you? And why does he have a grudge?"

"A two-part question? That's a cheat."

"The firefighter promotion exam is full of them. If I can handle them, you can."

She buried her face in her knees. Jacob had sworn her to secrecy—in blood, no less—but she was so tired of it. Everything in her longed to share the story with Vader. Maybe then he'd understand. Maybe then she'd stop hurting him.

It'll be okay, Jacob. It's time.

"His name is Frank Mackintosh. He's a friend of my father. And I struck him on the head and nearly killed him."

Speaking it out loud felt so strange, like stepping onto a new planet. One with lighter gravity, where you might take big, goofy missteps before you got the hang of it.

"Did he hurt you?" The icy rage in Vader's voice made her shiver.

"No." She shook her head quickly. "Not like that. He tried, but he didn't get that far. Jacob and I had it all plotted out. He wanted to run away too, because he'd figured out he was gay and our father would have killed him for that."

Vader growled low in his chest. Cherie could have kissed him for that. Protecting Jacob was such second nature to her. She loved that Vader felt that way too.

"Not deliberately killed him," Cherie said quickly. "Prophesize would have performed an exorcism on him. Really gruesome. If Jacob had survived, he would have had to get married and try to be fruitful, like the rest of us. From the age of thirteen he knew he'd be leaving. But we were always close, being fourteen months apart, and he wanted to stay and look out for me."

"Were things that bad in your family?"

"My father lives in his own crazy world. He's not a bad man, he's just kind of a natural-born cult leader. Some of his beliefs make sense. He believed in growing our own food, being as self-sufficient as possible. All us kids know how to do stuff like pickle collard greens and slaughter pigs. If I had to, I could rig up a pee bucket that would knock your socks off."

"Pee bucket?"

"We lived out in the woods. With fourteen kids, we were digging new outhouse holes every other year."

She glanced at Vader, suddenly aware of how strange it must sound. "You want to take your question back now?"

"Hell no," he answered quickly. "It's just getting good. So your dad was some kind of survivalist?"

"Sort of. Mostly he wanted to raise his kids away from TV and school and other bad influences. He called it brainwashing. Only one person could brainwash us, and that was him."

"But it didn't work out so well."

She shrugged, amazed by how much she was telling him. It didn't feel wrong either. The opposite; it felt right. "It did for some. Most of us are still there. It wasn't a terrible life. Lots of fresh air and healthy food. We had fun, us kids. I learned some interesting skills. I can shoot the tail off a squirrel from two hundred feet."

"And here I thought you were the ultimate girlie girl."

"Oh, I am at heart. I'd choose brunch at the Lazy Daisy over a squirrel any day."

Vader reached for her, found her calf, and began massaging the muscle there. Maybe he was trying to keep her relaxed and talking. If so, it was working. She let out a sigh of pleasure.

"I have to say, I'm impressed, Cherie. I mean, you were already supremely hot in my eyes. Throw in the sharpshooting, and damn."

"Don't forget the pee bucket."

"I'm trying to, but you keep bringing it up."

She giggled, feeling giddy. "Maybe it's not so bad, telling you this stuff."

"Like I said, the truth will set us free. But I'm still not connecting all the pieces here. Your father was a wacko who set up camp in the middle of the woods and started spitting out children."

"Well, he had some of us already. Seven. My mother died having Humility. Then my dad married Lily, my stepmother, and she started multiplying like a bunny in heat. She was always either pregnant or recovering from being pregnant. I grew up watching the little ones from the age of about eight."

"Okay, so far so good. How did the man come into it? Mackintosh. What happened with him?"

Darn it all, she'd been hoping he'd get distracted by her oddball family history. She nervously twisted the sheet between her fingers. "Well, see, my father wanted his little kingdom to expand as much as possible. He wanted us girls to get married right away and add our children to the cause. So he struck up some friendships with a few other people who thought like he did. He wanted to find us the right kind of husband, one who would stay close by and live the same sort of lifestyle. My older sister got married the day she turned eighteen. Her husband had done some work for Prophesize. We all knew him and liked him okay. Grace seemed happy enough. She got pregnant right away. Trixie told me she has three kids now. I'm surprised it's not more."

Realizing she was babbling, she took a deep breath, flicking one more cautious glance toward him. "Then it was my turn. The man he picked out for me, Mr. Frank Mackintosh, was completely different. He was older, and his wife had run off. He owned the adjoining land to ours. He had a bunch of kids, and they were terrors, let me tell you. The oldest one, Robbie, was only a little younger than me. My father decided I should marry Mr. Mackintosh. But that man scared me. There was something off about him. I heard rumors he'd been part of some sort of standoff with the FBI. I overheard him talking about do-it-yourself bombs once. He . . . well, I didn't want anything to do with him."

She swallowed hard. Here's where things got difficult.

"I told Prophesize I didn't want to marry that man, but he had his mind fixed on it. I think he worked out some kind of deal with Mackintosh. Me for Lord knows what. More land or something. Maybe a few milk cows."

Vader shifted forward and cupped her elbows. "He couldn't make you marry someone you didn't want. This is the twenty-first century."

"Not in Prophesize's world. To his mind, we were his kids and he could do what he wanted with us. He said I was marrying Mackintosh and that was that. He went ahead with all the planning, and I made my own plans."

He ran his thumbs along the insides of her forearms. "Your plans to run away."

She nodded, then lowered her head to her knees. Her hair fell across her shoulders. He scooped it out of the way, so her face was exposed. She couldn't hide anything from him.

"Are you sad because you had to leave home?" he asked gently. "Do you miss it?"

What a strange question. She'd left in such a state of terror, and that fear had tainted all her thoughts about her family. But now that he mentioned it . . . "Sometimes." She lifted her head. "But I had Jacob. I never could have managed without him. Being on our own was kind of exciting. We came to California because it was such a big state with lots of farms. We knew farm work. We camped out in a tent and got jobs nearly right away picking oranges and strawberries."

"How'd you end up in San Gabriel?"

"We wanted to try something different. I had all these other things I wanted to do. Dancing and getting educated. Someday I want to work with kids, like I told you."

He snapped his fingers, as if something had just clicked. "All your jobs pay cash. I can't believe I didn't see it earlier. Is that why you can't work with kids?"

"Yes. I don't want anyone checking into my background. We didn't want to leave a trail. We saved up some money for rent. We looked at a map. As soon as I saw San Gabriel I had a good feeling. I liked the name. I grew up with all those crazy Old Testament names, but Gabriel felt more like an angel who'd look out for us. I was always fascinated by angels. They can be pretty powerful."

"So you came to San Gabriel."

"And that's pretty much the end of the story."

From his bullheaded expression, he wasn't buying it. "Except Mackintosh holds a grudge."

She gave a microscopic little nod. "I don't think my father knew what he was dealing with. Mackintosh is scary. He acted like he owned me as soon as my father and him started working out their deal. I had to watch his horrible kids. He wanted me to do his laundry. All sorts of little chores like that. He'd come over to our place with presents like dish towels and yarn from his brother's sheep. That was bad enough, but he also brought me a new dress, new underwear. It was so disgusting. He expected me to put them on right then and there. He didn't bother waiting for the wedding."

"He didn't bother waiting," Vader repeated. She turned her head away. "You mean he . . ." He started to say the word "rape," then seemed to gag on it. "Violated you?"

"No! No. I already told you he didn't get that far. I hit him on the head. I gave him brain damage and now he hates me." She scrambled backward until her spine touched the headboard. She'd said too much. But she couldn't help it. Once she'd started talking, it had been so hard to stop. "That's enough answers. You said one question, one answer."

"What am I missing here?" He dragged his hand through his hair. "Why is this such a big secret? Why didn't you tell me before?"

Oh, what a mistake this was. Jacob was right, she should never have said one word. Because once she told him a little bit, he'd keep asking questions. More and more questions. "I never said I'd tell you *everything*. You said one question, and I answered it."

"You're dreaming if you think I'm going to just leave it at that, Cherie. I'll be back here tomorrow night, and the night after, and maybe some of the hours in between too. Something's not right here." He pressed his hands into his thighs, which made her think he was going to come closer.

If he did, she'd lose it. She felt too raw, too exposed. The thought of how she'd broken her promise to Jacob made her want to throw up. She flung up a hand. "Don't touch me."

His head snapped up. He fixed her with a look of outrage. "Are you nuts, Cherie? I haven't moved one finger. I'm not forcing you to do anything." His voice shook with passion. "I've never hurt you. Never done anything but love you from the moment I saw you."

"I didn't ask you to!"

"No, you didn't ask me to. I did it, all on my own, because that's just the way it is. I can't help it. I love you, Cherie, and it's not going anywhere. I'll love you tomorrow, and the next day, whether or not you ever decide to let me in on all your secrets. Or even one secret."

"Vader." Her voice trembled. "I've just told you more than I've ever told anyone. More than Soren, more than Nick, the Hendersons, my friends, anyone."

"I'm supposed to be satisfied with that? I beat out the emo boys and the babysitting family. Now I get to sit in a corner until you call on me again."

"That's not fair!" Furious, she scrabbled for a pillow and hurled it at him. He caught it in one hand and tossed it to the side.

"Fair?" He scrambled off the bed and surged to his feet. "*Fair?* How does 'fair' come into any of this? Was it fair for your father to try to make you marry someone you didn't want? Was it fair for my mother to get hit by a car? Was it fair for my dad to run off because he couldn't handle it?"

She gaped at him in shock. Where had that come from?

"Yeah. He came into my bedroom and explained that he hadn't signed up to take care of a cripple for the rest of his life." He struggled for a ragged breath. "It's not about 'fair.' It's about taking what life dishes out and doing the best you can, giving it everything you've got." He pointed at her. "You're hiding, Cherie."

She wanted to defend herself, tell him how wrong he was. But was he? She hugged her knees close to her chest, needing her own body heat.

"There, now you know my story." He upturned his hands in a helpless gesture. "I just gave you the perfect excuse to push me away. It's too much to handle. It's not what you want in your life. Go ahead, say it."

A heavy, electric silence vibrated between them. Was that what he thought of her? How could she make him understand . . . without telling him everything?

But she couldn't do that.

But she had to.

Oh Jacob, I'm sorry.

"You feed me little crumbs, Cherie. All I want to do is love you and take care of you and . . . and . . ."

"I can't. Marry you." Low and abrupt, with a passionate tremor, her voice barely whispered into the moonlight.

"You keep telling me that. But you still haven't made—"

"I can't because I'm already . . . sort of . . . married."

Chapter Twenty

Vader took a stumbling step backward. Of all the things Cherie could have said, nothing could have shocked him more. She was *married*? And she'd never told him? And what the hell did "sort of" mean? Through the thick fog of betrayal, he grabbed on to something he'd learned from firefighting. Keep your feet on the ground. Deal with what's in front of you.

"What are you talking about?"

From his position, standing near the foot of her bed, she was a dark lump huddled against the headboard.

"I mean, I signed something that made me married. Prophesize arranged it. I didn't agree to it, not consciously," she said in a voice so shaky he could barely hear it. "I was confused. I'd never drunk any alcohol before, and Mackintosh brought a bottle of champagne to celebrate. We were in our old henhouse, me, Prophesize, and Mackintosh. I only had a few sips, but I got kind of woozy after that. It was like I was floating up on the ceiling away from my body. He had some documents and a pen, and I signed where he said to. And then he said, 'Welcome to the Mackintosh clan.' My father and him shook hands, then my dad left. Mackintosh started talking about stuff like what he liked for dinner—I remember he mentioned Sloppy Joes, because I started picturing hot dogs and chili beans and feeling so queasy. I wasn't floating anymore, I was right there in my body, feeling sicker and sicker. Then he changed the subject to sex, and how many times a week he liked to do it, and I just lost it. Everything was spinning around like I was doing cartwheels. When he came after me and grabbed me, I threw up a little, and caught it in my hand. He said I was disgusting and told me to go outside and take care of myself."

"He drugged you," said Vader flatly. He knew it as clearly as if he'd been there himself.

She clenched the bedcovers as if they were Mackintosh's neck. "Oh sweet Lord. I think you must be right. Two sips of champagne won't make you throw up. I can't believe I never thought of that before! What a lowlife scum he was. Is."

She shuddered. Vader cracked his knuckles, wishing Mackintosh would walk through the door so he could beat him up.

"Anyway," she hurried on, "I went outside to puke my guts out, and there was Jacob, waiting for me. He had our little rucksacks, and the money we'd been saving. Mackintosh came after me, and I grabbed an old piece of pipe and smashed it over his head. Jacob kicked him in the groin, and maybe in the throat too. It's all pretty blurry. I thought maybe I'd killed him. After that, we ran. I was so ill I could barely move, but every time I thought about what was waiting back there, I made myself do it. Jacob half carried me part of the way. When we got to the highway we hitched a ride with a trucker who took us all the way to Texas. I lay down in the backseat of the crew cab. I kept throwing up, but I didn't want the trucker to stop so I'd do it in my rucksack, really quiet. First thing we did when we got out of the truck was wash everything in that bag. It felt like I was washing away that slimy man."

Before he realized what he was doing, Vader was at her side. She was gripping the sheets tightly enough to rip them. He sat on the edge of the bed and gently enclosed her hands in his. A weird sort of relief filled him, because that didn't sound like any sort of legal marriage to him.

"What happened next?" he asked. He sensed that she needed to spill the whole story, now that she'd started.

"Texas didn't seem far enough away from Arkansas, so we kept on going, hitchhiking until we got all the way to California. That was a great feeling—all that space, all those fields going on forever and ever, those wide highways. We figured they'd never find us here."

He ran his thumb along the pad of her palm. "So no one tried to find you? Was no one worried about you?"

"Well, about two months after we left, we took a bus to Nevada and found a phone booth. My hands were shaking so hard I could hardly dial the number. The Harpers don't even have a phone, you know. You have to leave a message at the feed store, 'cause the owner's a friend of my father. That's how I found out that Mackintosh was in the hospital and the police had filed charges against us."

"Charges?"

"We weren't there to tell our side, were we? I was too afraid to go back. We just decided to stay here and never go back to Arkansas. And hope Mackintosh didn't come after us. And never tell anyone about what had happened. We made a pact, Jacob and I. And I just broke it."

She took in a shuddering breath, but right now Vader wasn't worried about some idiotic pact with Jacob.

"This Mackintosh . . ." Even the name tasted bad in his mouth. "If you were forced into marriage with him—an illegal marriage—why don't you just file for divorce?"

"Because of my sisters."

He looked at her with complete incomprehension. "Is this more Harper family craziness? You're going to have to spell it out for me."

"In my eyes, Mackintosh is not my husband. Why, it was never even consummated. But if Prophesize *thinks* me and Mackintosh are married, then he won't let the man near my sisters, once they start coming of age. Bigamy's a sin. See what I mean?"

He scrubbed his hand through his hair. "Not really. Keep going."

"Mackintosh only wanted me because I'm a Harper. He made a deal with my father. Humility or one of the others would be a perfectly fine replacement. The only reason he didn't go after Humility was that he thought his son was going to marry her. But she ran away. So now I don't know what he's going to do. But I know that Prophesize doesn't believe in bigamy, and he doesn't believe in divorce. So as long as my father thinks Mackintosh and I are married, my sisters are safe. Get it now?"

"Yeah. I get it. You're sacrificing your future to protect your sisters. You know what, Cherie? This is the craziest story I ever heard. But I'll tell you one thing. You're not married." His certainty rang through the room like church bells. "First of all, how old were you? Seventeen, you said?"

"Yes. Seventeen."

"That's not even legal."

"It is, with parental consent. I checked the Arkansas statutes online. My father was there and I signed the paper . . ."

"I don't care what you signed. Did you sign it in front of anyone official? Like a clerk or a judge?"

"No. Just a few stray hens."

Vader brushed a strand of hair off her face. "Hens don't count. On top of that, you were given some kind of drug and you were unwilling. No judge in his right mind would consider that a legal marriage."

"I know that. But it doesn't matter," she said in a firm voice. "As long as Prophesize thinks it's legal, Mackintosh can't touch my sisters. Besides . . ." She let out a deep whoosh of breath. "You might as well know everything. There's probably still a warrant out for my arrest in Arkansas. I don't want to go near the legal system. I have Jacob to think about too. Mackintosh hates him even more than me. He's a terrible homophobe."

If Vader ever met this Mackintosh face to face, he'd tear him apart. "There has to be a better way to deal with the situation. Why don't you file charges against him?"

"What do you mean?"

"He drugged you and forced you to sign something. You were defending yourself when you hit him. *He* should face charges, not you. I know a lawyer who helped my mom with her insurance stuff. I'll make an appointment with her."

"*Vader.*" She scrambled to her knees, the bedsheet falling off her bare shoulder. She grabbed one of his hands. "I don't want you to charge in like some sort of warrior king. This isn't your problem."

He frowned. From where he was sitting, it sure as hell was. This crazy situation had kept him and Cherie apart all this time. "How can you say that? You say you can't think about marrying me because you're already married. Why isn't that my problem?"

"Mackintosh is scary. And if Trixie's right, he's even scarier now. I made him worse when I knocked him on the head. I don't want him coming after you. It's between him and me."

Vader leaned forward, his hands on either side of her, making sure she met his eyes and saw how serious he was. "Believe me, I'd love it if he came after me. Bring it on, Farmer Dude who drugs girls he wants to marry."

She gripped his forearms, her fingernails digging in. "This is exactly why Jacob didn't want to tell you. He was afraid you'd make a big fuss and alert the legal system, and then Mackintosh—"

"Calm down, Cherie. I'm just trying to help."

"Listen. I'll think about calling that lawyer. But you have to promise me not to do or say anything. To *anyone*. I don't want you involved."

He flinched. "I'm already involved," he said tightly.

"Yes, okay. I know. And I know I haven't been fair to you. I should never have gotten involved with you. It was wrong and I'll probably rot in hell, but it would make it so much worse if you got hurt somehow, and . . ."

Vader couldn't stand to listen to another second of her so-called reasoning. *She* was trying to protect *him*? Didn't she understand anything about him?

He stood up, fists on his hips, unconcerned with the fact that he was still stark naked. "First of all," he said, in clipped syllables, "I wouldn't fucking get hurt. If you don't trust me on anything else, trust me on that. Do you know why I have these muscles?" He thumped his chest with one fist.

She shook her head, as if stunned into speechlessness.

"I built them. Me and my free weights. I started at fourteen and I never slowed down. I wanted the strongest body I could get. Why? So I could keep *bad things from happening to people.* Same reason I became a fireman. And it works. Not always, but sometimes. I can carry my mother from the van to the house. I can carry a downed fireman. Two, probably. And I can take on some loser idiot from the backwoods. And you're going to tell me, 'Thanks, but no thanks' because you don't want me to get hurt? That's insulting. Don't you know what I'm all about by now?"

She opened her mouth, closed it. "What's wrong with not wanting you to get hurt?" she asked in a small voice. "I don't want anyone to get hurt. I never did. That's why I kept saying no to getting married."

He slammed his jaw shut, pressing his mouth into one tight line. How could he explain this to her? "You should have told me before. Straight up. But I can see that your so-called pact with Jacob got in the way. I can live with that. I can live with you keeping your sort of, not-even-close-to-legal, forced marriage to yourself until now. But that was before. This is now. You and me. And you have to start trusting me, Cherie. You have to *let me help.*"

When she stared back at him, silent, her eyes huge and silvery as twin moons, he felt a leaden weight in his gut. He turned up his hands, let them drop, then bent to retrieve his clothes. "I'm going to go check on my mom. She still isn't sleeping well. You think about what I said. Think hard."

Hand on the doorknob, he turned back one more time. "And Cherie. I love you." Then he was gone.

After Vader left, Cherie cried into her pillow for a good long while. Emotion piled on emotion until she felt confused and completely overwhelmed. Reliving that night, and the time afterward, was never easy. And then dropping the bombshell of her "marriage" on Vader had been horrible.

Of course, he was right, and it wasn't a real marriage. It probably didn't afford much protection to her sisters, but just in case it did, she refused to rock the boat. And that's what he wanted her to do. Rock the boat. File charges. Stir up the hornet's nest back home.

And yet, a huge part of her ached for what he offered. What if she could turn to him? What if he could protect her—and her whole family—from Mackintosh? What if she didn't have to feel so alone and frightened? What if she had someone fighting by her side? If only, if only . . .

She set her jaw. No. She'd been wrong to fall for Vader, wrong to let things go as far as they had. Wasn't she right to try to limit the damage? She'd created this mess and she should solve it.

First things first. She found her phone and called Jacob. Now that she'd broken her promise and told Vader their story, she'd better alert her brother.

He reacted as badly as he possibly could. "You took a blood oath, Cherie! Does that mean nothing to you?"

"Jacob, that's not fair. Our pact was stupid, it was because we were afraid of Mackintosh. I don't want to be afraid anymore. I've been wanting to tell Vader for so long, you know I have. It was destroying our relationship."

"You don't know what you've done, Cherie."

Cherie fought back against the tears. If Jacob turned against her, she didn't know what she'd do. "What do you mean? Vader's not going to say anything."

"How do you know?"

"I know him. I trust him."

"All you know about him is that he gives you screaming orgasms."

"Jacob."

"Don't 'Jacob' me. You *promised*. If Mackintosh finds you, he'll just take you back to Arkansas. But you know what he'll do to me and—" He broke off, as if interrupting himself before letting something else slip. "What's wrong with you, Cherie? I can't believe you would do this."

He hung up on her. She'd never heard him so angry before. How could she have made such a mess of things? In total despair, she buried her head under the pillows. Vader was furious with her. Her brother hated her. Mackintosh was lurking out there somewhere. What in blue blazes was she going to do now?

Vader approached his promotional exam with a sense of doom. He'd gotten barely any sleep thanks to the blowout with Cherie. The things she said kept running through his mind, until the answers to questions about fire ops turned into rants about henhouse weddings under the influence of roofies, or whatever the backwoods equivalent was.

Even though he knew he was tanking, he gritted his teeth and finished the exam. He wanted it to count as his first try, pathetic though it might be. After a couple of hours hunched over the pages, he called it good, stalked out of the room, and knew he'd been shot down for the second time in twenty-four hours.

Then he drove his truck to the reservoir where he

liked to run. It was a green oasis in the desert, pleasantly shaded with willows and aspens fluttering like girls in green lace. He parked in the gravel lot, cracked the window, and leaned the seat all the way back. A slight overcast filtered the normally blazing sun. The air wafting through his window was warm and smelled of sagebrush and eucalyptus, with an overlay of failure.

Nowhere with Cherie. Nowhere on the captain front. Temporarily homeless. What else could go wrong?

Normally he didn't waste time feeling down. He had no room for self-pity in his life. But hell, if he was doing something wrong, he needed to figure out what it was and fix it.

He closed his eyes. A little sleep, and he'd be back on his game. He'd take the exam again, and this time he'd pass. It wasn't as hard as all that. He knew that shit cold. And "homeless" might be going too far. As soon as the insurance money came, he and his mom would find a place. No biggie.

Cherie? Yeah, things were a mess once again. So what else was new? At least he'd gotten some details out of her. Now he knew why she kept putting the brakes on. What he couldn't understand was why she wouldn't let him help. For fuck's sake, he was a living, breathing, helping machine. That's what he did at the firehouse and at home. He helped people. So why wouldn't she let him do the same for her?

Well, there was one thing he could do. Setting his teeth, he drew out his phone and looked up Ginny's lawyer's number and texted it to Cherie.

There. His big hero act of the day. Texting a phone number.

Sleep dragged at his eyeballs. He had to catch a few Zs before he went home, because God only knew

Chapter Twenty-One

Before it was a restaurant, Firefly had been one of the original firehouses in San Gabriel. It had been decommissioned in the late nineties when a newer, larger station had been built nearby. A couple of enterprising retired San Gabriel firefighters had taken out a loan and turned it into a bar and restaurant. Vader had been one of its early and loud supporters, and he'd brought lots of business there since they'd opened. The owners, Pete and Jack, had told him he never had to pay for a drink there again, but he did anyway. For the most part. Unless he was having so much fun he forgot. Then he usually came back the next day and settled up.

Pete and Jack had kept many of the original details from Firefly's firehouse days, including the pole, which was the focus of the dance floor. Since, like many firefighters, they were handy with tools, they'd done much of the interior woodwork in the place. The centerpiece was a gorgeous hardwood bar that curved like a spaceship console around the edge of the space. Pete's wife, who had a green thumb, had contributed pots of ficus and even a miniature orange tree, which lit up one corner. Tables were clustered around the edge of the huge space, most of which was devoted to the dance floor, which was always mobbed.

For Vader, Firefly was a home away from home, or, more accurately, a firehouse away from firehouse. He loved every inch of the place. The food was perfect, burgers and salads. The beer was reasonably priced. The music was rocking. And the girls were friendly. Firefighters were always welcome. He even had his own personal tankard, in the shape of a Darth Vader helmet, stashed behind the bar—a gift from the Station 1 crew.

Tonight, his tankard wasn't getting much action. Vader didn't need to drink to have fun. He wanted to party to oblivion, and that meant throwing himself onto the dance floor and letting the music smash his brain into semi-conscious bits. He started the evening with a bunch of firehouse guys doing tequila shots, but by ten he was out on the dance floor tearing it up. Fred left by eleven, muttering something about his studio.

The dinner crowd left by eleven-thirty, and that's when the dancing got out of control. The servers shoved the tables to the very edge of the space. Jack cranked the music up and turned on the colored lights, so the writhing bodies on the dance floor were lit with orange and purple flashes. The smell of beer mingled with fruity shampoo and girlie perfume—sheer heaven, if you asked Vader.

Word of the party must have spread around town, because more girls arrived, crowding the dance floor with bare arms and itty-bitty microskirts. Vader danced, and laughed, and hooted, and let the wild party break him apart and put him back together.

At midnight, Pete cleared off the bar, blasted Firefly's signature song, and gave the signal to Joe the Toe. "Everyone follow the black guy," bellowed Joe. Vader threw his head back, laughing until his throat hurt. Then he joined the line of dancers doing the conga onto the bar.

"Boooo-yah!" he shouted, kicking one leg to the side, then the other, his hands on one girl's waist, another girl's arms tight on his hips.

By twelve-thirty, Vader's shirt was long gone, lost somewhere in the crowd, and six girls were taking turns gyrating against his body like strippers. At one in the morning, he took a break and fueled up with two gigantic hamburgers slathered in mushrooms and ketchup; Pete had set a plate aside for him before the kitchen closed. The waitress brought his Darth Vader mug filled with dark ale.

Mulligan, accompanied by a pepperoni pizza and three girls, collapsed into the chair across from him.

"What are you still doing here?" Vader asked him.

"Fred left me in charge."

"In charge of what?"

"The fun." The way Mulligan said the word "fun," the police couldn't be far behind.

"Where's Joe?"

"Hell if I know."

"Some wingman you are." He waggled a finger at the pretty redhead nibbling at her slice of pizza. She reminded him of Cherie, which made him want to warn her off. "Watch out for that guy. Not to be trusted."

Mulligan glared and leaned forward on his elbows, shoving his face into Vader's. "You want some of this? You been on my ass since I got to this town."

"Take it easy, dude. This is family here." Vader had a buzz on, but not enough to mess up his favorite bar with a brawl.

"Fine. We'll keep it clean, then." With his wrestler-tough squint, he glanced around the bar and the packed dance floor. "Dare you to come down that pole like the guys used to do it."

"You serious?" Vader knew how to shimmy down a pole with the best of them, but Station 1, being of more modern vintage, didn't have one.

"Yess!" The redhead clapped. "Slide down the pole, Vader!"

The two other girls chimed in. "Pole, pole, pole!"

Vader narrowed his eyes at Mulligan, who was cracking up between bites of pizza. The guy was an instigator, no doubt. "The pole's blocked off. Insurance requirement."

"You know how to get to it, right?"

"Of course I do." He'd helped remodel the place, after all. "If I slide down the pole, what'll it get me?"

"You mean besides fame and female adulation?"

"I already have that."

"Pole, pole, pole," chanted the girls.

"Something else." Vader pretended to ponder the issue. "I got it. If I slide down the pole, then at the next lineup, you raise your hand and say you have an announcement to make. Then you say, 'Vader is the captain of my heart.'"

Mulligan snorted. "You sure about that? That ain't going to help you make captain."

Vader waved his tankard, and a bit of foam lipped out of the edge of Darth Vader's head. "My chances of making captain are about as good as this beer's."

"Don't count yourself out, dude. No one passes the exam on the first try."

"Pole, pole, pole . . ." The chant was now spreading across the room. The crowd on the dance floor had stopped gyrating and started clapping along. "Pole, pole, pole . . ."

Mulligan and Vader exchanged a look, half horrified, half amused by what they'd created.

"Oopsie," said Mulligan, covering his mouth and widening his eyes, as if he were a schoolgirl caught smoking. "You're in for it now."

Vader took another swig from his tankard and plopped it on the table. "Do we have a deal?"

"I don't know, Vader. Think about your career."

"My career can fuck itself. And you too. *Do we have a deal?*"

"If you put it that way, then hell, yes. Just for free, I'll throw in a personal recommendation from a dedicated committee member."

"No lies. Nothing you don't believe."

Mulligan lifted his bottle of Corona and toasted him. "That's a guarantee. Lying ain't ever worth the trouble."

Through his party-fueled buzz, Vader knew a kinship had finally been established. "Then clear the way."

Mulligan stood and formed his hands into a megaphone. "This is the fire department speaking. Safety regulations require that we clear the area around the pole. Please step toward the edge of the dance floor. If you really need a pole, I got one right here. In my pants."

Vader was happy to hear the crowd boo Mulligan's crass joke. While the dance floor slowly and chaotically cleared, he made his way up the side stairs that led to the second floor, which served as a storage area. Since he'd helped Pete and Jake remodel the place, he knew exactly how to access the top of the pole. They'd left the original hatch in place, merely covering it with a specially cut foam donut so no one would accidentally slip through.

The upstairs was quiet except for the thumping of the music and the continuing chants of "Pole, pole, pole." He lifted the foam insert away from the hole, releasing a blast of music and warm, beer-scented air.

He hesitated. What was he doing, making an ass of himself before a bar full of half-drunk customers? He wasn't captain material. Who was he kidding? No wonder no one ever took him seriously, because he kept pulling stunts like this. He should put the foam back, walk downstairs, slip out the side door, and go study for the fucking exam.

The chant below tugged at him. "Pole, pole, pole." Laughing faces tilted toward him. Everyone down there was having a good time. But if he came sliding down that pole, they'd have more than a good time. They'd have a story to tell. Their faces would light up when they remembered it. They'd feel special that they were at Firefly the night some big, goofy, shirtless firefighter came down the pole to the tune of . . .

Oh hell. Pete, that son of a bitch, had put on an Elvis song. "Heartbreak Hotel." Everyone knew he could never resist an Elvis tune. The crowd was clapping again, as if wondering why he was hesitating. "Pole, pole, pole . . ." and "We love you, Vader."

In that moment, in that deserted, dusty upstairs room, something clicked in Vader's heart. He was, and would always be . . . Vader. An excessively muscled guy who liked a good laugh. A man who didn't mind playing the fool if it brought a smile to someone's face. He wore his heart on his bulging sleeve and he'd lay down his life for a brother fireman, or his mother, or even a total stranger if fate required it. He was Vader, and he'd make a damn good captain and a top-rate husband. If Cherie couldn't see that, then she was blinder than a bat in a belfry.

Or something.

Casting all second thoughts, second guesses, and last regrets to the wind, he gripped the smooth metal of the pole and wrapped his legs around it. To the tune of a million catcalls and hollers from below, he loosened his grip and glided down the pole. He kept his bare chest away from the metal, letting his legs, in their loose khakis, do the work. The music got louder as he went, the sweaty heat of the dance floor welcoming him like a sauna. Happy, laughing faces greeted him, male and female. When his feet touched the floor, he struck an Elvis-like pose, holding on to the pole with one hand, turning his head the opposite way, hand over his forehead. Then he switched hands, as if the pole were a tango partner swinging him into a dip.

"Whoohoo!" The crowd screamed with one voice. Several girls clutched at each other, fanning themselves as if he were the real King. Even the guys were laughing and high-fiving each other. Was this what it felt like to be a rock star?

He did one of his favorite Elvis moves, getting up on his toes, thrusting his hips forward, and scissoring his legs in and out. As the King sang about Lonely Street, he switched hands again, flipping his body to the other side of the pole. This time he twined one leg around the pole and arched his chest backward, moving his hips to the music and deploying his Elvis lip curl on a plump brunette he'd seen there before.

She shrieked, clutching her hands to her chest. "Oh my God, oh my God!" she babbled hysterically. "He kissed me!"

He hadn't done any such thing, but that didn't stop the other girls from going nuts.

He felt hands touching his chest, hot breath fanning his skin. It was hot and crowded, and the music was still blasting, and he couldn't breathe. He saw a girl sag into the arms of her friend, as if she'd fainted. And was that someone licking his shoulder?

He jerked his shoulder away from the strange touch, but right away someone else put a hand on his abdomen. This was bad. Things were getting out of control. He'd been in some wild scenes, but he'd never had girls fainting over him. In the middle of the crowd, he spotted Mulligan, and mouthed the word "help." But the crowd was so thick Mulligan could make no headway—Vader wasn't even sure he was trying hard. Mulligan probably thought he was having fun.

This was definitely not his idea of fun.

Then a firm, cool hand grabbed on to his. With some kind of Jedi dance maneuver, the hand swirled its owner into a tight embrace between Vader and the pole. He looked down into Cherie's beautiful gray eyes.

"Hey, hot stuff," she murmured.

"Where'd you come from?" He blinked at her, as if she'd popped out of a genie's lamp.

"Mulligan texted me. He thought you might need a rescue." She did another of her magical dance moves, so they were back to back. She must have made some sort of gesture to the crowd, because all of a sudden he had a little more space to breathe. Cherie whirled around again, pushing him into a position next to the pole, holding on to it with one hand, the other hand free to wave to the crowd.

"Give them a nice bow," she murmured. "And then we're getting out of here."

Best news he'd heard all night. He bent at the waist

in an elaborate bow, then rose again, to cheers from the crowd. Cherie waved and curtsied, despite a few nasty glances from the other girls.

"Unless I got it all wrong, and you want to stay," she said out of the corner of her mouth.

"Hell. No," he said, with complete certainty. "My work here is done."

"Spectacularly so." She winked, then took his arm in a way that screamed possession. As she made a path through the crowd, no girl in the place could mistake the way she leaned against him, the way she hooked her thumb in his belt loop. Every move she made signaled ownership. Vader reciprocated by wrapping his arm around her shoulder. When they reached the door, as a final punctuation mark, he lowered his hand to her butt and squeezed.

"You know this is one step away from going steady," he murmured in her ear, highly amused by her behavior. "This is going to be all over town tomorrow."

"I'll take my chances," she said with a crooked smile as they stepped into the starlit night—or was it early morning by now? "I'm pretty sure everyone's too drunk to remember. Including you."

"You got that wrong. I didn't even drink much. You know me, high on life." He followed her across the jam-packed parking lot to her ancient Mercedes, which she'd parked at the last remaining spot, if it could be called that. The poor car was crammed onto the grassy verge, a graceless position for such a dignified-looking car.

He pulled her around the Mercedes to its dark, sheltered side. With a quick survey, he made sure no one could see them. Using his own Jedi move, he swung Cherie into his arms and pinned her against the car. "Nice parking job. Looks like you were in a hurry."

"When my guy's in trouble, there's no time to waste."

He lowered his head to nuzzle her sweet-smelling hair. "Your guy?"

"You know what they say about saving someone's life. I'm now responsible for you."

A little starburst of warmth detonated in his chest. "I didn't know it was a life-or-death situation. But I'm fine with that. Are you responsible for kissing me too?"

She cocked her head. "I think that's probably included." He bent to her lips and helped himself to a long kiss, a life-giving, cock-hardening, world-righting kiss. Before he lost all common sense, he pulled back. "Hang on, though. It's okay for you to rescue me, but I can't rescue you? What kind of sense does that make?"

Clutching his upper arms, she sagged against the Mercedes. How he loved that drugged, happy look in her eyes. "All I know is, when I got the text from Mulligan, I jumped at the chance to turn the tables and feel like a hero. I guess it's a two-way street."

Of course. How could he have forgotten that the way to Cherie's heart was to need her help? "Two-way street. I can live with that. It's better than Lonely Street."

She wrapped her arms around his waist and leaned against his bare chest. He gave a passing thought to his missing shirt, then decided it didn't matter.

"I don't really like Lonely Street either," she murmured. "How about Let's Try This Again Lane? It's at the intersection of I'm Sorry and Please Kiss Me Again."

Yes, he knew the spot. They'd been there before. "Have you thought about what I said last night?"

"I have. And I got the number you sent me. I decided I'm going to take your advice and talk to her about filing charges. There can't be any harm in finding out what she says, right? It's all confidential."

"Yes. Although you can tell me if you want to."

The fact that she'd listened to him, that she was following his suggestion, made him want to kiss her until he forgot his own name. As he dipped his mouth to her lips, a movement at the edge of his vision caught his attention. He stilled and scanned the parking lot carefully. Nothing moved, but he'd bet anything someone had ducked behind a car. In any case, they had no business making out like teenagers in a dark parking lot.

"Let's go home," he said against her hair. "I'll text Joe the Toe. He's my ride."

"I think he figured it out." She searched in her little fish-shaped purse for her keys. The handle was shaped like a fish hook and fit on her wrist perfectly. She wore a tight-fitting deep purple dress that showed off her gorgeous cleavage. She was beautiful. And she'd come to his rescue without a second thought.

"I . . ." He wanted to say he loved her, but every time he said it things got screwy. "I thank you, Cherie."

She stared up at him with night-shadowed eyes, as if she knew exactly what he'd left out. "It's my pleasure, Vader. We should get back. I left your mother alone with Trixie."

"Right."

Chapter Twenty-Two

"You have to come look at this, Cherie," Trixie called from her room on the second floor. "You're famous!"

Cherie, who was making coffee in the kitchen, groaned. She had to make it to her shift at Healing Hands in half an hour and she'd gotten only a few hours of sleep. She poured herself a cup of not entirely brewed coffee and hurried upstairs to Trixie's room. When she'd given her sister access to her computer, she'd created an addict. YouTube and Trixie were made for each other.

Trixie was bouncing up and down in front of the old Dell. "You're already on YouTube! You and Vader. Well, mostly Vader. Wow, I knew he was hot, but not that hot! It already has ten thousand views. And look at all the comments. 'He sure knows what to do with that pole.' 'He can come rescue me anytime.' 'What's up with the fat chick ruining the—' Oops. Never mind that one."

Cherie stared at the computer screen, where she and Vader were bowing to the cheering, shrieking crowd. "The camera adds ten pounds. Everyone knows that. Of course, in Vader's case it's ten pounds of pure muscle. Holy smokes!"

Even if she did look plumper than in real life, she thought she looked okay. Vader obviously thought so too, judging by the way he pulled her into a smoking hot clinch at the end of the dance.

"You shouldn't be reading those comments, Trixie. They're rude."

"I like them. People can say anything on the Internet, can't they? It's awesome!"

"Poor Vader. I sure hope this doesn't mean trouble for him at the station." Surely a video like this would create all kinds of problems for someone trying to make captain.

Trixie clicked play again and there came Vader, sliding down the pole like Superman at a strip club.

"Whatever. It's worth it. He could quit the fire department and go into the movies or something. You know what, he should! We should send this to a movie person. Maybe the actress who's a firefighter now. Sabina Jones. I read about her when I was checking out the Bachelor Firemen."

An odd sound caught Cherie's attention, like something getting knocked over outside.

"Shhh."

"What, it's a good idea!"

"*Shhht.*" She motioned for Trixie to shush. "I heard a sound," she whispered. They both went still, listening to the creaks and whispers of the old house.

"It was probably Mrs. Brown," mouthed Trixie.

"She's still sleeping. And it was outside. Hang on." Cherie tiptoed to the window and peered into the backyard, which was nothing but a patch of brown grass bordered by rose bushes. Since the roses had stopped blooming in June, the yard was a pretty sad sight. And a completely empty one. "It's nothing, I guess. Maybe the cat bumped into something."

She turned back to Trixie, an uneasy feeling settling over her. "I wish I didn't have to work today. What are you up to? Can you stay with Mrs. Brown today?"

Trixie scowled and propped her bare feet on the desk. Each of her toenails had been painted a different shade of neon. She must have raided Cherie's makeup stash again. "Isn't she supposed to have a home health care nurse or something? How come I always get stuck with her?"

"Yes, she does, but she told me their insurance ran out and Vader's been paying the whole bill. If we can save them some money, why not?"

Trixie grumbled some more, but finally gave in. "Fine. Maybe she'll let me do Izzy's fur in pigtails again. That was fun."

Cherie checked her watch and bustled back to the kitchen. After her Healing Hands massage shift, she had a Singles Tango class to teach, and she had a feeling she was going to get plenty of heat over the Firefly video. Somewhere in there she had to make time to call the lawyer, even though the thought gave her a queasy case of the butterflies.

How had Vader managed to forget they'd entered the electronic era? As soon as he walked into the station to meet with the School Liaison Committee, the whistled versions of "Heartbreak Hotel" began. The B shift could have been a freaking barbershop quartet, the way they belted it out in four-part harmony. He bore the whole thing stoically, shoving his hands in his pockets and keeping his shades firmly planted on his face.

"Chippendale's called," said Lane, the B shift nozzle man. "They're reserving a spot for you."

Brett, the engineer, added, "I heard you're giving pole dance lessons at the strip club."

The B shift captain 1 paused, coffee cup in hand. "My wife sent the video to all her girlfriends. I told her she could put your phone number at the end. You okay with that?"

"No, sir," said Vader. "I wish to remain anonymous."

"It's a little late for that." Captain Brody emerged from the captain's office. Vader did a double take, since Brody wasn't supposed to be on shift either. The captain stepped to the side, revealing another man just behind him—the highly intimidating Chief Renteria, head of the entire San Gabriel Fire Department. The man looked like some kind of avenging Aztec warrior with that scowl on his face.

Vader got that horror-movie feeling, the one where everything was about to go to bloody hell. There should have been a soundtrack playing.

Had Vader's insane little show gotten Captain Brody in trouble? Had Chief Renteria dragged Brody in on his day off? Forget making captain. He'd be lucky if he didn't get suspended.

"Is this the newest Bachelor Fireman to hit the news?" the chief growled.

"Strictly speaking, he hasn't made the news. I think we can all be grateful that Ella Joy has the week off."

Channel Six, the local station, and its anchor Ella Joy seemed to have a lock on all embarrassing Bachelor Firemen stories.

"It's just a matter of time," said Renteria, with a heavy sigh.

"I'm sorry, Chief," said Vader. "If I'd known there was a camera . . ."

"There's always a camera."

"Yes, sir."

"Chief, let me introduce you officially. This is Firefighter Derek Brown. He's been leading the committee on revising the community relations manual. Remember that section you called a stroke of genius? The one dealing with Bachelor Firemen questions? Well, this is the man responsible." Brody clapped Vader on the shoulder.

"Maybe I should put you in front of the cameras when they come asking about pole dances."

"Yes, sir."

Keeping his posture military-straight, he stole a glance at Brody. His captain gave him a ghost of a wink. Would it be okay? Was the situation salvageable? Was there anything more he could add?

"Sir, I realize a fireman's pole is not something to play around with—"

Someone snorted behind him. The entire B shift was probably pretending to refill their coffee cups so they could witness the show. The chief tilted his head, as if he hadn't heard quite right.

Vader tried again. "What I mean to say is, firemen's poles are important tools for—"

This time, an outright hoot echoed through the kitchen. *Fuck it all.* Vader ignored his fellow firefighters and barreled onward. "Even though we don't use the poles as much as we used to—"

In the kitchen, a guffaw got stifled mid-snort. Vader fondly pictured a dish towel being stuck in someone's mouth.

"—we should still treat our poles with respect, since they're a treasured part of our firefighting past," he ended with as much dignity as he could muster.

The chief's fierce black eyes drilled into him. Out of the corner of his eye, Vader saw that Brody's face was bright red, as if he too was struggling not to laugh.

Well, he'd always known how to entertain the crew. Why should anything change? He waited stoically for the chief's verdict.

"Well put," Renteria said, finally. "It's nice to see the next generation appreciating the traditions of the past. Now let's sit down and see where you are with the handbook. Brody says you've been doing good work."

Vader allowed his shoulders a tiny slump of relief. He already owed Captain Brody in so many ways; now he could add this incident to the list. He followed Renteria and Brody into the office. As he closed the door, he looked back at his tormentors. Lane was doing the world's most ridiculous lap dance with a metal folding chair. Brett was dry-humping the doorjamb.

Vader drew a finger across his throat in the universal sign meaning, *You're so dead*. He mouthed the words too, for emphasis. Then he stepped into the office, followed by the very faint hum of another Elvis tune, " . . . a little more action, please."

Brody gave him a quick head shake, as if warning him not to react. Vader knew better. The only way to end the ribbing would be to wait it out until something even better came along. He didn't care about that part anyway, as long as Renteria didn't hold it against him. So far, so good. If he could wow Renteria with his handbook prowess, maybe the chief would let the pole episode slide.

Vader sat down in the chair that Brody indicated.

Chief Renteria placed one ankle over the opposite knee and leaned back. "So tell me where you are on this. Can you get it to the printer's by next week?"

"Sure can." Vader had no idea if that was possible. But if ever a little white lie was called for, this was the time.

"Of course we want to run it by the Public Information Department and the union, maybe even the Widows and Orphans Fund," said Brody smoothly. "They have a lot of experience dealing with the community. Best to allow a few extra weeks for all that."

"Bureaucracy," said the chief in disgust. "It's enough to make you run for dictator."

"Next time they put that on the ballot, I'll write you in," promised Brody. Both men laughed. Vader shifted awkwardly in his chair, which was much too small for his muscular self. The other two men were so at ease, so comfortable with their positions of authority. Would he ever be like that? Would he ever be someone others looked to for leadership?

Unless it was leadership down a slippery pole into a screaming crowd, of course. He'd be the go-to guy for that mission.

His cell phone beeped with an incoming text message. Damn, he should have turned it off before he came in here for this meeting. The phone was in the lower pocket of his khakis, practically all the way down at his shin. There was no way he could subtly turn it off without anyone noticing.

The chief was already giving him the stink-eye.

"Excuse me," he said. "Thought I'd turned it off." He reached down to his pocket, extracted the phone, and saw that the text was from his mother. Scanning the first line, which read, *Trixie wants you to . . .* he decided it was nothing important. He almost turned the phone off, but the truth was, he never left his phone off. A dead phone would make him so worried about his mother he wouldn't be able to concentrate. Instead, he switched it to vibrate and put it in a more unobtrusive pocket.

"Family matter," he told Brody and Renteria, trying to make it sound important, like something a politician might say.

"You're a family man, are you?" asked the chief.

"Well . . ." Vader faltered. Did taking care of your mother make you a family man? The chief was probably talking about kids and a wife. He'd heard Renteria was divorced. "Family is very important," he equivocated.

His phone vibrated, making his leg jump. He clenched his jaw. This was all Trixie's fault, he just knew it. Trixie was going to single-handedly torpedo his promotion without doing anything other than being herself.

Renteria turned his attention to Brody and asked him about Melissa and their new baby. Vader grabbed the opportunity to slide the phone from his pocket. This time, he'd freaking turn the thing off, for the first time in his life.

Another message from his mother. This one also began with the name "Trixie." *Trixie called Cherie but got no answer . . .*

Why did Ginny have to inform him of every little detail of her day? Especially irritating since so many of those details involved Trixie.

He plunged the phone back into his pocket and turned his attention to the conversation.

" . . . finally starting to sleep through the night, as long as you define night as the hours between midnight and four in the morning. I'm going to bring him into the station next week and give him his first tour. Show him the locker I have picked out for him." Brody winked one charcoal-gray eye. It did Vader's heart good to see the captain so happy.

Once again, his phone vibrated. That was it. Off it would go. He dug it out once more and poised his thumb over the power button. But first he'd better check to make sure it wasn't his mother reporting a heart attack brought on by Trixie.

Get over here now! the text screamed. *A man came looking for Trixie and Cherie. Trixie's terrified. I think it might be my fault.*

Vader bolted to his feet, knocking over the chair. The two men swiveled to stare at him.

"I have to go. Problem at home," he muttered.

"We're having a meeting," said Renteria imperiously. "I have a limited amount of time and this is it."

"I get it. And I'm really sorry. I'll send you a complete report, I'll come to your office for another meeting, whatever you need. What's your e-mail address?" Vader backed across the office as he talked. "I can send everything to you the day after tomorrow."

The chief scowled.

"Tomorrow," he revised. "But I have to get home right away." He reached the door, stumbling as his back hit the wood.

"Vader's mother was recently in a house fire," Brody told the chief. "They're still dealing with the aftermath."

Add another item to the long list of nice things Brody had done for him. The chief nodded with a show of understanding. "Good luck to you, man."

"Thanks, Chief. Thanks Captain." Vader threw in a military salute for good measure and flung open the office door.

"One more thing, Brown," called Renteria. "Make sure to send me that YouTube link. I need to know what we're dealing with."

"Yes, sir."

And he was gone, flying down the corridor toward the parking lot. He passed a firefighter from Station 6 arriving for the school liaison meeting. "Meeting's canceled," he yelled. "Spread the word."

And this, he thought, as he sprinted across the parking lot toward his truck, *is what a wannabe fire captain going down in flames looks like.* Maybe he could have survived the Firefly video. But the video, on top of running out of an interview with the fire chief, on top of canceling another meeting, on top of the legendary backlog of Vader deeds and misdeeds . . . he could kiss that promotion good-bye.

Some things were more important than the fire department career ladder. Though Renteria might not agree.

Chapter Twenty-Three

Vader bounded up the walkway of the Gardam Street house. Through the open front door, he saw all three women in the entryway. Trixie was babbling a mile a minute, his mother was wheeling her chair back and forth, and Cherie, white as one of her bedsheets, was questioning the other two. The combined decibel level was off the charts.

Before stepping into the madness, he did a quick, methodical check of the premises to make sure the intruder had left. When the search came up clean, he strode into the house, closed and locked the door behind him, and steered everyone into the living room. There, he planted himself in the middle of the room and called on all his firefighter training. Firefighters, especially captains leading their crews, had to project calm. Any hint of panic and everyone would freak out and accidents would happen.

"Trixie." His deeper voice managed to cut through

the cacophony. "You first." He figured she was going to talk anyway, he might as well start with her. "What happened?"

Trixie shot a frightened, questioning look at Cherie, who nodded. "Tell him," she said. "He knows about Mackintosh."

Cherie, actually advocating sharing information with him. Would wonders never cease?

"It was Mr. Mackintosh," said Trixie. "He knocked on the door and called out Mrs. Brown's name. He said she'd contacted him by e-mail about a new home health care insurance policy."

"I never!" Ginny gasped, but Vader stopped her with a commanding hand gesture.

"One at a time. Go on, Trixie."

"So I opened the door and there he was, just as putrid ugly as ever. Of course I told him to go back to Arkansas and leave us alone."

"Was he looking for Cherie?"

"No, sir." Trixie had never called him "sir" before; he kind of liked it. "That's the weird part. He wanted to know where Jacob was."

Cherie gasped. "*Jacob*? What did you tell him?"

"I said he didn't live here anymore."

"Did you think about calling the police?" Vader asked.

"I had my finger on my medical alert button the whole time," said his mother, with a hint of pride.

"He said not to call the police." Trixie began to sob. "He said if anyone called the police he'd report Cherie to the authorities."

Cherie's hand flew to her throat. She sank onto the couch, so pale Vader was afraid she would faint. "Did he say what he wants with Jacob?"

"No. But he looked mighty mean when he said it. We can't let him find Jacob."

"How did he know about Mrs. Brown?" Cherie asked the room at large. "Has he been spying on us?"

A sob burst from Ginny's direction. "It's my fault." Everyone looked in her direction. She wheeled her chair over to Cherie. Tears streamed down her face, usually so cheerful. "Oh hon, I'm so sorry. I was curious about you girls and started nosing around online. You know me and my Internet. Mackintosh was listed as your family's contact, so I sent him an e-mail, but I never said anything about health insurance and I certainly never gave my address. But I must have tipped him off. I'm truly sorry. He's a bad man, I saw it as soon as he marched in here with his lies."

Vader clenched his hands into white-knuckled fists. If only he'd been here . . . if only he could get just one chance to knock that man into the next century . . .

Ginny was still talking, half sobbing. "You opened your home to us and this is how I repay you. I'll never forgive myself. We should leave, Vader, you hear me? We shouldn't impose a minute longer."

Vader froze. That aspect hadn't occurred to him. His own mother had reached out, somehow, to Mackintosh and brought trouble into Cherie's home, turned Cherie into a white-faced, trembling bundle of fear. One thing was for sure; he wasn't leaving the house unprotected again. He'd put his mother in a hotel, maybe, or somewhere else safe. But he was staying put.

Impulsively, Cherie snatched up Mrs. Brown's hand and held it to her heart. "Don't you dare even think something like that, Mrs. Brown. It's no wonder you were curious. Vader's your son. 'Course you wanted to find out more. I don't blame you one bit for anything Mackintosh does. He's crazy, always has been. And it's my fault as much as anyone's. I shouldn't have kept so much to myself. You all are staying right where you are, hear? That is, if you want to after all this."

Her Arkansas accent had never been stronger; Vader had never loved her more.

Ginny cradled Cherie's hand against her cheek. "You've got a sweet heart, hon."

Vader might have cried, if he weren't a big, strong fireman in the midst of handling a crisis. "A sweet heart" was Ginny's highest compliment. He cleared his throat. "Has anyone called Jacob yet?"

Everyone's gaze turned toward him. Cherie jumped to her feet. "I'll call him right now. Where's my phone?"

Trixie tossed her own cell phone to Cherie. She punched in a number, her fingers shaking. The room went quiet as she placed the call.

When he answered, everyone went quiet as she spoke. "Jacob, it's Cherie. We just had a visit from Mackintosh."

"What?" Even over the phone, everyone could hear him. Someone else said something inaudible in the background.

"Where are you?" Cherie asked.

"I'm driving. What happened? What did he say?"

"He said he's looking for you. Oh Jacob, be careful. I don't know why he's after you, but he's getting crazier and crazier."

Jacob let loose a stream of curse words that made Trixie clap her hands over her hears. "Didn't I tell you this would happen, Cherie?"

Vader saw tears start in her eyes. Without stopping to think, he plucked the phone out of her hand. "Hi Jacob. It's me, Vader."

Surprised silence greeted him.

"I know you didn't want Cherie to tell me anything, but to be honest, that's just dumb. If this Mackintosh is really that dangerous, you need all the help you can get. Especially if you guys don't want to call the cops."

"We don't," Jacob said quickly. Vader knew Jacob pretty well, and had always liked him. He had a wry, live-wire style and was intensely protective of Cherie.

"I think that's a mistake. You're the one he's after, apparently. Don't you want some protection?"

"I'll be fine." He said something to whoever was in the car with him. "I'm on my way to Las Vegas. We've got a long weekend coming up. It's a good place to disappear."

"You have someone with you?"

"A friend. Don't worry about me, just take care of Cherie and Humility, okay?"

"Trixie."

"I'm not calling her that ridiculous name."

Vader winked at Trixie, who made a face at him. "Keep your cell phone charged."

"Guaranteed. And thanks, Vader. Maybe my sister knew what she was doing after all. I hope so."

Vader handed the phone back to Cherie. She spoke a few more soft words to Jacob, then hung up, giving him an odd look in the process. "Three days ago he was furious with me."

Vader shrugged. "He's got bigger worries now."

Trixie piped up. "Did he say Las Vegas? Why's he going there?"

"He said he has a long weekend. He's got a friend with him."

Cherie tossed Trixie's phone back to her. "So what do we do now?"

It felt so good to have Cherie turning to him for advice. He could definitely get used to that.

"We should consider calling the police," he said. "If Mackintosh made threats and came onto the property, he broke the law."

"No," said Cherie firmly. "Jacob doesn't want us to, and he's the one Mackintosh is after."

Vader rubbed the back of his neck. "For all we know, Mackintosh could change his mind and come back tomorrow. We'll book a hotel room. A suite."

"No," said Cherie, again. "I've been scared of that man for too many years. If he comes back, I want to be here. I want to find out why he's after Jacob." She shot a glance at Vader. "First thing I'm going to do is call that lawyer. Maybe you were right about those charges. Maybe we need to go on the offensive."

"Much as I love those three little words, 'You were right,' I'm not sure about this, Cherie. I don't want you dealing with him alone if he shows up. And I have one more shift to work this week."

"I have a brilliant notion." Ginny raised her hand. "How about we invite some Bachelor Firemen over for dinner? If there's a bunch of strong men rattling around, he might think twice about coming back."

Trixie clapped her hands together. "You're a genius, Mrs. Brown! I vote for that idea. We can make my special squirrel chili, except with beef, of course . . ."

Vader tuned her out. His mother might be on to something. He had no intention of leaving Cherie unprotected for so much as a minute, and he wouldn't mind some backup from the San Gabriel firefighters, since the police weren't an option. But he also liked the idea of going on the offensive and tracking down the bastard before he tried anything else.

First things first. He knelt in front of his mother, noting the high color in her cheeks and the feverish brightness of her eyes. "Maybe you should go for that hotel room, Mom. I don't want you dealing with all this stress."

Ginny whacked him on the arm. "Don't you dare, Vader. This is my fault and I'm not going anywhere. Besides, you all might need me. This wheelchair can do some damage, especially if he's not expecting it."

Cherie laughed. "You heard her, Vader." She put her hand on Ginny's shoulder; Ginny reached up to cover it with hers. Despite his worry, Vader could have danced a jig at the sight. If this experience ended up bringing his mother and Cherie together, he might have to give Mackintosh a big thank-you. After he kicked his ass, of course.

The panic of knowing that Mackintosh had actually *come into the house* kept hitting Cherie with new waves of gut-wrenching nausea. This was exactly what she'd feared all these years, except even worse. Why was he looking for Jacob? She could handle threats against her, but not her loyal, vulnerable brother.

Maybe Mackintosh had figured that out. Maybe it was all some kind of trick. If only she knew what Mackintosh was thinking.

"So here's the plan," Vader said.

Trixie propped her feet on the coffee table. "Who put you in charge?"

"Me," Cherie said firmly. She knew she wasn't thinking clearly. Thank the merciful heavens for Vader. Especially this sure, in-charge, decisive side of Vader.

Vader continued as if no one had spoken. "Trixie, you don't leave my mother's side. You both keep your cell phones with you at all times and put 911 on speed dial. Any sound, anything the least bit suspicious, you call 911. I don't care what Jacob wants, if it's an emergency, you call 911. Got it?"

Trixie nodded and started punching numbers into her phone.

"Cherie, you call that lawyer and tell her you need to meet right away. Use my name this time, please. I did some work on her house and she owes me. See if she can give you some kind of legal-looking document you can wave at Mackintosh if he comes back. I'll be here tonight, but starting tomorrow I'll set up a rotation with the guys. Someone will be checking on the house every hour. If anyone sees a strange man, they're going to call me."

"Vader, surely we can do more than that," Ginny complained. "Why don't we try to find out where Mackintosh is staying? I could do some searching online. If he found me, I bet I can find him."

"Internet searching is fine, but nothing more than that," said Vader.

"I'll call the lawyer right now," Cherie told everyone, then realized she had no idea where her cell phone was. Everything had happened so fast. She'd gotten the panic text from Trixie, she'd broken all the speed limits to get home, she'd burst into the house . . .

Right. She'd dropped her tote bag in the entryway. Shakily, she made her way into the relative quiet of the little foyer, with its coatrack and catch-all table and the fish tank, where the oblivious banana fish and reef fish were gliding peacefully to and fro. Somehow, the quiet of the room brought out all the accumulated adrenaline in her system. Her hands trembled so much that she had trouble searching her bag. When she finally fished her phone out, it slipped through her fingers onto the polished floor with a dull clunk.

It winked up at her in its silver case, as if reminding her of how crazy things had gotten. An hour earlier, she'd been fielding calls from tango students about her newfound YouTube stardom. Then the message from Trixie had come. How could things fall apart so fast? She bent down to retrieve the phone, the YouTube video running through her mind. What if Mackintosh saw it? Would he forget about Jacob and attack Vader?

"You okay?" Vader crouched next to her. His strong thighs flexed under the khaki of his pants. She caught his scent, that essential Vader combination of firehouse and body soap, comfort and strength. With a sob she turned and buried her face in his chest.

"Shhh," he soothed. "There's nothing to cry about. It's going to be fine. No one's going to let anything happen to you."

"But . . . what about you? If he sees YouTube, he'll know I'm with you, and if he goes after you, I'll never—"

"Shhh."

He gathered her into his arms, so the rest of her panicky words were buried against his huge chest. After snagging her phone, he rose to his feet. Taking the stairs two at a time, he carried her up to the third floor. As always, his sheer strength astonished her. Inside her bedroom, he kicked the door closed and settled onto her bed, cradling her in his lap. "It's a lot quieter up here. Trixie and my mother are still jabbering away down there. My mom's been through a car accident, a house fire, a runaway husband—not to mention childbirth. It's okay for Trixie, but I thought my mom would keep her cool a little better, being a future fire captain's mother." He winked.

Typical Vader, trying to lighten the moment. It was incredibly sweet, though probably doomed. She wiped the tears off her cheeks and tried to get a handle on everything spinning through her mind. "Since Trixie showed up, everything's upside down. Soren and Nick are gone, you're living in my house, Mackintosh is in San Gabriel, I'm on YouTube, and Jacob's barely speaking to me! What is going on?"

Vader nodded wisely. "I read it in the paper. Mercury's in retrograde. It's the only explanation."

At his solemn expression, she let out a giggle. "You win. You're trying to make me laugh, aren't you?"

He encompassed her in that warm brown gaze of his, as if filling her veins with honey and comfort. "You're so beautiful when you laugh," he said simply. She gazed back at him, struck with wonder that someone like Vader had stuck by her through all this craziness.

"Now are you going to make that call to the lawyer or are you going to let the big strong fireman do it?"

She gave a loud sniff. "No, I can do it. Thanks, Vader. I—" Emotion churned in her heart. There were so many things clamoring to get out—love, gratitude, awe—but she had to sort them all out first. Before anything else, she had to talk to that lawyer. "I'll be down soon."

"I'm going to check all the windows and doors, make sure everything's locked up. Then I'm going to swing by the firehouse and gather the troops. I'll see you later." He lifted her off his lap, set her onto the bed, then gave her a sweet, lingering kiss, as if he was pressing a chocolate drop to her lips.

After he left, she stared at her bedroom door for a good five minutes before she remembered what she was doing with her phone in her hand.

The next day brought nothing but tension and waiting. Cherie called in sick for all her jobs. The hours ticked by, but Mackintosh made no appearance. Cherie wasn't sure if this was good or bad. Not that she wanted to see him, but if she did, at least she'd know what he was up to.

The waiting was agonizing for all of them. Ginny wrote a month's worth of blog posts. Trixie spent a lot of time on the computer, looking up information about Las Vegas. Or something to do with Las Vegas, anyway. And the lawyer finally called Cherie back.

The conversation brought Cherie bittersweet relief. The woman told her she had no need to worry, that the "marriage" wasn't remotely legal. The flip side was that if Prophesize knew that, it wouldn't keep Mackintosh from going after one of her sisters. As for filing charges against him, the lawyer said she would discreetly check with someone in the Arkansas legal system before deciding what step to take next.

"Say hi to that big bear Vader, would you?" the lawyer said wistfully, just before they hung up. "Tell him if he wants to cover this session with more work around the house, I'm open to that."

"That's okay," said Cherie quickly. "It's my problem, my responsibility." She didn't add, *my man*, but she thought it.

It took her long hours to fall asleep that night. For six years she'd lived with the aftermath of that crazy night in Arkansas. Why hadn't she talked to a lawyer earlier? She could have fought back through the legal system instead of hiding out, afraid to make waves. It was probably too late to file charges by now. In a stupid effort to shield her sisters, she'd turned down Vader's proposals. She'd allowed Mackintosh to steal her chance at happiness.

It's not stolen, she told herself, as drowsiness finally crept through her. *The next time I see Vader, I'm going to tell him how much I love him. Have loved him, all along.*

Maybe he'll try that proposal again. This time I know exactly what to say. "Hell, yes!"

On that thought, she fell asleep.

Barely an hour later, Trixie was shaking her awake. "We have to go. Now."

"What?" Cherie rubbed her eyes, struggling from the nest of sheets twined around her body. "What are you talking about?"

"It's Jacob. We have to go."

Nothing was guaranteed to make Cherie move faster. She leaped out of bed, staggering from her tangle of sheets. "What about Jacob?"

Trixie thrust a bundle of clothes at her. "I was thinking about Mr. Mackintosh and remembering everything he said when he was here. First he said, 'Where is he?' I said, 'I don't know what you're talking about.' He just stared at me with this mean look. Then I said, 'If you mean Jacob, he doesn't live here anymore.' He said, in a horrible voice, 'That spawn of Satan will pay.' After that Mrs. Brown was about to press her alert button, so he left. Please, Cherie, get dressed, we have to go!"

Cherie tried to make sense of Trixie's jumble of words. "He hates Jacob. He hates everyone gay." She pulled on a skirt, with no idea if it was right side around or not.

"That's the thing. When he first came in here and said, 'Where is he,' what if he didn't mean Jacob? What if he meant Robbie?"

"*Robbie?* His son Robbie?"

"Yes. What if he thinks Robbie is with Jacob?"

Cherie fumbled with the top Trixie had given her. "Why would Robbie be with Jacob?"

"Weren't they friends back in Arkansas?"

Cherie didn't remember any particular friendship, but that didn't mean anything. The implications were rocketing through her brain, spreading panic in their wake. "If Mackintosh thinks Jacob's helping Robbie, he'll kill him."

"Exactly. That's why I woke you up. I tried to call Jacob but he didn't answer and I'm really, really scared."

Cherie examined her sister's face. Was she really scared? Or was this a ploy of some kind? "Are you up to something, Trixie?"

"No! What do you mean? I'm worried about Jacob, that's all!" The worry on her young face seemed completely genuine, and Cherie suddenly felt bad for doubting her.

By now adequately clothed, though she had no idea which clothes they were, she grabbed a random pair of shoes from her closet and headed for the door. Trixie followed.

"If Jacob's in trouble, we should call the police," Cherie told Trixie over her shoulder.

"I thought about that, but what are we going to say? We don't even know if Mackintosh is in California or Nevada. We don't even know what car he's driving. Or what car Jacob's driving, for that matter."

Cherie ran down the stairs in her bare feet, with Trixie right on her heels. When she reached the ground floor, she paused. "We have to tell Mrs. Brown what's happening."

"Let's leave her a note. She had a rough night, we shouldn't wake her. She'll be safe because the firefighters have been stopping by all night long."

"A note works. I just don't want her to worry." Cherie ran to the entryway, where she grabbed a pen from the jelly bean jar and scribbled a note that read,

Dear Mrs. Brown, Jacob might be in trouble. Call us as soon as you wake up. Don't worry about us, and keep the door locked. After a quick second of deliberation, she added, *Warmest wishes, Cherie and Trixie Harper.*

Trixie came up behind her and gave her a little push. "Come on, I have your purse right here. Hurry!"

Cherie ran for the door and burst outside. The night was cool and dark, with a sliver of a moon tangled in the tops of the eucalyptus tree. All she could think of was Mackintosh finding Jacob and beating him or shooting him or using one of his do-it-yourself bombs on him. The panic pounded through her like a deafening horn section.

One thought managed to penetrate through her fear. "I should call Vader."

"He's on shift tonight, remember? I already called him and asked if we could use his van. He told me where the keys were." She jingled them in the palm of her hand.

"His van? You mean the Suburban for his mother?"

"Well, we can't take your old rattletrap. We'd break down before we hit the highway."

They'd reached the sidewalk. Trixie hurried toward Vader's dark-blue Chevy Suburban, which he'd modified to transport his mother to doctor's appointments.

Cherie stopped dead. "Highway? What's your plan here, exactly?"

Trixie rolled her eyes. "What is wrong with you? We're doing the logical thing, of course."

The combination of Trixie and "logic" had to be trouble. "Which is . . . ?"

"We're going to Las Vegas."

Chapter Twenty-Four

Vader had never worked a longer shift. Even though he knew Cherie's house was locked up tight, and that Joe the Toe and several of the B shift guys were planning to cruise by at regular intervals, he could barely sleep. Should they all have gone to a hotel, just to be safe? Just how wacko was this guy?

As he lay on the narrow bed that never seemed quite big enough for his frame—at home, he went for the California-king size—he looked back over everything that had passed between him and Cherie and made an important decision. Mackintosh's appearance had made her strange, ambiguous situation all too real. Cherie was going to have to deal with her past before things went any further. He couldn't do it for her. If she didn't know his heart by now, she never would. The ball was in her court.

He'd still do everything he could to keep her safe, of course. He'd still be there for her and Trixie. But—

even though it killed him to think this way—the next move belonged to her. He needed to give her space to sort out the situation with Mackintosh. Not easy for a macho, take-charge guy like himself to take the back-seat and let someone else do the steering. But he'd just have to shut up and go with it.

He checked his cell phone. Two in the morning. The last text from B shift Brett had come in at one—*All clear, Chippendale.* Joe the Toe was going to drive by on his way to work, around six the next morning. That left five hours when no one would be stopping by. But he'd checked all possible entry points and made sure the house was secure. Besides, his mother never slept particularly well. If she heard anything strange, she'd text him right away.

Rolling onto his side, he turned his back on his phone. If he had any brains, he'd get some sleep before another call came in. Maybe he should have joined the police force instead of the fire department. He could pull some strings, find out where Mackintosh was staying, hunt him down and pistol-whip him all the way back to Arkansas.

"Down, boy," he muttered to himself. His primitive side was never far from the surface, and this situation was definitely bringing it out. "Keep it real, Vader. Keep it real."

Nonetheless, the pleasant fantasy of knocking Mackintosh, who took the form of a heavyweight boxer in his head—someone who would put up a sat-isfying fight—into a bloody heap lulled Vader to sleep. Dream images took its place. In one of them, Mack-intosh rode to town in a hay wagon that burst into flames. In another, Vader, as captain, called Mack-intosh into his office and suspended him. Mackintosh fell to his knees, pleading for mercy, but Vader turned his back while Fred dragged him out of the office. In all of them, Cherie was crying and begging for help.

The ringing of his phone woke him up in a cold sweat. On autopilot, he swung his feet over the side of the bed as if an incident call had come in. Then he realized the red light in the hall wasn't flashing and no tone blared over the intercom.

He snatched up his phone. "Yeah?"

"Vader, I think Trixie and Cherie are gone." It was his mother.

"What?" He bolted to his feet.

"I heard a noise—you know how lightly I sleep— and heard them whispering. Then I heard the door open and close. I came out into the hall and called up the stairs but no one answered. I'd go upstairs and check if I could. This darn wheelchair. I can't be sure, but I don't think they're here, hon."

Vader rubbed his fist across his eyes, trying to clear his thoughts. "Did you hear a man's voice too?"

"No. Just them."

"Maybe they went out to run an errand or some-thing."

"At four in the morning?"

Vader grunted. He was trying to think of someone to call upon at four in the morning. If he skipped out on his shift, not only would he never make captain, but he'd face disciplinary action.

"Have you tried calling their phones?"

"Yes. Neither of them answered."

"F . . . udge."

"I'm sorry to bother you during your shift." His mother sounded wretched. "I just didn't know what else to do. If they're upstairs sleeping, I'm going to feel just awful."

"No, you did the right thing, Mom. Give me a

minute. I'll see if I can rouse someone. Hang tight, I'll call you right back."

In his shorts and t-shirt, he took his cell out to the parking lot so he wouldn't disturb anyone. As he dialed Joe the Toe's number, his mind raced. How could he leave his shift five hours early? If Truck 1 was called to a fire, they wouldn't have a tillerman. He'd be potentially putting everyone on his crew in danger, not to mention the citizens who got less than a full crew fighting their fire. He couldn't do that. It would betray all his principles as a proud San Gabriel firefighter.

But how could he just stand by if something terrible had happened to Cherie and Trixie? Maybe he could quickly run home, check on things, then make it back before anyone noticed. Or maybe Joe would answer.

But Joe didn't answer. He must have turned his phone off for the night. Just for kicks, he tried both Cherie and Trixie. Neither answered. With a feeling of inevitability, Vader began dialing another number. Maybe he was making the wrong choice, but it was the only one he could make. Cherie was going to hate him for it.

Cherie put the key into the ignition of Vader's van while Trixie practically jitterbugged in the passenger seat. "You're sure this is all right with Vader? What if his mother needs the van?" And wouldn't he be worried about her and Trixie going off alone?

" 'Course I'm sure. He trusts us. Well, not me, but you."

That rang true. But still, she hesitated.

"Just drive, would you? Do we have to just sit here like sitting ducks? Mercy above, look back there. I think that might be Mackintosh's old Buick."

Cherie glanced in the rearview mirror. Everything seemed quiet, nothing but cars and bushes and streetlamps and telephone poles. She couldn't spot a Buick. But just then, a movement caught her eye. Someone stood up from behind a car across the street. In the darkness, she could see only the outline of his body—wide, stocky chest, deerhunter cap.

Mackintosh had always worn a cap just like that one, made of grease-stained tweed.

Cherie started the van and slammed her foot on the accelerator. The man stalked after them. She floored it. The Suburban went screaming down the street, taking the corner so fast the van nearly tilted onto two wheels. Trixie bumped against the passenger side door.

"Buckle your seat belt, you ditz," yelled Cherie.

As she buckled, Trixie twisted around to look behind her. "It's not Mackintosh!" She gasped. "I got a good look at him when he stepped under the street-light. That man's much younger."

"That's good, but let's get the heck out of here anyway." Cherie drove toward the closest main road, her heart racing from the scare about Mackintosh. She tried to collect her thoughts. "Okay, now that you've scared the life out of me, let's talk this over. Do you know for sure that Jacob's in some kind of danger?"

"If he's with Robbie, he is."

That much was true. "But we don't even know exactly where Jacob is. What's this brilliant plan of yours? And why do we have to leave in the middle of the night?"

"The plan is this. We know Jacob was heading to Las Vegas, so we'll head that way too. As soon as we know where he is, all three of us will be together so we can protect each other. Harpers stick together, right? It's a good plan because it gets us out of San Gabriel and away from Mackintosh. Also we stop putting Mrs.

Brown in the middle of our crazy family drama. The reason we have to leave tonight is in case Mackintosh comes back tomorrow."

Cherie shook her head as she veered around a slow-moving station wagon. "I don't feel right leaving Mrs. Brown alone."

"She has all those firefighters watching out for her. Jacob doesn't have anyone."

Cherie had a quick vision of her brother's wry smile and teasing blue eyes. She and Jacob had always watched out for each other. She felt an overwhelming urge to be with him, to protect him.

But leaving without Vader didn't feel right. She thought about all the times Vader had given unstintingly of himself, his time, his heart. And all the times she'd pushed him away. Wouldn't he want to be part of this trip?

She handed Trixie her phone. "Do me a favor and ask Vader if he wants to come with us."

"Cherie! He's on shift. He can't come and he's probably asleep. How about if I just text him? He'll get it when he wakes up." She was already tapping out the words.

"Read it to me before you send it."

The whoosh of an outgoing text interrupted her. "I already sent it," said Trixie. "I said, *We're on our way to Las Vegas to find Jacob, thanks for the van. If you want to come with us, call us as soon as you get off shift. Love you always.*"

"*What?*"

"Well, it's true, right? You love him."

"That doesn't mean I want to tell him like that, with a text that I didn't even write!"

"Oh, pooh on you." Trixie shrugged in her carefree way. "If it was up to you, you'd wait until he was dead in his grave. He's a fireman, you know. Something could happen any time he gets called to a fire. He could be in trouble right now, trapped in a burning house, screaming . . ."

"Trixie," Cherie said sharply, unable to tolerate the images popping into her head. Not now, not when she had a dawn road trip to navigate. "I'm about to kick you right out of this car. Did Vader answer the text?"

Trixie looked at her phone, which made the "dinging" sound of an incoming text. "He just answered. He said he'll call first chance he gets."

Cherie relaxed a tiny fraction. Whatever else this crazy trip held, she wouldn't be skipping out on Vader. She squinted at the road up ahead, on which green highway signs loomed next to a freeway entrance. "I have to think about the best way to get to Las Vegas."

"Highway 5," said Trixie promptly. "The on-ramp's right up there."

Cherie shook her head. She had to hand it to her sister; when she wanted something to happen, she did her homework. "See any cars behind us?"

"Nope. No one followed us. We're safe. And we're going to Las Vegas!" Trixie bounced in her seat and hooted.

Cherie thought "safe" was overstating the situation, but as she turned onto the entrance of the southbound 5, she realized it felt good to be taking some kind of action. Much better than sitting in the house waiting for Mackintosh to show up.

Vader had dialed half of the San Gabriel Police Department's number when he got Cherie's text. He ended the call, since there was no point in reporting two girls deciding to drive to Las Vegas.

"Vegas? In my van?" he said out loud, to the empty cars. "You're fucking kidding me." Right away he texted Cherie back. *Call me right this second.*

When two minutes passed during which she didn't call, he called her. No answer. Then he called his mother back. "Can you look out the window and see if the Suburban is gone?"

After a pause, he got his answer. "Yes, how odd."

"Can you check to see if the keys are in my room? I left them on the dresser."

Another pause, accompanied by the soft squeak of her wheelchair and followed by a gasp. "Your keys are gone!"

Vader nearly threw the phone across the parking lot. Cherie had snuck into his room, taken his car keys, and headed to Las Vegas without a second thought. While he'd been debating ditching his firefighting career to run home and see if she was safe, she was running off to Vegas.

But wait. What if Cherie hadn't done all that? What if her demon seed little sister was behind all this? How could he find out? Face it. He wouldn't know what was really going on until they freaking called him back.

"Hang on a minute, Mom."

He put the phone on mute, stuffed it in his pocket, clenched his fists, threw his head back and roared at the night sky. Then he did it again. His howl of frustration vibrated in his chest, every muscle in his body tight as steel cable. When he was done, when he'd taken the edge off his fury, he picked the phone up again.

"They've gone to Las Vegas, Mom. Don't worry about them. Just go back to sleep and I'll see you when I'm off shift."

"*Las Vegas?*"

"Yup. Cherie texted me that they're going to find Jacob. It makes sense. They're close."

"Well, of course they're close. They're all part of the Heavenly Harpers."

"Huh?"

"When I was poking around on the Web, I found out that the family used to perform at county fairs as the Heavenly Harpers. That's how I found Mackintosh's e-mail. He used to book their performances."

"They were harp players?" Vader was starting to wonder if this entire episode was a surreal dream. He'd probably wake up at any second.

"No, no. They sang. Gospel and country. They were so good they got offered a recording contract, but the father turned it down. They stopped performing after that."

Vader clawed a hand through his hair. "It must be someone else. Cherie doesn't sing."

"Are you sure about that? I listened to one of their songs online and they sounded beautiful. Voices like crystallized honey. The Heavenly Harpers is a good name for them."

With a silent howl of frustration, Vader decided he had an even better name for them. The Deceitful Duo. The Little Liars. He couldn't believe Cherie would hide something like that from him, something so little and yet so big.

If she could do that, why couldn't she steal his van behind his back? Had anything about her ever been real?

"I can't even deal with this right now, Mom. Look, go back to bed. We've lost enough sleep over those two. I'll be off in a few hours."

"Are you all right, Vader?"

"Snazzy." Except it might be time for another midnight howl. "Call me if anything else comes up."

On his way back into the apparatus bay, he nearly collided with Double D, who was stepping into his turnout boots, wearing nothing but his boxers and a baggy white T-shirt.

"Whatcha doin', D?"

"Heard something," the veteran mumbled. "Heard a yell. We catch a fire? Wait for me. I'm up. I'm up."

Vader tried hard not to crack up, and failed. "It's all right, Double D. No fire. I was just letting off some steam. Come on, let's get you back to bed."

"Okey-dokey, Mr. Pokey."

Vader, smothering a snort, considered whipping out his phone and taking a quick video of Double D. Maybe a sleepwalking fireman in his underwear would make people forget about his pole dance. Instead he led the man gently inside and steered him toward his room.

No one else had heard his crazy early morning caterwauling. He got back into bed, then texted Cherie again. No answer. She was probably driving on the highway and couldn't look at her phone. Or she and Trixie were blasting the radio and singing at the top of their lungs.

Because they were freaking *singers* and not only had Cherie never mentioned it, but she'd actually told him she *never sang*. And he'd believed her, like the sucker he was. Every time he thought he knew her, something else surfaced. He looked at the text she'd sent him. *We're on our way to Las Vegas to find Jacob, thanks for the van. If you want to come with us, call us as soon as you get off shift. Love you always.*

Yeah, right. She might as well have texted, *Ditched you, stole your van, made an ass out of you, love ya!* Even if Trixie was somehow behind the whole thing—which he suspected—Cherie had gone along with it. The least she could do was answer her damn phone. A slow burn of anger made his stomach pitch. How was he supposed to explain to the guys that they'd been dragging themselves over to Gardam Street to watch over two girls who were now on their way to Vegas? And how *could* they have taken his van? What if he needed it to take his mom to the doctor?

He punched his pillow. There was nothing more he could do tonight. *Go to sleep, asshole*, he told himself. And this time, he did.

He made it through the rest of the shift without incident. A grease fire at a donut shop woke him up around six. It was quickly dealt with, and he got back to the station around nine. For the hell of it, he tried Cherie again. Still no answer. He was changing back into civilian clothes when his phone rang. He snatched it up. Finally, she was calling him. Boy, he was going to let her have it.

"Vader, there's something else I just thought of," said his mother before he even said hello. Vader could barely speak through the sharp disappointment.

"What, Mom?"

"Yesterday I was trying to get Izzy down from the front windowsill—you know how he likes to play with that curtain fringe—when I saw a car cruising past, nice and slow. It caught my eye and I was going to mention it but forgot in all the excitement. It was an old make of Buick, a tan color."

"Okay." A car had driven past the house. So? He bit back his impatience.

"Well, its plates were coated with mud. It's been so dry here, I don't know why they would have been muddy."

"Muddy plates. Hmm." Vader yawned, and took a swig of Red Bull. "Maybe the dude just finished a road trip."

"Well, but you couldn't read what state it was from. Just out of curiosity, I checked the weather online and it's been raining a lot in Pine Creek, Arkansas. It must be very muddy there."

"Did you ever see it again?"

"No, because Izzy lost interest in those particular curtains and started stalking the fish tank again. But Vader, what if it belonged to that Mr. Mackintosh? What if he was watching the house and now he's chasing after them? Or what if he made them leave somehow?"

Vader went silent. He ran through everything his mother had told him, Cherie's text, her unusual behavior. Something wasn't adding up. For all her wariness about sharing her secrets, Cherie wasn't a thoughtless person. She'd never take off and leave him without a way to transport his mother in an emergency. Maybe it was just Trixie pulling one of her stunts. Maybe it was Mackintosh. Either way, he didn't have a choice. He had to go after them.

He swung the wheel of his truck, making a U-turn toward the highway. "Mom, will you be okay for a day? I think I'd better go to Vegas. I'll make sure the crew keeps checking on you."

"You go. I'll be fine. As a matter of fact, I'll be the envy of every girl in San Gabriel. I bet I'm the only crippled lady with a complete list of the personal phone numbers of the Bachelor Firemen."

"Rawr. You naughty cougar. You be careful and call me if you think of anything else."

He tossed the phone aside and floored the accelerator.

Chapter Twenty-Five

*W*hile Cherie, at the wheel, fought the fatigue that threatened to make her veer off the road, Trixie sent off a flurry of texts on her cell phone.

"Who are you talking to?" Cherie asked.

"I'm just trying to find out exactly where Jacob might be. And I'm trying to locate Robbie too."

"Any luck?"

"Nothing yet. But it's still early."

Cherie inhaled the slightly antiseptic scent of the Suburban's interior. It held only a trace of Vader, since he used his truck ninety percent of the time. "I sure hope Vader comes. I'd feel a lot better if he was with us."

Trixie looked out at the sunrise gilding the world with beams of pink and gold light. "Maybe it's better this way. Why should anyone else be in danger because of us?"

That question hit Cherie hard. Putting others in

danger was exactly what she'd been trying to avoid all this time. "You mean, because of me."

"I mean because of *us*. If Mackintosh can't get you back, he'll move on to me." Cherie glanced over at Trixie. All the flightiness, the carefree teasing, had dropped away. With the just-rising sun kissing her face, she looked much older than eighteen.

Cherie gripped the cloth-covered steering wheel. "We won't let him."

"You've been scared of him all this time, haven't you? That's why you don't really get involved with anyone, even someone like Vader."

"I'm involved with Vader."

"Not as much as you want to be," Trixie said in a knowing voice, as if she'd seen a million relationships come and go in her time.

"Well, that's because it's complicated."

"You make it complicated because you're afraid of Mackintosh. What makes you think you're so much safer alone?"

Cherie gritted her teeth. "You're barely eighteen and you've spent your entire life in the backwoods. What do you know about it?"

Trixie either ignored that or hadn't heard it. She was busy texting again. "You know what I don't understand? Why didn't you just marry Vader? You'd be a lot safer that way."

Cherie drew in a deep breath. Trixie didn't have the whole story. She didn't know that Cherie's signature was sitting on a piece of paper somewhere, and that piece of paper meant she couldn't just do whatever she wanted.

"I might be married to Mackintosh," she blurted.

"What?" For the first time, she had Trixie's full attention. The girl even dropped her phone onto the floorboards.

"Well, it turns out I'm probably not, but they made me sign a document and they drugged me and . . ."

"Holy catfish on a spit. Does Vader know?"

"Now he does."

"That changes everything." She chewed on her lip. "If you're actually married to him, then he's definitely going to come after us when he's done with Jacob. He's demented about his possessions. We borrowed his mule and he came over to check on it like three times a day."

Cherie didn't care for that comparison. "I'm not a mule. Or one of his possessions, for that matter. And I'm not actually married to him. The lawyer said it wasn't legal."

"But you're not thinking like Mackintosh. In his eyes, you're not only married to him, but you belong to him just like a runaway mule would." She snapped her fingers. "I know! We have to find a hotel room."

"What? Why?"

"Duh, we have to change our appearance. Plus we have to ditch the van and find another vehicle. Oh, I just thought of something! What if Mackintosh is following us and we lead him to Jacob? We can't let that happen. We'll definitely have to ditch the van."

Cherie put a hand to her forehead, where a nagging ache had appeared. The road seemed to be wavering back and forth before her eyes. She counted up the hours of sleep she'd gotten in the past few nights and didn't pass single digits. "Trixie, you're being crazy. I'd say you've watched too many episodes of *Law & Order*, but I know you've never even seen TV."

"I've seen enough. They play *Law & Order* at the feed store, in the back. We need a rental car and some hair dye. Unless you brought some with you."

"Yes, because the first thing I grab when I'm woken

up in the middle of the night is hair dye. My bag is full of it. Oh wait, what bag? I didn't bring *anything*, Trixie, remember?"

"Of course you didn't. That's because I brought everything we need. Everything I thought we'd need, that is. I have to admit I didn't think of hair dye." She frowned, concentrating. "That's okay. We can find a hair salon."

"I'm not going to sit under a hair dryer while Mackintosh goes after Jacob."

Trixie waved a nonchalant hand. Her brief moment of seriousness had sailed past and now she was back to teenage ditz. "So we'll get stuff at a pharmacy. No biggie. At least you can't deny we'll need different clothes."

"Why, are we disguising ourselves as sane people?"

"Your attitude could use some work, Cherie. At least the clothes part will be fun. I think we're going to pass some outlet stores. It's a good thing I brought all your tango money."

"You *what*?" The cash from her tango students constituted her emergency fund. She kept it in an old Crock-Pot in the kitchen.

"I knew you wouldn't mind. If anything's an emergency, it's trying to rescue Jacob."

Cherie was starting to wonder if the true emergency was Trixie's mental state. Maybe she ought to be driving straight for a psychiatrist's office.

"I just had another idea," Trixie continued. "Instead of a rental car, which is going to totally wipe out the tango money, maybe we should just trade in the van for a different car. You know, the way Justice-Denied is always trading in one junker for another."

That was it. Cherie threw up her hands, then clamped them back on the wheel. Trixie had clearly lost her mind. "Are you nuts?"

"Hey!" She sniffed. "You don't have to be so rude just because you don't like my ideas."

"I don't like your idea because it's stupid, not to mention illegal."

"Stop staying such mean things!"

"Trixie." Was there any way to get through such obstinate cluelessness? "Have you forgotten this is *Vader's van*? It belongs to him, not us."

"So? If you'd married him, it would be your van too."

"If I'd married him, I might be a bigamist!"

Trixie laughed. Cherie swiveled her head to look at her little sister, who clapped her hand over her mouth. Her blue eyes widened over the top of her hand. She spread her fingers apart to release a smothered "Sorry."

And then Cherie was laughing too, with an edge of hysteria she couldn't control. The absurdity of the entire situation sank home. She laughed so hard that tears leaked out of her eyes and she could barely see straight. "Did you really say we should trade Vader's *van*?" The last word came out as a shriek of laughter.

Trixie took her hand away from her mouth. "Maybe . . ." she gasped, "that was going . . . a little too far . . ."

"You think?" Still shaking with big gusts of laughter, Cherie alternated hands on the steering wheel so she could swipe the tears off her face with the free one. The highway kept blurring in and out.

How long had it been since she'd laughed with her sisters? There was no one in the world with whom you could giggle the way you could with a sister. When the gusts of laughter finally subsided, she drew in a deep, still shaky breath. Everything seemed lighter now, and much less terrifying.

She was trying to protect her gay brother from her

crazy, homophobic possible husband in a borrowed van with her madcap little sister—but things could be worse.

She let out a sigh and smiled at her little sister. "I think I needed that laugh."

Trixie returned a sunny smile, as if she were already concocting more crazy plans.

Cherie spotted a billboard advertisement for a Best Western off the next exit and decided it was a sign from above. "You did get one thing right, though. We need to get some rest. I'm not safe to drive right now."

Trixie peered out the window at the upcoming rest stop. It contained a Chevron gas station, the Best Western hotel, a Sizzler restaurant, an I-HOP, and that was about it. The place was as unglamorous as you could get. Her face fell. "Best Western? That's not what I pictured at all."

"Too bad. We're done doing this your way. Sorry, Trixie, I'm firing you as cruise director. We're going to get ourselves a room. We're both going to get some sleep. We're going to eat something. We're going to fill up the tank, because we're on empty. Then I'm going to make some calls and figure out what's next."

"Calls?" Trixie said nervously.

"Calls," Cherie repeated, more firmly. No doubt about it, Trixie was keeping something to herself. "We need to find out where Jacob is before we just go barreling blind into Las Vegas. This'll give Vader some time to catch up with us. I'll feel better once he's here."

She pulled off the highway and into the parking lot of the Best Western, which was comforting in its sheer generic familiarity. She and Jacob had splurged one night on a Best Western during their flight from Arkansas. Somehow it seemed appropriate to repeat the indulgence with Trixie.

When the clerk asked for her driver's license, she hesitated for a moment. But then she decided she was being overcautious. Even if Mackintosh was following them, he wasn't with the CIA. He was a farmer from backwoods Arkansas. He wouldn't have access to the hotel records. The bigger risk was that he would recognize Vader's Suburban. She'd make sure to park out of sight.

The hotel was nearly empty, so they had their pick of rooms. Cherie debated the issue of what sort of room would a fugitive choose? Isolated or surrounded by people? Ground floor or top floor? Near the ice machine or near the pool? It all seemed so ridiculous that she gave up and chose a room on the second floor, in the back. After she'd parked the Suburban in the most inconspicuous spot possible, she and Trixie let themselves into the room. Eyes gritty from fatigue, she'd barely put her head on the pillow before she was deeply asleep.

She was so exhausted, she forgot to call Vader and tell him which hotel they were at.

Luckily, Vader had LoJack on his Suburban.

He didn't want to report it stolen, because that would implicate Cherie—not that she didn't deserve it. But he knew that if he couldn't track them down, as a last resort, the police could. He also knew that the Suburban was low on gas. If they were leaving town in a hurry, in the middle of the night, they probably wouldn't have stopped for gas until they'd left San Gabriel. But just in case, he stopped at the few gas stations between Gardam Street and the southbound 5. No one had seen a big navy-blue Suburban.

He did the same thing at each gas station he passed.

Since he knew the license plate number and even had a recent receipt for his car registration in his wallet, he had no trouble questioning the gas station attendants. The problem was that each time he described Cherie, the angrier he got. Describing her was a humiliating reminder of how much truth she'd withheld from him.

"Red hair—well, usually. I'm not sure of her actual hair color because she always dyes it. The younger girl has light brown hair, except that right now it's dyed blond."

Since both sisters changed hair color on a whim, who knew what color it was now?

"One red, one blond?" The Pakistani clerk couldn't have sounded more bored.

"I guess they could have changed hair color, so never mind their hair. They both wear . . . I don't know. Dresses." This was why he was a firefighter, not a detective. You didn't have to take note of people's outfits while you were saving their houses. "Pretty ones. No jeans or anything like that. Unless they were traveling, you know, incognito."

The guy frowned. "Are these girls celebrities?"

"No." Unless you counted the Arkansas country fair circuit. "The Southern accent is a definite, but sometimes it's stronger than others. Mostly when Cherie— the redhead—is tired or upset."

Which she might be, if Mackintosh really was on their tail. The more he heard about the man, the more worried he got.

"So you're asking about two girls, who may or may not be red-haired and blond, who might or might not be wearing dresses, and who might be upset or tired?"

"They have names. Cherie and Trixie. No, hang on. Their real names are Chastisement and Humility."

It occurred to him that each could use a little dose of her own first name. Maybe he should change his name to "*Futility*."

The Pakistani clerk had nothing for him, nor did the attendants at the nine other gas stations he stopped at.

He stopped for lunch about halfway between San Gabriel and Las Vegas and wolfed down a turkey sub and a giant Red Bull. After all his years in the fire department, he knew how to operate on not much sleep. He also knew that he tended to get crabby in such situations.

Crabby was definitely on the menu today, sandwiched between anger at Cherie and worry about Mackintosh.

But the farther down the highway he got, the more the worry about Mackintosh dominated. He tried Cherie's cell phone several times, and even called Trixie's. But neither one of them answered. What if Mackintosh had caught up with them and they couldn't reach their phones? What if he was using them to lure Jacob into some kind of trap?

Toward evening, at a gas station just over the Nevada border, he finally got a tip. A Suburban had driven into the rest stop earlier in the day. The young attendant had seen a redhead and a blonde in the car, though he hadn't heard them speak or gotten a look at their clothes. Both were hot chicks.

Bingo. Though he himself wouldn't put Trixie in the "hot" category, unless "hot" included "radioactive."

The attendant didn't think the girls had left yet. Logic told him to check the hotel, since they were very likely as exhausted as he was. He drove slowly around the Best Western, scanning the parking lot. And there, all the way in the back, snuggled in a corner, he spotted his Suburban. The sight brought his simmering rage to a boil.

What if his mother had needed the van?

Many things he could forgive—had forgiven—but interfering with his ability to take care of his mother wasn't one of them. Cherie had better have a really, really good reason for what she'd done. He couldn't wait to hear it.

After knocking on all the nearby ground floor rooms and coming up empty, he bounded upstairs to the second floor. At the third knock, he heard scampering feet inside. His whole body went on alert, like a hunter who has finally spotted a deer.

He heard whispers, and something that sounded like a giggle. It was Trixie and Cherie. It had to be.

And that giggle was the last straw.

The two Harper sisters were laughing at him. At what a fool they'd made of him. At how they'd jerked him around like a lovesick puppet on a string. At how he'd thought he was rescuing them from Mackintosh, when they were perfectly safe the whole time. He thudded his fist on the door with one sharp blow.

The door swung open. Two pale, alarmed faces stared up at him, but all he saw was Cherie. Cherie with her voluptuous body and eyes full of secrets. Cherie with the generous nature but the barricaded soul. The woman who had snagged his heart from the very beginning, and who'd never taken him seriously.

And in that moment, he knew that he was done. Really, truly done. Once and for all.

Chapter Twenty-Six

*C*herie nearly fainted in relief at the sight of Vader. When the banging on the door had woken them up, both she and Trixie had been sure that Mackintosh had tracked them down. She'd scrambled out of bed, a current of panic running through her as she collided with Trixie, who'd started giggling hysterically. After the terror came a rush of fury that one man could still make her feel so vulnerable—that she'd let one nasty man control her life for so long.

At that point, she'd let go of Trixie and marched to the door. Trixie had scurried after her, either for protection or support, she wasn't sure. She peered in the peephole, but instead of Mackintosh's thick-jowled, squinty-eyed face, there was strong, handsome, *good* Vader silhouetted with the setting sun behind him.

She threw open the door, but before she could throw herself into his arms, he started talking. He didn't sound at all like the playful, ardent Vader she was used to. This Vader spoke with implacable cold-ness.

"I'm here for one reason only," he said. "Mackin-tosh. My mother thinks he might have followed you. Have you seen him?"

Numb, Cherie shook her head.

"Good. I'm going to be keeping watch in my truck. I would consider it a real favor if you wouldn't run off again behind my back."

"Behind your back? But you said—"

He threw up a hand to stop her. "There's no point. I'm done, Cherie. Even I have my limit, and you finally crossed it. I kept thinking I couldn't feel so much for someone who didn't feel anything for me, but I guess I don't know much about love."

Cherie tried to protest, but he kept going.

"I was so stupid, I thought loving you with all my heart would be enough. I was a big, goofy-ass fool. But I'm done now. As soon as we deal with Mackintosh, my mom and I are moving out. And you can go on with your life. In the meantime, I'll be out in the truck. And you might want to turn your freaking cell phones on."

He swung away from the door and disappeared down the outer balcony that wrapped around the back of the Best Western. Cherie stood frozen as the door clicked shut on its own.

"He looks pretty mad," Trixie said. "Are you all right, sis?"

She didn't answer. Whatever she was, the word "okay" did not apply. She wanted to check her body for broken bones, pierced organs, actual injuries that might explain why she felt mortally wounded.

Brushing past Trixie, she dug in her purse for her cell phone. She hadn't intended to sleep so long. Most of the day had disappeared. Maybe her cell phone had died. But no, it still had three percent battery left. It also displayed an array of missed calls and messages from Vader.

"I didn't hear any calls," she said, puzzled. Then she turned the phone over, and saw the little button had been pushed, the one that kept calls from coming through. She frowned at it, thinking it must have gotten clicked by accident. Then, just to torture herself, she listened to Vader's last message. "I got your text. Call me, Cherie. This is *not* cool. Not cool at all."

She looked up at Trixie. "You said he offered us the van."

Trixie stuck out her chin. She was still in her underwear, little panties and a ribbed baby T that made her look like an underage model in a Calvin Klein ad. "He loves you. He would have offered it."

Cherie drew in a deep breath. "I told you to tell him to join us." Even as she said it, she scrolled through her text messages until she found Vader's answer. "*Call me right this second,*" she read aloud.

Trixie dropped her head in shame.

"And then, what'd you do, turn the ringer off so I wouldn't hear his calls?"

A microscopic nod.

"What about the note I left for Mrs. Brown?"

"Fish tank," whispered Trixie.

"What in blue blazes are you trying to achieve, Trixie? You're trying to make Vader hate me? What evil little plan are you working on?"

Trixie's head swung up, eyes spitting fire. "I don't have an evil little plan. I have a good plan. Anyway, what do you care? You don't want Vader anyway!"

"Why, you little— Let me get this straight. You lied about getting Vader's permission to use his van, then ignored his texts? He must have been frantic. He's been nothing but good to you and that's how you treat him? That's how you treat *me*?"

"Who are you to talk?" Trixie stamped her foot in a passion. "If I had someone like Vader who loved me, I'd never let him go!"

Cherie waved the phone toward the door. "You just took care of that for me, didn't you?"

"Oh, you're always going hot and cold on him. If you're so worried about Vader, what are you doing standing here talking to me?"

Cherie stared at her little sister, who could drive you crazy one moment, and hit on the most important thing in the world the very next. She checked her phone, which still had only three percent battery, and decided to leave it on the charger. "We're not done here. I'm so upset with you I could scream. You lied right and left! What were you thinking?"

"I didn't mean any harm! I didn't want to wait. I wanted to leave right away. Then you made us stay in this stupid hotel and—"

Cherie threw up her hands and turned toward the door. "Don't go anywhere."

"You're leaving me here alone?" Trixie asked anxiously.

"Lock the door. Don't open it unless it's me. Then again, *I* might strangle you."

Cherie ran out the door, onto the second floor landing, and leaned over the railing. She didn't see Vader, but his baby-blue truck was parked conspicuously on the other side of the parking lot. It was empty. "Vader," she called, but he didn't answer. She wouldn't blame him if he never answered her again. If he thought they'd run off to Vegas in such a screw-you way, no wonder he despised her. She would have deserved it.

But she hadn't, and she at least deserved a chance to explain.

"Vader," she called again, louder, feeling like Juliet calling down to Romeo from her balcony. When she still got no answer, she headed for the stairs that would take her to the ground floor. Maybe he hadn't gotten to his truck yet. Maybe he had put the seat back to take a nap.

Twilight was descending onto the anonymous stretch of highway that soared overhead. The steady roar of the nearby 5 sounded like an especially noisy ocean. It reminded her of the time Vader had taken her to the beach in Santa Barbara, and how much fun they'd had playing in the waves. He'd let her ride on his shoulders and helped her swan dive into the water. Vader had been as excited as a kid, showing her how to float on her back and dog paddle. All Vader ever wanted to do was enjoy life and lavish love on her. And she'd been too afraid to let him.

The parking lot lights blinked to life as she hurried across the asphalt to his truck. Peering in the passenger side window, she saw that the driver's seat and spacious crew cab were both empty. The sight of the Ford's interior sparked another little surge of emotion. She spotted Vader's beloved ram horn necklace hanging from the rearview mirror. It had been gifted to him by the so-called Goddesses he'd helped out in Loveless, Nevada after the wildfire. They'd informed Vader that the ram was his totem animal, which made sense to Cherie. The cup holder still held a Red Bull. His car charger was still plugged in.

Everything Vader, except Vader.

She pulled back from the truck and scanned the lot. Maybe he'd gone to the Sizzler for some food. He probably hadn't eaten much, what with pursuing two thoughtless girls across the California border. "Sorry, Vader," she whispered to his totem necklace. "Sorry for everything."

She decided to just call him, then remembered she'd left her cell phone charging in the hotel room. No problem; she'd dash over to the Sizzler and check for him there. She squinted toward the restaurant, where red neon lights shone through the blue twilight. If Vader wasn't at the Sizzler, she'd just wait by his vehicle. He had to come back sometime. He'd said he was spending the night in his truck, and he always did what he said.

A bit nervously—it was getting dark, and she supposed it was possible that Mackintosh had followed them, though unlikely—she crossed the parking lot and headed down the sidewalk that hugged the wall of the Best Western. She'd feel a lot safer once she reached the busier thoroughfare between the restaurant and the hotel.

But she didn't even make it that far. As she rounded the corner, she slammed into a large, male body that stank of nervous sweat, old car, and tobacco juice.

Mackintosh.

Numbly, she looked up at the familiar, squinty-eyed face. Six years hadn't changed him much. They'd added a bit of extra flesh to his jowls, sunk his eyes deeper into the ruddy elephant folds of his leathery face. He was sweating like an old hog and breathing heavily, as if he'd just expended a tremendous amount of energy.

"What'd you do?" she asked, nonsensically. But a horrifying suspicion was dawning. No sign of Vader, and here was Mackintosh, looking like he'd just run up a mountain. "*What'd you do?*"

"Taught that boy a lesson. He needs to stay away

from my rightful wife," said Mackintosh, in his broad, backwoods cadence. He wiped his hands on his overalls. "You think I didn't see the video the whole town's talking about? I'm not buried in the last century like your father."

"Where is he?" Strangely enough, after all these years of fearing Mackintosh, now that he was right here in front of her, all she could think about was Vader. "What did you do?"

"What had to be done."

"You're crazy as a sick rooster."

He reached for her, but she wrenched her arm away before he could touch it.

"I'm not your wife. I checked with a lawyer and that so-called wedding was not legal."

"I got signed papers." He patted his jacket, the same sort of waist-length denim workingman's jacket he'd worn ever since she could remember. Under it he wore a limp-collared once-white shirt. The sight of the frayed edges brought back the suffocating atmosphere of Pine Creek.

She nearly gagged. "It doesn't matter. I was underage, you drugged me, and there was no official witness. You can't get away with any of this, Mackintosh."

He squinted at her, his mouth working. She knew he had a serious tobacco addiction, but wasn't chewing any at the moment. Maybe he'd run out. *That* would do wonders for his mood.

"We'll keep this real simple. Your daddy gave you to me. We signed the papers. I held up my end, but you didn't. I told him the only way to make it right, since I had a missing bride, was if I could have Humility. Prophesize said it would have to be my son who got her. But then she run off too. So did Robbie.

Now I want my damn son back. So you're coming with me."

Holy spit on a cracker, Mackintosh was even crazier than she remembered. He wasn't even making sense. "I don't know where Robbie is. Neither does Humility."

Blotches of red mottled Mackintosh's face. "No, but I'm betting your spawn of Satan brother does. If Jacob knows I have you, he'll come running. I should have grabbed Humility at your house. But that wheelchair witch had her hand on her alert button."

So he wanted to use her to lure in Jacob. Cherie had to admit his plan would work. If Jacob knew Mackintosh had her, he'd come running. She quickly ran through her options. Mackintosh was strong enough to easily overpower her. She could yell and hope that Trixie heard her—or someone else. But by the time anyone could do anything, she'd probably be unconscious in the trunk of his car. Besides, she didn't want Trixie anywhere near the man.

Her best hope was to keep him talking until someone happened to walk by. And it was time to go on the attack.

"Mr. Mackintosh, if you leave here right now, without making any more trouble, I promise I won't file charges against you."

His eyebrows, so bushy that a few hairs wandered a good three inches from his face, pulled together. "What are you going on about?"

"I told you I saw a lawyer. What you did was illegal and I can prove it. You gave me drugs."

"There's no proof of that."

"Jacob was there. He saw me right afterward. And whatever we did to get away from you was in self-defense, so don't even waste your time talking about the charges against us. They'll never stand up in court. The lawyer said so." She couldn't believe her voice was holding steady. She actually sounded legitimate.

Behind him, between their corner and the Sizzler, a steady trickle of customers drove into the restaurant parking lot and strolled toward the door. If only one of them would look in their direction! But what would they see? It probably looked as if she and Mackintosh were having a pleasant conversation. But if someone paused even for a second, she could scream or run or do something dramatic that would draw their attention.

And then she saw it. A police cruiser easing through the lot, heading right for the restaurant. The officers in the car were probably interested in a meal, not a rescue, but she'd take what she could get. She wished she could take a step back, out of Mackintosh's reach, but if she did they wouldn't be able to see her. If she darted forward, she'd run smack into him.

She opened her mouth to scream, but Mackintosh was too quick for her. He grabbed her and spun her around so her back pressed against his front. He clamped his hand over her mouth. She tried to scream anyway, but it came out as a muffled squeak. He squeezed her face so hard the flesh bunched up around her eyes, distorting her vision.

But she could still hear. She strained for the sound of the cruiser's tires on the pavement, longed for a concerned voice to ask, *Everything okay over there?*

Nothing but Mackintosh's harsh rasping in her ear. "Thought you were so clever, didn't you? Think I don't remember what your pretty mouth looks like when it's about to sing? You were about to call out to someone, weren't you? Well, it can't be your cheating friend. I knocked him out good. He ain't waking up for a long time. And I'll do the same to you if you don't stop makin' a fuss."

Cherie struggled for air. She felt as if she were drowning in fear and dread. This was every nightmare she'd had over the past six years. Fear of this, exactly this, had been hanging over her all that time. And now it had all come true. Mackintosh had caught her. And worst of all, he'd hurt Vader.

What had he done to Vader? She would have heard a gunshot. Mackintosh had all sorts of stuff on his farm. He could have knocked him out with some sort of animal medicine. Rat poison. Or worse. Mackintosh had faced down the FBI, if the rumors were true. Who knew what he was capable of?

For months she'd tried to push Vader away so he wouldn't get hurt. Now he had anyway.

Sudden anger seared through her like the edge of a sword. All those times she'd practiced her self-defense techniques in the privacy of Move Me—she'd never had to use them in real life, but this seemed like an excellent moment to try.

She lifted her foot and slammed her heel onto Mackintosh's instep. Unfortunately, he wore heavy work boots while she wore strappy sandals. But the move took him by surprise and his hold loosened. She sank her teeth into his forearm as hard as she could, the flavor of disgusting, sweat-soaked denim filling her mouth.

"You little sneak," he growled. "Now you done it. I didn't want to knock you out but now I have to."

His body shifted behind her, as if he was raising his arm. Her next move should either be to swirl around, now that she'd hurt his arm, or grab on to it and try to lift him onto her back, then toss him over her head.

Yeah, right. He was like a big old sack of buck-wheat. She bent at the waist, holding tight to his arm, but nothing much happened, though he did give a big grunt. He might have risen onto his toes, but she really couldn't tell. A whoosh of air warned her that a blow was coming. She turned her head to the side to provide him with as small a target as possible. Scrunching her eyes shut, the way she always had during beatings at home, she held her breath and braced herself.

An ugly grunt came from behind her, and then Mackintosh collapsed on top of her. She crumpled to the sidewalk, the heavy weight of him nearly crushing her. What had happened? Where was the slash across her cheek, or the slam across the back of her head? Before lack of oxygen could knock her out, she squirmed out from under Mackintosh's weight, and peered upward.

There stood Trixie, holding a signpost that read "Rooms 11–31."

Cherie tried to scramble to her feet, but couldn't quite manage it. "We have to find Vader. Mackintosh did something to him."

Trixie held out her hand so Cherie could grab on to it. "He's under a bush around the corner. I found this signpost on the ground right next to him. It was all bloody. Come on, hurry!"

Chapter Twenty-Seven

Vader swam up through swirling, red-laced darkness to find Cherie's face just inches from his. Her eyes seemed to take up the whole world, as if he was surfacing into a gray mist. A streetlight behind her made a reddish halo out of her hair.

"Vader, thank heavens! You're awake. Can you hear me?"

It would be hard not to, she was practically screaming in his ear. But when he opened his mouth, nothing but a croak emerged. She darted an anxious glance behind her, and he tilted his head to follow her gaze. A bulky body lay sprawled on the ground, half on the sidewalk, half on the woodchips under some tidy shrubs.

That's right. The man had jumped him from behind. He'd jabbed an elbow in the man's ribs, cracked a few, then gotten him in a headlock. The man had yelled at him enough to make clear it was Mackintosh. He'd shoved the man away and told him to get the hell out if he wanted to avoid the police. The man had dragged himself off, while Vader had pulled out his phone to call Cherie and warn her. Then he'd turned just in time to see a wooden signpost come down on his head and that was it for memories.

He struggled into a sitting position. "Is he . . . did he . . ."

"Trixie knocked him out, but I'd rather get out of here before he comes to again. He's a little crazy."

Even in this hazy state, Vader had to agree with that. He also remembered vaguely that he was angry with Cherie, that she'd crossed some sort of line and he was done with her. But that sounded so unlikely. Done with Cherie? When she was bending over him with that anxious look, using her beautiful cream-colored sweater to wipe the blood off his face?

He frowned. This was all backward. He was supposed to be taking care of her. "Are you okay? Did he find you?"

"You don't remember?" She seemed worried by that. "It looks like he attacked you. I thought you were dead. You scared the blazes out of me."

He put a hand to his throbbing head. His thoughts still seemed sort of random and sketchy. Things wavered in and out of focus. But if he kept his attention on her eyes, everything steadied. He grabbed her wrist to stop her from patting his face. "Your sweater. Ruined."

She let out a sad little laugh. "You really think I care about the sweater? I care about you, Vader. I just hope you'll believe me."

He frowned, but that movement hurt his head, so he stopped. Even though the pain in his head was remarkably bad, he was enjoying being fussed over by Cherie.

"Vader, Trixie ran back to the room to get a phone. Should we take you to an emergency room?"

"Not necessary. My head's not that bad."

She frowned dubiously. "It sure looks bad."

"Trust me. I'm a paramedic. Head wounds bleed a lot but the big fear is concussion. I'm not seeing double, although two of you would be twice as nice." He closed one eye in a wink, which seemed to relieve her. "You're supposed to keep an eye on me to see if I become disoriented and start calling you Lindsay Lohan or something. We clean it, slap on some ice, and you make me rest. That's it."

A smile curved her lips. He'd bonk himself on the head with a signpost for that smile.

"Can you move yet?"

"Give me a minute." As he gingerly assessed the lump on his head, everything came back to him; the theft of the van, the lack of communication, his anger with her. "You stole my van."

She crumpled her ruined sweater into a ball. "It was Trixie. She told me you offered it to us."

"Trixie." He groaned. "I should have known. I knew something didn't add up, but I was out of my mind with worry."

Cherie winced. "Don't get me wrong. I can't totally blame Trixie. I should have insisted on talking to you myself instead of giving her my phone. I should have known she was up to something. I'm really, terribly sorry. I was wrong. About everything. Will you give me another chance?"

He watched the vulnerable bones of her throat shift as she swallowed. Her eyes were going all misty again, as if she was trying hard to hold back tears. The words "of course" hovered on his lips, begging to spill out. But he hardened his heart against the urge. He always slid back to her side so easily.

Not this time. Something really had shifted inside him. If she wanted him, she was going to have to prove it. "Another chance to what? I need specifics."

She swallowed again. "A chance to prove to you how much I . . . I love you."

The fog in Vader's brain went warm and golden. She loved him. He knew it! He'd known it all along. Finally she'd caught on too. About time. He attempted a goofy, bloody grin, but that hurt, so he stopped.

And a warning bell rang in his mind. *Don't be a sucker. Let her prove it.* "Prove it, how?"

She shook her head. "Later. Let's get you up to the room. We'll call 911 and let the paramedics handle Mackintosh." She indicated Mackintosh's unconscious body. "We need to get some ice on your head. Can you walk?"

"Of course I can walk," he bluffed. He had no idea if he could walk. But he was Vader, strong as an ox, and he'd walk if it fucking killed him. He tried to roll over so he could get his feet under him. It wasn't graceful, but by leaning heavily on Cherie he managed to come onto his knees. From there, all those leg lifts and abdominal strengthening sessions paid off. He stood up, reeling from the dizzying pain.

Cherie dusted woodchips off him. "It takes a lot to keep you down, doesn't it?"

He grinned. "A lot of guys have tried, few have succeeded. A signpost's a first though." Mackintosh stirred slightly. "You might want to make that call to 911 now."

"My phone's in my room. Come on." She draped his arm over her shoulder. Even though his head was clearing, he had to admit it helped to have someone supporting him. He took a tentative step forward, happy to find it didn't hurt too badly.

"I should get brained more often." They side-stepped Mackintosh's prone body. "I have my phone somewhere, I think. Try my front pocket."

"Cute, Vader."

"What?" He tried on an Elvis lip curl for size, and found that it lifted his mood significantly. "You have such a dirty mind, Cherie. Try to get ahold of yourself."

She laughed, a lovely, throaty sound with an edge of worry to it. "You must be feeling better if you can make dumb jokes."

"I can do that in my sleep. Or unconscious."

They reached the stairway that led to the balcony. "I can't believe no one noticed both of us getting attacked."

"It's dark." Vader shrugged. "People are focused on their own thing. Personally, I'm glad no one saw it. With my luck, I'd end up on YouTube getting hit on the head with Rooms 11 through whatever. I'd never hear the end of that."

She giggled. "Maybe someone was hiding in their room with a camera. You never know. I tried out my self-defense moves. I'd love to see how that looked."

He froze, his imagination suddenly going wild. "Self-defense moves?"

"Just basic stuff. You know, the instep smush. I bit him."

"Did he hurt you?" A dangerous spinning sensation came over him. If Mackintosh had been there at that moment, the man would have been splayed out on the ground in two seconds flat.

"No. Not really. He scared me, but you know something? It was good. I mean, it was better than being scared the way I was before. Facing him was a lot better than *thinking* about facing him, if that makes sense. I'd probably be stuffed in the back of his old Buick by now if Trixie hadn't shown up."

He gritted his teeth. That image was definitely not helping his head. She helped him up the first stair-step.

"Why did you and Trixie run off?"

"To find Jacob. At least that was my intention. I'm not completely sure what Trixie's up to. Maybe you should ask her yourself. Threaten to charge her with grand theft auto, maybe then you can get a straight answer. But she did save me, so I hope you take it easy on her." Luckily, the flight of stairs was short, and their room wasn't far. She knocked on the door while he recovered from the journey.

Turning on the paramedic part of his brain, he assessed his condition. Double vision? No. Disorientation? Hard to say, since the whole situation was so weird, but he didn't think so. Headache? Most definitely. Acquisition of a painkiller was a definite priority. After he yelled at Trixie for her utterly irresponsible behavior.

But when she opened the door and burst into tears at the sight of him, all his accusations fled his mind. "This is my fault," she wailed, as she flew around the room, gathering towels and smoothing out the bedspread so he could have a place to relax. "I didn't think he was following us. Do you need ice? You need ice. I'll get some ice." She grabbed the cheap ice bucket that came with the room.

Cherie snaked out a hand, grabbing her wrist before

she vanished out the door. "Hang on. Mackintosh might have come to by now."

"Nine-one-one," Vader reminded her as he settled with a groan onto the bed.

But Trixie, who was already out on the landing, shook her head. "Mackintosh is leaving," she called. "I see his Buick pulling out of the parking lot."

"Okay, you can go as long as the coast is clear. But come right back." Cherie released Trixie's wrist and the girl vanished down the balcony. She left the door open. They both heard the rattle of ice hitting the cardboard bucket. Vader let his eyes close. What looked like red and black fish swam back and forth in his vision. Sleep. He could definitely sleep. How long had it been since his last solid sleep?

But Cherie's soft voice was pulling him from the deep pool that beckoned. She sat on the edge of the bed, leaning over him, one hand next to his chest, the other clenched in her lap. "Don't go to sleep yet, Vader. We have to ice your head, and then I need to tell you something. I don't know when I'll have another chance with Trixie bopping around. But I got the life scared out of me down there, and I can't wait any longer."

He blinked at her, amazed by how heavy his eyelids felt, as if they carried the weight of two frying pans. "What is it?" He felt slow and thickheaded.

"I love you. I mean, really truly love you. I've loved you for an awfully long time, but I was too afraid. I couldn't let myself admit it. I was afraid for myself, afraid for you. I know I hurt you, but it really was never my intention. I'm just . . . well, I guess I'm a bit of a coward. I couldn't bear it if I got close to you and then it turned out I was married and Mackintosh got mad and . . . it just all seemed impossible."

He watched the little dimples rise and fall next

to her mouth as she talked, the way her lips curved around the words. Her hair had come loose and hung in a tangle around her shoulders. A smear of something that might be grease slashed across the fresh-petal skin of her cheek. She sure was beautiful.

"Do you hear what I'm saying, Vader? I know this isn't the best moment to dump this on you. But I don't want you to go another moment without knowing how I feel."

Everything she was saying . . . it was all he'd ever wanted from her. So why wasn't he jumping with joy? Aside from the fact that jumping would make his head split into jagged pieces? Maybe he didn't quite believe it. Maybe he'd gotten too used to her pushing him away. This just didn't feel real.

"Am I dying?" he asked abruptly.

"What?" She went white. "What are you talking about?"

"Is there some gigantic wound I can't see, but you know it's going to kill me so you're being nice to me on my deathbed?"

She stared at him, her mouth open in a little O of shock. "How can you even think that? You don't trust me at all, do you?"

The thing about trust was, it had to be earned.

His silence provided her answer. Her face closed off as though a pale velvet curtain had been drawn shut. "Maybe we shouldn't be talking about this kind of thing right now."

"What kind of thing?" Trixie appeared at Cherie's shoulder. She held the overflowing ice bucket clutched to her chest. "Should we call a doctor, do you think?"

"No." Heartsick, Vader shook his head. He knew he'd made a wrong move, but his head was pounding too much for him to sort it out. "I just need some ibuprofen and that ice. And you have to wake me up every few hours. Any more big escapes planned for tomorrow? Can I sleep in?"

Cherie and Trixie both spoke at once, then Trixie piped down so Cherie could answer. "No one's going anywhere until you feel well enough to drive."

From his position, Vader caught the flicker of rebellion that passed over Trixie's face. But what could she do? She didn't even know how to drive. Like it or not, she'd have to abide by Cherie's decisions.

Trixie wrapped some ice cubes in a towel and pressed it against his head. The cold penetrating through the cloth brought sweet, welcome relief. "It's all about you now, Vader," she said. "Hope you don't mind being waited on hand and foot."

Cherie found a bottle of ibuprofen in her purse and brought two tablets along with a glass of water. While he was downing them, she disappeared into the bathroom, then returned with a wet washcloth. "I'm going to clean the rest of the blood off you, then you can sleep," she told him, all business.

Fuck. He'd screwed up. He'd thrown Cherie's declaration of love back in her face. But hell, it wasn't fair. She shouldn't have sprung it on him when he wasn't fully functional. And hadn't she said before that she was going to prove how much she loved him? That's all he needed. A little proof.

Under Cherie's gentle dabs at the mostly dried blood on his face, the drowsiness came back for real. He nodded off, then woke partway to find his arms over his head and his T-shirt being stripped off.

"He's really strong, isn't he?" Trixie whispered.

"No looking. He's asleep, so that's cheating," answered Cherie.

"Oh pooh on you. I can see him on YouTube anytime I want."

"Shut up and help me with his shorts."

The two sisters got his board shorts off and maneuvered him under the covers. He probably could have helped them, but he was incredibly exhausted and it was entertaining listening to them bicker with each other in whispers. He could tell that Cherie was still mad at Trixie. But he was beyond anger himself. How could he be too angry about a situation that inspired Cherie to tell him she loved him? Her words, and the completely serious expression on her face, kept coming back to him in quick, surreal flashes.

As he'd instructed, Cherie woke him up several more times. Once when a pizza arrived and it smelled so good he thought about trying a bite, but fell back asleep before he could mention it. The next time she woke him, his favorite *Friends* episode was on, the one with Ross and Rachel's wedding in the bombed-out old chapel in London. Trixie was watching like a kid, crouched on her knees about a foot from the TV. Cherie lay back down in the next bed over.

He beckoned to her, wanting her in bed with him. She shook her head, glancing toward Trixie, but he gestured again, more urgently.

She slid off the bed and padded over to his.

"I'm cold," he said, pathetically. "Someone should keep me warm. It's in all the manuals."

As soon as she slid under the covers, he nestled her up against him. Her delicious warmth immediately seeped into his body, relaxing him like a drug. Sleep tried to tug him under, but he resisted. "What was that you were saying earlier about proving your love?" he whispered into her hair. "Rooms 11 to 31 might have jumbled things up a little in my head."

He felt her snort. Then her mouth traveled up his neck, using kisses like stepping stones. When her lips reached his ear, she breathed, "We'll talk about it tomorrow. Now go to sleep. I promise I'll stay right here in bed with you."

Talk about it tomorrow? What kind of answer was that? That "talk" better include some of that proof she'd promised. And "proof" better include . . . He fell asleep.

Chapter Twenty-Eight

*C*herie spent the night tangled up with a deeply slumbering Vader. She didn't sleep much as she ran through everything that had happened in the course of their relationship. How every choice Vader had made was based on the generosity of his big heart. While every choice she'd made was based on fear.

Okay, maybe not every choice. She'd been trying to protect her sisters. And she'd had the good sense to let Vader into her life in the first place. But after that she'd pretty much made a mess of things. Worst of all, she'd let her fears from the past hurt the most important person in her life. Because that's what he was, she realized as she basked in the warm, reassuring rumble of his snores. Vader, somehow, without her realizing it, had become the person who mattered to her the most.

Trixie stayed up late watching the *Friends* marathon, then crawled into the other double bed. "Don't you dare do anything sinful," she said, before laying her head on the pillow and virtually passing out.

Cherie wanted to point out that Trixie's deceptions weren't exactly earning her a pass into heaven, but snuggling next to Vader made her feel too good to complain. But her sister did have a good point, so she wore a nightgown to bed and tried to think chaste thoughts.

That effort ended when she woke up to find Trixie's bed empty except for a note written with eyeliner on a piece of hotel stationery. *Cherie—The free continental breakfast is calling my name. I'll be in the lobby. No rush. Hint, hint. P.S. You deserve to be happy. Love, Trixie.*

Cherie glanced over at Vader, who was still asleep. He looked good. Not only in his usual manly way, but in the sense that he didn't look so pale and he was breathing easily. She went into the bathroom, and washed her hands and face. Then, remembering Mackintosh's denim-clad arms grabbing her, she stripped off her nightgown and hopped in the shower. As she let the hot water wash over her, as she scrubbed every bit of him from her skin, she thought about Vader's reaction to her words of love yesterday.

He hadn't believed her.

It hadn't gone at all the way she'd expected. She'd imagined him lighting up with joy, his whole world transformed by the fact that finally, *finally*, she was giving him the same loving words he gave her. As if she were a fairy granting him his heart's desire.

Instead, he'd had a perfectly reasonable reaction. After everything that had happened between them, he was going to need more than pretty words. And how had she responded to that? She'd shut down and nearly pushed him away. The same exact thing she always did. She'd responded out of fear.

No more. With sudden determination, she turned off the water. After she'd dried herself off, she walked naked into the bedroom. Just to be safe, she opened the door a crack, turned the door hanger so it told the world, "Do Not Disturb," and adjusted the blinds so they were completely closed. Then she slid back into bed.

She began by placing her hand on the left side of his chest, where solid muscle formed a sort of shield of flesh. Maybe he had his own defenses against hurt: the spectacular conditioning of his body. She let her hand sit for a long moment as warmth seeped into it and the pulsing of her own veins tangled with the steady rhythm of his heart. Vader might rely on his muscles, but she knew his true strength lay in the vital organ beneath.

She ran her hand down the rippling pattern of muscles covered in warm, silky skin. As much as Vader prided himself on his toughness, his belly was tender to the point of being ticklish. Even asleep, his skin gave little flinches as she dipped her hand into the valley between his hipbones. His hips were narrow compared to the breadth of his shoulders. She wondered what his physique would have been like if he hadn't started lifting weights as an overwhelmed teenager. She wondered what sort of person he would have become if he hadn't had to take care of his mother alone.

She couldn't imagine him becoming anyone better than he was. He'd taken a crappy turn of the dice and made something beautiful out of it.

She pressed her lips to his shoulder. It felt like kissing a sun-warmed boulder. Those huge muscles were a work of art, honed to their peak. She darted her tongue against his skin and sucked in quickly, adding a little nibble. Not for the first time, she wondered what someone as obsessed with fitness as Vader saw in her. She wasn't one of those tight, athletic girls. Her shape was more womanly, always had been. As much as she loved to dance and move her body, she'd never felt compelled to lose a lot of weight. Tango didn't require it, neither did movement therapy.

But maybe her relative softness was what drew him. If he wanted someone to lift weights with, he could have hooked up with one of the girls at his gym, Toned. She'd walked in there one day, turned right around, and never gone back. Not her world at all. She liked moving to the music, losing herself in the rhythm, letting the melody sweep her away.

Dancing was the closest she let herself come to singing. Well, maybe not the closest, she thought with a dreamy smile as she sealed her naked body against Vader's. *This* might come even closer.

Hearing the opening beats of her favorite tango number echo in her head, she subtly undulated her body against his side. Her hand drifted to the iron curve of his upper thigh. Even in repose, the power of those legs took her breath away. She spent some time running her hand back and forth across the mountainous territory from outer to inner thigh. The slight covering of little hairs made the motion pleasantly, mildly abrasive. The sensation of growing heat in her palm inspired an answering glow deep in her belly.

Was any of this having any effect on the Sleeping Beast? Time to find out. As if her fingers were curious explorers hiking across familiar terrain, she inched her hand into the thicket of curls between his thighs. Ah yes, there it was, that rigid rise of flesh soaring skyward. She glanced down, seeing the definite tent that had formed under the bedsheet. Then she let her gaze travel upward, across the dunes of his chest to the smile hovering over his mouth. His eyes were closed, but something about that smile . . .

She wrapped her hand around his shaft. Saw his eyes shift back and forth behind closed eyelids, the corner of his mouth lift. So he was secretly awake, just as she'd suspected. And he wanted to play.

In one swift movement, she stripped the sheet from his body. She took a moment to appreciate the thick, eager erection rearing between his legs. Then she swung her body on top of his and straddled him.

His chest rose as he drew in a sharp breath. She squeezed her legs around his hips, so the soft flesh of her inner thighs clung to his erection. She watched his lips tighten, then relax as he let out a snore.

A *snore*? So he was going to play it that way, was he? She leaned forward until her breasts pressed against his hard chest. She nipped his chin, trying to surprise a reaction out of him. When that didn't work, she eased her tongue across the coffee-dark stubble on his chin. Sucked his Adam's apple. Pressed her lips into the divot between his collarbones. As she did so, she turned her body into a full-length, life-size Magic Hands, massaging with her breasts, her hips, her skin.

These detailed sensual attentions usually came from him as he worshipped her body with his. This time, it was her turn to swirl kisses along the swoop of a rib, to bring his nipple between her lips, flick it with her tongue. Each muscle received its own careful delineation from the steady march of her mouth. No inch of his upper body escaped her avid, appreciative suckling.

Immersed as she was in his physicality, she knew when his pulse quickened, when his shaft hardened in the tight grasp of her thighs. But a surreptitious glance upward showed he was still holding firm. His breath might be hissing through his teeth, but his eyelids were clamped shut.

"This means war, big guy," she murmured. She shifted her body downward, her knees on either side of his. A light stroke of her fingertips along his erection brought a groan that he quickly tried to mask as another snore. She smiled, followed her fingertips with her tongue, from root to tip, then blew on the wet trail she'd left. His hips flexed, as if greedy for more.

"Something you want to say?" she said, her lips brushing against his penis.

This time his fake snore had a pleading quality. She could relate. Handling his body like this had set off a hum of arousal inside her. Her nipples were swollen from brushing against the rough hair on his chest. Her inner thighs tingled, her sex quickened. Even her mouth throbbed from the contact with his hot skin.

"I see what's going on here. You want me to do the talking. Fair enough." She swirled her tongue around the flange on the head of his shaft. "I love you, Derek 'Vader' Brown." Taking the entire head in her mouth, she closed her eyes, savoring the intimate connection, his vulnerability. When she drew her mouth away, his erection, wet and glistening, sprang toward his belly. She spread butterfly touches along it, along his thighs, his springy hair, his sensitive belly.

"I know I wasted a lot of time and I hope you can forgive me. It's okay if you don't believe me right away. Just give me a chance, that's all I ask. I'll keep saying it and trying to prove it until you just have to believe me. And if it turns out you don't love me anymore, well, I don't know. I'm not going to worry about that now. I'm going to throw everything I have into showing you how much you mean to me."

She raised herself on her knees, risking a quick

check of her pretend-sleeping lover. A broad smile had spread across his face and his eyes had opened just a slit. Enough so a brown ray of warmth shone through. Her heart stuttered, then resumed in a kind of joyfully skipping rhythm she didn't recognize. She felt . . . free. Unafraid. Open. In love.

She reached up and gave him a playful flick on the uninjured side of his head. "Is any of this getting through or do I need to break out the signpost?"

"Follow the signs. Into the fire," he murmured, which might have sounded like aftereffects of a concussion if it hadn't made sense to her. When it came to love, you just had to make the leap into the fire. Anyway, there was no need to be afraid of the fire between them. He was a fireman; she'd be safe with him.

"Into the fire," she agreed, shifting her knees closer together. "Or onto it." And she took his erection into her hand, guiding him into her body. Not that he needed direction; his shaft settled into place like an arrow into a quiver. Everything in her world settled into place along with it. If he had doubts about her love, he would have stopped her. But he hadn't, and a sweet sense of harmony rippled through her. She let out a long, luxurious sigh as she clasped him in the clinging depths of her core. "I've got you now, Vader Brown. Don't even think about going anywhere else."

She lifted herself up until his slick length nearly left her, then lowered herself back into place.

"Sweet Lord," he breathed, his hands going to her breasts, those big thumbs teasing her nipples. It felt so good she groaned, which didn't sound at all graceful. "You are the sexiest woman in the world."

"Oh, come on."

"Hey. You're the sexiest woman in *my* world. You know what else happens in my world?" Taking charge, he thrust his hips upward. The sudden surge of masculine power shot through her like a bolt of lightning.

"What?" she gasped.

"In my world, you take your compliments and smile nicely and say, 'Thank you, Vader, you know best.'" He transferred her hands to her hips so he could intensify the rhythm of up and down. "Bend closer."

She lowered her torso and braced her hands on either side of him. With quick, glancing flickers of his tongue that sparked little shocks of pleasure, he lapped at her nipples.

"That feels insanely good, Vader," she said, in a not entirely steady voice.

"This is only the beginning, Cherie," he answered, hot breath whispering across her sensitized breasts. "I'm going to love you so hard, you'll be looking at insane in the rearview mirror."

Flames rushed from her face to the backs of her thighs, where his hands were now playing. "Promises, promises," she muttered, arching her back to give him more flesh to work with, to tease, to consume.

"Oh, it's a promise all right." He ran his hands along the globes of her ass, his big palms making her feel beautiful. Not too big, not too small. "I never break a promise. You can ask anyone."

She didn't have to. Some things were like bedrock, and that was one of them. Vader, strong as a ram, loyal as a hound dog. Lovable as a kitten, though she'd never tell him that. Instead she let her body do the rest of the talking. Let her moans and quivers show him how much he moved her. Gave herself over to him, her breasts to his talented mouth, her hips to his powerful grip, her core to the intimate invasion of his shaft.

The music began again, and even though it was

only in her head, he seemed to hear it and move to the same rhythm. They flowed against each other, thrust and counter-thrust, move and countermove, each step stoking the passion that flared ever more vibrant. A low hum began in her throat and she didn't stop it. Didn't even try. She hadn't used her voice this way in so long, it felt almost rusty. Letting her voice carry her emotion into the light, letting it fly free and wild—it felt like the most magnificent gift the heavens could grant.

Shivers of pleasure swept through her. Not just bodily pleasure, but that of the soul too. The inner drumbeat increased its pace, demanding its due, marching toward release. She felt cleansed by joy—the joy of feeling the barriers fall, letting the sweetness of another being join with hers.

When he arched into her, clamping her hips against his, glory burst over her in blinding waves. She sang his name, or maybe she hollered it. All she knew was it spiraled from her throat like a clarion call. He answered by gathering her against him and wrapping himself around her, as if their combined release fused them together into something new.

It took a while for either one to attempt to move. Vader wondered, with half of his potentially concussed brain, if he'd died and gone to heaven.

"Want to tell you something," Cherie mumbled from the direction of his chest.

Seriously, maybe he had gone to heaven. All this time she'd spent *not* telling him anything, and now she wanted to talk. "Now that's what I like to hear. Tell me anything you want."

"You didn't realize it, but I was a virgin when I met you."

"What?" He sure hadn't expected that. He struggled to sit up, but she kept her weight squarely on top of him. He fell back against the pillows.

"I was afraid of men and afraid of Mackintosh. I'd just planned to avoid the whole kit and caboodle. But when you came along, I couldn't help myself. I'd still be a virgin if it wasn't for you." She kept her head buried in his chest. "That's why I kept you waiting all that time at the beginning. I had to read up on it."

"You read up on it?"

"Educated myself. We didn't get much information in Prophesize's house. For certain, I never would have imagined it felt so good."

"A virgin," he repeated, marveling. "I feel stupid that I didn't know."

"Why would you know? I hid it pretty well. I'm only telling you now so you know I always loved you. I wouldn't have gone to bed with you if I didn't."

A quiet sort of hush fell over the room as Vader digested this. "You loved me," he said finally, in a voice roughened by emotion. "But you kept saying no."

She raised herself onto her forearms, splayed across his chest. He tilted his neck up to meet her suddenly serious gaze. "First, there was the situation with Mackintosh. But that wasn't the only thing. I'd never even been to your house. Vader, you never mentioned your mother's accident, or her wheelchair, or your father. Is it any wonder I didn't really believe you were serious? I hid stuff, but you did too."

Unable to keep from touching her, he brushed his thumb across her cheek. "Maybe I don't like people seeing I'm not Superman."

She turned her head to kiss his thumb as it passed. "You are to me. But until that fire at your house, I never thought you needed me."

"Oh, I need you," he said in a hoarse whisper. "I'll never stop needing you."

"I love you so much, my dearest sweetest Superman." And they lost themselves in a kiss that felt more real and sweet than anything Vader had dreamed of. Then he rolled her over and sealed it with something more than a kiss.

After that satisfying interlude, Cherie slowly formed the thought that a good portion of the morning must have passed. "What time is it?"

"I'm the wrong person to ask. It is daytime? Nighttime?" He lifted his head a bare inch off the pillow. "Blinds are shut tight, but I see some light under the door. Must be daytime."

"Trixie said she went for breakfast in the lobby."

"Breakfast. Now you're talking. I never had dinner last night."

"You must be starving." Vader, Cherie knew, required a lot of fuel. "Maybe she'll bring us some muffins or something."

"You want to bet?"

At his skeptical look, she laughed. "Trixie has her moments. She saved me from Mackintosh. And she let us do this, didn't she?"

"Let us?"

"Yeah. She left a note that said, 'I'm in the lobby, hint, hint.'"

"Well, if I know my Trixie, and I've kind of gotten a crash course since she moved to San Gabriel, she did that for a reason."

Cherie squirmed out from under him. "She probably wants us to get together. I mean, for real."

"It was always real for me." He said it matter-of-factly, with no hint of accusation. "Can you reach your phone? I've got a goddess on top of me and I can't budge."

Cherie gave him a little swat, then scrambled across him to grab her phone, which teetered on the edge of the nightstand. "Wow. It's five minutes to eleven. Checkout's at eleven."

"That must be one long continental breakfast."

"I'm calling her." She dialed Trixie, but the call went straight to voice mail. "That girl is going to drive me crazy."

"I'm going to take a shower. Why don't you go check the lobby? I don't want her running into Mackintosh when she least expects it."

"He left last night. We saw him."

"Still. We know he's persistent. And that he knows how to improvise a weapon."

A knot of dread began to form in the pit of her stomach. It did seem like a long time for Trixie to be gone. She hadn't checked the clock when she first woke up, but at least two hours had passed, probably three.

Quickly, she pulled on her clothes—this made the third day in the row for her pistachio-green checkered dress—grabbed her phone and card key, and hurried down to the lobby. The breakfast bar had been cleared away. An older couple sipped coffee at a table as they watched the TV mounted in the corner.

Trixie was nowhere to be seen.

Ordering herself not to panic, she approached them. "Excuse me, I'm looking for my sister. She's thin with blond hair and big blue eyes, and she was eating breakfast—"

The woman smiled up at her. She had a kind face wrinkled by years of that lovely smile. "Yes, Trixie. What a sweet girl. You must be Cherie."

"Yes." Relief made her grin widely. "Do you know where she is?"

"She left a short time ago. Her cell phone was dead, so she said to give you a message."

"A message?"

"Yes. She said she was rolling the dice. That was it."

The man, who wore an old-fashioned derby hat with a jaunty little feather, chimed in. "I thought I saw her at that bus stop over there, and I said, Minnie, is that her? But before Minnie could look that way, the bus pulled up and she was gone."

"Bus stop?" Cherie realized she was stupidly repeating everything the couple said, but she couldn't help it.

"The Greyhound Bus Lines. One goes north, one goes south."

Cherie was almost afraid to ask. "Which did you see?"

"South. Toward Las Vegas. Oh, my goodness. Rolling the dice. Do you think that's what she meant, Minnie? We've been trying to figure out what her message might have signified, and . . . Oh! There she goes, Minnie. They move so fast in their family!"

Cherie, already halfway across the room, waved at them. "Thanks for passing on the message! Have a lovely day."

"Good luck to you, Cherie!"

Oh no, not me, Cherie thought grimly. The one who needed luck was Trixie, when Cherie got her hands on her.

Chapter Twenty-Nine

*C*herie tried to convince Vader that he didn't need to come to Las Vegas. But he was at the start of a four-day break and flatly refused to let her go alone. He did agree to let her drive, since he was still a bit woozy from his knock on the head. While she drove, he manned the phone.

First up was Jacob. "Humility-Trixie is on her way to Las Vegas. Alone. In a Greyhound bus."

"It's too early for funny jokes." Jacob sounded sleepy, as if he'd been up all night playing the slots.

"It's noon."

"Sweet mercy, noon already? All right. Let's have it. First of all, where's Cherie?"

"She's driving."

"And Humility's on a bus? Why? Why's she coming here?"

"Who knows with her? She said she was trying to

find you, but we think she has something else going on. Otherwise, why'd she ditch us?"

"No doubt. Alrighty then, I'll head for the Greyhound station. I'll call you when I find her. After I wring her neck."

"Cool. Also, Mackintosh caught up with us here at a rest stop off the 5. So watch your back."

"Mackintosh?" Jacob's teasing tone dropped abruptly. "Did you see him?"

"I didn't see much of him. He knocked me out from behind. Then he tried to grab Cherie, but Trixie knocked him out." Vader ground his teeth as he recounted that fairly mortifying sequence of events. "Cherie said he's looking for his son Robbie. He's driving a tan Buick. Cherie told him you don't know where his son is either."

Silence on the other end of the phone. Then Jacob said a tight "Thanks for the heads-up," and hung up.

"Does he know where Robbie is?" Cherie asked.

"Didn't say. But Mackintosh definitely has him spooked. Or something does."

Next he called Joe the Toe and asked if he could pick up the Suburban. Joe grumbled, but when Vader offered to put fifty bucks on red at the roulette wheel for him, he agreed. Finally Vader called his mother to give her an update and told her to keep her cell phone charged and in her hand.

"I wouldn't dream of anything else. This is so exciting!"

"I'm glad someone's enjoying it." But no one could possibly be enjoying this more than he was, with Cherie finally by his side, the way he wanted her.

Well, maybe not exactly how he wanted her. He'd prefer the driver's seat. He loved Cherie, but watching her drive his truck was worse than getting hit on the head with a signpost. She kept taking her hands off the wheel as she ranted about Trixie. "I knew she had something else up her sleeve. You know what I think she's doing? I think she's taking my tango money and playing the slots. Finding Jacob was just an excuse. She can't drive so she lied to me. And stole your van. That girl has more angles than a geometry class! Would you stop that?"

Vader had snuck a hand to the steering wheel so she couldn't veer into the fast lane.

"If you drive at this speed in the fast lane, someone will lynch you."

"I'm a cautious driver." She always drove about ten miles slower than anyone else.

"My truck is crying right now. You hear those sobs? *Save me, save me.*"

"Do you mind if we stick to the point? I'm really worried about Trixie. She has no clue what Las Vegas is like."

"I thought you were mad at her."

"Yes. Mad and worried. That about sums it up when it comes to Trixie."

She kept talking, while he laid his head back and watched, basking in the joy the morning had brought. He was now entirely convinced that Cherie loved him, though making her prove it some more might be fun too.

Just as they reached the outskirts of Las Vegas, Jacob called. Vader put him on speaker so Cherie could hear too. "Found her. Well, I don't have her yet, but I know where she is." He sounded grim.

"Where?"

"Are you ready for this? She's either on her way, or

already at, a wedding chapel called the Chappelle de l'Amour. Some kid picked her up at the Greyhound station."

"What?" Cherie cried.

Vader whipped a hand to the steering wheel to keep her from driving clear off the road.

"She's getting *married*? Oh, I'm an idiot. I should have put that one together right away!" Cherie slapped herself on the forehead. "All her flirting and going online. When she heard Jacob was going to Vegas she must have jumped on the opportunity. Oh, that girl, I'm going to . . ." She brandished her fist in the air.

"Hands on the steering wheel, Cherie. I'm begging you. Jacob, we'll meet you there."

"Absolutely. Whoever gets there first gets to strangle Humility."

While Cherie fumed, Vader looked up directions to the Chappelle de l'Amour, which, according to its Web site, offered classy weddings for every lifestyle.

It turned out to be a modern, brand-new-looking building with hardly a cheesy touch to be seen. Inside, the floors were polished hardwood, the decor clean and simple. A few couples gathered in the waiting area. Jacob and Trixie were nowhere to be seen.

At the far end of the chapel, a closed door bore a sign that read, "Wedding in Progress." They ran toward it.

"I sure hope we're not interrupting anyone's special day," Vader whispered as Cherie reached for the door-knob.

"Too bad." And she pushed open the door.

Three people were gathered inside the quiet, light-filled space. Trixie stood at the head of the aisle, face to face with a clean-cut, skinny boy Vader had never seen before. He wore an ugly green blazer several sizes too big for him. Even Vader could tell that it clashed with Trixie's sunflower-yellow sundress and sequined flip-flops. An official-looking man in a black suit glared over his half-moon glasses at Cherie and Vader.

"You'll have to wait your turn like everyone else," he told them. Trixie spun around.

"Cherie?" Trixie's eyes went wide as Vader's tire rims.

Cherie stalked up the aisle, her dress swirling around her legs. "What are you *doing*, Trixie?"

Trixie jutted her chin forward in a gesture Vader had come to know all too well. "What does it look like?"

"It looks like you've lost your ever-loving mind. Who is this?" She gestured at the painfully young groom, who took a step back, nearly stumbling over a folding chair.

Trixie shrieked and lunged for the kid, snagging him before he fell. "Now look what you did, Cherie! Dale and I are in love and you're trying to ruin everything."

Cherie cornered the two of them. "How old are you, Dale?"

"Eighteen," he quavered. "I'm old enough to get married."

To Vader, he looked more like fourteen, max. A shock of sandy hair stood straight up from his forehead.

"But why would you want to do that? Is it a religious thing? You can't have sex until you get married?"

Dale flushed as red as the carnations on the altar and looked to Trixie for help.

"He's marrying me because he wants to keep me safe," she said defiantly.

"Safe?"

The wedding officiant spoke up. "If both parties are willing and both are eighteen, and there's a valid wedding license, we don't have a problem."

"*I* have a problem," said Cherie. "She's getting married for all the wrong reasons." She turned to Trixie. "No offense to Dale, but how in blue blazes is he going to keep you safe?"

Dale huddled further into his oversize blazer. Peering more closely at the jacket, Vader noticed it bore a name pin from a car rental agency. At a guess, his father worked there.

Trixie stomped her foot, making the hardwood floor echo. "You think I'm just a kid, don't you? I know more than you what's going on! Soon as I saw you with Vader, I knew you'd end up with him. I started looking for a husband right away. You know I'm right, Cherie. You slept in that bed with him last night, with me in the room, and I know you wouldn't have done that if you don't mean to marry him."

Vader snapped his head toward Cherie, who refused to meet his eyes. "We're not talking about me right now."

"Me, you, it don't make any difference to Mackintosh! Once he knows you're taken by a big strong fireman, I'm next on his list. The only way to stay off it is to get married! I told the whole thing to Dale online and he agreed. A wedding ring and a marriage license, that's all I need to keep me safe. I just want to be safe. That's all."

With a little sob, she shoved at Cherie, who stumbled backward. Vader hurried forward to catch her in his arms. His poor love was shaking. He heard the chapel door open, but was too preoccupied with Cherie to see who it was.

"If all you want is to get married, why didn't you just marry Robbie Mackintosh?"

"Are you kidding me?"

The chapel door closed with a solid thump. Everyone turned. Vader recognized Jacob right away. He'd always reminded Vader of a wiry, twinkly-eyed elf, one he might accidentally crush if he took a wrong step. But he didn't know the dark-haired young man at his side. The stranger spoke into the surprised silence.

"She couldn't marry me because I'm gay and I'm in love with her brother. Always have been."

Cherie's jaw dropped as she stared at Robbie Mackintosh, whose stocky, muscled frame had filled in since she last saw him. He was a couple of years younger than she, so he'd only been fifteen when she'd left home. Now he was holding Jacob's hand, and Jacob looked happier than she'd ever seen him. A glow seemed to surround the two of them.

"You two are *together*?"

"Yep," said Jacob. "For good, this time."

"This time?" She clutched at Vader's arms, which were still wrapped around her.

"We had a thing going on back home. Mackintosh caught us kissing and came damn close to killing us." Despite his light tone, Jacob's expression tightened with the memory. "I wanted Robbie to leave with us, but he wasn't ready."

"Not then," said Robbie. "But I'm here now. That's why my father's on a rampage. Sorry you all got caught in the middle."

Cherie still couldn't wrap her mind around it all. "Why didn't you ever tell me, Jacob?"

"*No one* knew. We didn't tell anyone. Deep, deep dark secret. Deepest and darkest. Anyway, when I left Pine Creek, we thought it was over. I tried to forget about him. It was only when he showed up in Santa Cruz that I knew I'd never stopped loving him. When us Harpers fall, we fall for good." Her brother gave Robbie such a tender kiss that Cherie's heart melted. Jacob's usual wry, joking attitude had completely disappeared, as if the clouds had moved away from the sun, revealing the true glory beyond.

"Is that why you freaked out when I broke our pact and told Vader about Mackintosh?"

"Yes. Robbie was already with me. We knew Mackintosh would be looking for him. The last thing we needed was a complication like Vader. But I was wrong. I admit it. Forgive?" He pulled a comical, apologetic face, the one she could never resist. How could she not forgive him? They'd stuck together through everything. This would be only a tiny bump on the road.

Trixie stomped her foot. "Can we get back to business here? Mr. Preacher, Dale and I have a wedding night to get to."

Dale blushed a painful fuchsia.

"Technically, I'm not a preacher," explained the officiant, who seemed to be a stickler for accuracy. "I am a licensed minister, but I have no religious affiliation."

"Trixie," Cherie pleaded, untwining herself from Vader's arms and approaching them. "Dale seems like a really sweet guy, so why don't you take some time to get to know him?"

"We know each other on a soul-deep level, don't we, Dale?"

Dale finally spoke his second sentence. "Uh-huh."

"Listen, both of you." She took both of their hands in hers, though Trixie immediately snatched hers away. "Look at Jacob and Robbie over there. Now *that's* true love. Don't you want real love, a real relationship? Dale, how will you ever know if you really love each other or if you're just getting married to protect Trixie?"

"Dale doesn't care!" Trixie burst out impatiently. "He just wants to get laid!"

Her groom let out an appalled gasp. "We're in a church, Trixie."

"Shut up, it's not a church, it's a Chappelle. Says right there." She waved at the sign over the altar.

"But you said it would be a church wedding. And that man said he isn't even a preacher."

"Do you have to worry about every little detail?" Trixie snapped. "I hope you're not like this when we're married."

Cherie stepped between Trixie and Dale, forcing her sister to look at her. "Listen to me, Trixie. You don't have to worry about Mackintosh. He can't force you to marry him."

"Yeah? Who says I can't." A deep, twanging voice spoke from the far side of the chapel.

Cherie spun around toward a little side door that she hadn't noticed before. Mackintosh filled the doorway with his burly, denim-encased presence. He held something black in his hand.

Before anyone else could move, Vader launched himself into the aisle, herding Cherie, Trixie, Dale, and the officiant behind him. "Don't do anything crazy, man."

Cherie felt as if she was teetering on the edge of a tall cliff. What was Vader trying to do, be a human shield? Block Mackintosh's bullets with his own body?

Mackintosh looked across the chapel, where Robbie and Jacob had stopped halfway up the aisle. "Robbie, get away from that devil's spawn."

The acid hatred in his voice nearly made Cherie's heart stop. Her brother looked so vulnerable and exposed, standing there in the aisle of a wedding chapel holding hands with another man. Jacob's blue eyes stood out in his suddenly white face.

"No. I'm staying with Jacob," Robbie said. His voice quavered, then held firm. "I won't let you hurt him." The two of them gripped each other tight, so there was no separation between them. To shoot at one would be to shoot at the other.

Mackintosh averted his eyes, as if he could barely stand the sight. "You're asking for hellfire and damnation, boy. And it's coming." He gestured at the officiant. "You. Preacher. You're gonna change the groom's name on that marriage license."

Trixie gasped and huddled behind Cherie. "What's he doing?" she whispered.

With an offended expression, the officiant peered over his glasses at the grim-faced intruder. "I'm afraid it doesn't work that way. Altering an official document is a crime, and certainly against Chappelle de l'Amour regulations."

"Excuse me." Vader took a firm step in Mackintosh's direction, so that suddenly everyone's attention shifted to the big fireman. Cherie clutched at the back of his T-shirt, trying to stop him. "I've been staring at that thing in your hand, and it doesn't look like a real gun."

"It's a lot better than a gun." Mackintosh opened his

jacket and slipped the black object into a sling wrapped around his chest. "This here's a remote control. I ain't just an ignorant farmer. I can go online like anyone else, and I got fertilizer coming out my ears. There's what you call an explosive device out in that waiting room, big enough to smash up this sinful homo chapel and everyone in it. Question is, who gets to leave and who's gonna stay right here and get blown up?"

Chapter Thirty

Into the shocked silence, Vader addressed Cherie. "You know something? I'm starting to get why you were scared of him."

But no more than a tiny smile twitched her mouth. She, along with everyone else, was riveted to the sight of Mackintosh's hand hovering over his alleged remote control. Vader cocked an ear toward the waiting room, but the soundproofing in the chapel was so good, he couldn't hear anything from outside the room. A crowd could be gathered out there, waiting for this endless not-quite-a-wedding to finish.

Vader thought rapidly. *Keep everyone calm. Get control of the situation. If possible, contact the Las Vegas PD.* Within seconds, he'd formulated a rough plan.

First step, keep talking. "I'm sorry, I hate to keep saying this, but how do we know it's real? I think I saw something like it in my captain's daughter's toy box."

"Is that what you think?" Mackintosh snarled. "Want me to test it?"

Vader lifted his hands. "No, no. You only get one shot at this. Once that bomb goes off—if it's actually a bomb—all hell breaks loose, and no one gets what they want. Tell you what. Why don't you let me look at the bomb? You know I'm a firefighter, right?"

"Saw you on YouTube shaking your ass."

"Then you know I can probably confirm it's a real bomb." He had no expertise in explosive devices, but chances were Mackintosh didn't know that. "Once I've confirmed that it's real, then we'll come back in here and take care of business. No one will have any doubts then."

Mackintosh sneered at him. "You're going to try something. Get me alone, then jump me."

"No I'm not. Tell you what. You can tie my hands behind my back." Demonstrating, he crossed his hands behind his rear, which had the benefit of giving him access to his back pocket, where he'd stashed his phone. Next step in his plan: Call the Las Vegas PD.

"No," said Cherie sharply. "Don't go anywhere with him, Vader. He'll hurt you. We can't take a chance. What do you want, Mackintosh?"

"I want my son to renounce his disgusting ways, I want that devil's spawn to go to hell, and I want one of you Harpers to make good on Prophesize's agreement. Humility'll do just fine. She's younger."

Trixie, huddled behind Cherie, let out a little scream. Vader took advantage of the sound to reach deep into his back pocket for his phone. Luckily, his khaki pants were on the baggy side. He managed to maneuver his phone enough to flip it open.

"No," said Cherie. "I'll do it. I'll marry you. It's better that way so Prophesize doesn't worry about bigamy or divorce. I'll marry you if you let Robbie and Jacob alone and if you promise not to hurt anyone."

"No, Chastisement." Robbie hurried down the aisle toward his father. "Jacob's the one he hates. Pops, I'll come home and marry whoever you want if you let Jacob live."

Vader felt the situation slipping away. Once Mackintosh felt he had complete control, there would be no options left. He shifted into commander mode, calling on the authoritative tone he'd heard Captain Brody and Chief Roman use so well. "Stay where you are, Robbie."

Robbie stopped in his tracks.

"No one does anything until we know what's what with that so-called bomb. Right now, it's an empty threat."

He met Robbie's frightened gaze, then Jacob's, then Cherie's and the others', making sure everyone heard and understood. The poor officiant looked as if he were about to faint.

"Now." He turned back to Mackintosh. "There's one problem with your plan. Everyone here can testify that you coerced Cherie into marrying you. And you can't alter a marriage license. The marriage won't be valid. Right, Preacher?"

The officiant opened his mouth, possibly to point out once again that he wasn't a preacher. But at Vader's pointed look, he closed it again, and nodded. "That's correct."

"Hear that, Mackintosh? What good is a wedding that's just going to get undone later? I suggest we make a deal. You let me check out that bomb, and everyone here will agree not to contest the marriage. As a gesture of good faith, Cherie will tie my hands behind my back so you know I won't try anything."

He crossed his wrists behind his back again.

Mackintosh's suspicious gaze traveled from one to the other of them. Vader had no idea what was going on behind his back. Hopefully no one was staring at his ass, because his search for his phone must look pretty funny. He got his fingers around his phone and pressed the button that would speed dial his mother. He debated calling 911 instead, but a dispatcher wouldn't be able to make heads or tails of the overheard situation. His mother would recognize his number and she knew enough of the story to put everything together. At least, he hoped and prayed it was so. Besides, he'd told her to keep her phone handy, and she would.

As soon as he heard the faint ringing from his pocket, he started talking again to cover the sound.

"Think about it, Mackintosh. If the news gets out that you rigged up a bomb in the waiting room of the chapel of . . . what's it called again? Cherie? Trixie? Anyone?"

"Chappelle de l'Amour," said the officiant. "Weddings for every lifestyle."

"Hear that, Mackintosh? A homemade fertilizer bomb at the Chappelle de l'Amour is going to be tabloid catnip. The news'll be all *over* this shit. You think that YouTube video was popular, wait until this hits. No one will hold Cherie to that marriage. No, sir, the only solution is for you to show me the bomb and let me confirm that it's the real thing. If you do that, we won't make a fuss. Right, everyone?"

He pleaded silently that they'd follow his lead. Cherie spoke first. "That's right. As long as you don't hurt Vader when you show him the bomb, I'll do whatever you say, Mackintosh."

The man glanced around the chapel with loathing. "This place needs to get smashed right into hell. You do homo marriages here, don't you?"

"Weddings for every lifestyle," repeated the officiant, faintly.

"When I trigger that bomb, you'll get what you've earned." Mackintosh snarled the words in Jacob's direction.

Vader spoke quickly, afraid the whole thing was about to go off track. "But you can't trigger it yet, mister. You have to pick the right moment. Who's in, who's out, remember? You want your son back. Godly, like he was before. And you want a bride. You want things to go back the way they should be. Am I right?"

He spotted a gleam of agreement in the man's deranged eyes.

"If you let him check the bomb, I'll go with you, Pops," said Robbie. "Without making any trouble."

A smothered protest came from Jacob's direction, but he clapped his hand over his own mouth to stop it.

"We have an agreement, then," said Vader with all the supreme confidence he could muster. "Cherie, go ahead and tie me up so he knows I won't make any wrong moves. Then we'll take care of this situation."

"Don't move, Chastisement," said Mackintosh.

Vader held his breath. Would the man balk at his proposal? Maybe it didn't matter at this point. Either his mother had heard everything and was already hopping online to contact the Las Vegas PD, or she'd never answered and he'd have to come up with Plan B. He carefully closed the phone so Mackintosh wouldn't notice the strange lump in his rear pocket.

The minutes ticked away while Mackintosh deliberated. As far as Vader was concerned, he could take all the time he needed. Ginny would need time to contact the police, and the police would need time to get here.

Finally, with one hand hovering over the remote control, Mackintosh gestured to Cherie. "Do it."

She stepped next to him. "Take your time," he said under his breath.

"You'd better have a good plan," she answered in the barest whisper. Something silky came around his wrists.

Under other circumstances, this could be interesting.

Cherie, bless her, took an ungodly amount of time tying his wrists. The first time, she pretended to mess it up, then had to try all over again. Vader kept mental track of the time. By now, the Vegas PD should have gotten Ginny's call. It would take them another few minutes to get to the chapel.

She raised her voice. "Don't you dare do anything reckless, Vader. You look at that bomb and you come right back."

"You're so bossy. Mackintosh, are you sure you want such a bossy woman? Explain something to me, sir. How come you're so set on one of these two? Take it from me, they're a lot of trouble."

Mackintosh shifted his shoulders, exposing more of the remote control. The more Vader saw of it, the more real it seemed. In his mind, the stakes ticked higher. An unstable, vengeful man with a bomb was nothing to mess around with. "I been defied, conked on the head, brain-injured, and made a fool out of by those Harpers. Then they stole my son from me. They're going to pay for what they did. Every last sinful act."

Vader inwardly flinched at the thought of what Cherie would face under Mackintosh's control. He couldn't let the man win this. He'd die first.

"We didn't mean to make a fool of you," said Cherie. "But you can't just make people marry someone they don't want to. People should be able to choose who they want."

Even though she didn't mention Robbie, her meaning was crystal clear, and the worst possible thing she could say. Mackintosh's face went dark and ugly. "No one should defy their own father. Not you, not no one."

Distract him, distract him. Vader pretended to wince. "Easy there, cowgirl. What are you using on my wrists back there?"

"It's Trixie's wedding garter."

Mackintosh gestured impatiently. "Enough of all that. Get over here, Fireman. Walk in front of me."

With his hands fastened, Vader stepped away from Cherie and skirted around Mackintosh. "I always said it would take handcuffs to get me down the aisle."

"Big joker, aren't you?" Mackintosh prodded him in the ribs, which made him stumble to his knees.

Cherie cried out. "You leave him alone or the whole thing's off!"

"Women," Vader muttered to Mackintosh. "Always squawking about something."

"Same goes for me, Pops," shouted Robbie. "You treat him fair, or I stay here with Jacob."

Mackintosh growled something vicious. Vader dragged out the process of righting himself as slowly as possible. By his mental calculations, someone ought to be on the scene by now. Hopefully they'd cleared the waiting room and the perimeter. But a little more time wouldn't hurt.

When they reached the door, Mackintosh poked him in the back again. "You open it. Use those big muscles of yours. Look in the potted plant under the middle window."

Heart pounding, with all his senses on high alert, Vader did as the man said. He pushed the door open a crack, enough to see lights flashing outside the window. Since he had a good six inches on Mackintosh, he immediately stepped forward to block his view. That gave him a glimpse of a dark bomb squad suit.

And that was all he needed. He spun around and bonked Mackintosh with a vicious head-butt, which sent stabs of pain through his own still-aching head. Then he kicked at Mackintosh's right hand as it reached for the remote. The man crumpled to his knees. Vader kicked him onto his back, then stepped hard on his shoulder. Maybe the resulting crunch shouldn't be satisfying, but it sure as hell was.

"All clear out there?" he yelled.

"Disarming the device," someone shouted back.

When Mackintosh heard that, he tried to reach the remote with his left hand, but it was too late, because by now not only was Vader stepping on both arms, but Cherie was pinning Mackintosh's hand to the floor with the weight of her entire body.

She looked mad enough to rip the man's head off. "You said you wouldn't hurt him, you fucking asshole," she yelled at Mackintosh.

"That's profanity," said Vader primly.

"Hell yes, it is."

No one could get Cherie to let go of Vader. Not the police, who stormed in and handcuffed Mackintosh. Not Trixie, who shadowed her like a scared kitten, even though Cherie kept telling her they never had to worry about Mackintosh again because he'd be in prison. Not Jacob or Robbie, though she did give them both a fierce, one-armed hug. Not Ginny, who insisted on a complete account of the episode over the phone. Luckily, Vader didn't even try to make her let go. He kept his hand firmly latched to hers while he gave a statement to the police and fielded questions from the media.

A slew of TV cameras had appeared with astonishing speed. "Mr. Brown, the police are saying that your quick thinking likely saved many lives today. How did you know what to do in this dangerous situation?"

"Well, I'm a firefighter back in San Gabriel, California, and we're trained to respond to all sorts of crazy situations. I didn't want anyone to get hurt, and luckily it all worked out."

Cherie, hanging back, marveled at how calm and cool he seemed. He was a total natural in front of the camera.

"You're certainly the hero of the hour, but apparently there's a heroine too. Is it true your disabled mother called 911 from her wheelchair?"

"That's right. Virginia Brown is my mom, and my personal hero." Was he choking up? The cameras all seemed to zoom in a little closer. "I knew she'd know what to do. Since I can't always be with her, we do safety drills back at home. It's important to be prepared for any emergency. Even if you don't have a fireman at home"—he winked—"you can do a lot to protect yourself."

Honestly, it was as if someone had scripted it for him. And that wink . . . Cherie could just imagine all the females in the Las Vegas viewing area going gaga.

A female reporter with shellacked blond hair stepped forward. "My producer just informed me that you are one of the famous Bachelor Firemen. Is there a reason you're here at the Chappelle de l'Amour? Something you'd like to share exclusively with our viewers?"

"Well . . ."

Vader turned toward Cherie and raised his eyebrows in a question as clear as if he'd spoken it aloud. She beamed back at him with all the love she never wanted to hide again. He grinned, then began to sink onto one knee.

"No!" she burst out. "Stop, Vader. Don't."

He straightened up and shoved his hands into his pockets. The slope of his shoulders, the tension of his jaw, the wariness in his eyes just about killed her. Quickly, she went on. "I know this is a wedding environment and you can't ever resist those. But it's my turn."

His quickly indrawn breath echoed through the suddenly still chapel. She stepped forward and drew his hands from his pockets, clasping them between hers. Those broad, strong, blunt-fingered hands had always made her weak in the knees.

Okay, so doing this in front of a television audience wouldn't be her first choice, but as a firefighter's wife, she'd have to respond to all sorts of crazy situations.

"Derek 'Vader' Brown," she said in a low voice. The camera people stepped closer. "I love you more than you could ever imagine." She searched for romantic words that would convey what was in her heart. "You're the sunshine I want to wake up to. You're the earth under my feet." Wait, that didn't sound right at all. The cameras were throwing her off. "What I mean is, with you, everything makes sense. Except me, I guess I'm not making much sense." She drew in a deep breath, almost hoping a reporter or someone might interrupt, but no one breathed a word. Vader's rough-hewn face gave nothing away. "You're like a . . . an element. Earth, fire, water, and Vader. It's like the planet would be unlivable without you." Okay, now she was getting into some kind of environmental speech. She stumbled onward. "At least my planet would. If you let me, and if you'll forget the dopiest proposal ever made, I'll spend the rest of my life loving you, taking care of you." Maybe she could salvage things with a lighter touch. "Save the planet, Vader. Will you marry me?"

She stopped talking and pressed one hand to her hot cheek. Was it possible for an entire body to feel embarrassed? Because hers was flushed from head to toe. But it didn't matter. None of it mattered, not the fact that Trixie was jumping up and down next to her, or the fact that one of the camera people was muttering, "And we're here live at the Chappelle de l'Amour . . ." or the fact that even the grinning bomb squad had stopped to watch. The only thing that mattered was Vader.

"I love you," she whispered. "Please be my husband, and I'll be your wife and love you and cherish you every day until death do us part."

The officiant chose that moment to butt his head between them. "That part's my line. And the Chappelle de l'Amour would be delighted to waive all wedding fees as a gesture of thanks for the groom's courageous actions today."

Vader put out a hand and, gently but firmly, pushed the officiant out of their line of vision. Impassive no longer, the look on his face sent starbursts of excitement through her system.

"No," he said.

Before the shock could register, he caught her up in his arms. "I mean, yes, I'll marry you. But not here, no offense to the Chappelle. After all it took to get you to fall for me, I want to make this wedding count. I want to get married back in San Gabriel."

In one fell swoop, her world righted itself. Giddy with joy, she clung to his shoulders. "I fell for you that first night," she told him. "You know I did."

He smiled down at her, those warm, lit-from-within eyes infusing her with a feeling of rightness. "Yeah. I know. Everyone thought I was being dense. But I'm smarter than they think. I knew all along this day would come." With a glance at the chaotic scene around them, he added, "I gotta say, I didn't picture it like this though." He gestured to Jacob and Robbie. "Hey guys, the Chappelle is offering up a free wedding. Know anyone who might be interested?"

Jacob went bright pink, then white. Robbie, who was pressed about as close to Jacob as Cherie was to Vader, whispered something in Jacob's ear. The waves of color kept coming and going, until her brother, red as a strawberry, said, "We would. Yes. We'd like to get married."

"Can you do it?" Vader asked the officiant.

"We'll need a properly notarized marriage license from a state that recognizes same-sex marriage, but yes. Of course we can do it. What date works for you?" Huddling with Jacob and Robbie, the officiant whipped out an iPhone and began tapping.

Still holding Cherie in his arms, Vader turned his back on the cameras and walked her a few feet away, where they could be marginally more private.

"How does four months from today sound?" Vader said, brushing his lips against hers. "Does that give us time to make our wedding as beautiful as you are?"

"Sure. I'll see if I can find a henhouse that hasn't been booked yet." And with that little joke, she knew she'd left the past behind, for real this time.

Lights flashing, Engine 1 pulled into the parking lot of San Gabriel Fire Station 1. Strangely enough, Double D, the engineer, wore a tuxedo. He braked the engine to a stop and climbed out, joining the crowd of onlookers. He tweaked his white bow tie into a perfect line.

A tone sounded and a female voice spoke over the intercom. "Ladies and gentlemen, firefighters and guests, please welcome our bride and groom, Cherie Harper and Vader Brown."

Fred, wearing a black blazer over jeans, marched to the engine's door and opened it with a flourish.

Vader, an awe-inspiring sight in his black, swallow-tailed tuxedo, stepped out. He gave the crowd an incandescent smile, then turned back to his bride. He lifted Cherie as if she were crafted of swan's down and set her on the pavement, where she stood in a floating cloud of purest cream. A sigh fluttered through the group and everyone applauded.

Cherie had worked for months on her dress—four months, to be exact. Its filmy layers of dreamlike chiffon were adorned with little pink flowers lifted from a vintage cashmere sweater. Its tight bodice had made Vader's eyes go bright as flares when she'd first stepped into the fire engine.

Trixie had loaned her a bracelet of sweetgrass from home. The wistful scent brought to mind her father, who'd called from the feed store with something almost resembling an apology. He'd wished her well in her marriage; it was enough.

Ginny Brown had gifted her with a glass hair ornament shaped like a blue butterfly. It sat above her ear, keeping Trixie's masterpiece of an updo in place. Trixie had been studying wedding hairstyles for weeks, and had come up with something ridiculously elaborate that had taken her all morning to accomplish.

Cherie was too happy to mind. Trixie could have shaved her head and painted "Marry me" on her scalp and she would have been delighted.

Fred, with a solemn accompaniment from Mulligan on bagpipes, shepherded the guests toward the rows of folding chairs on the lawn behind the station. Everyone except Vader and Cherie trooped that direction. The bride and groom were supposed to wait until everyone was seated so they could proceed down the aisle between the chairs. At the last minute, Danielle remembered that she was the flower girl, and ran to Cherie's side.

Fire station weddings didn't happen very often— Station 1 had never hosted one—but since Vader had just earned his promotion, acing the "three whole score" interview, with the entire Las Vegas police force vouching for his leadership qualities, Chief Renteria had made an exception.

Captain Brody took his place under the "arch," as everyone had been calling it. The guys had made the structure out of PVC pipe, and a few of Cherie's tango students had volunteered to decorate it with lilies and white-petaled hydrangea. The captain wore a nice black suit and looked extremely handsome. But Cherie couldn't tear her eyes away from Vader, her strong, loyal, stubborn ram of a husband-to-be.

Before she wheeled to her position in the front row, Ginny Brown twitched a wrinkle out of Cherie's dress. Even Vader hadn't required as much proof of her love as Ginny had. But over the past few months, Cherie had won her over with much baking and yarn rolling and baring of her heart.

"Do you know, hon, I think my feng shui worked

after all," Ginny whispered. "If I hadn't set the house on fire, we might not be here right now."

Cherie stifled a laugh in her bouquet. Ginny winked and rolled down the aisle to her spot.

Trixie, as maid of honor, already stood on one side of the arch, holding a simple bouquet of lilies with a trailing pink ribbon. Joe the Toe towered on the other side. Vader had been torn between Joe and Fred, until Fred had obligingly volunteered to be a sort of master of ceremonies instead.

Brody cleared his throat, signaling the beginning of the ceremony. "Welcome to the wedding of Derek Brown and Chastisement Harper, known to those who love them as Vader and Cherie." Brody looked down at the pages he held in his hands. "Before we start, I'd like to add my own personal thoughts about this wedding."

Cherie's eyes widened. Brody was going off the planned script.

"I've learned a few things about love in the last couple years." Everyone glanced at Melissa, his wife, who cradled their new baby boy in her arms. She beamed back at the crowd. From what Cherie could tell, she pretty much alternated between beaming and sleeping these days.

Brody continued. "I've been humbled many times by love. I've had my eyes opened, I've had the sense knocked out of me. Some people say this firehouse is cursed. That every time one of us falls in love, it's like stepping onto a roller coaster. I'm not going to disagree with that. But I'm here to tell you that it's not a curse. It's a blessing. It makes us recognize true love when we see it shining in front of us, the way we do with our brother Vader and his beloved Cherie. It's a true honor and joy to be part of this moment in their lives."

Cherie's eyes hazed over. Oh no, this was her worst fear. She'd lectured herself on the ride from her house. *Don't cry, don't cry.* But the tears insisted on slipping down her cheeks, and she decided to let them.

Fred beckoned to Danielle, who skipped down the aisle, tossing rose petals with wild abandon, as if they were confetti. White and pink fluttered through the air, falling on upturned faces and suit jacket sleeves.

Even though Cherie laughed along with everyone else, her tears didn't stop. As she and Vader walked hand in hand down the aisle, she knew people noticed her face was wet. She made sure they also saw her brilliant smile. *No more fears. Only love.*

When she and Vader had taken their places and faced each other, Ryan Blake got to his feet and read the Firefighter's Prayer, which Vader had selected as the opening prayer. "*When I am called to duty, God, whenever flames may rage. Give me strength to save a life, whatever be its age. Help me embrace a little child before it is too late. Or save an older person from the horror of that fate . . .*"

And here came another hot trail of tears down her face. The moving words, the solemn silence, the occasional chatter of voices from the B shift still at work inside the station, the gentle scent of lilies blessing the air with their essence . . . she'd never forget this moment, and how it felt to be standing up before the world revealing her love for the man across from her.

The tears kept coming, off and on, throughout the simple ceremony. But they didn't keep her from saying the most important word of her life, "Yes."

Yes to love, yes to life, yes to Vader. Such a simple word, "yes," but it could change your whole life. Vader said it too, with an expression of bone-deep seriousness. She wondered how many of his fire crew had seen him like this before, his devotion and commitment so clear, not a hint of playfulness to be seen. She loved him to the core, through all the different layers of heat and fun and rock-solid loyalty.

Joe the Toe reached into his pocket and pulled out a vintage square-cut diamond ring in a rose-gold setting. Vader had combed through San Gabriel's shops until he found something he thought suited her. He'd been a hundred percent right. Trixie extracted Vader's ring from the little bag attached to her wrist. Cherie had designed it herself, with three interlocking bands: gold for permanence, copper for good luck, and iron for protection. She'd poured many prayers into that ring; she was counting on it to keep him safe. That—and the firefighters here today, every one of whom she trusted with her heart's life.

When Captain Brody declared them man and wife, an expression of such tender emotion came over Vader's face that Cherie started crying again. Ginny rang the ceremonial fire bell, and amid its solemn, joyful tones, he drew her toward him and kissed each tear away.

"I'm so happy," she sobbed, worried he might think the wrong thing. "I'm crying because I'm happy," she called to the guests, who were rising to their feet. "I always cry when I'm happy."

"She does," agreed Trixie. "But I've never seen her cry this much before."

Everyone laughed, and Cherie shot her a look of pure gratitude. And then Brody was hugging her and she was thanking him, and Ginny was wheeling her chair toward them. Tears streamed down her face as well. "I always cry when I see other people cry," she explained. "I can't help it."

Cherie laughed, and that helped chase the tears away.

By the time they'd all reached Firefly, where the reception was being held, she was ready to throw herself into the party. Former Chief Roman had volunteered to man the grill and was churning out cheeseburgers and chicken wings at a rate only a party of firefighters could consume. The bar held platters of the legendary Harper family molasses-ginger-chocolate-chunk cookies and Vader's favorite peanut butter brownies, which Trixie and Cherie had spent days baking.

But the real showpiece was the wedding cake, which had been donated by the Chappelle de l'Amour and could only be considered a work of art. It sat in a place of honor on a table in the middle of the dance floor, surrounded by admiring guests. It was two cakes, really, the larger one decorated to look like a house on fire, with flames made of red and orange frosting licking up the sides. The smaller cake looked exactly like a fire engine. A candy ladder linked the two cakes. On the very top of the bigger cake, a miniature fireman held a white-gowned bride in his strong arms.

Guests sipped beer and champagne and oohed and ahhed.

Since Cherie knew the schedule inside out, she knew that her big surprise had to happen right away. She extracted herself from Vader's tight grasp. "Be right back," she told him. She gestured to Jacob, who was manning the bar with Robbie, and Trixie, who was flirting with Ace again.

With her brother and sister at her side, Cherie made her way to the microphone that had been set up near the old fireman's pole. "Hello everyone. Thank you so much for being here on the happiest day of our lives. It means so much to me and to my wonderful, beloved husband, Vader."

Husband. Amazing how easily the word rolled off her tongue.

"My brother and sister have kindly offered to help me express my joy. So here we go. Introducing, for one day only, the Heavenly Harpers."

She cleared her throat, and began to sing.

The first note vibrated in Vader's belly as if Cherie had reached in and plucked a string he hadn't known existed. The second note sent a shivering thrill down his spine. He wasn't even sure what the words were. All he knew was that ravishing beauty existed all around him, and he'd never known it until her voice had struck the match that illuminated it.

He closed his eyes as her singing reached across the room and curled around his heart. Two other voices joined hers, one high and ethereal, like a fairy's, the other bright and vibrant, enthusiastically capering through the hushed, spellbound atmosphere.

At last, her love had come, Cherie was singing.

And she was talking about him.

He opened his eyes to meet hers, to let the full power of his love show. But she was way ahead of him. Love radiated from her being, vibrated in each glorious note, danced around the room to include everyone present . . . and found its way to him.

He realized he was gripping someone's hand. His mother's. The look on her face must have echoed his—incredulous bliss at witnessing something so splendid. If he hadn't already loved Cherie with every particle of his heart, he would have loved her even more, for putting that expression on his mother's face.

Later, after Cherie and Vader's first dance—they wowed the guests with a tango they'd been rehearsing, or pretending to rehearse, when they weren't falling into bed—Vader found himself alone with Jacob.

"You sing like a freaking angel," he told his new brother-in-law. "Why don't you do it for a living?"

"Ohhh, that's what we should call ourselves. 'Freaking Angels.' Just kidding. None of us wants to sing professionally. We do it for love, that's all. But I won't be surprised if Cherie starts using music in her work with kids."

Vader nodded. He could picture that. He could also picture Cherie singing to their children, raising them with music and dancing and peanut butter brownies. There would be several children. He knew it, the same way he'd known Cherie was the one for him. "I've been wanting to ask you, Jacob. What's the deal with Soren and Nick?" Both members of Optimal Doom were out on the dance floor, stumbling their way through a tango with Cathy and another of Cherie's students. "Are they really such good friends of yours?"

"I know what you're really asking. You want to know why I made such an annoying pair of losers move into the house when I left."

"Yeah."

"To watch out for Cherie, of course. I couldn't leave my sister unprotected."

"But *them*?" Vader watched as Soren squished Cathy's foot, making her hop around in agony. "What were they supposed to do, irritate intruders away?"

"In a way. I figured any guy who could put up with those two must really love my sister. Think of it as a labor of Hercules." Jacob winked, and headed off to dance with Robbie, his own brand-new spouse.

Vader had to think about that for a minute. Feats of strength were his stock in trade. Feats of putting up with irritating housemates . . . he'd never considered that.

"Frickin' Hercules," grumbled Stud, who stood at his elbow, holding a bottle of beer. Frankly, he looked a little drunk. "It's always the big, strong guys who get the girl. Look at you, Vader. You know what girls think when they see you?"

Vader didn't care what any girl except Cherie thought, but he humored him. "What?"

"They think 'hero.' Like Hercules. You're strong, you can lift anything, you have that manly look they go crazy over. They all want a hero. That's what they see when they look at you. If I could have just a tiny bit of what you have . . ." He trailed off, shook his head sadly, and tilted the bottle to his lips. "Ignore me. I've got a buzz on."

Vader clapped a hand on his back. "Freddie, I'm going to get mushy right now, because it's my wedding day and I want everyone to be happy. You ready?"

Fred, looking a little alarmed, nodded.

"If the girls knew what a hero you are in here"—he thumped Fred's chest—"you wouldn't be able to take a step without some chick falling for you. So be careful what you wish for."

Fred stared at him, the beer bottle stranded halfway to his mouth. Vader could practically see the wheels churning.

But now Vader had run out of patience with being separated from his bride. The need to be with Cherie propelled him across the crowded dance floor. Today, now, after everything they'd been through, he didn't want to be apart from her. As he made his way to her side, the final words from the Firefighter's Prayer echoed through his mind.

And if, according to my fate, I am to lose my life; Please bless with your protecting hand my children and my wife.

His wife. It had been at least four minutes since he'd

touched her, or even seen her. But as usual, he knew exactly where she was, without even looking. It was as if an invisible lamp glowed in her soul, lighting his way back to her.

Life was pretty simple, as it turned out. All you had to do was follow the light.

Next month, don't miss these exciting new love stories only from Avon Books ♥♥

Moonlight on My Mind by Jennifer McQuiston
Months ago, Julianne Baxter wrongly implicated Patrick, the new Earl of Haversham, in his older brother's death. Now, convinced of his innocence, she's tracked him to Scotland. But a clandestine wedding may be the only way to save her reputation—and his neck from the hangman's noose.

Between the Devil and Ian Eversea by Julie Anne Long
The moment American heiress Titania "Tansy" Danforth arrives in England she cuts a swath through Sussex, enslaving hearts and stealing beaux. But Ian Eversea, the only man who fascinates her, couldn't be less interested. Eversea never dreams the real Tansy—vulnerable, brave, and achingly sensual—will tempt him beyond endurance.

Wallflower Gone Wild by Maya Rodale
Lady Olivia Archer's marriage prospects are so bleak that her parents have betrothed her to Phinneas Cole, a stranger with a dire reputation. If he wants a biddable bride, perhaps Olivia can frighten him off by breaking every ladylike rule. Soon the newly provocative Olivia discovers there's nothing so appealing as a fiancé who's mad, bad, and dangerously seductive . . .

At Avon Books, we know your passion for romance—once you finish one of our novels, you find yourself wanting more.

May we tempt you with . . .

- **Excerpts** from our upcoming releases.

- Entertaining **extras**, including authors' personal photo albums and book lists.

- Behind-the-scenes **scoop** on your favorite characters and series.

- **Sweepstakes** for the chance to win free books, romantic getaways, and other fun prizes.

- Writing **tips** from our authors and editors.

- **Blog** with our authors and find out why they love to write romance.

- **Exclusive content** that's not contained within the pages of our novels.

Join us at
www.avonbooks.com

AVON
An Imprint of HarperCollins*Publishers*
www.avonromance.com

FTH 1013

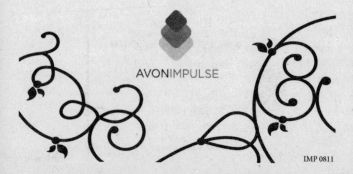